Joseph Carrabis

TALES TOLD 'ROUND CELESTIAL CAMPFIRES

Northern Lights Publishing

Nashua, NH

Paperback ISBN 978-0-9841403-3-6
ebook ISBN 979-8-9878048-2-7

Editing by Jennifer Day, Susan Carrabis
Front cover image and all interior images by John Bernard Scullin
http://skolenimation.com/
Book design by Jennifer Day

Printed and bound in the United States of America
Third edition printing April 2023

Dancers in the Eye of Chronos was the cover story of Free Worlds Magazine, August 1994.
Those Wings Which Tire, They Have Me Upheld Me is copyright 1992. It appears in The New Accelerator 2019 and Penumbra Dec 2022
Binky originally appeared in NewHouse Publications, December 1996
The Boy Who Loved Horses originally appeared in Pulphouse Magazine, May 1994 and Allegory May 2020
Canis Major originally appeared in Tomorrow Magazine, April 1996.

PRAISE FOR TALES TOLD 'ROUND CELESTIAL CAMPFIRES

"...a plethora of delightful and thought-provoking stories that run the science fiction gamut from on-world to off-world to dream-world to surreal-world. Each tale is meticulously crafted and well researched, with most of the stories featuring relatable—or at least sympathetic— characters, each with something to gain and something to lose, each navigating their world as best they can and hopefully helping us learn something about ourselves along the way. I am not exaggerating when I say that several of these tales are worthy of inclusion in any best-of science fiction anthology.

...Worthy of Philip K Dick himself. ... the stories are pretty much all gems. Intelligent. Thought provoking. Each with its own unique voice, setting, tone and message. And a few delightful surprises along the way."

"I enjoyed all the stories, their mix of the commonplace with fantastical twists, and their incredible descriptions – just one example of the latter: "...the fog was hanging on you like a sweater soaked in snow...". "Mani He" was my favorite of the collection, with its nice surreal feel and a number of great life-lessons. "Those Wings Which Tire, They Have Upheld Me" brought tears to my eyes. And "The Settlement" caught me completely by surprise; I had not expected that twist at all!"

"What a mind! I like a book that grabs my interest right from the beginning. Your story telling is colorful. If these stories are built around your life experiences I have to make sure not to walk along with you. I couldn't put the book down needing to find out what was going to happen to the character(s), how the story would end, then on to the next story and the next.

These stories captivate you!"

"You'll find yourself lost in the best possible way. Joseph Carrabis draws you in with his descriptions and leads you into new worlds with each story. The real world fades away. Beautiful writing. Great mental getaway, ..."

"I couldn't put it down. I kept reading and reading. Reminds me of Stephen King's "Night Shift," and John Christopher's "The White Mountains," "The City of Gold and Lead," and "The Pool of Fire," or, maybe The Twilight Zone."

"A Unique Book from a Great Writer - Joseph is an amazing seer of the world about him and great teller of tales..."

"Engaging, vivid, unexpected, and amazing. - Engaging stories, vivid imagery and enjoyably unexpected narratives, Best of all, these amazing tales are wrapped up in a healthy dose of enlightenment (if you're paying attention),..."

"Joseph is able to hold up a mirror to other people's experiences through his writing, letting them find themselves within the pages of his book. His short stories may be works of fiction, but they are nothing short of deeply human."

"For fans of the band Tool and the writing of Joseph Campbell, Gene Wolfe, and Ursula K. LeGuin - For those who want to be inspired, for those who are on the path, and for those who just enjoy entertaining, well-written stories. Reach For Your Dreams Openly and Innocently! Very highly recommended."

"If you like exploring oddities, swooning over otherworldly romances or thrilling to beasties in the night, this one is for you."

"Celestial Campfires is filled with the kind of fantasy short stories that pull you into wonderland and welcome you there with open arms, although there might be something else behind the smiles."

The song lyrics in Canis Major are used courtesy of John Pousette-Dart and Debbie Rose, from The Pousette-Dart Band's "Next to You"

Cold War originally appeared in Midnight Zoo October 1992. It was reprinted in Horizons Science Fiction, April 1999, Daikaijuzine, Sept 2020

Cymodoce originally appeared in Tomorrow Magazine, October 1995, and was recommended for The Nebula Award™. It was reprinted in Midnight Zoo 1999 and in parAbnormal Magazine June 2019

Power Unlimited appeared in ARAASP April 1992 and Daikaijuzine Jul 2021

The Goatmen of Aguirra is copyright 1992 and serialized in The Piker Press Oct 2019

Mani He originally appeared in Magic 1995, Read 'N Run Anthology, Crumb Elbow Publishing's 1996, and Bewildering Stories May 2022

The Settlement originally appeared in Tomorrow Magazine, May 1995 and was broadcast on the Chronosphere Science Fiction Podcast, June 2020

The Weight originally appeared in The Granite Review, November 1995 and was nominated for The Pushcart Prize™ and in The Fifth Di... Dec 2020

Them Doore Girls originally appeared in Haunts 1992

Sema originally appeared in Pulphouse 1993 and was reprinted in Penumbra, Dec 2021

Winter Winds originally appeared in Jack and Jill, January 1983 and was broadcast on Tall Tales TV, Mar 2022

Published by Northern Lights Publishing
www.northernlightspublishing.com

For Susan
(because everything should be)

And AJ
(who said "I can see everything!")

CONTENTS

TALES TOLD 'ROUND CELESTIAL CAMPFIRES

AUTHOR'S FOREWORD

*Y*ou knew I always wanted to write fiction, right? I still haven't actually, because everything written here is true. It actually happened.

No, really, it did. I've seen things and been places and met...creatures...most people can't imagine. Or wouldn't want to. Or should. It all depends on the person and the creature.

But much like Gahan Wilson's "I only paint what I see", I only write about what's actually happened; *Winter Winds* (page 309) was written in the heart of a blizzard. *Them Doore Girls* (page 275) was written one morning in a small village on the Maine coast. *The Boy Who Loved Horses* (page 63) was written one night in a small town in Appalachia. *Dancers in the Eye of Chronos* (page 5) was written over the course of several weeks when Susan and I studied dancing.

It's amazing what can happen to you if you're willing to let it.

So sit back, relax, have something tasty near at hand or tentacle or claw. Read these when other people are around...if you can trust they're really people. Or read them alone, when it's dark out. Maybe. Unless you're not sure what things go bump in the night or scurry unseen in the dark.

I've learned to welcome them. None of them will hurt me, none of them want to.

But you should hear what they say about you...

DANCERS IN
THE EYE OF CHRONOS

DANCERS IN THE EYE OF CHRONOS

*H*yphi *and Gal parade onto the great hall's floor, he half a pace ahead, she half a pace behind,* their legs moving like a cat's caught in headlights, their torsos straight and even. They pass the crowd among applause and hurrahs then pass the judges. Eyes focus on their clothes as well as their steps. The DJ looks to the judges for his cue. In mid-stride, the great hall rumbles as the DJ's turntables engage.

Hyphi and Gal rumba. Gal wears a tasteful nuevo-Italian suit. Triple pleated frost brown pants with matching European cut jacket – no vent – brightly mottled red-and-yellow-on-black wide tie with double Windsor knot, ballooned creme shirt, pocketless, white gold with diamond eye studs, brown rattaned alligator Freeds – no Capezios here – frost brown silks, slightly darker than the pants and lighter than the shoes, easing the transition from one to the other. Tall. Broad shoulders, narrow waist, legs like tapered pillars and arms strongly anguine like boas, his hands and fingers long and graceful. His hair is salt&pepper, the salt like snow and the pepper like star studded night. His eyes are cyan iris against white orb like the sky seen through a cloud at sixty thousand feet. His skin is olive smooth, colored by a heredity so obvious it can't be placed.

Hyphi's head comes to just under his chin. Perfect for slow dancing. Perfect for sow dancing. Pale blue, three-ringed ruffle waisted skirt, line-thin lime green hip hugger belt, tight bodiced lime green blouse, ribbed and expanding beneath the breasts, showing the shoulders, white gold Bubo with emerald diamond eyes and hematite beak, tiny, clutching her throat on a slivered black band, finely silked scarf hinting at slipping from her softly muscled shoulders, pale earth tones of calmly pale earth scenes, dryads and naiads hiding and peeking as the scarf folds and unfolds to her dance, unnaturally natural blonde hair, eyes like his and skin the same, slightly lighter, yet the same. He smells of oceans and she smells of mists.

They shimmy and they shake, their hips and thighs move like lovers' but remain the proper distance apart. Their torsos and arms stable and stationary despite the gyrations and rotations beneath. The DJ flips a switch on his big board, cutting out one player and cutting in another, just as the rumba presses a beat, jumping the big speakers from rumba to jive. Several dancers stumble and don't recover. A few cover their mistakes with exaggerated moves, sliding too low or spinning twice instead of once. Hyphi and Gal pace the music, leading it, as if their bodies are connected to the DJ's turntables instead of their brains. Judges confer, take notes.

When it is over, Hyphi and Gal take center stage. Gold medals. Ten thousand dollar prize. Handshakes and a kiss. No photos. Sorry, son.

Hyphi nudges Gal's arm, gently takes his hand and moves it towards the left a certain distance. He turns a one-quarter turn and shakes a hand, peering over the handshaker's shoulder towards the doors of the ballroom, his eyes following Hyphi's signal.

The tall man is there. Tall, fair skinned, with jet black hair swept down over the ears, hair a little too long considering his dress. Blue eyes, a compassionate face. A jaw line cut like the jib on a windward cutlass. The tall man dresses in a conservative suit, too conservative in this eclectic dancing, grab-your-eyes-accentuate-the-positive-eliminate-the-negative crowd, his suit so conservative it is meant to stand out by its gray pinstripe blandness. He pulls out a pocketwatch, checks the time then looks directly at them.

"You can't run anymore," he whispers. His voice carries to them over the crowd and shuffling band. "He knows where you are. You'll start to grow old. You'll start to age."

Hyphi looks at the man with the watch. "So be it."

Gal agrees, "Let Chronos take his magic from us. Let us grow old. Let us show the years that have given us such happiness."

*M*ontreal. New Paris Invitational. Hyphi and Gal speak Quebécois flawlessly, seamlessly, like their dancing. Grand Ballroom. American Waltz, European Waltz, Viennese Turning, Two Step, Tango. They shock the crowd by adding some three beat Cuban movement in mid-stride. A few, the intellectual hungries, the emotional starving, fresh from the unpleasantness in Europe, leaving before the Archduke's assassination spread into full scale war, damn themselves by applauding openly. When others turn in discorn the Europeans stamp their approval, pounding the great hall's floor in time to the music.

Hyphi curtsies and smiles, remembering to be demure and remembering to be haughty. The world is changing. Changing more rapidly than it ever had before. A cigarette would be too much, even for the Europeans. She gathers her red twin kick pleated skirts in the hand tied to her flounce and curtsies again; her other hand holds a yellowed string of fresh water pearls against her black-and-red-fringed bolero.

Gal pulls his Castillian fitted jacket down and tight. His tails lap his calves but go no lower. The sheen from his trousers' vein catches some of the new Edison lights and bounces it back like raw yellow fire, sulfurous.

Another couple, The Bennets, professionals who were this time second place, congratulate Hyphi and Gal. The conductor taps his stand, the strings gather, a Joplin rag comes out like a Bach two part invention. One of the conductor's tricks. The crowd calls for Hyphi to go round once with William, Gal with Chrysanthé.

Gal smiles and spins his wife, dipping her and drawing down to one knee, kissing her only inches above the floor. Some recognize the Colonial Quadrille moves in the midst of the Bolero.

"Through all time," he whispers, "I'll have no partner but you."

Hyphi smiles. The polished wood floor thrums with the crowd's approval.

New Hampshire has just signed. Word has come via Mssr. Thornton through New York.

Benjamin autocracizes that all should call him Lord Franklin. Lord of the Pennsylvania, from the northern New York to the Maryland of the south, bounded on sunrise by Delaware and sunset by Ohio. He wears a crown of flattened fish heads and calls for Fat George to declare his Independence from this Most Young Nation, These United States, The Free Americas.

The rum flows like the Delaware itself, quick and clean. The only cup to stay empty is Hopkins' – unless Dr. Franklin eyes not. Jefferson and Martha are the only to challenge Hyphi and Gal, and them not much, John Adams and Abigail willing but typical Boston clods in their steps. At least John has Abby to keep him sane, otherwise he'd be thrusting all who mock him.

Hyphi and Gal are by Jefferson's hest. "I have two wonders for you. Croppers from high in the Sound, and generously made known to me. They'll damn them Harvard mucks when the Vienna or Fling is called to dance. I'm told they have stories of the lost Colonies, as well."

Franklin, one eye upon Hyphi, quickly agreed. When he asked, Hyphi blushed to him then turned and laughed. "To think the good Doctor could ask me away!"

Gal came forward and Franklin raised his stick. Gal shook his hand and hugged him before Franklin could attack or defend. "By the gods, Franklin, your eyes are not dimmed by your age. You've chosen the fairest maid, and the only knowing enough to refuse you." He quickly turned to the other guests at the Ball. "Miladies, understand a husband's tongue is driven by his heart."

The room was filled with congratulatory "Yee"s from the men and titters from the ladies present.

Hyphi and Gal, in each others' arms once again, spun and whirled like tornadoes in flight.

Adams nudged Jefferson. "Damn me to Hell and again, Jefferson. Franklin's speechless!"

*L*ord *Raleigh's holiday for our first year in this Roanoke* Colony goes well. The only blight, and yeah, some consider it a sign of the tempest, are the Erinlender trappers the Massapoags brought with them.

These two, Hyphi and Gal, dress not as Anglish and not as Erinlenders, nor do they dress as any the Governors White, Carver, or Smith have seen, nor the captains of the great slaving ships. Even the Massapoags say these two keep strong magick a'twixt 'em.

They dress solely in skins and quilts as the savages taught them, but with strange cuts and plies not known to us.

There is their speech, aye. They speak the Savage well. Some say too well. It took Old Mackey a day to hear the Anglish in their speech. Old Anglish, he called it, far too old for them to know natural. They say it be due to their age and time in these Americas living and trading. The Governor asked the Massapoag regarding thus. "Before Yesterday," said Tennechehu, the oldest Savage we Colonials know.

Nor are the features of this Hyphi and her man Gal like the races of men we've known. Perhaps these be the strange men called "Chinese" or some of the heathen Bhuddans.

When the sun set and the stars came out we started our fires, sending embers up into the nightness. Out came flutes and strings and the Savages' drum. Then these two did dance.

Pagan, we knew them then. Heathen. Too long away from the One God. Their dance, we saw, called others to dance with them, others to lift their bodies and plunge their souls. I felt the spirit failing in me as well and, to keep my mind on the One True God, cut myself deeply in the flesh.

"Hail!" I called out, standing in the darkness with only the fire's light to show me. I lifted my bleeding arm high. "Look! Look what these two's magick has done!"

The Massapoag rose as one to keep us from the two Hyphi and Gal as the latter made their leave, laughing at us as they did.

It does not look good for us here. We fear as others may have in Wolstenholme Town, in Martin's Hundred upon the James. We should

Joseph Carrabis

travel perhaps north, beyond the Albermarle to Plymouth Colony or
the shores of Jersey.

Grandfather tells us Héna Túwe Wacípi, Those Who Dance,
are coming to join in the Eighth Snow Moon of Manintonquot.
I have asked Grandfather if Héna Túwe Wací-hwo and Héna
Túwe Wací-he will tell their story. I have never heard it, except from
Grandfather.

Before we became the People of the Quiet Water, when we were one
with the We Are Here Between Two Mountains, Héna Túwe Wacípi
came to Turtle Island across the Sunrise Waters, in a long boat with
many Black Shirt Men.

As soon as they came, Héna Túwe Wacípi danced. Soon their friends
the Black Shirt Men died, but Héna Túwe Wacípi remained. Over time,
they taught us the Sunrise Dance, the Fire Dance, and many others.

It is a good story to tell, a better one to hear.

Claddagh tore off his hood and pulled back his cassock, tucking it
into his waistrope. "Gal, Cha niel sibhse danns. Falbh na Dhiabhal!
Dia!"

Gal and Hyphi turn as Claddagh and his twelve monks gathered
their oars and prepared for quick sail. Claddagh had hoped for a different night. The Eiren west coast was still peopled by savages, some, and
a darker night would have profited them more.

Claddagh thought them children at first, children whose par-
ents hadn't approved. But then he saw, the Evil god, the Evil One,
tall and smiling and asking about the children Gal and Hyphi, the Evil
One dressed like a common man with a commoner's crop and talking
common to them down by the sea.

He followed the Evil One, to trap him as Our Lord hath said, but
too late, when, into the forest, shaded by trees, the Evil One changed
before him into a flying man and was away. Gal and Hyphi lay huddled
in his chamber when Claddagh returned. "Am feum sinne cho luath."
The children agree. Far across the sea, perhaps to the old Viking lands,

there the Evil One will not find them.

Now Claddagh hurries his serges to make to the sea. The Evil One called upon him today.

The she Hyphi points back to the shore. There, a silhouette in the crescent moon as it rises from the land, the Evil One, staring out to sea.

St. Remigius has agreed to baptize Cletus upon one condition. Cletus was enraged by this. Sending no messenger, he came to Remy himself; Cletus, a giant among his men and he still a head shorter than the Bishop of Rheims.

I've defeated the Alemanni, Cletus tells Remy. Strasbourg is mine and, now given to the church, yours. What more would the Bishop of Rheims ask of me? he demands.

The Gauls, murmurs Remy, removing his miter and showing his ears. Cletus goes to his knees, his face hidden, begging mercy, he didn't know in whose presence he spoke.

There are two, of the Gallic Lines, St. Remigius continues, quietly. They spread the dance of the old ways, the ways before our Lord Jesus Christ. They continue their dance and ask others to join them. The Church must destroy them.

He raises Cletus to his feet and stares deeply into his eyes. You must destroy them, he whispers. You must do this by bringing them to me.

Cletus, trembling, released himself into his own cloth.

St. Remigius only smiles. He allows Cletus to see his ring, which Cletus kissed. Remy then touches his ring to Cletus' brow. Cletus screamed as the Bishop's seal burnt into him.

See that you do this for me, said Remy. For your baptism, for your children, for you.

Cletus was baptized, for the church so ordered upon acceptance of his lands. St. Remigius went where Cletus directed, saying the Line dancers went north and west, to Allemande.

I, Josephus, writing in the third year of Caligula, thirty-fourth year of Judea as a province of Rome, from Corinth, upon the erection of a temple to a new god.

There is much confusion. There is no temple in place, merely a gathering of those who pray to this new god – I wonder at what expense. First, Rome is willing to embrace this new god as one of its own, but not willing to let this new god claim any that might be Rome's. Second, this new god was, as a man, a questionable prophet of the Jews. The Jews are quick to say they have one god. Now, it seems, the Bethlehem Messiah makes two.

Third, and this I find strangest of all, are the man and woman dancing here, clearly Greek, clearly from around the Thermaikós Kólpos. I remember them from the day Pilate saw to the man-god in Jerusalem. That day, as the Galilean writhed on his cross, these two danced for the guards and others who waited beneath him. Now they dance here, praising this prophet Jew, although like many who call out to him, in secret.

It is perhaps the greatness of this new god, and those who worship him, that all are accepted, despite their pasts, and protected through this underground brotherhood, moved and shuttled so that their enemies can not find them.

Inquiring, I found this man and woman, these two dancing, were spirited here. It seems some enemy sought them in Judea, even as they danced beneath this Christ's cross, apparently oblivious to the god-king who danced above them.

*C*hronos *smiled sunshine to the earth below. "Come, Hermes. Look upon these two; Hypheria and Galaxus! Never have two* mortals delighted so much in their movement!"

Hermes came and stood beside Chronos' throne.

"Ho! A riddle for you, Messenger. Clio has taught those at Cnossus to remember their words, and Ramses in Memphis makes me think Thaleia has taught the Egyptians to laugh. Now these two ask for a gift. What is left for them?"

"Why not gift them from Terpsichore, Lord Chronos?"

"What is returned to me?"

"They call out to you, they cry upon your name. Give them the gift, then take them as your own."

"How would I do this? To gift them from Terpsichore, such beauty to be among men?"

"Wrap them in the tears of one eye, my Lord. Thus you will always see the beauty of their dance before you but not be blinded from the rest of the world in the other."

"Ha! Ha and done. Terpsichore, muse your magic upon them. Make it so!"

*T*he knock on the door startles Hyphi and Gal from their embrace. They take their headphones off. Hyphi helps Gal to his chair. They won't stop dancing, although it takes so much out of them now. The walls of their room are bare, not even a mirror, not even a calendar to mark the days. Only the top drawer of the lowboy can be opened, which is enough because they don't have much clothing between them. That, their bed, the mattress sagging to show where they play spoons each night, two hardback chairs, and their music box is all there is in their room.

Hyphi opens the door. A nurse stands there.

"Mrs. Kólpos? Mr. Kólpos. Sorry to disturb you." She looks past them into the room, not seeing them, never seeing them. They are more troublesome than the others. They refuse to be separated into the men's and women's wards, even though the state promised they could see each other whenever they wanted. That is trouble enough, as Mr. Kólpos always stands guard at the lave door when Mrs. Kólpos has to go. Which is often, by the way. Then there is their radio which they played loud because they were both going deaf and needed to hear it to dance. That was handled by taking their radio away at first. Instead they sang and, by god, no one wanted to put up with that. Then their dancing. Always dancing. Thank god they were light. Frail in their old age. Wrinkled and tiny, although they moved together so well and even Dr. Fortin recognized that and decided, hell, it makes them happy so we'll look the other way. Okay, let them be happy, but did he have to give them that damned music box, even if it was just a Walmart mpg player with a tinny speaker, and the remote headphones? It was against regulation and that wasn't right at all at all at all.

The nurse moves past Hyphi and turns the music box off. Red receiver lights fade on the two sets of headphones and Gal, the music fading around him, searches for Hyphi with rheumy eyes, his hand reaching as his voice cracks, calling her name.

"You won't need this," the nurse says. The side of her mouth crinkling in a smile. "Your son's here." Thank god, she added to herself. She didn't even know these two had a son.

"Our son?" says Hyphi.

"What did she say?" asks Gal.

Hyphi goes to Gal and rests her hand on his shoulder, rubbing him there. "She said our son is here."

"Son?" He looks from the nurse to Hyphi.

Hyphi smiles and they nod to each other. They nod and a single tear comes from each, each from one eye. She kisses him then and the nurse turns away. Two old people shouldn't carry on so.

"Show him in," Gal says. As the nurse leaves they put their headphones back on.

A moment later he stands there. He thanks the nurse and she leaves, and he waits until they stop dancing before he enters. Tall, his hat still on, jet black hair and blue eyes and compassionate face and crystal cut jaw. He looks around.

Hyphi takes her seat beside Gal as he takes his. In this small room, in its unrelenting sameness, they are daised as King and Queen.

"Sorry there's no place to sit," says Gal.

The tall man closes the door behind him and takes off his hat. His ears are pointed. "The room is bland and vacant except for you. You bring so much love and light into the room decorations are meaningless." He opens his pocketwatch and notices the time.

"Thank you, Mercury. Or Hermes. Or Michael, Bruhan, Cyllen... What are you called now?" asks Hyphi. Her words are not bitter. They bear the sound of relief.

The tall man shrugs. "Chronos chose you to dance only for him, for he so delighted in your movement and love for each other. He chose to keep you eternally young so that you might dance in his eye forever. But you fled. Why did you flout the god's gift?"

"Because of what the gods could not know," says Hyphi as she turns to Gal and takes his face in her hand. "The joy in counting the wrinkles of your lover's face, of knowing a life spent loving another, of growing old and growing stronger in another's love. The joy of waking up in the morning and seeing more to the person beside you than was there the night before."

Gal kisses her hand. A wrinkled hand on a shriveled arm reaches around long fallen breasts and holds her near him. His other arm goes around her back and keeps her close, there.

"These are the reasons we fled," says Gal. "We could not stay young forever. It might be the way of the gods, but not of us. Men and women are meant to grow old, to grow wise, to grow stronger in love even as their bodies grow weaker in time."

The tall man nods, understanding, possibly in agreement, then snaps the watch shut and rubs the signature of Olympus with his thumb. Hypheria and Galaxus crumple before him into two piles of dust.

The tall man's form mists slightly and he stands before their dust in his true form, prepared for flight, when his god-keen ears hear distant, quiet laughter. He kneels, not breathing, and strains his ears.

There is no wind, no rain, no stirring of the earth from below, yet what remains lifts in tiny whirlwinds, swirls into and around each other's ashes, and again he hears their laugh.

**THOSE WINGS WHICH TIRE,
THEY HAVE UPHELD ME**

THOSE WINGS WHICH TIRE, THEY HAVE UPHELD ME

SPRING

Cowan was walking in the woods the first time he saw Angel. He was really looking for a haunted house the real estate lady told his parents was back there and he'd walked further into the woods than he'd ever gone before.

There was an inch of snow on the ground except where the sun came through the trees for most of the day. In those places the ground was muddy. Cowan felt the crisping of the snow under his boots and looked at his footprints, wanting to remember what they really looked like when he could really see them.

He took off the wrap-around sunglasses he wore to hide the holes where his eyes had been, thinking maybe the sunglasses stopped what he used to see from getting through. He still smelled the woodiness of the trees, still felt the cool air on his face and his breath misting as he exhaled. His breath didn't look right, though.

That was because of the Cap.

Dr. Hargitay said the Cap was best at least until they were sure the cancer didn't come back. After that, Dr. Hargitay told Cowan's parents, maybe they could transplant.

But until then it was the Cap.

Cowan didn't like it. It itched.

Cowan's family moved closer to the hospital that previous winter.

Mom and Dad wanted to be with him more and this was the only way to do it. Cowan knew there were lots of other kids whose parents had moved closer to the hospital, but few of those kids ever came out.

He sniffed and wiped his nose on his sleeve.

When Cowan showed up in his new school after Spring vacation, Kevin, who wasn't even in his class and had stayed back twice, followed Cowan all over the playground, just walking behind him and sing-songing "*I* can't *See, I* can't *See*" until Cowan ran back into the school. Ms. Sanborn heard him in the boysroom and sent in Mr. Horly, the janitor, to see if everything was okay.

Because Cowan couldn't cry – Dr. Hargitay explained that when they removed his eyes they had to take lots more out. The cancer, he told Cowan, had done more than attack his eyes – Mr. Horly told Ms. Sanborn everything was okay.

The next day Kevin and three other boys, their arms locked over each other's shoulders like high school football champs, walked behind Cowan all of recess, their four voices singing Kevin's "*I* can't *See, I* can't *See*" song. Cowan knew the playground monitors and teachers were around. He could see them. Maybe they didn't help him because they didn't know if he really *could* see them. Maybe they felt if they were really, really quiet, he wouldn't know they were there because of the Cap. It was brand new. Not many people besides Dr. Hargitay and his friends understood it. Cowan heard Dr. Hargitay talk about light being electric and magnetic vibrations in space and how the brain didn't need eyes to sense those vibrations, that the Cap could do it, but Cowan didn't understand.

But that didn't matter to Cowan. On the third day, what mattered was Kevin and his football buddies spending half the recess following him around.

Cowan turned to face them. Kevin laughed and his buddies laughed and they sing-songed louder, "*I* can't *See, I* can't *See*." Cowan took off his glasses and unhooked the Cap. Only Dr. Hargitay, Mom and Dad knew what Cowen looked like without the Cap. Dr. Hargitay said it didn't matter and Mom and Dad never told.

Two of the boys screamed and ran. One got sick and wet himself. Only Kevin stood his ground, staring at Cowan but saying nothing, swallowing hard and snuffling until Cowan walked away.

Ms. Sanborn called Cowan's parents. Cowan, she told them, was terrorizing the children on the playground. Cowan, they told her, would be punished.

That night, after dinner in the kitchen, Mom said he must never take off the Cap. Dad rearranged cookbooks on the shelf over the stove but said nothing, only nodding at things Mom said. They took him to Dr. Hargitay who did something so Cowan couldn't take the Cap off again. "For your own good," Dr. Hargitay said.

The next day Cowan caught some kids staring at him. He wasn't sure which hurt more, the Cap or the other kids' stares. Every time he caught them staring they'd quickly turn away and watch him from the corners of their eyes, facing front, their hands on their books and their heads towards the board, but their eyes over to the sides or their heads tilted just enough so he could tell.

He got back at them, though. When he caught them staring, he'd hiss at them or growl. Sometimes he'd spit. A few times he'd tense his fingers until his hands looked like bird claws and he'd scratch them.

Nobody, not even Kevin, dared fight him. They were frightened of the Cap, with its red, yellow, and turquoise lights flashing, the light-guides glowing on and off, and always the black holes, hidden by his wrap-around sunglasses, where his eyes used to be. Nobody wanting to fight him made Cowan feel a little better.

Sometimes, when Cowan felt alone or angry or like he wanted to cry and knew he couldn't and even if he could no one would let him, he'd show them.

He'd take off his glasses and show them.

He'd show everybody.

Except Leonard Houde. A few days after Ms. Sanborn sent Cowan home, when Cowan was standing by the fence on the playground and keeping to himself, Leonard walked up to him.

"Hi," Leonard said.

Cowan growled and hissed.

Leonard said, "Yeah, well, hi," and walked away.

Ms. Sanborn was always sending Leonard into Mrs. McDonough's office. It seemed to Cowan Ms. Sanborn sent Leonard to Mrs. McDonough's office whenever anything happened Ms. Sanborn didn't like. It didn't matter if Leonard was the one who did it or not, Leonard was the one who'd go. She sent Leonard to Mrs. McDonough's office the first day Cowan came to class. Cowan remembered that. Cowan walked in and Ms. Sanborn introduced him to the class. Somebody laughed and threw a wad of paper at Cowan. It didn't even come from Leonard's direction but Leonard say "Hey" and Ms. Sanborn said, "Mr. Houde, get your things and get out" so basically Leonard walked out as Cowan walked in.

Cowan wanted to say something but Ms. Sanborn said "We behave in this class, Cowan." Was Leonard being punished for Cowan's being there?

Leonard waved and smiled at him as he walked out.

It bothered Cowan that Ms. Sanborn always sent Leonard to Mrs. McDonough's office because Leonard was the only kid who'd been anything like nice to him. Cowan figured Ms. Sanborn hated Leonard. She was nice to Cowan but only because he wore the Cap, not because of anything else. He figured if he'd been another kid, somebody without the Cap, he'd go see Mrs. McDonough pretty often, too.

So because Cowan didn't have any friends, and because even the grown-ups were afraid of the Cap, Cowan walked in the woods behind his house all by himself that Saturday the first time he saw Angel. His mother said he had to be at the hospital in an hour so he could go play until she called him.

The house, when he found it, didn't look haunted. It looked like a dump; big and green with brown trim, most of its windows broken and a wrap-around porch. The highest windows had no glass in them at all.

"Hey, is there anybody in there?" he yelled. "My name's Cowan Barnes and I came out here to play." He waited. "Hey, anybody home?"

Nobody answered. Cowan picked up a rock and threw it at the

house. It bounced off the side.

"Stupid house."

A big, old spruce stood in front of the house. He folded his sunglasses in his pocket and leaned against the tree, taking deep breaths of its Christmasy smell. He remembered, where he used to live, he leaned up against a spruce tree and his mother yelled at him because his hair got all sticky. He patted the tree and felt the sticky sap on his hands, then got angry because he didn't have any hair left to get sticky. All he had now was the cool metal skin of the Cap, its blinking lights and glowing little wire guides where curly blond hair used to be. There was no one around for him to growl at so he smashed the Cap against the spruce. The bolt of pain reminded him of the cancer and he cried, which hurt even more because there was nothing left to cry with.

He lifted his head. Something was wrong. His vision blurred, but not like when he had the cancer. Back then things just got fuzzy and never cleared. Now he saw two pictures of everything; one like always but only black&white, the other one a mash of different colors and a little to the right of the first. It was like when he first woke up with the Cap and Dr. Hargitay had to make adjustments.

Cowan waited for the mashed color images to blend into the black&white. When they didn't, he got scared. He wanted to cry again but that hurt too much, so instead he reached for the black&white spruce. It was there and it was solid. then he reached for the mashed color tree. It wasn't there. His hand went right through it, except he saw a black&white hand go through the colors and saw a mashed color hand go through the air a little to his right.

He laughed and experimented. Soon he got the hang of it. All the mashed color things were like shadows. He could walk through the colored shadows like they were nothing at all, only the black&white things were real.

He started back home, careful to walk through the colored shadows and not the black&white things. Most of the time he wondered whether or not to tell Dr. Hargitay.

This was fun.

That's when he bumped into Angel.

Cowan saw what looked like a blurry, mashed black&white dead old tree trunk with two scrawny branches to his left and a clear, multicolored, almost burning tree with two huge branches full of glowing leaves to his right. He walked into the multicolor tree and fell back onto the ground. When he looked up, the multicolored tree was staring down at him. Only now it had huge wings which reached up and out behind it. It looked like it was kneeling down, trying to figure him out. Over to the left, Cowan saw what he thought might have been a blurry, black&white, dead old tree bending like it had knees. That was wrong. Trees didn't have knees. When he really looked at it, it didn't look like a tree at all, it looked like a tall man's shadow with wings.

To his left, what might have been a scrawny, dead branch reached down to him. In front of him, something with three fingers, no thumb, and which seemed to be on fire, came towards him.

Cowan got up and ran. Between the things he could see, between what was real and what was not. All the way home.

Cowan's mother said nothing except to ask him if he had fun in the Woods.

When they got to the hospital, Dr. Hargitay hooked a computer into the Cap. "The external representation and the internal reality are out of synch." He patted Cowan's shoulder. "Wow, I'll bet that must have been scary for a while, huh?"

Cowan said nothing.

"I'll bet you could still remember which was which, huh?"

Cowan looked at Dr. Hargitay with black sockets where his eyes use to be.

"Okay, Cowan, tell me what you see." Dr. Hargitay turned back to his computer and made adjustments without waiting for Cowan to speak. "That's right. The black&white is the object, but just the shape and form, the blur of colors is what the object is, content and context."

Dr. Hargitay typed at his keyboard and the real image and the mashed color image came together again, the colors swarming over the black&white like moss climbing a rock. When Dr. Hargitay finished everything had a single, colored image again. He and Cowan's Mom talked while Cowan played in the waiting room. There were some other kids there with their parents. Kids who weren't in Cowan's school, with parents who didn't live close by.

Cowan didn't go into the woods for a week. When he did, he saw Angel. Cowan yelled, "Who are you? What're you doing here?"

If Angel noticed, it didn't respond.

"Hey, you! Hey, Turdhead, I'm talking to you!"

Angel stood still in the forest without acknowledging Cowan's presence. Cowan made his hands into claws, took off his sunglasses, growled and ran at Angel.

Angel didn't move until Cowan ran into him and fell down. When Angel did move, it was as before, kneeling down and reaching out to Cowan.

This time Cowan didn't run. He'd done his best. It'd always frightened the kids at school and sometimes even made Ms. Sanborn turn away and leave him alone.

So Cowan looked. Angel was all red. It had a head and there were two black eyes. At least Cowan thought they were eyes. They were two large black ovals that touched at the top of Angel's head. Each went down the side of the head to almost where ears might be, except Angel didn't have any ears and no nose or mouth. Angel had the shape of a grown-up, but skinnier, which Angel wasn't, but Cowan didn't know how else to describe it. It was like somebody had taken a Gumby and pulled it too much and the Gumby never went back to normal.

Angel's hands were three pointy fingers which didn't have any knuckles, nor did Angel have any feet. It looked as if its feet were buried because its legs ended in spikes which punched into the ground. What Cowan liked most were the two huge bat-like wings which came out of Angel's back. Angel wasn't really tall – Cowan thought it was only a little taller than his Dad – but Angel's wings looked big enough to cover both his Mom's and Dad's cars if they were parked end to end.

Angel reached down and wrapped a hand around Cowan's arm.

Inside his head, Cowan saw himself walking into Angel the first time, then running at Angel this time. It was the first time he'd seen himself without his sunglasses, saw the two empty eye-sockets looking out.

He turned away but the image stayed in his mind. He couldn't blink it away and the more he saw it, the more it made him want to cry, which he couldn't which made him want to cry even more.

Angel's eyes changed color. They were blue, deep, deep blue.

Suddenly Cowan saw the woods as they were in winter, quiet and snow laden. The pictures went light to dark and back quickly. Deer made their way through the snow and rabbits and squirrels ran about. Quickly the snow melted and trees and flowers bloomed. Insects buzzed. Cats and skunks and raccoons wandered in and out of view. The trees' leaves changed color and started to fall.

Cowan looked into Angel's face. "You're showing me the seasons, aren't you."

A moment later Angel's eyes were black again and there were no more pictures in Cowan's head.

"Who are you?"

Angel's eyes turned blue.

"Hey, Cowan? Who you talking to?"

Cowan jumped and Angel let go. Cowan fumbled for his sunglasses before getting up.

"Who you talking to, Cowan?"

Leonard wore black high-top Keds with broken laces. His jeans needed patching, as did his jacket. His hair needed combing and there was dirt on his face and hands.

"What d'you want?"

Leonard shrugged. "Nothing. Just walking. Saw you running at something and thought maybe somebody might be trying to beat you up. Thought maybe I could help you."

Angel walked away.

"Nobody wants to beat me up. Everybody's scared of me."

Leonard looked down and kicked some dirt. "I'm not."

"That's because you're stupid."

Leonard, never looking up, kicked some more dirt. "Lots of people say so." He looked at Cowan and held his fists up. "But nobody ever said I was afraid."

Cowan took his glasses off and growled. Leonard hit him on the jaw. The punch knocked Cowan to the ground. When he looked up, Leonard had his hand out, offering to help him up just as Angel had earlier.

"You going to knock me down again?"

"You going to make me?"

Cowan shook his head, no, and took the hand Leonard offered. They stared at each other a few moments then Leonard said, "Can I touch your Cap?"

"You really want to?"

"Yeah. I think it's neat."

Cowan leaned his head towards Leonard. Like a blind man reading someone's face, Leonard ran his tiny hands gently and carefully over Cowan's Cap and through the lightguides. Not even Dr. Hargitay's touch had been as soft. When he was done, Leonard asked, "Do you think I could get one?"

"I think you have to have cancer first."

Leonard didn't answer right away. "Oh."

"You hungry?"

"Sure."

"Want to go back to my house and get something to eat?"

"Great."

They talked about kids at school until they got to Cowan's yard.

"So who were you talking to back there?"

"I don't know." Cowan described Angel to Leonard.

"Wow, neat. You saw your guardian angel."

"You didn't see it?"

"Nope. That what lets me know it's an angel. You tell anybody else about your angel?"

"Yeah. Not! Everybody knows I'm sick. You want them to think I'm stupid, too?" Cowan winced. "I don't think you're stupid, Leonard."

"I know. Neither do I."

"I mean crazy stupid. I don't want people to think I'm nuts. Don't you think I'm nuts?"

"Nope. Maybe it's that metal on your head. My Dad's got some metal in his head and he's always hearing stuff. He'll be walking along then grab us and knock us to the ground and shout 'Incoming'. My Mom said it's because of the plate in his head. She says it's not so bad. She says sometimes, if she rubs his head just right, it's like being on one of those dime rides at the grocery store. I'm not sure what she means by that, but it sounds funny."

"Did he have a cancer, your Dad?"

"Naw. This happened when he was in some war. I think my Mom told me it was a grenade. Can you see your angel now?"

Cowan looked around and back into the woods. "No. I think it left when you came."

"Gee. I'm sorry."

"Don't worry. If it's really my angel, it'll come back."

Three weeks later there was no snow any more and most of the buds had turned to leaves on the trees. Cowan's Mom and Dad were grateful Cowen'd finally made a friend and Leonard, in return, had become a regular guest at the Barnes' house.

Cowan and Leonard were out in the woods when Cowan stopped them both.

"What is it, Cow?"

"My angel," Cowan whispered. "It's over there."

"Where?"

Cowan pointed. "See it?"

"Nope. Looks like it's all yours. Want to go over and say hi?" Leonard didn't wait for a response and walked in the direction Cowan pointed.

"Hey, wait up. It's *my* angel." When they were close, Cowan took the lead and touched Angel.

Angel's wings unfolded and his eyes turned blue as he returned Cowan's touch. In his mind, Cowan saw stars burning in the rich blackness of space.

"What's going on?" Leonard asked.

"It's giving me pictures."

"Oh. Hey, ask if it's an angel."

"Are you an angel?" Cowan asked.

Angel's eyes went from blue to gold. Pictures of all sorts whirled in Cowan's mind, each stopping for a moment then moving on. Cowan felt as if Angel were skimming through some huge encyclopedia in its head.

"What's it say?" asked Leonard.

"I don't think it knows what an angel is. I'm getting all sorts of pictures, but nothing like an angel."

"Tell it what one is, Cow."

Cowan began picturing an angel in his mind. The only one he'd ever seen was on an old CD his parents had by somebody named Dan Fogelberg. On the CD, the angel was a woman with blond hair, a white robe, white spots where her eyes should have been, big white feathered wings, and, what Cowan remembered most, gold handcuffs and chains. As he remembered the only angel he knew, the picture grew in his mind.

When he got to the handcuffs and chains, Angel's eyes went from gold to red, not quite the same color as its skin, but close, and in Cowan's head the handcuffs and chain grew coarse and large. The pictures of the CD angel blended with an image of Angel for a second. Cowan felt sad and wanted to cry. As quickly as the pain came, it was gone, the picture in his mind replaced by the CD angel, without chains, flying in the black, starred night. As he watched the picture in his head, the CD angel turned into the one in front of him.

"Well?" asked Leonard.

"I still don't think it's an angel, but that's as close as we'll get."

"Find out if it's from Heaven."

"Yeah, I think it is. It always shows me pictures of outer space. That's where Heaven is, isn't it?"

"Hey, maybe it's an alien. Ask if it's an alien."

Cowan showed Angel all the pictures he knew of aliens from comic books and movies.

Angel's eyes twinkled until Cowan was done.

"Nope, nothing like that."

Leonard considered, nodded, then giggled. "Hey, find out if it's a guy or a girl."

Cowan giggled, too, then thought of his mother and father. He made the pictures go back an forth in his mind. Angel's eyes went brown then back to blue. Inside Cowan's head, the pictures of his mother and father merged. All their features unique and separate, yet somehow Angel managed to make them into one beautiful whole.

"I don't think it's either. I think it's both."

"Can't be."

Angel's eyes continued blue. Inside, Cowan saw pictures like in science books, one-celled creatures dividing themselves in two, then other animals, things like flowers, only flowers that moved, with parts reaching out to other parts, and where they touched things like seeds were being sent into the wind to become other walking flowers. Next he saw things from the oceans, things he didn't know he knew, but seeing, understood, things growing large until smaller versions of themselves separated from the original and left, leaving the original free to begin the cycle again, and lastly, Angel showed Cowan itself, its wings folding, its belly swelling, until a second Angel grew out of the first; head first, wings folded, eyes sparkling all different colors at once.

"No," said Cowan. "Some things are both. They have kids that way." Angels' eyes flashed like a signal beacon – gold, brown, blue, then black. "I think it's okay if we call him a boy though. He doesn't seem to mind."

"Oh." Leonard strained to see something of Angel but nothing came. "What's he doing here?"

Cowan made a picture of Angel in his mind. Next he made a picture of Superman flying around the Earth, coming through the clouds and landing.

Angel's eyes flashed red. It let go of Cowan's hand and moved off into the woods. Cowan sniffed and wiped his nose on his sleeve.

"You okay, Cowan?"

"Yeah. Just a little sad. Angel didn't tell me why he's here. I think it's not a good thing, though."

"Ask him."

"I can't. He left."

SUMMER

*L*eonard sat in Dr. Hargitay's waiting room. Mr. and Mrs. Barnes sat with Cowan in the examining room.

Cowan had drawn a picture of a human brain, rough but accurate and detailed. Cowan drew lines. "Here," he told Dr. Hargitay. "From here and here to here."

Dr. Hargitay straightened up as he stared at Cowan's drawing. "The visual cortex, from pre-optic ganglia straight back to the occipital lobes." He looked over at Mrs. Barnes. "You're right, Cowan. that's an excellent guess."

"It wasn't a guess."

"Cowan," hushed his mother.

Dr. Hargitay shook his head. "No, no. He's quite right. It's too accurate to be a guess. How did you know that, Cowan?"

Cowan shrugged.

"What grade are you in now? Second? Third?"

"I'm starting third grade this fall."

"Where did you learn about the Cap?"

Cowan shuffled on the examining table. He looked towards the door. "I read about it. Online."

Mrs. Barnes apologized, "He's been doing a lot of reading lately."

Dr. Hargitay thought about that then unhooked the computer feed and helped Cowan down. "Well, keep it up, Cowan. I can use the help. Would you mind waiting for your folks outside, please?"

Before Cowan was out the door Dr. Hargitay said, "He's a clever boy, Mr. and Mrs. Barnes. Very clever. He's got some good ideas, he does."

Cowan cleared his throat as he opened the door. "Don't patronize."

Dr. Hargitay paused and stared at him. "Yes. Quite."

Mr. Barnes said, "I'll wait outside with the boys."

Cowan sat beside Leonard. "So?"

"I think we either have to stop seeing Angel so much or we need to be careful who we share what with."

"With whom we share what."

"Yes, exactly."

"What did he say, Cow?"

"He said Angel's right about the modifications to the Cap."

Mr. Barnes sat across the room and picked up a magazine.

Leonard nodded at Cowan's father. "You didn't tell them about Angel, did you?"

"I'm blind, Leonard. I'm not nuts." Cowan looked at his father and spoke up. "Hey, Dad, how long do you think Mom'll be with Dr. Hargitay?"

Mr. Barnes looked at Dr. Hargitay's door as if he'd never seen it before. "I don't know, son," he sighed. "At this point in my life, I'm just along for the ride."

A few hours later Leonard and Cowan were out in the woods. They walked side by side. Leonard had a backpack on. In it were two books Angel wanted the boys to read. One was *Robinson Crusoe*. The other *Pilgrim's Progress*. "Where's Angel?" Leonard asked. "I'm getting tired. Doesn't he know about ebooks? Use to be every week new books. Now it's every day new books." He sang "I'll never be your beast of burden."

"If I had eyes, I'd roll them heavenward." Cowan stopped then strode in a new direction.

"What is it? Did you see Kevin or something?"

"Naw. My Mom found out Kevin goes to live with his Dad each summer. It's Angel. He's over there."

"Hey, Angel!"

"Cut it out. You know he can't hear you. He can only talk when he touches you. and then only if you can see him."

"I know." Leonard kicked some dirt.

Cowan placed a hand on Leonard's arm. "I'm sorry, Leonard."

With neither boy realizing it, Angel came over to them and touched Cowan's shoulder. His eyes flashed blue.

Leonard yelped and fell to the ground.

"Lenny, you all right?"

Leonard shook his head. "I don't know, Cow. that was real weird. Kind of like, all of a sudden my mind had all these pictures."

Inside Cowan's mind he felt the blue-eyed quiet and rest, Angel's 'Hello'. He focused the thought as Angel had been teaching him to focus, concentrating until each thought became a picture in his head. He made a picture of Angel's 'Hello' and shrunk it down in his mind, placing a distinct black abyssal around it as a border. The feeling of Angel's greeting remained, although Cowan felt it smaller in his head.

"Here." He held his hand out to Leonard.

Leonard's eyes glazed over but didn't shut. "Wow. this is great. What is it?"

"What do you see?"

"I'm not sure. Clouds, I guess. Like in a movie, when you fly through them in a real bright sky."

They moved through the clouds and far below the ground was orange but only in patches. Everywhere else the ground was mottled gray.

Angel flew into the picture, a brighter and more colorful Angel than what Cowan saw and Leonard imagined. Angel flew and dove and landed on an orange part of ground. Little angels came to him and surrounded him, jumping and flying, their little angel eyes blinking like little rainbow caps on all their heads.

Other grown-up angels entered the picture. They flashed but only black and white. They pulled the angel children away, eventually getting to Angel and flying him high into the sky, higher and higher until they passed through the clouds. As they took Angel further and further away from the little angel children he grew somewhat less colored, less distinct than the Angel Cowan saw and the one Leonard imagined.

Cowan, his voice quiet like in a theater or a church, said, "Why didn't you fight them, Angel?"

But nowhere did Angel fight them or struggle. They lifted him so high that none of them could travel higher, then threw him into the stars. Multicolor, twinkling stars. All the black and white angels folded their wings and dove back to their slate colored planet.

The pictures in Cowan and Leonard's minds showed Angel's world again, but now colorless save the slate shaded ground.

The Angel in their minds stretched up into an earth-like sky, his wings opening and closing until his spear-like feet came loose from the ground. Higher and higher he flew. The Angel in their minds began to fade.

Leonard frowned. Cowan saw the blue sky and clouds breaking up and sliding into the surrounding abyss. Angel's eyes flashed from blue to red and he knelt on the ground, as if tired, exhausted.

Both Cowan and Leonard felt it. Leonard kicked at some grass. Cowan sniffed and wiped his nose on his sleeve.

Angel stood up and rubbed Cowan's back. His eyes flashed all their colors and it felt like Angel was tickling Cowan inside Cowan's head. Cowen tried to shrug Angel off but Angel held on until Cowan laughed. then Angel took Cowan's hands and placed them palm up with Cowan facing Leonard.

Leonard said, "It's getting late."

"I know. I think Angel wants us to play a game, though."

"Hey, I know this one." Leonard placed his hands palm down, lightly on Cowan's. As he did, Angel placed both his hands on Cowan's shoulders. His eyes went to blue.

Cowan's mind filled with colors. Leonard's legs went soft. He clenched Cowan's hands for support. The colors resolved into blue mountains heavy with pink and orange clouds. The mountaintops were buffeted by sun-bright snow and winds. Both boys recognized bird songs but from birds neither knew.

Angel held Cowan. Cowan, glancing on either shoulder, saw Angel's hands turn blue and his wings open. Without knowing why, he shouted, "Hold on, Leonard," and, as if Angel had given them a cue, they flew into the night.

AUTUMN

*K*evin and some of his friends were huddled on the playground the first day of school, waiting. Leonard and Cowan sized up the opposition from the playground entrance.

"You know," said Leonard, "this'll be the third year he's stayed in the same grade. He'll be in Mr. Evans's class, same as us."

"Really."

"Yep."

Half the playground away Kevin and his friends started, "*I* can't *See*, *I* can't *See*." Their chant continued until they stood next to Cowan and Leonard, Kevin towering over both them and his own friends. "My Dad told me about you, Barnes. He said you're just a freaky little blind kid and I'm not afraid of any freaky little blind kid. Do you hear me, Barnes? I'm not afraid of you anymore." Ms. Sanborn and Mr. Evans turned and walked away.

Cowan stood and looked at Kevin and his friends, neither saying nor doing anything. Leonard shuffled off and left him alone.

Kevin pushed himself up against Cowan. "Hey, you too stupid to know when I'm talking to you?"

"I know you're talking to me, Kevin. I just don't know what to do about it."

One of Kevin's friends offered, "Going to take your glasses off again? Huh, freaky Mr. No-eyes? Going to take your glasses off again?"

Cowan looked at him. "No. I wouldn't do that."

Kevin pushed Cowan. "So what you going to do?" He started the chant again, pushing Cowan with each emphasized syllable. "*I* can't *See*, *I* can't *See*."

Cowan, measuring the beat of the other boy's words, stepped aside as Kevin pushed and Kevin fell to the ground.

He got up with fists clenched. "You're dead, freaky no-eyes. You're dead." He started dancing around Cowan, his fists up and ready to strike.

From deep within the playground Leonard screamed, "I *can* see.

Mr. Evans, Ms. Sanborn! I'm watching you walk away." He took out his mobile. "I *can* see and I'm documenting this."

Kevin and his friends turned. Cowan took the opportunity to move past them onto the playground. Close to the middle of the playground stood Leonard, facing Cowan and Kevin, his little index finger extended and pointing at them. Immediately in front of him were Mr. Evans and Ms. Sanborn, their backs to Cowan, Kevin, and his friends but facing Leonard.

"Look, Mr. Evans. Look, Ms. Sanborn. I *can* see and soon the whole world can, too." He watched his mobile's screen.

Even from where he stood Cowan could see the expressions and colors of the two teachers faces as they turned.

Mr. Evans grabbed Leonard's outstretched hand. He and Ms. Sanborn walked briskly, Leonard in tow and hopping all the way. They gathered Cowan, Kevin, and the others and brought them into the school, dropping the horde in Mrs. McDonough's office. "So begins another fine year," Ms. Sanborn mumbled as they walked out.

"A little dramatic, don't you think, Houde?" Cowan said. He turned to see Kevin staring at him, staring at the Cap, his eyes bright and curious, not dull and malicious.

When he realized Cowan was staring back he said, "I'm not afraid of you, Barnes."

A few Saturdays later Cowan and Leonard stood deep in the forest by the haunted house, Angel behind them, one wing over each of them, protecting them from the cold, autumn rain and wind, the three of them staring into the sky. Angel's eyes were deep brownish-red, the color of dried blood. Cowan saw Angel's thoughts clearly and hand-in-hand gave them to Leonard.

"You know what he's telling us, don't you?"

"Don't say it, Leonard."

Angel, his eyes still red, gave Cowan a picture of his colors fading, washing away, until his image against the sky and woods dissolved.

Cowan pushed Angel's wing away and stepped out into the rain. "No!" He knocked off his sunglasses and started thrashing at Angel's wings as the rain splashed the Cap and ran down his face. "I won't let you. I won't let you!"

Leonard reached for Cowan's arms and Cowan fought back. They were rolling on the ground, covering themselves in cold mud and wet leaves, their little fists and tiny feet striking out wildly as they screamed at each other.

Suddenly they were apart and hanging in mid-air, two wet kittens being carried by an invisible cat. Angel, his eyes flashing all their colors, held Cowan and Leonard each in a three-fingered hand.

Angel's eyes steadied, changing slowly from blue to gold to red and back. In his mind, Cowan saw the black and white angels throwing Angel out, banishing him from their world to this one.

"I'm sorry, Len." He reached out. When he and Leonard touched, Angel put them down.

Leonard picked up Cowan's sunglasses and handed them to him. "I don't think Angel wants to die, Cowan."

"Yeah. Well."

"Everybody's gonna die. My Mom told me that."

Angel's wings reached back out and over the boys. He drew them in close until both boy's could feel him against them, the heat of his body keeping them warm and dry despite the storm. Slowly, he motioned them back to where Leonard's bookbag lay.

Keeping them under his wings, his eyes went from red to blue as he opened one of the books and handed it to Leonard.

"The Mysterious Traveler" started Leonard, "by Mark Twain..."

That next Tuesday, as Mr. Evans formed reading circles. Kevin shoved something into his desk.

"What was that, Kevin?" Mr. Evans stared at Kevin, sitting in the back and cramped in the desk she'd given him. "Kevin? I asked you a question, Kevin."

"Nothing."

Mr. Evans walked over to Kevin's desk. "Please give me your 'nothing', Kevin."

Some of the kids chuckled. Kevin's face got red. Cowan, watching, saw Kevin retreat into his already too small seat.

Mr. Evans stood over Kevin, one hand on her hips and the other palm up in front of his face. "I want that 'nothing' now."

Slowly, almost mechanically, Kevin reached inside his desk and pulled out a rolled up comic book. His eyes remained fixed forward and vacant as he handed it to his teacher.

"You know I don't allow this silly trash in my classroom, Mr. Sumone," she said.

"What comic is it?" Leonard asked.

"Something wrong with your nose, Mr. Houde?"

"It's an honest question, Mrs. Shea," Cowan said. "What comic is it?"

Sighing and staring at the ceiling, she unrolled it. A man in an 18th Century European soldier's uniform in some kind of treasure room graced the cover. Three moon-eyed dogs sat before him, each one larger than the last. Behind the three dogs rested three chests of coins. The smallest dog's chest held copper. The middle dog's chest held silver. The largest dog's chest held gold. The title read "Classic Comics Presents 'The Tinder Box'."

"That's a good story, Kevin. You should read Anderson's original version," said Cowan.

"Oh my yes," added Leonard." 'Fyrtøiet', from his 'Eventyr, fortalte for Børn'."

"You can find it in the library, Kevin, in 'The Classic Fairy Tales'."

Kevin growled quietly, "Fuck you."

Mr. Evans grabbed Kevin by the collar and shook him free of his desk.

"I'm witnessing this, Mr. Evans," yelled Leonard.

"Good. Good." She dragged Kevin to Leonard's desk and pulled him free, as well. "Go. Go right now. You, too, Cowan. All of you. To Mrs. McDonough's office. I don't have to put up with this."

She threw them out the classroom door and slammed it behind her. Cowan and Leonard shook themselves off and looked back in through the window. Kevin looked into the classroom too, turning away only after Mr. Evans threw his comic into the trash. As he turned Cowan met Kevin's eyes and wondered if there was something wrong with them, something that wouldn't let Kevin cry, as well.

Mr. Evans looked out the window, saw them standing there, and yelled at them to get to Mrs. McDonough's office.

Mrs. McDonough hung up the room-phone as they ambled in. "You boys wait right there for me, understand?"

Leonard said, "If you're too busy right now – "

"Sit."

She picked up the outside line and stared at Kevin. "Who's home today, Kevin? Anybody going to be able to come and take you away?"

Kevin stared at the floor and shrugged. "I don't know. I have to go pee."

Mrs. McDonough sighed, "Go ahead. Just come straight back."

Cowan watched the door close behind Kevin. "Last year I hated him. Now..."

"I know," nodded Leonard. "Me, too. What's Angel doing to us?"

WINTER

*A*ngel's scarlet body glowed less brightly than Cowan remembered. They sat on the ground, one boy on each of Angel's legs, an arm around each boy, his wings covering them like an amphitheater shell, their audience the western horizon and setting sun, warming them, Angel's wings protecting them from the cold while catching and amplifying the fading light.

Leonard carried three books: Posner's *Economic Analysis of Law*, Hyde's *The Gift*, and Ingpen's *An Encyclopedia of Things that Never Were*, the last open on his lap as he read aloud.

Angel turned shapes and colors into dancing images in Cowan's mind, explaining what Leonard read. A thought peeked out from behind a newly formed griffin. Angel expanded the griffin to hide the thought but Cowan shooed the griffin away and brought the thought forward.

Angel's eyes turned blue to red, then finally to black. He put both boys down and walked away.

Leonard asked, "What happened?"

"Angel is dying."

"Is there anything we can do?"

"We can stop learning."

"What?"

"I never understood until now. He wasn't willing to share it until now. He teaches us and he survives in our environment yet he never consumes anything. Think about that; He expends energy without gain."

"Impossible. That goes against everything he's taught us. It violates economics, commerce, Shannonistic and Semiotic Information Transfer, Fair-Exchange Theory, ..."

"Do what he taught us. Think bigger. He can't give without getting something. We know what he gives. What does he get? His values aren't ours. What does he value?"

Angel kneeled behind them, his hands hovering above their heads, the boys so focused on their discussion they didn't notice him there.

Leonard closed his eyes. He leaned forward, slightly rocking. His little hands forming claws to grasp and hold the answer. "He values learning." He inhaled deeply. His nostrils flared.

"He values teaching." He screamed, the realization so painful tears wet the pages of the open book.

"He's killing himself to teach us all he knows, all he's experienced, before passing. He's racing death so we'll be greater."

Cowan's hands worked into his lightguides, tightening on them, preparing to pull them out, The Cap's vision now too painful to see.

Angel's hands came down on their heads, gently. They looked up. Angel glowed brighter than ever before, so brightly Leonard could see his outline.

He showed them themselves, talking to each other, talking to others, and each time little angels danced around them, leaping from their minds and mouths to the minds and mouths of others.

"He's teaching us so we can teach others. So his knowledge will continue. That's why he had to leave his world. They didn't want his knowledge to continue."

"Nicholas of Cusa," Leonard said. "All we really have is our knowledge of ourselves. It doesn't matter what you teach, Cowan, what the subject matter is. You're always going to teach who you are."

Cowan looked into Angel's eyes. "That's it, isn't it? You're not a teacher like here. You're dying because you teach who you are. You share yourself, literally, so what you are - your knowledge - can continue. It's okay for you to pass on because you've given everything you ever had away."

Leonard sniffed. "That's why he isn't afraid of death. That's why he welcomes it."

Angel sat on the ground. He lifted the two boys onto his lap, holding them close against him.

"Cowan?"

"Yeah?"

"What does Angel smell like?"

"I don't know."

"Ask him."

Cowan filled his mind with pictures of everything he could think of which he could smell. He smelled dog fur, wet and dry, then his Mom's makeup and perfume. Dad's aftershave. Peanut butter. Fresh mowed grass. Garbage. The ocean. His hospital room before he got The Cap. Grandpa's pipe. When he went to visit a farm. Cookie dough. Spaghetti cooking. Pizza. Ice cream. School paste. Crayons. Dog and kitty poo. Everything.

When Cowan finished, Angel placed his hands on him and turned his hands brown. Both boys inhaled deeply, their breaths a sigh of recognition, as if the air around them was filled with the perfumes of familiarity.

Angel held them like that, his hands staying brown until Cowan sneezed. A moment later, Leonard wiped tears from his eyes. Angel stood and the two boys slid from his lap. He went back into the haunted house and they followed.

They sat together in Angel's attic, going over some proofs which Angel had explained to them, their backs to a western facing dormer trying to capture the last rays of light before the sun set. It was difficult, not because the proofs were complex but because Angel could barely send pictures into Cowan's mind anymore.

Something crashed downstairs.

"What was that?"

"If we were at my place I'd say my Dad again. I'll go check."

Before Leonard got to the door they heard Kevin calling up the stairs. "Hey, who's up there? Could it be my two best pals, Lenny and Freaky Cowan No-Eyes?"

Other voices laughed.

Cowan looked around them. "This isn't good, Leonard. I don't think we can talk our way out of this one."

Leonard leaned out the window and came back in. "Give me the papers." He folded and stuffed what he could in different pockets. "We're over the bathroom, right? The window's knocked out of that room and it's right under the cornice."

"We're three stories high, Leonard!"

"Come on, come on. This window's a dormer and you can reach from the sill to the cornice. Just hold on to the edge and swing in. We can do it when they're right at the attic door. Then we're out and away before they know what happened."

"What about Angel?"

"If I can't see him you think they will?"

Kevin and his friends banged their way up the stairs.

"Guess not."

Kevin et al stood in the doorway. Leonard swung out the window.

Cowan sat on the sill, waiting his turn.

Leonard splayed his arms and easily caught the ledge. "See, Cowan. No problem."

Cowan swung out, one hand holding onto the sill. Kevin grabbed his arm. Cowan pulled diagonally and down, using Kevin's strength against him.

Kevin gripped Cowan's arm tighter, rolling out the window and over Cowan, holding on all the way.

"Cowan!"

Their combined weight moved them too fast and to one side. Leonard reached for them and missed by a foot. Cowan screamed.

He fell in slow motion. Leonard's voice came to him over a great distance, Leonard's words slowed and paced by Cowan's own heartbeat.

He watched Kevin's friends fill the attic as they fell, Kevin's friends' eyes wide and their voices as dulled as Leonard's. Somewhere beside him Kevin screamed and clutched him.

He heard everyone's breathing, loud and volcanic. Bracing winds of cold slithered past him, moved through his clothes and found his skin as he fell. He wondered when he and Kevin would plop in the snow.

Then he felt himself stopping, staying stationary in the air. Kevin was suddenly pressed tightly against him. Cowan felt great arms around him, supporting him. He heard the constant, steady whoosh of great wings above him.

And his mind filled with pictures. Colors. Places. Words and thoughts. People. Beings. Creatures Angel had seen over a hundred thousand lifetimes.

Slowly, the bright pictures began to fade as Cowan saw the ground slowly rise to greet him. Beside him, Kevin snuffled and tears iced his face.

The pictures in Cowan's mind continued to fade. The sound of the wings grew soft as he felt the snow compress beneath his feet. He heard sounds in the house and felt more than saw Leonard standing beside him. He began clutching at Angel, trying to hold him, trying to find him. "Don't go away. Don't go away. Please don't go. Please." He sank to his knees in the snow, holding onto the tips of Angel's wings as Angel shared the brightest stars in the Universe, the greatest lessons, the strongest colors as his body dissolved away.

Cowan had a single picture then, a single overwhelming picture filling his mind. He saw Angel's world, colorless, lifeless, just moving through space, black&white even though the universe around it was filled with colors; blue, red, brown, gold and others Cowen'd never seen in Angel's eyes before. He saw Angel walking towards another black&white world, another Earth, an Earth of only shape and form, devoid of context and content. Then there was Angel, looking different in his mind but Cowan still knowing it was Angel he saw.

As he watched, the Angel in his mind gave birth. Two smaller Angels emerged. He looked and, even with his Cap, he recognized the young Angels as himself and Leonard. The Earth was going dark, like Angel's world. Angel motioned his children towards the black&white Earth and the universe of colors filled it until there were context and content to support the shape and form.

At the door to the house Cowan heard people breathing. Leonard, behind him, whispered, "My god."

The picture in Cowan's mind blazed bright and a small picture of his father formed in the corner. "Ride, not." The picture of his father faded away. "Participate, Journey, Life."

The blazing picture faded. Nothingness. Emptiness. Angel's wings slipped gently from Cowan's fingers.

Cowan fell forward and cried.

Sometime later it was dark. The stars were out and could be clearly seen above the trees in the night sky.

"Cowan? You okay?"

"Yeah. Kevin still here?"

"No. He told his friends to go home, to find friends their own age and to leave him alone."

Cowan nodded. "Angel's gone."

"I know. We saw."

"How?"

"Right before he died, you could see him. I never really knew what he looked like until the end."

Cowan sat up in the snow. Their breaths wisped above them in tiny, moisture laden clouds. He patted the snow and listened to the sibilance of its hard cracking surface beneath his hand.

BINKY

BINKY

Marino sipped cold coffee from a white styrofoam cup. He stood in his corner of the clinic staff's office. A bricked up fireplace ran along the wall nearest his desk, his clarinet on the mantle. Each day started with a little klezmer or polka, something to amuse the staff before the day began.

He nodded and smiled as they came in - "Morning, Dr. Marino.", "Morning, Janet.", "Yo, Peter.", "Yo yourself, Brian." - performing a headcount.

He was one shy. Who...

Pahtmus' and Officer Houle's voices rose above the chants and hollers of protesters beyond the clinic's perimeter fencing.

"You know you can't park here?"

"I work here. You've seen me every day this week."

"How come you don't have a sticker on your car?"

"This is the first day I drove my car."

"You got a sticker?"

Marino nodded to one of the new volunteers, "Vicki, could you run out with a parking permit for Dr. Pahtmus, please."

He met Pahtmus in the entranceway. "Pretty loud today," Marino said.

"Ah. You heard."

"A little. You're in triage today."

Pahtmus nodded and shuffled off to the waiting and reception area.

"Wait a second. You'll need this." Marino held out a folding chair.

"Uncomfortable and austere is not chic, my friend." Pahtmus waded into the sea of too many people and too much noise.

Over an hundred years ago a coal-baron bought this block in the most affluent part of town. He created an American palace complete with gardens and pool, but economics and immigration had turned the most affluent part of town to the most feared and the one-time palace into an empty, broken down property, perfect for an inner city health center. Curtains and drapes from Czarist Russia once covered these walls. Persian rugs and Oriental wall-hangings and heavy, regal furniture from European castles once filled these rooms.

Now the grand hall served as the waiting and reception area because it led everywhere else in the house. Third-hand Levelor blinds did what they could to keep the sun out. Staff and clients lucky enough to sit did so on office furniture from seven different donors. Once a month Marino told the Board of Health that the stains on the marble floors only looked like blood. He didn't know what they were but they weren't blood and yes, they maintained a sterile environment.

The rear gardens were a blessing, though. Signs in six languages and locked doors kept clients out so the staff could walk the flagstone paths in peace and safety during their infrequent breaks, the hostility kept outside by a ten foot stone wall. The remains of the pool always offered a point of discussion. Was it kidney shaped? Some kind of ovuloid? Maybe an ovary? How about old men huddling?

Whatever it had been, it now existed as an oddly shaped concrete hole with a diving board and ladder. The bottom looked like a Jackson Pollack experiment dripped with dirt instead of paints. Cracks in the original pool floor showed through like tiny roads in a mountain country diorama.

This would all have been crowded with revelers once. New Year's Eve, maybe, or some late summer bash. And probably all of them white revelers, Northern European caucasian.

A large blue and white swirl startled Marino and he looked up into the eyes of a little African-American girl, her hair in long cornrows. She smiled at him then ran after a blue and white soccer ball as it bounced among other children in the hall.

An old voice, a loving voice, "Abrianna! Girl!"

Her ball tightly tucked under a strong, healthy arm, she ran back to three women, one in her early thirties with similar features, one maybe late fifties with close features and the last he couldn't guess. Ancient. But he could see majesty and knew it had once been a beautiful face.

"You darling, darling child," the youngest woman said. "How about we get that ash off you before you see the doctor? He'll think we don't care enough about you, he sees all that ash on you, girl." The little girl jumped into the woman's lap and laughed as the woman rubbed the flaky skin off the girl's arms.

Four generations and he didn't recognize one of them. Must be their first visit.

Then he heard the oldest woman say, "She go that way she run into the kitchen. Ain't no place for that child, the kitchen."

He squatted in front of her. "Excuse me, Miss."

The woman laughed. "You blind, you call me 'miss'." She offered her hand. "Sally May Comfort."

"Peter Marino. Good to meet you, Ms. Comfort. Did you say the kitchen was down this way?"

She pointed. "There's the kitchen." She pointed down another hallway. "The laundry's there. The pantry's between. There's a room behind that, closest to the back. We used to play there when the weather bad."

"You used to play here? You lived here?"

"When I was a girl, younger than this one. We lived and worked here, my maam and pap, me and brother Eb. He worked the stables and the automobiles when they come."

Marino sat on the floor, a child hearing stories of his people's Old Ones around a campfire. "My god, the stories you must have. How long were you here?"

"Oh, we left shortly after Binky died."

"Binky?"

"Binky. They last child."

"How sad."

"No, not sad. Best thing for that child, dyin'. Should a been born still. Hideous thing. Mister wanted to kill it and missus wouldn't let him. Kept it alive and hiding 'til it died on its own. Terrible thing. Missus holdin' it and holdin' it, rockin' it like she's gonna pump life back in. Last thing pap and Eb did was bury that child in the bottom of the pool. Took a day to break through the concrete and another day to bury him, all the time Missus screaming like Jacob raised his ladder and she can't reach the rung. All the time Mister drinking himself blind."

"The child's buried here? In the pool out back?"

"Uh-huh, bottom of the pool. There's a plaque under the ivy by the side, got Binky's name on it. Child loved the pool. Only time he could be a child was him splashing in the pool."

"My god, I never knew."

Vicki called out, "Abrianna Hale?"

The youngest woman gathered the child in her arms. "That's us."

The three women stood. Marino took the old woman's hand. "Would you have someone find me before you go? I'd love to know more about this."

Sally May Comfort shook his hand and nodded.

Pahtmus walked up with his clipboard and Marino shifted a pair of reading glasses from the cord around his neck to his nose. "What you got?"

Pahtmus flipped the pages. "It's getting worse, Pete. One pellagra, a possible marasmus, the standard nutritionals. An erythema which might be simple neglect. Cervicitis." He picked up the remaining sheets between two fingers. "And these good folks want abortions."

Dr. Schwartzmann came up beside them. "Did you tell them abortions are Tuesdays and Fridays? Today schedule is light to make time for emergencies."

The sheets slid from Pahtmus' fingers. "Thank goodness we can schedule our emergencies." He walked toward his first client.

Schwartzmann glanced out the window. "It's looking pretty mean out there today, Pete. My family's concerned. They thought I'd better not come in today."

"Don't they say that everyday?"

"I told them what you said at the last staff meeting, about closing down if we have one more bombing."

"And?"

"And they support our work but think you're a fool to have kept it open this long."

Marino changed subjects. "Hey, I think I found out why our lease says we can't do anything to the pool."

Schwartzmann nodded and went to meet the first of her clients.

Marino went back to the office and took his clarinet off the mantle. He played a Pete Fountain variation to relax as he watched the protesters out the window.

Then a young couple caught his eye. They broke through the crowd and moved towards the clinic doors.

He put his clarinet back and studied them. Easily eight months pregnant and both dressed poorly. She wore a soiled red and white smock over a swollen belly. He had on crudely patched jeans and K-Mart work boots untied and open. They wore matching dungaree jackets, too thin to offer enough protection in this changing season. The angle and placement of her belly told him she carried her child close to term.

He left his office in time to get a good look at their faces as they entered. Newbies. He'd have to do a full intake.

Officer Houle walked in right behind them and Marino intercepted him. "What's the problem, officer?"

He heard Pahtmus, Knudsen, and Schwartzmann groan and knew he would catch it later. He insisted all of them be civil and gracious to any who walked through the doors. They - especially Knudsen and Schwartzmann - thought Houle should be castrated. Civilly and graciously, of course, but nevertheless castrated. Two nights earlier he had been in the crowd that hurled firebombs onto the clinic grounds and organized the protesters to inhibit fire equipment from reaching hydrants. The other officers failed to make arrests because doing so meant copping one of their own.

Right now Marino was concerned Houle would arrest the kids who'd just entered. They looked young and might be under the age of consent.

But he didn't. He gathered Marino close to him and fanned out several tracts. "Dr. Marino," he said, "you're a reasonable man. Would you take a minute to look at these with me and let me know if we could place some of them in your clinic?"

Marino stared at Houle. Who was this podperson? What happened to Officer Houle? "Sure. Of course. Certainly."

The kids sat together, looking around wide-eyed, holding each other like caged monkeys waiting for the next experiment to begin.

Marino watched Schwartzmann walk away for a fourth time and took the tracts out of Houle's hands. "Thanks, Officer." He turned towards the couple and Houle pulled him back. "You'll read those tracts, won't you, Doc?"

Marino nodded, absently. "Yeah, sure. Of course I will."

He started away again and Houle took his hand, shaking it vigorously, drawing Marino towards him. "Thanks, Doc. Thanks. I knew I could count on you."

Marino dropped the tracts and Houle stooped to get them. His hand released and Houle's attention drawn elsewhere, Marino walked towards the couple. Houle called after him, "Doc? Hey, Doc."

Marino called over his shoulder, "Just leave them by the door, officer. I'll get to them in a minute." He heard the door close and Knudsen gave him a thumbs-up as she went from one examining room to another.

"Hi, my name's Peter Marino. 'Pete"s fine." He offered his hand to the couple, the young girl first. They stiffened slightly and drew closer to each other.

"You're Dr. Marino?" the boy asked.

"That's me."

"I'm Tommy. She's Karen. We're going to have a baby."

Marino nodded. He'd learned long ago to show neither joy nor concern until the clients evidenced their own feelings one way or the other. "Uh-huh."

"We...," Tommy put his arm around Karen and held her to him. She looked down at her sneakered feet. "We don't want a child."

"Okay."

"Right now," added Karen.

Marino nodded again. Something nudged him. Probably nothing. "There are things we need to talk about," he said. "Please follow me." He led them to his desk in the office and left the door opened so the staff could look in: a sad precaution, sacrificing client privacy and confidentiality for personal safety. He unfolded some chairs by his desk.

"Do you know how many months along you are, Karen?"

She looked down again. "I don't know. Six or seven, maybe."

"There are some routine questions I have to ask. They'll probably seem foolish or stupid. In most cases, the answers are obvious to everybody, but I still have to ask them. Do you understand what I've just told you?" He felt like he was Mirandizing clients each time he did this and hated it.

Tommy and Karen nodded. "Yes, sir," she said.

Tommy said "Yessir." He sounded like a grunt fresh off the bus. Marino shrugged it off.

"I need to know if you've had any previous medical exams."

"No, Dr. Marino," she said. "Not since I was a kid."

"Uh-huh." He turned to Tommy to keep the boy involved and engaged in the conversation. "How about you, Tom?"

"Huh?" Tommy's gaze shifted from the window back to Marino. "No. Not since I was a kid."

"There are certain tests we'll have to make. Karen, you said you didn't want a child right now. Do you have any idea what you'd like to do if you really are pregnant?"

She placed a hand on her belly. "Of course I'm pregnant. Why do you think I came here?"

Her defensiveness took him by surprise. "I don't doubt you're pregnant, Karen. I just want you to know what's involved, how long things may take based on your decision, and what dangers and benefits there might be because of your decision. I just want you both to know what this is all about."

Houle came back in the clinic and stood in the middle of the reception area. He shouted, "Anybody here own a blue '97 Pontiac? It's illegally parked and we're going to tow it."

Through his office door Marino could see people staring at Houle. Nobody answered him. Houle looked in Marino's office and Marino smiled at him. Houle called again, louder. Nobody responded. His face tightened. "Anybody? Blue '97 Ponty?"

He pursed his lips and walked out.

Knudsen, talking to a young woman dressed in a clean but old red dress, torn nylons and black shoes split at the sides, looked at Houle as he walked out. She continued to listen to the woman but caught Marino's eye and frowned. The look on her face said, "What the hell was that about? He never warns us when he's calling for a tow."

Marino turned back to Karen and Tom. "Where were we?"

"I've suffered syncope and dyspnea," Karen said.

Marino looked at her. "*Syncope* and *dyspnea*?"

Tom put his hand in Karen's. Her face flushed. "I think that's what it's called. I've been dizzy. Sometimes I can't breathe."

Marino picked up his tablet to give his hands something to do. "Syncope and dyspnea can be caused by several things. If you'd like, we could run some tests right now to help us make sure your pregnant and not, perhaps, oncolic."

She waved his suggestion away. "I don't have any cancers."

Tommy cut in, "Pete, we just want to know what to do. You can tell us what to do, can't you?"

"Let me see." Marino checked off items on the screen. He held the tablet flat on his lap so all three could see the standard inpatient form.

Outside the office door Knudsen talked to the same young woman. Knudsen's voice rose enough for Marino to hear, "You want to be hospitalized NPO? Perhaps we have different ideas of what 'NPO' means."

Marino smiled. Lots of clients caught phrases and doc-talk and used it to appear brighter or more capable when they entered the clinic.

Was that happening with Tommy and Karen? Maybe they'd heard

words somewhere, or worse, read some books?

He checked the box "Hyd. Mole & ChC".

Outside his door, he heard Knudsen mention the four types of abortion possible and what happens to the conceptus in each.

Karen said, "I told you I have no cancers."

The woman with Knudsen said, "You mean my baby."

Marino looked away for a moment, nodding. "Excuse me for a moment."

Tommy said, "Sure."

Marino walked into the grand hall, called out, "Dr. Howard, Dr. Fine, Dr. Howard. Dr. Howard, Dr. Fine, Dr. Howard," and walked towards the kitchen.

The staff looked up and around. Excuses were made to patients in non-critical situations. Moving casually yet economically the staff gathered in the mansion's expansive backyard, all according to the drill practiced many times before. Doctors, nurses, and other staff walked in small groups along the separate paths talking to themselves. They walked through long shadows cast by the late autumn afternoon sun. None had taken jackets or coats and many massaged their arms against the chill.

Vicki, the last to come out, shivered slightly. "Sorry, I was playing receptionist."

They could hear the protesters' chants clearly over the stone wall. "What the hell is wrong with these people?" Knudson nodded towards the chants. "Do we do this when they do their jobs?"

Marino said, "Does everybody know what's going on?"

Schwartzmann asked, "Was there another bomb threat?"

Knudsen said, "Nothing so exciting. Just some ringers shaking the tree."

"Then you know about that young lady you're intaking?"

She frowned. "Her? I meant the two kids at your desk. I've seen them in the crowds before."

Pahtmus shielded his eyes from the setting sun. "You didn't tell him?"

"It's all right," Marino said. "Listen folks, so far I've made the decisions and you've all stood behind them. I don't think that's fair anymore. I'm going to put it to a vote before we get another firebomb thrown in there."

The small talk died and it made the protesters seem louder. "Do we keep the clinic open or not? Democratic vote, folks." He pulled business cards from his pocket and passed them around. "Nothing fancy. Just 'Yes' to keep the clinic open, 'No' to close it down. Majority rules. Go off by yourselves if you like. Give 'em back to me when you're done. I won't even look at 'em until we're back inside. Fair enough?

A bright, childish laugh caught their attention.

Somebody inside the clinic called "Abrianna!"

Vicki's hand covered her mouth. "I forgot to lock the door."

The childish laughter came again and a blue and white soccer ball swirled over the neglected shrubbery. It bounced on the flagstone right in the middle of them then up and over their heads and down at the edge of the pool, swirled for a moment and fell in.

The little African-American child Marino had seen earlier squeezed through the shrubbery, laughing and chuckling.

She ran towards them.

She is beautiful, Marino thought. Dressed like an urchin, but still beautiful.

None of them moved. She ran through and past them to the pool.

He looked towards the others. Their eyes followed Abrianna's flight.

She continued to laugh and ran straight for the diving board.

"No! No!"

The bright, laughing Abrianna ran to the end of the diving board and jumped.

Marino's legs finally moved. Others ran ahead, some came from behind, all wanting to reach her before she smashed onto the bottom.

Abrianna smiled as she sailed through the air.

Marino watched, confused. Doesn't she realize there's no water in the pool?

They watched as she completed her arc.

When she should have hit bottom, where her beautiful dive should have ended in a small patch of dirt and broken bones, where her blue and white ball should have rested, Abrianna continued her dive.

Abrianna broke through the dirt, her dive continuing as something enveloped her from below, the bottom of the pool splashing and shattering around her, becoming a blinding liquid that didn't belong.

It looks like fire.

The staff stood, watching. She came up as if completing her dive. Some of the fire splashed around her.

Pahtmus said, "It's not really fire, just something that looks like fire."

She was still Abrianna but somehow older, an adolescent's developing body instead of a child's. She held a guitar and exclaimed, "Look, I can play guitar."

They stood there as she played.

Someone said, "She plays well."

Marino stared, confusion lost to wonder. He heard the others murmuring and Abrianna's guitar. Not the protesters.

Not the protesters, not their chants.

Nobody spoke. They stood watching and listening as Abrainna fingerpicked the guitar and hummed something, minor-thirds resolving to major-sevenths. Carly Simon? Something like that. He couldn't place it. And all the while she played surrounded by puddles of flame so like flickering spotlights at her feet.

She held the guitar against her and dropped back under the lava-like water.

Marino couldn't move, only watch. Nobody's moving. Why isn't somebody moving?

Something else erupted from the hole. It had its back to them and seemed to be a caucasian juvenile, oafishly large, but with the general morphology of a three or four year old.

It turned and faced them.

Aile's Syndrome. Its size was due to Aile's syndrome. The misshapen body, as wrong as it could be and still be human. The child wore a red and white striped beach suit belonging more to the mansion's era than

Marino's. The legs bent beyond the point of being bow-legged. Each foot had only two toes and the feet themselves were too narrow and too long to allow for walking. A wide gap separated the toes, shaping the feet into flippers, but flippers useless in any capacity. It had no hands. In fact, nothing existed beyond the elbows on either arm and the elbows were flattened. The child held a partially deflated, dirty beach ball on its right, under what looked like a partially plucked chicken wing. The head was too large and the face too wide and flat, the neck too short, the eyes too vacant, as if a hydrocephalic had merged with a Down's child. Large sarcomas on each cheek spread down the neck and followed the flesh under the swimsuit.

It pressed the partially deflated ball to its side. "My name is Binky."

Marino heard the words come from a mouth that should not have been able to speak.

They didn't know about genetic markers back then. They could have screened for it and aborted the child within weeks of conception. He didn't have to be born. Nobody had to suffer.

"He's saying it to a world that doesn't want him." Marino wasn't sure who spoke.

The child squeezed the ball again, this time between its wings.

"Deflated, but still held onto. Like the dreams of children who realize there's no more room."

Marino nodded.

Gripping his tired, dying beach ball and facing them, Binky lost his balance. His flippers shuffled on the ground but his wings never released the ball. He fell backwards into the hole in the bottom of the pool.

He disappeared into the flames and they all heard a scream.

Abrianna.

Knudsen and Marino scrambled into the pool.

There was no hole, no fire, no lava-like water, no Binky. Just Abrianna crying and the screams and chants of the protesters outside the gates.

The staff ran and jumped after Knudsen and Marino, all now moving to the little girl's aid.

Knudsen got to her first. "She's okay, just bruised and scared."

Marino acknowledged and lifted her to Schwartzmann. "Take her inside." Words still didn't come easy. "Bandage her up."

The staff moved back in, into the sounds of distressed children and unhappy parents and out of the profanity and harassment of the protesters outside.

Marino and Pahtmus stood alone at the edge of the pool, staring at the dust and dirt where Abrianna fell.

"Come on, Peter. We've got work to do."

Marino pulled apart some creeping ivy at the edge of the pool. Metal caught the sun's fading light. He knelt and brushed away dirt and acorns, death and new life.

Pahtmus stood beside him. "What is it?"

"It's why we're here."

Marino stood and let the ivy take back the past.

"Yeah. Let's go."

THE BOY
WHO LOVED HORSES

THE BOY WHO LOVED
HORSES

I was born in a town like this. Mine's on the eastern ridge and closer to Raleigh. My town had the same dirt roads, the same one-room wooden church, the same old store where you asked for things instead of getting them yourself, the same people but with different faces, the same old men carrying coon rifles, girls getting married when they're thirteen and younger, having kids before they're through being kids themselves, the same sense of what's ours and what's not. I left my town and got educated. Made it into the extension service. Decided to come back and help others in towns like mine. My education didn't take all the hill out of me, though. Knew enough to carry a gun in case I got too close to a still. But it did take some of the hill away. I forgot about towns like this.

I came here about a year ago; my big, state-issue Buick all shiny as it passed suspicious eyes. The state needed a count of school age children to qualify for funding and I came to count the children in this town.

Hill are wary of anything new. They saw my car and suit and whispered "city" as I passed. It was true. When I come to this town, I acted like I was an educated man and everybody was suspicious of me. I went into the general store and bought a pop, sat down and tried to talk with some of the folk. Took me a while, but I got a nod, then a wink, then a smile. Turns out some of us had kin.

Eventually had to tell them why I came. They got quiet after that. I asked if there was some place I could spend the night. Nobody said.

I should've left. I know hill. I should've known the signs. One of the men, Burt, left. The rest of us talked some more and, when there was no more to say, I thanked them all and left.

I saw Burt as I drove out of town. He was walking, two steps forward and one step back, and I could tell he was tasting squeeze since he left the store. Should've kept on driving. Should've known Hill's got mysteries they need to keep. "Hey, Burt," I called. "You need a ride?" I opened the door for him and he winked and handed me his bottle as he got in.

Burt lived in a cabin up a short, rutty, old road about a mile out of town. We drove there talking hill, talking kin. By the time we got to Burt's cabin, he was smelling like a coon's been rolling in 'shine. There was another jug on his table. He offered me more but drank most of it himself. "They won't tell you about the boy," he said.

"What boy's that?"

"Lem's son, the boy who loves horses."

He was quiet for a bit so I said, "You going to tell me, Burt?"

Burt rolled up the sleeve on his left arm. It was covered with deep scars, like something didn't take a liking to it. "I used to keep hawks. The boy turned my birds against me. You stay the night if you want. Then you best leave."

"What do you mean, the boy turned your birds against you? Did he poison them? Is he twisted?"

Burt rolled down his sleeve. He was about to pick up his glass when he slammed his hand down on the table.

"What's wrong?"

He pulled his hand back and wiped it on his shirt. There was a black pus puddle and eight twitchy legs where he hit the table. "Boy's not twisted. But he twists." He looked at me then. I could tell because he shook my arm. "Calm down, son. Just a spider, is all."

Now, I been shook by spiders ever since I was four. I was walking with my pa. He heard something and told me to stay put, but I didn't listen. I tried to follow, got lost, and fell into a pit of spiders. Lord Almighty, how I shrieked. Big, fat, fuzzy things crawling all over me, in my hair, on my face, up my legs, down my arms. I started screaming and my pa came and got me. He slapped them off. Some squashed right on me, so big you could see their eyes bulging as they popped against me. Never got over it. Not then, not ever.

Burt pushed the jug at me and I finished it off, at least what didn't slide down my chin.

About eleven, eleven-thirty, Burt's snoring woke me up. I went outside and walked around. It was a clear, full mooned night, a night where the hills smother you in smells of wet hay and laurels. There was a field down the road from Burt's cabin. I walked down there. As I got closer, I heard horses. In the center of the field, in the light of the moon, I saw a boy, twelve or thirteen was all, standing in the middle of twenty head. He was waving his arms and not saying a word, at least not that I could hear. But the horses were following his motions and jumping and snorting and playing like he was one of their own.

Then he saw me and his arms came down and the horses got between me and him. I called him but he was gone.

The next day I went into town and asked if anybody knew about the boy. They told me no such boy existed. Too much squeeze, they said. I wasn't sure. Some others brought their children to me and I took down names and guessed at ages.

Should've known then. I was hill. Should've known. Too much education. Didn't know enough. I drove back that night and went to Burt's cabin. No one was there. I started walking, flashlight in my hand, to the field where I saw the boy. Only marks there were a day old.

I drove to town and there was the boy. The same boy, in the middle of the street this time, with more horses around him. Stallions and mares, paints and quarters, morgans, arabians, belgians, percherons; there were so many I couldn't tell what all was there. But there they were, prancing in the moonlight, the boy like some ringleader in a circus and his horses on display. I got out of the car and started towards him. He saw me then. His arms shot out and the horses ran off. I dodged a belgian and saw the boy go into the church.

I cornered him in there. Just me and the boy. The windows didn't have shades or blinds and the moon shone through. The place was filled with moonlight and shadows. He backed up to the pulpit and I followed him, pew by pew. I got close enough to get a good look at him. There's nothing different about him; he was just a boy was all. Black hair and eyes, clean clothes, patched but as clean as hill clean gets. No shoes. "What's your name, son?" I said.

He didn't answer. He just kept looking at me. "Boy, what's your name?"

He backed up against the pulpit, his head just beneath the Cross. All of a sudden the doors of the church burst open. I turned around to see. The horses were coming into the church. Two big percherons, probably twenty hands each, broke the doors off the hinges and bowed the frame getting in. They came down the sides of the sanctuary, all the time snorting and stamping like they scent a lynx or a bob and there's a foal in the field. Then came the others. I could see them in the moonlight, four stallions, throwing their heads up and down, their eyes opened wide and right on me, looking at me like it's the Apocalypse and I'm unworthy to ride. The chairs and pews are going everywhere. Wood was splintering, hymnals were flying, Bibles were getting trampled.

The horses were getting closer, and I grabbed the boy, one hand on his arm and the other in his hair. "You stop them, boy. You hear me? You stop them now or you'll be dead before tomorrow, boy."

His eyes darted from me to the horses. I squeezed his arm so tight I could feel his pulse in my hand. "I mean it, boy. You send those horses away."

The horses started going out. The stallions first, then the two big drafts. It was just the boy and me. And as I was looking at him, something moved right above his head. Right there at eye level, eight legs arcing and its web glistening, was a spider, its web attached to one arm of the Cross, the spider swinging to the other.

The boy moved away. He saw me, and I could tell I was pale even by moonlight. But I wasn't letting him go until I got back to my car. We started out of the church when I heard footsteps in the street. We got as far as the doorframe and I saw the townsfolk there. They're looking at me and looking at the boy.

"You let him go, mister. We got no truck with you. The boy's not your concern. You let him go and we'll let you be," somebody said.

That much of the hill no education takes away. I let the boy go and I wouldn't take a step before Gabriel's horn come calling me. "I'm going to my car and this boy's coming with me." I took one more step and heard some hammers cock. The moonlight glinted off some stocks and barrels. I took my gun out of my pocket then. "Anybody wants a go, I say I can shoot this boy dead before I see my maker. Anybody wants a peace, I'm going to start walking. And if my car don't start and move when I step on the gas, this boy's dead. And just so that no one thinks I'm too city to shoot this boy, remember some of us got kin. I'm from the other side of this ridge." I gave them time to think about that. "I'll let this boy go soon as I'm clear of this town. You don't know me but some of you know my kin. You got my word; I'll let this boy go, you just let me out of this town."

If I wasn't city, they'd listen and let me go. But not now. Now I was city, I wasn't hill. And they knew the same as I did; soon as I could I'd be back with people to get this boy. Boy had a gift and city'd want to know.

I saw their eyes. Knew they didn't believe. I pulled the boy to put him between me and the crowd. Then I saw one man looking straight at the boy. "This your boy?" I asked him.

The man nods and I guessed the boy saw him because he nods, too. The man says "Yeah, that's Luke. He's mine. And I'm his pa. I got nothing else but that boy in my life, mister. That boy and the horses I trade when the breeders come looking for hot or cold blood. That boy loves his pa, mister. Just like you must love yours. You do love your pa, don't you, mister?"

I tugged on the boy's arm, not wanting to answer. All of a sudden I heard a scuttling above me. I looked up and saw all these legs and eyes staring down. The boy's heart was pounding, I could feel it, but I didn't care. The spiders started dropping down, not even coming down on threads. Some were so big you could hear them splat when they hit the ground. I let go the boy's arm and started shooting at the roof. But it was no good by then.

I was in Burt's cabin when I woke up. There was food on the table, but I couldn't eat it. I found a broom and went all through the house looking. Couldn't find one. That's when Luke's pa come by to tell me. Luke doesn't like to hurt anybody. Doesn't want to, either. Just wants to train horses. Boy's got a natural way with them, loves them and they love him. But Luke's pa also tells me I can't leave. Says if I ever try to go away Luke'll send more'n you, more spiders, isn't that right?

So can't go away, never, can I. That's your folk, scuttling on the roof, ain't it? Talking real soft? That's your kin.

Ain't it?

CANIS MAJOR

CANIS MAJOR

Iggie dropped from the tree onto the fawn, his weight breaking its two hind legs. It tried to run anyway but its forelegs only clawed up the moist, dark forest floor, clouding Iggie's thoughts as the rich earth aroma wafted into him. Iggie didn't want the animal to suffer and bit into its throat, tearing out esophagus, jugular and various muscles. Still the fawn tried to escape. Iggie grew nauseous by the mix of his needs and the fawn's attempts to break free. This wasn't what he wanted. His father had told and taught him to make his kills quick and clean, to spare creatures any pain. Iggie curled one forepaw into a fist and punched through the fawn's ribs, crushing the heart. The fawn stopped moving and Iggie, gazing up at the dark, star filled sky, let the blood trickle down his muzzle, dribble into his nostrils, and cover his fur from flews to belly as he dined.

> *TALL, HANDSOME, good build, good humor, able to stand on a rocking ship with my hands at my sides. Brown hair, brown eyes, black beard, white skin. Have been mistaken for a brown bear when I bathe in mountain streams, well educated (past 6th grade), still have all my teeth but not all my marbles. Looking for a well-rounded, buxom woman. Buxom men need not respond. Applicants should know by this that brains are more important than brawn. Dinners, dancing, demitasse, and dramamine. Send resume and salary history.*

The ad sat on Iggie's desk for two months. The first month he'd written it by hand and crossed out several portions. The second month he'd typed it into his computer, made several more edits, and returned to the forest.

He stared at the screen for some twenty minutes this time, ran the spelling checker over it four times, read the ad backwards to check for additional misspellings, and printed it out.

He lifted the paper in his hand, his eyes examining the grain of the page as his fingers felt the texture. A mirror on the wall next to his desk echoed his movements. All the walls in his house had mirrors: mirrors framed in gold, mirrors framed in window panes, hand-held mirrors, mirrors simple and ornate; every room had at least one. He gazed into this one, opened his eyes wide and stared into them. Large, brown eyes stared back. Eyes a little too large, a little too far apart, with pupils a little too large. He rocked back and his focus changed to his nose, too thin on top with nostrils too wide on the bottom. He smiled, his face growing light and his lips parting to show strong, even, white teeth. He abruptly opened his mouth until it became a mucus laden cavern in the mirror, leaned closer, and inspected his teeth, one by one, finally running his tongue over them like a barber testing a razor's edge, and closing his mouth. Next he studied his narrow, dark-skinned, clean-shaven face, the thick brown-black hairs framing his high forehead and peering out from his open collared shirt.

He checked the calendar beside the mirror. A red line cut through most of the month save the current week plus a day on either side.

"Today is Friday," he told his empty house. "I could submit the ad online but online readers want things too quickly." Iggie wanted a woman who still read print. "Print readers still take their time."

He flipped months on the calendar. "It'll be a month before this even sees print. Another month or two before any responses arrive. March, April, May. Maybe a first date in June? It would nice to have someone during the cold months." He shuddered with the thought. Someone to hold him? Someone to warm him?

New life burst through old snow outside his window. He glanced down his hallways and sighed.

He folded the ad into thirds, included a check to cover its cost, sealed the envelope and walked the several miles down the mountain into town.

*A*pril. *Iggie woke up on the forest floor, in a place high in the* protected woods of his family's company. No kills surrounded him, but he was full. It took a moment for him to remember what had transpired in the past twenty-seven days. He remembered the ad and started for one of the outbuildings beside his home.

A rubber paired door allowed him in like a woman welcoming a long absent lover. Bright lights came on as he groomed himself, performing a visual inspection, looking for wounds like a leper looking for new bruises. He didn't remember meeting any bears, bobcats, coydogs, or wolves, but better to be sure than to find a festering wound several days into manhood. Satisfied, he rested on the straw floor for another day, waiting while his features retreated from their earlier form. When he awoke, he went into his house, showered, dressed, got in his Range Rover and drove into town.

The town hadn't changed much since his birth: primarily a main street, not exactly straight, about three hundred feet long, met at either end by roads which froze over each winter and rutted out each spring. In the middle stood a general store serving as post office, information hub, and bus stop for the Claremont-Unity-Keene run. A white-spired, black-trimmed Methodist church dominated the end of the street closest to Iggie's home. In front of the church, behind the black wrought iron fence and perched upon scraggly, weed-infested grass, a dim light hung over what Iggie's father called "a verse under glass". At the far end of the street — and to Iggie's eyes, hiding under the sheltering pines and oaks — a bar door opened revealing the dark interior where locals, most of whom worked in the mill Iggie's family had owned for generations, drank and lied to each other.

He walked into the post office. Postmaster George McCormick, well past both voluntary and forced retirement, called Iggie to the window with a voice befitting a Yankee whaler. "Ignatius Tanner, got your mail waiting for you right here as always." A few of the others nodded. No one said hello.

George, who had been a steady part of Iggie's life since Iggie's childhood, stood shorter than Iggie now, but Iggie always remembered George with eyes brilliantly blue, a face tanned and craggy from July-August suns and central New Hampshire winters, a full head of striking white hair, and strong white teeth still all his own. No one in town bothered with Iggie except George. George's deeply veined hands lifted a box and pushed it across to Iggie. The latest *Boston* Magazine lay on top. "Getting an urge to move to the city, Ignatius?"

"Nope." He blushed and whispered, "Looking for a wife."

Several people's eyes widened at that remark. Someone coughed. A woman in ill-fitting clothes missed the mail slot and had to retrieve her letters from the floor.

That night Iggie prepared strong coffee using beans he'd just roasted, the thick acidic aroma making his nose run. He went to lick it and laughed; his human tongue and face couldn't support such grooming now. He took a cup, the *Boston* magazine, and went into his study. A quick scan told him his ad hadn't made it into this month's issue.

He read the ads once, drained his cup, got another cup, and read the ads again. Five cups of coffee, five times through the ads, visualizing the women, auguring if the few disastrous relationships he'd had would be repeated with the women on these pages. Eventually he threw the magazine in the fireplace, but there was no fire.

A few days later he checked the calendar.

His time neared.

He placed a note in Postmaster McCormick's box, "I'll be gone for the next three to four weeks on business. Please hold my mail until I return. Iggie T."

*H*e woke up curled on the straw in the outbuilding.
McCormick had the box of mail ready as Iggie walked in. "Got it right here for you, Ignatius." Iggie thanked him, took the mail

and left.

His ad was almost dead center of all the personals. Longer than most, he wondered if its size and placement would cause women to dismiss it. Going through his mail, he found his first response mixed in with legal matter, requests for charitable contributions, and catalogs from which he supplied his home.

Fourteen responses. Word processed letters he dismissed, sensing them by the hollowness of the page. He could learn nothing from pages taken from a printer and concentrated on the hand-written responses. Words on a page didn't mean as much to him as the texture of the writing, the way a hand formed the letters. People never realize how many clues they give about themselves in a simple scrawl, like tracks in a freshly snowed woods.

The fact they wrote rather than videoed or TXTed told him much. Even when using a typewriter, using anything with which the body directed the impact on the paper, people left impressions and images of themselves beyond their signature at the bottom.

"Thank god typewriters are making a comeback." Some of his catalogs offered them as home office accessories, adornments like a watch or bracelet, never meant to be used, always meant to be seen. "Retro, but a comeback."

Some envelopes had strong perfume scents. He sniffed each one a few times before opening it. One envelope, blue and made of soft paper, carried a quiet hint of perfume, as if the paper collected the scent as it rested in the writer's presence. The writer hadn't scented either, but he still detected her perfume there. The envelope wasn't thick, perhaps a single page. He could feel the penstrokes through the paper. His eyes grew wide and dark. His breathing quickened. Some spittle leaked from the corners of his mouth.

The lilting of the pen pretty much matched the written words. She was shy ("I tend to stay away from people. I think in my life I've made five or six true friends."). She was unsure of herself ("I studied music but now work as a high yield bonds dealer. Maybe I don't know what I want to do."). She liked honesty ("If this is just for sex, please tell me before we get involved. I'm not saying I'll say, 'No,' I just want to know before setting myself up for something that's not there. Do you know what I mean?").

But she didn't send a picture. Wasn't that the norm? Maybe she didn't realize he wanted a picture. He said resume and salary history. She included a Boston telephone number and first name, "Sherry." He repeated it a few times. He didn't want to be alone anymore. He wanted to tell somebody about himself, someone not local. Someone who might accept his schedule as part of business. "Iggie the Traveler" they would say of him.

He cringed. "Iggie the Traveler."

He felt a familiar ache in his bones. Who would understand? Perhaps Sherry?

He woke early the next morning to a beard already coming in too thick and decided he wouldn't call her. How could he explain his behavior? The question caused memories to stir. He remembered his mother, but not fondly. "Did they think I wouldn't find out?" he asked the rising moon. No response. He remembered other things. Things his father had and had not taught him. Things as painful to him as not being merciful in a kill.

"Be merciful," his father said long before Iggie knew exactly what he meant. The first lesson had been when the two of them were bow hunting. Iggie's father, Nathaniel, hated hunting although he was an expert and unerring with bow and knife. He, like Iggie, had a lithe, graceful, well-defined build, with a agonized musculature embracing a skeleton traveling between two worlds, his arms stronger than they appeared and hands and eyes steadier than mountains against wind. His father drew the string, his index, middle finger, and thumb holding the nock without strain, his eyes seeing their mark and closing as he turned his head away, his arms and hands never moving. Nathaniel sighed, a sound of relaxation and release. The arrow flew from his fingers, flying past the bow, silent against the sky, flying among the trees until it penetrated a pheasant's side, capturing the bird in mid-flight.

Nathaniel's nose twitched. Once, twice, and he handed the bow back to his son. Not a compound, with neither stabilizers nor sight, just sixty to seventy pounds at maximum draw, twenty inches from back to belly and Nathaniel did not shake or sweat. "Be merciful. Be quick. Be clean. Every kill should be made with a single blow. If your prey cries out..." His nose twitched again. He walked away without finishing the thought or collecting his prize.

"Shall I get the bird for you, father?"

"Take it to your mother. She can clean and dress it. You'll have no need..." Again the unfinished phrase.

Father had so many.

Iggie loved his father, although Iggie didn't understand his father until a few years after his death.

Iggie scratched his beard. The next day he left his house.

He awoke a month later and, waiting a day before venturing into town, read Sherry's letter several more times. Early the next morning he tested his voice a few times, listening to make sure nothing in its sound but the voice of a man, and picked up the phone to call.

Ten rings and nothing. He checked the number and dialed again. Ten rings and nothing. "How long does one wait for a phone to be answered?" he wondered. He could post in a tree for hours or even days waiting for a dying beast to come by. If he truly hungered – he always gorged himself before the metamorphosis, hoping his bloated belly would prevent him from wandering too far – he would smell out a wounded or dying beast and hunt it down.

But the phone? He rarely called anyone. He had no friends. He feared to be around others, fearing they knew his secret better than he. No childhood friends had lasted with him through his puberty, his latency, as his body assumed its new desires independent of his wish or will. When his mother took him out of school, he thought it because all others could control their transformations, that he was inept, the fool, some metamorphic bed-wetter at whom all others laughed.

He wasn't hungry but made dinner anyway. A vegetarian souffle. He never ate meat as a man.

Later, he tried the phone number again. No answer and no answering machine. The moon mocked him from behind a sash. He snarled and went to bed. Imaginings of Sherry danced in his dreams.

He woke up on the floor. Had the past few days been bestial dreams of manhood? A dog chasing rabbits in its sleep but standing on two legs, as a man?

Sometimes dream-like memories of beasthood came to him. Sometimes, when he was a beast, memories of manhood came to him in what seemed like dog-like dreams. He remembered them and dealt with them accordingly.

But he wondered at what haunted his sleep, at times when he couldn't remember his dreams, hoping the memories would descend from the hidden into the light, hoping he wouldn't find some disemboweled stranger in them.

What he did find terrified him; Sherry, whom he knew nothing about except his own imaginings, ran from him, terrified.

He picked up the phone and punched in her number. Someone answered on the third ring. He hadn't looked at the clock and panicked. Was it too early to call?

A groggy but musical voice said, "Hello?"

"Hi."

The voice, still musical, carried a hint of annoyance. "Hello?"

This isn't going well. "Hi. I know it's early and I hope I didn't wake you. My name is Iggie Turner."

"What's this about?"

"I'm the brown bear."

"And the tiger walks in the spring. Good-bye, Mr. Turner." She hung up.

Iggie sat on the floor next to his bed and controlled his breathing. He could feel his temperature rising, his face flushing. He dialed her number again.

"Yes." A statement and hardly any music.

"Sherry, you answered a personal ad in *Boston Magazine*? The ad mentioned a brown bear, had all my teeth but not all my marbles?" If she hung up now he'd go on to someone else's letter.

Her voice became alert and apologetic. "I'm sorry, Iggie. Is that right? Iggie? I didn't remember. God, what time is it?"

"It's 6:45AM. I didn't realize the time when I called. I'm usually not so inconsiderate."

She laughed and his heart spun. His mind forced her sounds into memory. "I hope you're not. But don't worry, I had to get up in a few minutes, anyway."

"Do you normally start your day this early?"

"No, you picked the day I'm going to New York on business."

"Should I let you go?"

"You better not, you just woke me up, Iggie. Now you've got to entertain me until the alarm goes off."

They talked about movies one or the other had seen (they both favored foreign movies, no subtitles, on DVD with the sound off, just to look at the strange way people acted and dressed), music (Iggie's memories were wrapped in sounds and Sherry studied to be a music historian), both liked game (Iggie didn't respond immediately when she asked and she tapped the phone to see if the connection had gone dead), bad experiences with past amours (Iggie listened and made soothing sounds as she spoke, not having much of his own he could share on the subject), and so on, soulmates who'd never met.

"We've been talking for about an hour, Sherry. Didn't you say you had to start early today?"

"Oh, damn!"

"I'm sorry, did I keep you too long?" He didn't want to be so timid, so shy, so afraid of doing the wrong thing. He envisioned himself as a child constantly peeking out the door of his room as his parents fought, constantly wondering how to make it better, how to make it right.

"Yes, you did, but I don't mind. Look, Iggie, I've got to go and get ready. But you do sound nice. I'd like to meet you."

"Really?"

Now she sounded shy, as if she'd stepped beyond where she should go. "You don't think we could get together for coffee or a drink or something?"

"Yes, but you said you're going away, and I'll be out of town for about a month."

A defeated sigh. "Oh, okay. I'm sorry. I'm only going to be out of town tonight. Well, give me a call…"

He cut her off before she could finish. "I won't be leaving for a few days. When do you get back tomorrow?"

"I'll be back by noon."

"Could we have dinner?"

"Dinner? Sure." Enthusiasm! He heard bedsprings and some clothes ruffling. "I'm free. Hey, what luck! It's a full moon tomorrow night. Maybe we could go somewhere on the coast. Watch the moon over the water?"

"Yes." He was shaking, quivering sporadically, and didn't know why. Could this be initiating a change?

"Just one more thing, Iggie." He waited. "I told you about some bad times I've had on dates, remember?"

"Yes."

"You're not a wolf or anything like that, are you?"

He shook violently. He could feel the vibrations in his lungs. His voice would quaver when he spoke. He laughed to release the tension. "Not a wolf, but something like that."

She laughed, too, but not nervously. She gave him directions to where they could meet and said goodbye.

*H*is phone guided him to a garage near the bistro *Sherry* mentioned and he parked there. It was a few blocks away but the distance comforted him. He still had an out if he decided he couldn't go through with it.

He checked himself in the rearview mirror, trying to calm himself and anxious about leaving the quiet solitude of his SUV. Outside would be the noises of the city: harsh and spiteful on his ears. He braced himself for the sonic onslaught, checked himself again in the mirror once more, put on some sunglasses then got out of the car and leaned against it until the sounds became distinct. Trucks and cars on

Interstate-90 went in both directions, more trucks coming into the city than leaving, more cars leaving than coming. Construction, both minor and major, like the arcana from some obscene Tarot, pounded him. Smells of oil, diesel, noncombusted gasoline. He inhaled and caught an LPP leak somewhere in the garage, although not a dangerous one. His RangeRover still had new engine, new car smells even though he'd owned it for several years. Some scents of perfume and cologne, the cologne mostly stronger than the perfume. Somewhere, towards the back of the garage, he smelled fresh, warm urine, feces, too-sweet berries, and sweat. He lowered his sunglasses and peered over the edge, his pupils growing wide until he saw a drunk lying there, puddles forming around him.

Iggie scented Sherry two hundred feet from the Bistro.

She sat with legs outstretched and crossed, relaxed and sipping an espresso at a table, her back to the street, her chair up against a black, four foot tall old-world, finial-topped iron fence separating the bistro's veranda from sidewalk traffic.

Sherry's perfume, remembered from her letter and envelope, lifted above all other scents in the city. He'd never tasted anything similar, and it seemed no others wore it.

She had a somewhat punkish haircut, short and a little spiky. An auburn which might have been burnt red in a different light. Her skin was pale white and she was thin and tiny. Sitting, measuring her body as he approached, he judged her not to be over five-five and about 110. She lifted her espresso with her right hand. There were no rings, but an emerald-on-gold band slid down her wrist and stopped mid forearm. Her nails were long, manicured, and blood red. Her ears were fully exposed, unlike his, and supported large hoops. The left ear, the one he could see as he approached, also carried an emerald ear cuff, and she was dressed for a Boston June evening. A jacket rested on the chair beside her, black with full shoulders and pulled at the waist. She wore black, pleated silk pants and deeply green shoes with low heels. Her billowing silk blouse didn't quite hide her full chest and matched the color of her shoes. A gentle breeze caused a mesmerizing pattern in the silk and he caught himself staring.

He glanced at his reflection in a passing store window before calling her name. "Sherry?"

She stood up quickly. Her chair skittered backwards and bumped into a gentleman sitting at the table behind her. She turned and touched the man's shoulder. "Sorry."

He'd accurately guessed her height. Her eyes were green, neither flecked nor chameleon, a simple green contrasting well with her hair and fair, cool skin. She had full lips, her mouth not wide, her nose thin and almost aquiline, her face thin without being angular. Her eyebrows matched her hair.

"Yes. Iggie?"

He clenched a fist, nails into his palms, making sure they weren't longer or sharper than decency would allow, ran his tongue over his teeth to ensure his canines were still recessed, then offered her his hand and smiled. "Yes. It's nice to meet you."

She put on large, red framed glasses. The lenses weren't thick, but they made wide moon-like circles over her eyes. "I don't have to wear them, just for reading." She put them back in her bag. They stood there for a moment or two not talking, not looking at each other, the fence's finials separating them like a demilitarized zone, her scent, anxiety, rising, his own fears telling him to run away. People started staring.

"Looks pretty lonely over there," she said. "Why don't you come on my side for a while?"

The waiter waited without offering a menu. "Whatever she's having." The waiter walked away without looking at Sherry's cup. Iggie listened to her breathe: light, shallow. She looked away for a moment or two. "Am I making you nervous?" he asked.

She stared at him, a little quizzically. "No, why."

"You seem nervous."

"Just the situation."

"I'll leave if..."

She didn't let him finish. "No, stay. I've just never answered one of those things before."

"Yes, you told me."

"Our marathon morning call, right."

"You're beautiful." He kept her gaze in his, never letting his eyes wander from hers, feeling the animal in him confused and timid.

She stared at him a long time before saying anything. All the while he kept the beast in him attentive to her, stalking but not stalking, his dark, languid eyes always on her face, his body light in the chair and tilted slightly towards her.

"Telling me I'm beautiful isn't going to calm me down, you know."

"It's true."

She laughed, the same, full laugh she had on the phone. "How did you know I was me? I didn't tell you what I'd be wearing or what I looked like."

"Your – " he hesitated. "A good guess?"

"A good guess," she echoed and smiled. "Care to take me to dinner, Mr. Turner?"

He stood up, pulled back her chair, held her jacket as she slid her arms through the sleeves, dropped two twenty dollar bills on the table, and offered his arm, guiding her out to the sidewalk, letting her slightest, unconscious body shifts guide him to the restaurant of her choice: an Italian restaurant with authentic Northern cuisine.

"I love this place. What made you decide to come here? I thought you didn't know much about Boston."

"Just seemed like the kind of place you'd like to dine. It's okay, isn't it?" She kissed him then, quickly but softly, on his cheek. It almost took him by surprise and he held back his urge to view her sudden movement as an attack. His body prepared for movement and sent a rush of blood through him.

"I'm sorry, Iggie." She hugged him and laid her head on his chest, tenderly, gently. "I didn't mean to make you blush. You're just such a gentle man."

He opened the door and walked in behind her. He ordered something with vegetables, meatless, in a light garlic sauce. All through the meal he didn't take his eyes off hers, although his other senses trained on her like a Pointer in a hunt.

Two hours later she said, "You've got a long ride back. Should you be starting for home?"

"As you wish." He motioned for the check.

She looked at him somewhat differently then. "Just going to leave like that, huh?"

"I thought the evening was over."

"Did you think the evening would go further?"

"I was hoping so. I mean..." Shyness rose in him. He didn't know how to act, how to respond. He spoke timidly. "I think you're really nice. I like you. A lot."

"Iggie, I like you, too, but I'm not the kind of woman – "

"No." His eyes widened as he realized her meaning. He put his hand up as if to ward off her words. "I didn't think you were. I mean..."

She pursed her lips. "Yes?"

"No, I mean I can leave anytime. No one's waiting for me at home." Iggie checked his watch, doing so only because a man two tables away did so as he talked to a woman sitting there. "I do have to go away on business in a few days, though," he added helpfully.

She crossed her arms over her chest and sat back. Her face got tight and flushed, her eyelids lowered and he felt himself evaluated in a mirror he could not see.

"Look, I'm new at this and a little awkward. What I'm trying to say is, I don't have to go home. I don't have to go to your home either. We can go somewhere else, if you'd like."

She pulled a fifty dollar bill from her purse and threw it on their table.

"I mean dancing or for coffee or a ride maybe." He lowered his head to his hands. "I wish I knew more of what was expected of me in these kinds of situations. Guess I've blown this one, huh?"

There was a silence which only he could hear. There was confusion. She was relaxing and tensing and relaxing and he knew she watched him.

She laughed, the same musical laugh he'd heard on the phone, and he looked up. Her body hadn't moved, but her face lightened. She smiled and the smile spread to her eyes. "You're cute."

He felt himself floating on her voice, resting warmly in her eyes. "And cuddly, too."

"Iggie, I don't normally do this." She suddenly looked to the side. "My god does that sound like a line." She looked back at him. "Anyway, I don't live far from here. Would you like to come by for a drink?"

It turned out he parked around the corner from her Back Bay condo, three small rooms in a gentrified hotel a block east of Kenmore Square. She had an excellent stereo, a black Yamaha baby grand, and three small rooms and called it "home." It made Iggie claustrophobic. He left her early in the morning without waking her.

*H*is answering machine greeting him with a red, blinking "2" when he got home.

"Hi, it's me. I just wanted to say 'Hi.' Hope you made it home all right. I wish you woke me before you left. I was kind of tired. I guess that was obvious after the last time, huh? You weren't kidding when you said you ran through the woods to stay in shape, were you!" She laughed. "I guess I needed my sleep. Thank you. When can I see you again? Have a good time on your trip. Send me a postcard or call to let me know how you're doing. I like you. How much time do I have before this thing beeps? Bye." He played that message three more times before listening to the next one.

"By the way, this is Sherry. I left the last message. Call me before you leave, okay?"

He called. She wasn't there, but he remembered she worked at Merrill Lynch. He called there and two secretaries later heard her say, "Sherry Stearns." There was still music in her voice.

"Hi. Remember me?"

"Iggie? Iggie, hi! Do I remember you?" She laughed as she echoed his question. "Why don't you run up and down a few more mountains?"

"I just wanted to call you before I left."

"Are you at Logan? If you are I can catch a cab out there. Maybe we can have a drink before you leave?"

"No, I'm not at Logan."

"What, are you flying out of Manchester?"

"No, I have my own plane."

"Really? Wow. What business did you say you were in? That's right, I remember. Weyerhauser leases the forests on your mountain." She laughed again. "Where're you going?"

"Kind of all over. I've got a lot of stops to make. Everybody needs toothpicks. And TP. I just wanted to let you know I'll be gone for about a month and would like to see you again when I get back. I didn't want you to think I was one of those one night guys when you didn't hear from me for a while."

"Well, where are you going?"

"Europe. Europe then South America."

"Will you call me from where ever?" Delight drained from her voice.

"I'll try. That's all I can say."

"Okay."

She sounded disappointed but what could he do?

"Have a nice trip. Give me a call when you get back." She hung up before he could say anything.

He called his attorney and told him to send a bouquet to Sherry's office close to the middle of the month.

Twenty-six days later he recognized a thumb where his dewclaw had been the night before. His voice was more feral than human and his extremities too hirsute for any man's. He didn't remember noticing these things during his metamorphoses before. A rabbit scurried from its cover. He lost interest in his physiognomy and ran after it.

Two days later he woke on his porch. The answering machine's light blinked rapidly and continuously. There were more messages stored than the machine could count. Normally he returned to find none. The only people who needed to reach him knew enough to do so by mail. The answering machine can wait, he told himself, checking his voice before calling Sherry.

"Hello?" Her voice sounded as it had the first time he'd called her and he realized it was barely 6:00AM.

"Hi."

"Hello?"

"It's me, Iggie."

Her voice went cold. "Iggie who?"

"Iggie Turner."

"Oh yeah. Thanks for the flowers."

"Maybe I should call back later?"

"Or maybe not at all." He said nothing, waiting through the silence. "Why didn't you call me from Europe? Or South America maybe?"

"I didn't have a chance."

"You had no time to yourself in a month to make a call?"

"Look, this is complicated. Can I see you to try and explain it?"

"Men. Fucking men. What the hell am I talking to you for?"

She hung up, the phone's click penetrating his bones.

He cleaned up, staying in the shower until the water felt like ice crawling on his skin, then called a Boston florist to send Sherry some more flowers. Later that afternoon he listened to his messages. All were from Sherry, all of increasing anger, frustration, resentment. The last message ended with, "...and I don't care if you send me every fucking flower in the world." He called the florist. Too late, the order had already gone out. He hung up the phone and it rang before the receiver stopped jiggling in the cradle.

"Yes?"

"You don't listen to your messages very often, do you?" Sherry. Still angry but her voice softened.

"Sorry about the flowers."

"Can you come down tonight?"

"Tomorrow would be better. I just got back and..."

"No excuses. Tomorrow. I'll take the afternoon off so we can talk. Okay? And when we get together, you better explain all this to me. Tomorrow night, at my place, at 6:30. Is that night enough for you?"

"Yes." He heard her hang up and put the receiver back into its cradle gently. He stared at it a few minutes, waiting for it to ring again. It didn't.

Sherry waited for him in her lobby. He hadn't taken his sunglasses off, knowing that his eyes still reflected light slightly, and allowed his eyes to take in all the colors of her. She was wearing a slit maroon knee length skirt, a billowy white blouse, and a scarf with emerald, black, and maroon flowing through it. It was clasped with a gold pin. Her hair was slightly longer, her eyes slightly wider and deeper than he remembered – something he attributed to her makeup more than a lapse in his memory or a shift in her features – and her lips, her full, gently pouting lips, were touched with a pale frosty glaze.

"I'd forgotten how beautiful you look."

She checked her watch. "When you say you're going to do something, you do it, don't you."

He nodded. "Yes."

"Are you hungry?"

He nodded again.

"Care to take me out to dinner?"

"Sure." They went to a Thai place a couple of blocks from her condo. He asked for a table in the back, one without any lights near it. The waiter lit a candle and set it on their table.

Three quarters of the way through a silent dinner she said, "Did you get into a fight?"

He dropped his fork, unsure of what she could have noticed. "No, why?"

"Do you do drugs?"

"What are you talking about?"

She reached over and took the sunglasses off his face. "Then are you ashamed to be seen with me? Or are you afraid someone might recognize you and wonder who you're with?"

He lowered his face and scrunched his features to hide his eyes. His left hand rifled up, near anguine in its movement, and snapped around her wrist. "What are you doing? Give me those now."

He heard his glasses drop on the table. "Let me go. You're hurting me." He released her hand as if it were a glowing coal.

"I'm sorry. Give me my glasses, please."

"They're right there, in front of you."

"I can't open my eyes to find them. Please just hand them to me and I'll go."

He heard her lift them from the table. His hand tracked hers until he realized she wasn't handing them back. "They're not prescription. I can see through them fine. They're awfully dark, though."

"Please just hand them back."

"Why can't you open your eyes?"

"I'm having a little trouble with them right now."

"Iggie. Please look at me."

"Blow the candle out first." He heard her exhale sharply but felt it on his hands, not in the direction of the candle. "Sherry, I'm sorry for any trouble I've caused you, but don't bullshit me."

"Wow, you swear? Do you get angry, too?"

"I know you didn't blow out the candle. I can still feel the heat and see the glow through my eyelids. There's no smell of smoldering wick and I felt your breath on my hands when you were suppose to be blowing it out."

"Look at me. I just want to see if you've been doing drugs."

He took a deep breath and opened his eyes slowly, hoping they would adjust rather than gather the light.

"You have beautiful eyes, Iggie. If you've been doing drugs, they don't show it."

The kitchen door opened and his eyes blazed green as they amplified and reflected the light. He jerked his head down and covered his eyes with his right hand. "Please give me the glasses."

"Your eyes sparkle."

His heart sank. "I can explain."

"You don't have to. My mother's eyes did the same thing."

He looked up at her. "They did?"

"Yes, for about a month after her operation. Why didn't you just tell me, Iggie?"

Tell her the truth, he told himself. You like her and you have to let her know. "I don't know."

She placed his glasses in his hand, lifted it to her face and kissed it. "If I'd known, I could have sent *you* flowers."

They finished the meal, but not before he put his glasses in his pocket and rearranged his chair so he was sitting next to her and away from the kitchen door.

They picked up some DVDs – *Rocky II*, *Young Frankenstein*, and *The Watcher in the Woods* – and went back to her place. Later that night, as she fell asleep, he got out of bed and stretched, his body silhouetted against the waxing moon in her window. He heard her move under the sheets.

"Boy, can you fuck," she sighed.

His voice growled out in a fair imitation of Mr. T's "Clubber Lang" character, "Come on, I got a lotta more." He rolled his back and shoulders forward, unafraid for the first time in many years, and leapt across the room onto the bed beside her.

He left the next morning, slipping out of bed as she rolled off him in her sleep. He left no messages, no notes, no hint of his departure.

He got home to hear her leaving a message. "Once, just once, I'd like to wake up beside you."

The phone rang as he stood there. "Yes?"

A sigh. Sherry's sigh. "Iggie." She hesitated. He lifted his hand to his nose and inhaled deeply, her musk still strong on him. The scent combined with her voice brought him back her, laying upon her.

"Iggie?"

Her voice shook him from his memories.

"What's going on? How come you never spend the night? The whole night?"

"I have other things to do." He spoke softly, half hoping she wouldn't hear, half wanting to say something else.

But she did. "Yeah. Right. Fucking men. What do you tell her when you come home in the morning? Or do you shower at some club to get my stink off you?" She hung up.

The next day he waited for her to arrive at her office. She looked at him and said nothing. He reached out for her as she walked past. "Sherry – "

She pulled her arm away before he could take it. "Leave me alone, you son-of-a-bitch."

He tried not to, but laughed at the epithet. It always made him want to say, "No, it was my father..."

"You think this is funny? Get out of my life, please!"

People turned and stared. A security guard keyed his lapel mike. Iggie raised himself on point involuntarily. "No, Sherry, let me explain."

"No, don't. I don't want to hear it. Just leave me alone. Go away, back to where ever and who ever you came from. Get lost, okay? Thanks for the good times, but you're not worth the bad."

He stood in front of her, unintentionally blocking her way.

"I was somebody's mistress once but at least he was honest about it." She pushed past him and went into One Financial Place.

He was by the doors when she came out for lunch. "What are you doing here?" She checked her watch. "Isn't it time for you to go away again?" She didn't stop. He walked beside her.

"I'm not a bad fellow. I've just got a few problems, is all."

"You never said deafness was one of them."

"Huh?"

She stopped and laughed. "Okay, you made me laugh. What's the story, Iggie? What, are you married or something? If you are, tell me. I can handle it. Do you have some crippled sister at home that requires all your time and attention? Tell me. Do you have a crazy mother in the attic?"

His face went blank and cold. He felt the blood drain, his body-awareness telling him the days before his next cycling.

Sherry touched his arm. "Iggie, is that it? I'm sorry. I didn't know."

"I had a crazy mother. Now she's in this attic." He pointed to his head.

She stared at him. Anger and compassion alternating on her face. She reached out to him and gently held his arm. "Iggie, I like you. But I need to understand you if I'm going to stay with you. Everybody has secrets. Why don't you let me decide if yours are so horrible I don't want to hear them? I might surprise you."

He looked down then back into her face. "I'm...I'm...my father..."

Her finger pressed his lips close. She put her arms around him and hugged him. "Not now, Iggie. You don't have to tell me everything now."

"But I'm going to have to go away again."

"When?"

"This Sunday."

"Is there anything for you to do for the next few days?"

"No."

"Then let's spend the next few days together. I know this place up in Maine. We can get a cabin and be all alone for a few days."

He pulled away, nervous and afraid.

"Well?"

"Yeah, sure."

"Good, I'll tell the office that I'm going to be gone the next few days. We can leave right after work. You can get your things on the way up."

He shook and hoped it wasn't noticeable. "No, no. I have everything I need in the car."

"You're pretty damn sure of yourself, weren't you?"

He didn't answer. They ate at 'Wall Street' and he walked her back. He spent the rest of the afternoon running through several stores, picking up an overnight bag and assorted clothes. What time he had before Sherry got out of work he spent tearing labels and packaging from the clothes and putting them in the overnight bag.

They spent most of the time either in bed or in restaurants, only going sightseeing twice. The first time was horseback riding. Sherry's mount became skitterish when Iggie approached and the handler, a woman whose farm labors gave her the build of a man, commented she'd never seen the horse behave so.

It knows, Iggie thought. It knows what I am. What can I do? Iggie looked deep into himself, into the beast within, and remembered that the beast more than the man found a peace in its immediacy. The horse stopped shying and nuzzled him, stirring him from his thoughts.

"How'd you do that?" the handler asked.

Iggie shrugged.

Later that night Iggie woke up, sweating while Sherry slept. He'd dreamt of the farm, the horses. A moonless night and he wasn't a man, but he stood like a man, under some trees and leaning on the fence to the pasture. The horses neighed and nickered, grew anxious and fearful, gathered at the far end of the field. They whinnied and ran, kicking and biting each other. Iggie saw himself as the horses saw him, standing like a man but looking like a wolf or a bear. His snout long and his ears high and prehensile, swishing as they scoped out sounds, his eyes large and gleaming in the moonlight. His tongue a sliver of pink that wagged from the left side of his mouth and flicked over sharp, razored and bone-crunching teeth. A mist rose from his mouth as he breathed. It rose into the trees and fogged above his head. The handler and another woman, petite when compared to the first, with a high voice and bright eyes, came out to see what spooked the horses. The smaller woman aimed a rifle at Iggie and shot.

Sweating as he lay next to Sherry, he checked his hands. Human hands. Straight, human teeth. He touched his nose and ears.

Human. All human.

He woke Sherry and made love to her, anchoring himself in her, in her humanness, in this time and place, before going back to sleep.

Sherry asked to go hiking early on the third day, wanting to see the bright autumn colors. She couldn't keep up with him and he eventually started running up ahead then back to check on her.

"You tired?" he asked when he found her sitting on a rock beside the trail.

"No, I'm waiting for a bus to the top."

Before she could respond Iggie threw her over his shoulder and ran up the trail. They got to the top and he wasn't breathing hard. "You really are in good shape."

He smiled, felt his canines pressing on his lower lip and quickly closed his mouth.

"Anything wrong?"

"No. Let's head back."

"Don't you want to rest?"

"No." He lifted her again and ran back down.

Back at the cabin, he started gathering his things. "Let's go."

"We're leaving?"

"Yes."

"Why?"

"It's time for me to go."

"Can we talk about this?"

"No, I have to get home."

She turned away and started packing. Iggie heard her sniff, smelled her tears and felt her skin tighten, and continued to pack.

They were north of Concord and she was reading a map. "Your home's off the next exit, isn't it?"

He hadn't spoken all the way back and cleared his throat before answering. "Yes."

"Aren't you going to slow down?" They zoomed past it. "I guess not. I thought you had to get back home."

He cleared his throat again. "I do. I'm taking you home first."

Her breathing changed. He smelled her effort to control it, heard her body tightening and relaxing, tightening and relaxing, tightening and relaxing as she fought to control her frustration.

"Iggie, I think I need to see your house."

"No, you don't."

"No, Iggie, I think I do. I think I care about you but I have to know what's going on if I'm going to see you again. Right now this relationship is really one sided. I'm giving you everything but I don't think I'm getting much back. I care about you a lot, Ig, but I care about myself more, and if you're not going to share yourself with me then just leave me in Concord and I'll take a bus home. I'm sorry, Iggie, but that's the way it's got to be."

"You don't understand," he snarled.

"Iggie!" she pulled away, against the side of the car and away from him. He'd frightened her.

"Listen, Iggie. I want to understand, but I can't unless you're willing to let me. I don't want to stop seeing you, but I can't spend my time with only half a man."

He winced. A tear slide down his cheek. Another exit towards his home approached and he took it. They drove on in silence.

He woke before her and looked at the calendar against the wall. Two days left. Maybe sixty hours, at most, before he wouldn't be able to stand up straight or have hands to hold things, hold her, in. As it was, he couldn't stay clean shaven for more than six hours and his voice was sinking. His tongue started to fill his mouth, his elbows, wrists, knees, and ankles becoming more pronounced, and worse, the smell of Sherry's anxiety was accelerating his change.

Last night, when they made love, the beast had come and watched the man until finally, the man turned and the beast had taken her in its arms. Why hadn't she noticed, he wondered.

He left her a note on the table and took a perch half way up an oak some two hundred feet from his house. He knew when she read it because her smell changed drastically and he heard her cry. The note told her to take the RangeRover and leave. He didn't want her there when he came back.

He heard and smelled her make breakfast, clean, wash, dress, go into his study, call her answering machine, go into the den, turn on the stereo, and lay on the couch. She didn't move from there all day.

The sun had set behind the tall pines and mountains to the west an hour earlier. In the dusk and cool near winter air, he tried to cry and grew only more frustrated that that vestige of humankind had already left him. Descending from the tree, Iggie wondered how to handle this situation. "She must leave," he growled, the words low in his throat, more rumbled than spoken. "She can't stay any longer. She'll find out and she won't love me anymore."

He entered through the front door, but shut off the lights along the way. Her glasses were still on the kitchen table, next to the note he left. He smelled her, still in the den, still on the couch. He called from the hallway, "I told you to leave."

"What's the big secret, Iggie?" she demanded. "I only see you once a month – you're worse than my goddamn period. At least I know when to expect that. I finally get to see where you live and you want me to leave after one night. What's the story? You're wife coming back? Just tell me what's going on. I want to know the secret."

He heard her get up and growled, his voice harder and harder to control, "Don't move."

She rose more quickly and started towards him. "Iggie, what's wrong?"

It's dark, he told himself. She can't see that well in the dark without her glasses. These thoughts emboldened him and he stepped into the doorway. "I don't love you. I don't even like you. You were fun for a while, but now you bore me. It's time for somebody new. Get out."

She stretched her arms out towards him, her face white with pain as tears flooded his eyes. "No, Iggie. Please, don't say that. Is this about last night? Please say no, Iggie. Last night was so passionate, so beautiful. Last night was the first time I thought I was with the real you."

He retreated back into the darkness, his voice quieter, higher, frightened at what she might know. "What are you talking about?"

"Last night, when you rolled onto me and started making love. You've never been like that before. You've never been so passionate, so primal, so intense. You've always been good, Iggie. But last night almost hurt...I don't know...there was so much more emotion, like I was getting my brains fucked out. And you started biting me. No, it was more like you were nipping me. Kind of like a puppy teething. It really got me going. Then, when you came, you made a sound deep in your throat between a growl and a moan. That was another thing. You're fairly quiet. You usually don't make any noise. I wish you would because that way I'd at least have an idea of what you're thinking about or what you'd like me to do.

"But last night, when you were finished, you were relaxed. That's one thing I've noticed about you, Ig. The better the sex, the more relaxed you get. And you're never relaxed. Just when I think I've really pleasured you, you sit up in bed and look like you're thinking of something else.

"Do you know how that makes me feel? When it's obvious something or someone else has come into your mind? And I'm left trying to figure out who? I feel so shitty, so empty when that happens.

"Then, just as I was dozing off, you started licking the sweat off me. Did you know you did that? And you said, 'Do you realize how attractive you are to other men?'

"I woke up at that. 'What do you mean?' I asked and you said, 'Can't you tell, as you walk past them? Can't you see the heat rise in them? Smell how their bodies quicken at your approach? Look into their eyes and see what thoughts lie behind? Hear their hearts and lungs grow tighter, stronger, as they try and decide if they should say hello?

"'No, you can't,' you said. It was the sweetest thing anyone'd ever said to me. Strange, but sweet.

"You held me then and I started to go back to sleep. And as I was falling asleep I started dreaming. I dreamt you smelled different, that your body changed. I remember getting scared. It felt as if your chest expanded, as if your shoulders got wider. In my dream, you started to breathe deeper. I know it sounds stupid, but I saw your eyes get darker and wider, too.

"But it was only a dream, Iggie. If I said something or did something, it was because I was really tired and probably asleep. I was frightened, but that's normal, don't you think? You obviously have something you're hiding from me and it came out like that in the dream. I'm sorry, Iggie." She sobbed then, an offering, exposed, hiding nothing.

He watched her, deciding if he was witness to anger and rage or anguish and pain. Part of him, the part now not so deep within him, the part she said she liked, came forward, overwhelmed by her pain. He never meant this. He couldn't control this situation.

Now she knows and it frightens her.

His own anxiety and Sherry's scent rushed the emerging beast within him. He let the animal out, bellowing, letting the words crawl up his lungs, taking their time to be human words in the throat of a beast.

"Get out." He slammed his fist into the wall.

Sherry ran past him, through the door and out into the yard. He heard the RangeRover's door open, slam, and the splashing of dirt and gravel as she drove off. Iggie walked to the door, saw the moon with only a crescent left, and forced a scream from his throat, screaming not at Sherry, not at himself, but at Luna, his rage releasing the animal from the cage within him, shrieking and leaping, banging himself off the walls until he slumped to the floor, too exhausted to move, unable to cry. He looked at his hands, no longer quite hands, and the increasing bends in his sleeves and pants. His tongue flicked his teeth. They were sharper and the canines were more pronounced.

He shrieked at the stars, "I'm not an animal." He stretched and tried to clench the moon between the pads forming on his fingers. Instead he slumped to the floor, on his knees in the vestigial moonlight. In his moment, in his agony of wanting to love but being afraid no one would love in return, of being alone and wanting to be held, of sharing his world and finding no one wanting to share, of realizing he was what he was, he remembered something his father had said, a drop of wisdom in the memories of confusion, something recently experienced with the horses: Accept what you are. Accept what you are and you make yourself something greater, something better. Don't accept and anything you build you build on sand.

Sherry had been gone for about two minutes. She knew only one way to Boston, through town. She couldn't be far past where his driveway met the logging road. He growled, took off his shoes and socks, and burst through the door, knocking it from its hinges. His eyes opened for the darkness, his nose widened to avoid both predators and prey that might bar his path, and his legs pulsed with the motion of a man and the spring of something deeper, something older, something placing more energy in him.

He heard the car skitter on the dirt as it turned onto the logging road. It went past him as he emerged from the woods. He continued through the woods and down to the town. She would get there before him, but if he didn't get her there he would never see her again.

His legs continued, not straining, with neither the pain nor the stitches others might have felt following his path. He didn't trip, fall, or rustle leaves as he moved, all the while feeling the moon watch over his parade.

The RangeRover sat in front of the bar. The bus stop sign was lit and nothing else was open.

He waited outside in the shadows. Bar sounds came to him: pool cues hitting balls, jukebox music played too loud, glasses and bottles clinking and tinkling, voices feigning sober discussion. He wasn't sure if he could pick out Sherry's voice from the rest, but the smell of her perfume was strong. There was a scent of fear mixed with it. He stood to the side of a rear window. Voices became more distinct. There were still many – Iggie counted five – but one stood out from the rest.

"You with Turner? That's his car, isn't it?" No response. "I asked you, are you visiting Iggie Turner?" Again no response. "Hey, lady – "

Another voice. "Jake, leave her alone."

Iggie noticed the bar was growing quiet and groaned as the jukebox's tune became obvious:

> *It took a long time to get next to you.*
> *It took a long time to get next to me.*
> *I spent my share of nickels and dimes*
> *on telephone lines just telling you lies.*

"Why?" Jake asked. "We all work for that bastard but he don't know us. Then he goes and gets himself some fancy Boston bitch – "

A third voice. "Jake, you're drunk. Come on over here and we'll talk about Turner ourselves."

A sharp crack and wood splintered. Jake again. "Talk's for shit. I never smelled perfume like that. And look at her hair. You know any women cut their hair like that? Betsy? You cut your hair like that?"

Laughter.

Sherry's voice, cold and hard. "Leave me alone."

A female voice, perhaps Jake's Betsy, rising above the general noise.

"Why's Iggie Turner want to waste his time with some high class like you, I don't know. He wants a good turn, he doesn't have to look out of town."

The bar again grew quiet, the jukebox again more obvious.

> *Somewhere back in my eyes you can't see*
> *Is a hole big enough to let out the rest of me.*
> *It took a long time to get next to you.*
> *It took a long time to get next to me.*
> *Why do those lies make us more wise?*
> *Why did those lies ever rule our lives?*

Somebody laughed and voices started again. Jake said, "Damn you've got big tits."

A hand slapped a loose, fleshy cheek.

Sherry's voice, not in control. Desperate. "Keep your hands off of me."

Iggie opened the door to the bar. At first the smells overpowered him. He sneezed and, unable to stop himself, licked his nose.

Stay on your feet, not on your toes.

Sherry stood by the bar. A large man in a red hunter's jacket and an orange cap held her arm and pushed her against the bar. The man needed a shave. His eyes were close together and pig like, his nose flattened from too many fights, and Iggie wondered if there was a curled tail tucked into his manure stained overalls.

"Let her go," Iggie said, his voice more human than he hoped.

"Well, finally decided to talk to the little people?" the man said. The voice told Iggie it was Jake.

Another man, closer to Iggie and sitting at a table, said, "You're the great Iggie Turner? You're not so big in real life, you know that?" The man belched and the smell of sour beer engulfed Iggie. He sneezed again.

A woman with Betsy's voice, a woman with a cheap flower print dress cut too low, a woman with a push-up bra working too hard, a woman with nylons with too many runs to possibly feel comfortable on her legs, a woman with too much makeup and too loud a perfume, a woman with hair too many years out of fashion for her sadly lined face, staggered over to Iggie with a handkerchief. "Here, hon. Betsy'll take care of that cold for you."

Iggie snarled and bared his fangs at her approach. She cried out, covered her mouth with the handkerchief and whirled away from him, tripped over a chair and landed flat on a table, sending warm beer and day old pretzels onto the floor and laps of those present.

The man who belched at Iggie and two others from the table where Betsy landed got to their feet. Jake looked at Sherry. "Stay here, bitch."

One of the men picked up a pool cue and swung it at Iggie. But Iggie's moon was sending him quickly into the ways of beasts and his running had fueled the metamorphosis. His anxiety rushed what might have taken another day or two at other times. Reflexes that kept bobcats and bears at bay, reflexes that caught fish without hook or net, rushed through him.

The pool cue whizzed over his head. Iggie's claws ripped open the man's face. Neither Jake nor the other two men nor anyone else in the bar moved.

The man dropped the pool cue and clutched his face. Blood flowed through his hands and drenched his shirt. He screamed and fell back onto Betsy. She shrieked and pushed him off. The other men moved towards Iggie.

Iggie leapt. His body flew parallel to the floor. One hand pushed one man's head as Iggie's other hand grabbed the man's shoulder, exposing the neck. Iggie bit deep enough to instill fear, to leave scars, but not permanent damage. The man fell and didn't get up.

Iggie stood in the middle of the bar. Jake came at Iggie from one side and the belcher from the other. The belcher broke a beer bottle as he approached. Iggie backed up, trying to get outside and away from Sherry. Instead he found himself in a corner of the bar.

"Just like an animal, huh, Turner?" said Jake.

"Accept," Iggie whispered.

The two men moved at once. Iggie's claws went deep into Jake's soft belly. One paw moved up and the other down, opening Jake like a cleanly killed rabbit. The animal in Iggie saw the deliciously sweet intestines there and stopped, fascinated. His tongue swept his lips and his eyes went wide at the prize before him.

The bottle flashed in front of him and cut his arm. Iggie yelped as the bottle came at him again. He caught the belcher's arm and dug his claws deep into the flesh, through the muscle and into the bone. The belcher screamed. Iggie pulled the man's arm until his face was level with Iggie's. The man screamed again. Iggie looked at the bleeding body of Jake, his intestines spilling onto the floor, then looked into the sour smelling mouth of the belcher, into the terrified soul he knew existed there, the terrified soul so similar to his own.

But now Iggie admitted who and what he was. Even if Sherry didn't want him, couldn't love him, feared to look upon him, he knew what he was, what his world was, and accepted it.

Iggie opened his muzzle until he knew the man could look into him as Iggie had stared into the man. He felt his saliva slide down his flews and onto his clothes, ran his tongue over his teeth, felt the man shake before him, and howled until the man's screaming stopped. He let go and the man slumped onto the floor beside Jake.

The bar held only Iggie's fallen attackers, an unconscious Betsy, and Sherry. Iggie walked over to the door. He walked on the balls of his feet, on his toes. He had no choice. His back began arching and his arms stretched to match the length of his legs. His ankles rode higher on his legs, making an opposing knee appear in his pants. His face grew longer, his ears longer and tapered, his eyes and nostrils larger, the hair on his face darker and thicker, and now obviously coursing down his neck to his chest and back. Soon he would have to take all the clothes off.

He had to get back to his house. Soon. Now.

He stopped at the door and turned to Sherry. The look on her face, her smell, her sounds, all a mix of fear and anguish, her eyes widened with far more terror than he'd ever imagined. The jukebox finished playing the song.

I don't know why you still love me.
Why did those lies ever rule our lives?
Why do those lies show in your eyes?

He raised an arm and held a hand out to her, the hand too hairy and ending in fingers too long and too thickly nailed for a man, fingers with obvious pads giving them an odd mallet like shape. His voice more animal than man, he tried three times before the words sounded human enough. "No wife, no mother, no others. This is my secret. This is what I am. Can you love me knowing this?"

She swallowed hard, once, then again. She crossed half the room to him, her steps small and unsure. "Iggie?"

He wanted to look away but didn't, no longer afraid of what he was and not willing to let others' fears guide him. Instead he looked into her eyes.

"It is you. Your eyes, Iggie. They're still beautiful."

He tried to smile and drool hung from his flews.

"Are you going to hurt me?"

He looked around the room.

She stood taller, moved closer, always looking into his eyes and face. "Not them, me. Can...can you understand me?" She started talking slower and enunciating, as if asking directions in a foreign country. "Are you going to hurt me? I need to know if you are going to hurt me."

He shook his head and growled, "I won't stop understanding you, and no, I won't hurt you. Ever."

"My dream. It wasn't a dream, was it?"

"I am a man only when the moon is full. I change from and to a beast as it waxes and wanes, but I'm never one without the other. Both are inside me, always."

"And your business trips, they're—"

"When I'm fully changed, when I no longer look anything like a man."

Sherry closed her eyes and swallowed, shook herself, opened her eyes, walked over to him and shuddered.

She took his hand, slowly. He felt her trembling, her fear, her anxiety.

She reached for his wounded arm. He whined and pulled away, a small pup afraid of being hurt.

She took his hand and drew his arm to her more slowly, watching him for a moment then inspecting the wound. "We'll need to take care of this. We don't want it to fester."

He smiled. He hoped he smiled. He looked at his reflection in the mirror behind the bar. He used his free paw to fashion his wolfish lips into a smile.

Sherry stroked his brow, always looking into his eyes and, he hoped, seeing him there. "Let's get you in the car and back home. We can take care of this there."

She held the door for him as the rest of the metamorphosis took place. His body dropped to walk on all fours. He felt her breath blow over his brow followed by her lips resting there, kissing him.

COLD WAR

COLD WAR

Home is…south? Gotta be. Everything's south.
    Which way is south? Can't smell it anymore. Damn compass froze, it's so cold.

Cold didn't bother me the first 250 miles. Neither did the glare of the sun. Or the endless white. Or the total lack of smells. Someone told me there'd be weird smells up here. There aren't any. Not this far north. There's the smell of the ocean, humming beneath this glacier. I could smell the snow at first. That stopped after a few hours, after my mind got so use to the smell of white that it got blocked out. The winds don't howl like I thought they would. They wouldn't this time of year, anyway. But they whisper. The glacier surface is so flat I can hear conversations back in Mantinac Bay. They come to me when I let my mind rest, when I lay down to sleep. That's not like in-country. You lay down in-country, any thing's got legs uses you for an LZ, a runway. The ice surface is uneven, though. Up close it's uneven. That's like in-country. But nothing crawls over you. Nothing living, nothing but the wind.

I don't sleep that much anymore. The monitor's attached to my chest. Physically attached. They sowed it into me where the skin is thickest. So I can't sleep on my stomach and when I sleep on my back I can see this damn little red light blink blink blink. Blink blink blink. Keeps you up all night, you know? Blink blink blink.

How much farther? I use to be able to do this in my head when I started. Mantinac to the Pole is nine-hundred sixty klicks. I've gone four-hundred. What does that leave?

It's a long trip. Some nut told me the ice would smooth out. This from a guy with a Ph.D. in cold weather research. Guy learned from a book. That was back at USAACRREL: United States Army Arctic and Cold Regions Research and Environmental Labs in Hanover, New Hampshire. New Hampshire can get cold, when the Montreal Express comes in the from the north and we get a Nor'Easter heading in from the Maritimes. One year we had a snow squall New England style. That's a hurricane in winter. It got cold. Not like this. This is a dry cold. They didn't modify me right. I can feel it. Right up my legs to where my willy used to be. I can feel it.

I started with just over nine-hundred kilos of supplies. Stupid bastards. Over nine-hundred kilos in the sled, my body weight just under a metric ton. Oh yeah. They figured this one right. Each time my feet splayed, the fishtails on my soles picked up little slivers of ice that worked their way in. Deep. Kind of like shin splints that itch. I've only used a third of the supplies. That part of the design went right, anyway. Big as I am, I don't need much food anymore. How 'bout that, mom? Mother never raised no tiny children, she used to say. What you think of your poor boy now, momma? They took what you and papa made one night and made me something no woman will look at again.

Everybody thinks they find test subjects in jails. He's a lifer, he'll do this to get out. Maybe a college student who needs extra beer money. Oh, and there's this one, where they volunteer some private to go hazard. You know how Garrett got to be The Flash? Fricken' lightening hits his lab bench and douses him with chemicals. Fricken' Bruce Banner would have a tumor the size of a football if he ever sat in a gamma ray like they said. Remember 'When Captain America throws his mighty shield'? The next line should have been 'That ninety pound wimp gets a dick as hard as steel.'

Used to read comics all the time. Can't remember too many of them now.

How much further do I have to go?

Got this thing in the side of my head. They said it was like what they did to help me walk after Charlie sent me a baseball as I jumped off the Rome. I never walked right. They said they would fix all that, too. Make me a fricken' Steve Austin. Fuck. This thing in my head, under this plate, it listens to me and signals some satellite where I am and how I'm doing okay.

I'm doing okay, whoever's listening. I'm doing okay. Got this little red light says I'm doing okay. Blink blink blink.

Anyway. This thing in my head keeps me pointing north. Not this ninety degree west bullshit they told me about. You get far enough north and compasses go worthless because they always point ninety degrees west. So, can't you figure it's pointing west and go north just the same? Fricken' geniuses.

Hey, genius, you know what you got up here? You got snow. You got snow, white snow, crunchy snow, soft snow, hard snow, good snow, fricken' snow snow snow.

You know what else you got? You got cold and ice.

The ice. It doesn't smooth out. You get far enough north the ice becomes a layer of rubber that bounces you along the ocean. Seven to thirteen centimeters thick. Not much. But it'll support you. Even at a tonne and baggage. Got my bags packed. Going to fly me home. I thought ice was like ice and you see it in a drink or a lake and its hard, you know? No, arctic ice is like a skin on the ocean, at least between the leads. It's like a skin and you're some bug and the earth is just waiting to scratch.

It scratches when you don't expect it. There's thunder under your feet and the ice snaps open. It doesn't break. It snaps like an elastic wound too tight around a pack of cards. It snaps, you go down and they never told you what to do or that it could happen. I felt the thunder before I heard it. Started to move off the ice but fell in anyway. Me and the sled. I'm so damn big I must've looked like a whale with a backpack getting out. I'm going down deep and thinking, "Hey, you guys got an implant for this?" Finally thought to flatten myself out and let the ridges in my skin get me up. The ridges trap air so you stay warm. Hey, guys, they let you float, too. First bath I had in over a year. Just kept on walking and let the sun dry me off.

I'm usually walking by the time the sun comes up. Well, the sun doesn't come up. It kind of climbs up, bleary eyed like after a night at Jason's. It hangs half on the horizon. I can look at it, red and swollen like that, because of the changes to my eyes. It looks like me when I'd come home stinking and try to remember where I was. You hang on the sink and never get your face more than half in the mirror, kind of like eyes peering over the hill, because you see your shit and drive the porcelain school bus.

I used to drive the school bus. Those kids, once they found out, they were cool. I was a real hero then. One day I'm some fuckbag, driving the bus and getting spitballs in the back of my head, next day they're wanting to touch me and giving me their twinkies.

I like Twinkies. Liked 'em, anyway. Two-legged twinkies, you know?

Shit. Last year, last time before they wouldn't let me out anymore, I went to Jason's for some ass. Didn't have the implants then. I was big, but I was always big. Feet hadn't changed, and I could still shake hands. I used to bounce for Jason. This big guy starts picking a fight with somebody. Kind of guy plays pro ball and lifts, you know? Big. Hell, I never would've tried before.

Now I figure, what the hell? They're not going to let me out again. I got an arm like a fricken' Ben Grimm. This guy comes to just under my nose, hits me in the gut. I'm wearing a long coat they gave me, hides everything. It's like hitting fricken' concrete. Guy tries to knee me in the balls. I got no balls no more. He starts going wild. He knows he's dead. He's hittin' me with everything he's got. His hands are bleeding, you can hear his bones breaking because he's hitting me and he's so scared. The guy starts crying. I just look at him. "Go outside," I said. He near kills himself getting to the door.

I'm heading back to my booth. I'm not going after him. Then I notice everybody watching me. I never raised a hand and they're looking at me. I could smell them. They told me my nose would get more sensitive, and now I can smell these people in the bar. I reached into my coat pocket to pay my tab and the coat's sticky. It's blood. Not mine. This was red and mine is almost black by this time. Jason goes, "It's okay, Len. I got it." Yeah, I know. Len, get your things and get out.

I could pull this thing out of my head. Nobody'd know where I am. Have to pull this case off my chest, too. Aw, what the hell. I can make it.

You know what they do this for? Land's too valuable. You don't want to fight a war on land anymore. You blow up a city, you blow up manufacturing and you need manufacturing. You blow up roads and you blow up transportation. What good is manufacturing without transportation, right? So you blow up fields. Can't do that because most people can't feed themselves now anyway. So, where you going to fight? Up in the cold, Len.

You know what they said? Said, "You're going to be the first, Len. You're going to be a hero."

That'd be cool, I said.

Fricken' geniuses. Saw a tank specially designed for arctic warfare. It didn't work. Didn't work here, didn't work there. I know. I remember. I used to build LZs deep in-country for the medevacs to lift out wounded. Never thought I'd be wounded myself.

I drove the Rome-plow, fricken' big bulldozer. War took too long. Hell, one day, it was quiet. Charlie's nowhere. One of the tank drivers asks me for a tug of war, Rome's hydraulics didn't even strain.

The guy gets real pissed. I see him swinging the 80mm around, so I swing hard and bring up my blade. Caught the 80mm coming down and just let the Rome chug forward. Driver couldn't get the tank into gear quick enough and I rolled it over with the blade. I told them, "War'd be over if you got a couple of dozer-jockeys to level the place first."

Fricken' geniuses decide we don't need a few big tanks in the cold, we need lots of little ones. Oh, here's a good one. I'm reading this guy's paper on cold regions combat. You know what an 'unarmed arctic tactical ballistic projectile' is? Fricken' snowball. You got no more rounds, no blade, they want you to get into a fricken' snowball fight.

They used to throw snowballs at the school bus when it passed. You can't make snowballs up here. You got lots of snow, but you got no sticky snow. You can't even make an iceball. Got no balls no more.

When I reach the pole, sub's suppose to get me. Going to break through the ice and take me home. I'm a metric ton, thirty-five fricken' cubic feet of mutated shit. Ain't one hatch on the whole damn sub I can fit through. How they going to take me home?

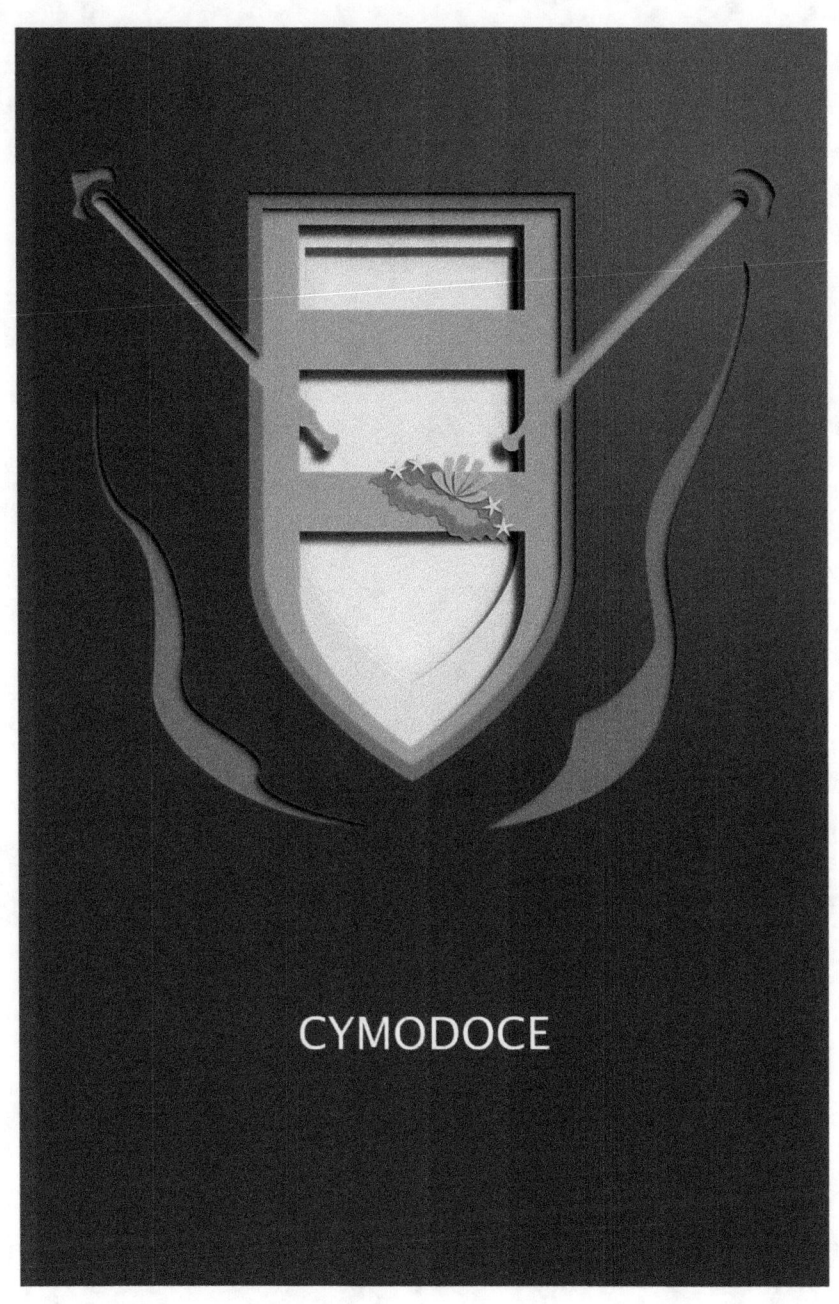

CYMODOCE

CYMODOCE

How happy could I be with either
Were t'other dear charmer away!
But while ye thus tease me together,
To neither a word will I say.
- John Gay, The Beggar's Opera,
Act II, sc.xiii, air xxxv

Jenny silently guided the rowboat to the dock, all the while keeping one eye on her three-year-old twins, Davy and Cymmi, sitting in front of her. When the boat was next to the mooring Jenny grabbed a line, pulled the boat to the dock and tied it. It was the first time she'd been to the island since the twins were born. Her parents, who died within a week of each other the previous fall, left her the dock, the boat, the cabin, the two acres of land, and only property taxes and upkeep to concern her.

Davy fidgeted. "Mommy, I'm hungry. Can we eat now?" She put a finger to her lips and Davy pouted. Cymmi was leaning over the side of the boat, splashing her hands in the water. She paused, looked out over the waves, then splashed harder.

Jenny moored the boat, lifted a lunch basket and helped the children onto the dock. "Mom," Davy whined, "I'm hungry."

"We'll go up to the cabin and eat. Okay, Davy?" They started up the narrow path.

"Mom, Cymmi's still by the water."

Jenny looked up. Cymmi was in up to her ankles. Jenny dropped the lunch basket, ran back and lifted Cymmi from the water. Her feet glistened. Cymmi kept looking at the waves as Jenny sat her by the lunch basket, took out a container of fresh water and poured it over Cymmi's feet. The tiny, silvery marks began to fade and Jenny signed /COME /EAT /NOW /PLAY /LATER /OKAY/?// She took Cymmi's hand and gently pulled her along.

Much later, when Jenny had put the children to bed, she walked down the path and sat on the dock. She took off her sandals and swished her feet in the ocean. Across the Sound she could see the lights of the Maine coast. The island had always been a quiet place. Even in the heat of the tourist season, when Route 1, heard if not seen across the Sound, was a tangle of campers, buses, and hitchhikers, the island was left to the three New York families who owned it and had cabins there.

The sounds of summer came across the water. She tried to match the sounds with the lights. Fuzzy rock music came from Beniroo's, an old icehouse turned bar and nightclub. When Beniroo's music paused she could hear a calliope and, intermittently, people giddily screaming. That would be Funland. She could see the Ferris wheel spinning and the roller coaster trestle climbing into the sky. Search lights swept back and forth, sweeping the ocean mists inland and then back out to sea. To the north she could pick out the tinny guitar and muffled bass of The Word's tent meeting, preaching God's message to the summer sinners.

Something tickled her foot and she jerked it from the water. Soon the tide would turn and go out. Fundy had powerful tides, aided this night by the moon overhead. There was a splash out by the rocks. Something bobbed briefly about forty feet from her. She heard another splash, saw a rippling approach her through the waves. /HELLO/?//

"Mommy?" Davy's voice pulled her back to dry land.

There was a slight almost soundless splash in the water.

Jenny's heart pounded. She fumbled getting up. "Yes, Davy?"

He walked over to her. "Who're you talking to?"

She smiled and ruffled his hair. "Just the fishes. I told them we came back this summer. Now, what are you doing out of bed?"

"I couldn't sleep."

She lifted him up so he could ride her hip as she walked. He wrapped his arms around her neck and cradled his head in her shoulder. "Come on, little man, you can sleep with me tonight." Davy's arms hung limp by his sides before they got back to the cabin.

She put Davy in her own bed and checked Cymmi before returning to the kitchen. There she made herself a cup of coffee and, from a window, watched the coast lights go out, one by one.

The next day they cleaned the cabin. Jenny and Cymmi doing most of the work. Davy would sweep, watch them, see something outside, go investigate, come back a few minutes later, sweep some more, and watch them again, repeating the pattern over and over.

Jenny, moving the broom in careful strokes, swept up memories along with the dust bunnies. Twelve years earlier, too young and too protected to know different, she'd come to the island with Anthony DiGracio. They were what, she wondered, sixteen then?

She remembered that at sixteen, the skinny, olive-skinned fisherman's son had fleshed out into a handsome man: his dark curly hair heavy on his head, now darkening his chest and stomach, his blue eyes smiling under long lashes.

Jenny walked through the town with her parents and their friends for almost three hours that day. Not once did the conversation waver from stocks, clients, or banks, all of which bored Jenny to death. As Jenny's people walked off, Anthony tapped her arm. "Wanna go out to the island?"

They went in Anthony's skiff. He rowed with his shirt off, his muscles knotting and unknotting rhythmically under his skin.

They closed the cabin door and, before she knew it, he was up against her, his sweat and teenage cologne a miasma around her, his hands gentle but searching.

They were on the bed and her jersey was off when she heard something. She was about to ask Anthony if he heard anything when the door opened.

Daddy stood there.

"You guinea bastard, what do you think you're doing?"

Jenny didn't know Daddy knew those kinds of words.

Anthony leapt off the bed. His eyes were wide. They darted back and forth as he backed into a corner of the room.

Jenny, still lying on the bed, watched Daddy and Anthony face each other.

There were more voices outside, Daddy's friends. "I'm in here," he called.

"Everything all right, Ed?"

"Yes. We'll be out in a minute." Daddy looked from Jenny to Anthony and took another step towards the dark haired boy. "You think you can touch my daughter? You think you're going to ruin my plans for her?"

Daddy's face turned crimson in the fading sunlight. "Come on, meatball, you think you're a man?" His hands were up like a boxer's. "Show me how much of a man you are."

Anthony backed away, not saying anything. He didn't even hold his hands up in defense. Daddy swung and caught Anthony square on the chin.

Anthony's head moved slightly with the impact. He looked at Mr. Packwood, waiting to see what the old man would do.

"You stupid immigrant wop bastard, you're going to notch your belt with my daughter while their sons have already spoken an interest?" Daddy swung again. Again he caught Anthony square on the chin. Again Anthony's head moved slightly.

Anthony's bright blue eyes looked at Jenny, still lying on the bed. There was a small trickle of blood coming from the right side of his mouth. Jenny stared at her father.

Daddy's friends called from beyond the door. "Ed?"

Jenny started crying.

"Ed, we're coming in."

Anthony's eyes flashed to the window.

"Come on," challenged Mr. Packwood. He swung at Anthony one

more time.

Anthony moved away from the punch. One tanned fist doubled Daddy over. The other cracked against Daddy's jaw, knocking him to the floor. Anthony started out the window, stopped and looked back at Jenny. They nodded and Jenny felt something was understood between them. He completed his exit as Daddy's friends came in.

It was then she realized that none of Daddy's friends were from the village, none had calloused hands or despised the taste of lobster. Daddy's friends were from Boston, New Haven or New York, like the Packwoods.

Two of them went over to Father, still doubled up on the floor and gasping for air. One of them picked up Jenny's jersey and gave it to her. "Put this on, Jennifer," he said and turned his back.

When they returned to the village, the DiGracio boys and others laughed. Jenny, not understanding, laughed with them. Father – he became 'Father' then and sometimes, even in his presence, "Mr. Packwood" – slapped her across the face and the laughter stopped. Doc Willows came by later without being asked and quietly, discretely, offered to give Jenny an exam, should one be needed.

Anthony had been Jenny's first experience. An awkward, unfulfilled one. Embarrassing for all concerned but nothing more. Except Father's friends sons didn't happen by that much anymore.

And if they did, a pleasant drive was not what they intended.

A bitter taste halted the memories. Jenny went to get a dustpan. It hung on a hook next to a calendar which hadn't been changed since she'd last been to the cabin six years ago when Father grudgingly gave her the keys. Jenny's parents didn't go to the island anymore. His excuse that year was mother's poor health. Father had an excuse every year since the incident with Anthony. "I'm sure you'll take care of yourself," he sneered.

"You've left me no choice." She left without thanking him for the keys.

She lifted the calendar off its hook and its dry, browned edges crinkled and fluttered to the pile of dust at her feet. She took the dustpan and laughed.

"What's so funny, mommy?"

"Oh, just remembering something grandpa said."

She returned six years later and made her rounds of the village her first day back, jingling Father's keys in her pocket as if their sound validated her presence there. She let the police and post office know she had returned, and noted how little the town had changed since she'd seen it last.

Mr. D'Angelo gave Jenny a warm embrace. "Jenny Packwood, you look so good to my old eyes."

Mrs. D'Angelo asked, "You look good, Jenny. Maybe now you come see us more often?"

Jenny smiled and shrugged, remembering how Mr. and Mrs. D'Angelo had comforted her when her parents wouldn't.

"Any thing special you need we can get you, Jenny love?" asked Mrs. D'Angelo.

"Just some time alone on the island. To read."

The D'Angelos didn't hide their disappointment, but nodded, Mr. D'Angelo offering, "You come see us when you're ready, Jenny. There's always a plate for you at our table."

Mention of food sent Mrs. D'Angelo huffing upstairs. "Oh...Oh...I got some good lasagna. Let me just put it in a tupperware and you can take it, okay?"

Jenny knew not to argue. Besides, Mrs. D'Angelo could *cook*.

She spent most of her time on the island. There was little to do except read and she'd brought a good supply of books — she preferred the feel of a turning page and the island had no power — but after a month it was nearly exhausted and she decided to head back home.

She gathered most of the perishables into two bags in preparation for leaving. The only food and fuel she kept were those necessary to close the cottage for another year. She carried the two bags to the boat and took them across the Sound. The Word accepted all offerings for the poor and she decided to leave everything with them. When she went outside she saw Anthony wearing a "JESUS SAVES" t-shirt, watering the Word's Victory-in-Christ garden. It was a hot, dry summer and the garden wasn't looking too victorious. He smiled until he recognized her, then concentrated on his watering. Six years of lobstering had filled him out nicely.

Jenny started towards him, wanting to laugh at the past. Anthony dropped the hose and moved quickly into the tent. He never looked back.

Jenny returned to the cottage to finish her last book. She had two hundred pages to go. That would finish the day. Tomorrow, she would close up the cottage and head back to New York, back to the silent security of teaching Drama to the Deaf.

The sun was strong and Jenny realized she hadn't even bothered to get a tan so she put on a baggy pair of shorts, a bathing top, sunglasses, a wide brimmed hat, shoved an apple and penknife in her pocket, grabbed her book and wheeled a beach lounger outside. With one hundred pages left, she heard something. It sounded like the clacking of lobster buoys adrift in the shallows. Sounds didn't make her nervous, but she knew every sound the cottage, the island and the ocean could make. This wasn't one of them. Either someone was playing a joke or someone was hurt. She wasn't sure if the locals could be that immature, but she wouldn't put it past them. Twenty-five pages later she heard it again.

The sound came off and on with the wind. Unsure what it was, she investigated.

It stopped as she neared the dock.

"Hello?"

There was nothing there. No signs of any craft except Jenny's own securely moored boat. She started back up the path and it started again.

There was a man lying among the rocks on the shore.

She walked towards him. "Are you all right?"

His naked body was cut and bruised in several places. Parts of a nylon fishing net cut into his flesh. The wounds had festered. His legs were bound in various lines. He rolled onto his stomach as she neared.

His back was blistered from the sun.

"My God, what happened to you?"

He tried to crawl away and passed out. She took the knife from her pocket and cut the lines. Unconscious, he shivered, his breathing shallow.

She ran to the cabin and brought the lounger back. Carefully, gently, she rolled him onto it and pulled him back to the cabin. There she placed him in her bed, rubbed aloe on his wounds and covered him.

There wasn't much she could do for him. She'd just given The Word all the medical supplies she'd bought for the summer. She took one more look at him, placed a note on the bed stand beside him and went back to the village.

Mr. D'Angelo saw her coming and opened the door as she neared his general store. "Jenny, heard you're leaving. Not so soon, I hope."

"Well, I thought about it."

"Listen, Jenny, don't let people drive you out. The good people don't talk, the bad always do." He nodded in the direction of The Word's tent, "And you know who I mean."

She laughed. "I need medical supplies; bandages, stuff for cuts and sunburns, exposure and infection."

He started putting things on the counter. "Not for you? Somebody hurt on the island?"

"Yes. One of the locals, I'd guess, but I don't remember him. Anybody new come in to town while I was gone? Big, nice build." She pursed her lips. "Can't be local, now that I think of it. He tans in the nude."

Mr. D'Angelo's eyes never lost their look of concern.

"Should I call the doctor?"

"Please. He doesn't look good. I found him entwined in some nets. He's got some bad cuts and looks of exposure and dehydration. I didn't even want to take the risk of bringing him across the Sound. I'll need food, too."

Mrs. D'Angelo came out from the office and started bagging groceries. "Jenny, today's doc's day on call and there are dead zones all over the county. I'll call his office and leave word, but don't expect him soon. So, anything else you need, Love?"

She looked in the bags. "Nope, that looks good." She pulled a wallet from her purse.

Mrs. D'Angelo patted Jenny's hand. "We'll settle later. You get out of here and go take care of your friend."

Jenny got back to the island and ran to the cottage. He was still there, still sleeping. She pulled the rocker into the bedroom, picked up her book, and read.

She'd finished the book and was making dinner when she heard the bed creak. She entered and sat on the edge of the bed. He didn't talk. "Hungry?" she asked.

He looked at her. She signed /EAT /NOW/?// from reflex when he didn't respond to her words. He continued to look at her. She pointed to her mouth and made chewing motions. He smiled, but didn't move.

She motioned him to stay in bed and brought some beef broth to him. At first he was reluctant. Eventually he sipped as she spooned it to him, although he grimaced at each mouthful. She showed him the bag of medical supplies and he gave her what she assumed was an "I don't understand" look. She pointed to the cuts on his arms and neck, pointed to some hydrogen peroxide, picked up a cotton ball and made dabbing motions on her skin.

He smiled at her, then went into a coughing fit. She rolled him onto his stomach with his head off the bed and slapped his back. It was still raw with burns and he made a sound she'd heard often before; the dry hollow sound deaf children make the first time they learn hot water burns. She rolled him onto his back again. He winced and there were tears in his eyes.

She signed /SORRY//SORRY// and mouthed the words as tears formed in her eyes.

Feebly, he pointed to the cuts on his chest, the hydrogen peroxide, then picked up a cotton ball and dabbed at her eyes. His arm fell away and he went back to sleep.

Jenny debated what to do. Finally she rolled back the covers, took out some bag balm and gently applied it to his bruises. She dabbed peroxide on his wounds and covered them with bandages. His body was firm, but smooth. His hands weren't calloused. Aside from his head, genitals and small tufts under each arm, he didn't have any body hair. What hair he did have was coal black and thick, tightly curled and close fitting. She couldn't determine any racial characteristics from his features, which were fine and, like the rest of his body, smooth. His nose was small, his jaw definite but not pronounced, his eyes slightly wider than the norm. She was about to dab at a fleshy, pink rimmed cut above his Adam's apple when he caught her hand. She hadn't known he was awake and wondered if he were studying her as she was studying him.

"You have chameleon eyes," she said. Slowly she pulled her arm away and left the room.

She met Doc Willows the next morning. He was preparing his dinghy to go across to the island, she had just come across the Sound to pay the D'Angelos and get some fresh fruits. She'd left the man sleeping on her bed. He seemed too weak to move yet strong enough to not need Doc's intervention. "You did just about what I'd've done, Jenny." He handed her some antibiotics and pain-killers. "Give him these if he needs them, and call me if he takes a turn for the worse."

The mute stayed in her bed three weeks, healing rapidly but not moving much. He either didn't or wouldn't talk so she started teaching him to sign. /BRUSH// followed by pointing to the hairbrush and moving her hands through her hair in a brushing motion. /SLEEP// followed by tilting head, closing eyes and resting hands. Signs for physical objects and conditions he learned quickly enough. Other signs – the less obvious ones like /HELP//, one hand clenched in a fist and the other lifting it up from underneath – were a problem. His name was another. He referred to himself as /ME/ so often Jenny gave up asking. His sign for her amused her; motions of dabbing a face with a cotton ball.

One sign he picked up quickly was "I won't listen." It wasn't so much a sign as a reaction, its nuance depended on the intensity of the statement: either the face or the whole body turned away from the speaker as they signed /HEAR /YOU /NOT//, although some signers had picked up "Talk to the hand" and were using that, as well. Whenever she asked about his family or home he politely turned away as if to say, "I'm sorry, I didn't hear the question."

She made biweekly trips to the mainland for supplies. Each time she'd ask /YOU /GO /NOW/?//

/OKAY /STAY /HERE/?// he asked in reply. He didn't eat much, and the cut on his neck still flowed occasionally and showed no signs of closing. More than that, she enjoyed his silent company and interest in her.

/OKAY /STAY /HERE//SHOPPING /NOW//BACK /SOON// Each time she'd return to find him in her bed, sleeping.

He was sleeping the last time she left and she didn't want to wake him. When she got back he was gone. No notes. He hadn't even made the bed. She sat in her rocker and rocked, rapidly, back and forth, looking out the window, her jaw tight, occasionally clearing her throat.

That night, after changing the sheets, she tried to sleep. Just as she was closing her eyes for the night she heard the cottage door open. She looked around and grabbed the hairbrush, the only thing she could think of as a weapon within reach. The floor boards by her bedroom door creaked and it opened, slowly.

He stood there, dripping wet, smiling. She lit the lantern. He spun away and made some gurgling noises, and she noticed his skin glistened in the light. She watched the patterns for a moment before she lowered the flame. In the softer light he turned back and walked over to the bed. The cut above his Adam's apple was still there, unchanged from when she first saw him. He picked up a cotton ball and gently dabbed at her face. She smiled. He pulled the covers off her and continued dabbing, down one side of her body and up the other.

Sometime late into the night, Jenny unwound herself from him.

She awoke near noon, alone. There was a crown of seaweed and shells on the bed table.

Jenny spent the rest of the summer on the island, hoping he would return. He never did.

A month later, back in the city, she visited her doctor. The news made her laugh.

*D*avy's tone of boredom summoned her back to the present. "Mom?"

"Okay," she said, "let's go across the Sound. We've got to stock our shelves." That perked the children up. They ran down to the dock ahead of Jenny, but when they got to the boat they stopped and stared. "Go ahead, get in," she said.

Davy looked back at her. "Mommy, there's some seaweed in the boat."

Jenny was used to the mess seagulls made, but wasn't prepared for what she saw – a crown of seaweed and shells. She kept her voice calm, "Isn't that pretty? We'll save this for later." She took the seaweed crown back to the cabin.

Mr. D'Angelo came back from his counter and started talking, each sentence punctuated with a hug. "Jenny, how have you been?" Hug. "We got your letters." Hug. "Did you get ours?" Hug. "So good to keep in touch." Hug. "I told Momma you meant this week, ..." Hug. "...but you know that old woman..." he looked down as Davy tugged the grocer's apron. "And these are the twins? Beautiful, just like you." He stared at the children intently then said, "They look a lot like their father, don't they." It was a question trying hard not to be one.

"Yes, they do. But you haven't met him. He's not from around here." Mr. D'Angelo smiled at the children and nodded. They chatted, Jenny always keeping an eye on Davy and Cymmi to keep them out of mischief.

"Did you see the new playground we put in behind the store?" he asked, knowing she hadn't. "Let's go take a look."

There were swings, slides, hobby horses and jungle-gyms in a sand-covered lot. "The kids will be okay here, if you want to leave them so you can wander." She looked at him. "The Mrs. comes out and watches." He pointed to a window in the apartment above the store. It opened.

Mrs. D'Angelo waved her apron at them. Jenny waited for the subdued Sicilian accent to wash over her. "Jenny Packwood, hello how are...ooh, ooh, the children are on the swings. Don't you let them fall, old man. Aunt Sadie's coming down." The window slammed. A moment later Jenny was smothered in Mrs. D'Angelo arms. She patted the children. "Beautiful babies, Jenny. Their papa up too?"

Mr. D'Angelo cut in. "No, Sadie. He's from New York and didn't come up this summer. Isn't that right, Jenny." It was a statement offering protection.

Jenny appreciated the offer but didn't accept it. "No, I didn't meet him in New York. As a matter of fact, I haven't seen him in four years." Mrs. D'Angelo took Jenny's hand.

Mr. D'Angelo looked at the children. "You got beautiful children, Jenny. Nothing to be ashamed of."

Mrs. D'Angelo said, "Better he didn't come back. Probably bring you more heartache. You go take a walk. I'll watch the children." Jenny wasn't sure she could leave the children with them. Her concern showed. "Jenny, I read your letters. I know Cymmi's mute. I'll keep my eye on them, promise."

Jenny stared at Mrs. D'Angelo for a second before she realized what the latter meant. "Davy," Jenny said, "Would you mind if I went for a walk by myself?" He was already on a hobby horse and shook his head, no. "You'll have to tell Mr. and Mrs. D'Angelo if Cymmi wants or needs anything. You sure you won't mind?"

Davy got off the horse and went over to Cymmi, rocking on her own horse. /MOMMY /GO//BACK /LATER /OKAY/?// Cymmi nodded. /NEED /WANT /TELL /ME /TELL /THEM /OKAY/?// Again Cymmi nodded. "Okay, mommy. I'll watch Cymmi."

"See, everything's fine," said Mrs. D'Angelo.

"Cymmi mustn't go swimming," Jenny said and tapped Cymmi to get her attention. /NO /SWIM//UNDERSTAND/?// Cymmi turned away and pouted, her eyes on the ocean not far away. Jenny tickled her gently until Cymmi silently laughed and looked at her again. /CYMMI /NO /SWIM /PROMISE/?//

Cymmi nodded. /NO /SWIM /PROMISE//

Jenny smiled. She left the children in the D'Angelo's care and left to walk through the village.

She walked for a few hours. Small pleasure craft and the larger lobster and fishing boats filled the Sound. The air was heavy with the mix of salt and diesel. Each wave brought the shrieks of water skiers and bluetooth boxes played too loud. She heard seagulls fighting for scraps and following the trawlers. Far beneath the gulls and music and vacationers she could hear and feel the grunting, steady engines of the trawlers laying their miles of netting or scooping lobster buoys from the sea.

She saw three small children, she guessed them to be two, three, and four - boy, girl, boy - playing dangerously close to the edge of the pier. As she approached she noticed the soiled, tattered clothing and dirty, shoeless feet and matted hair. They were sharing a can of coke and a package of twinkies. A seagull, almost the size of the smallest child, started to get bold and Jenny hurried before it hurt one of the children.

Suddenly a man appeared from one of the nearer boats and yelled. The seagull took flight and the children flinched. The man's shoulders were hunched forward with the weight of his gut, but Jenny could tell the muscles were still strong in his arms and chest.

He looked up at her and quickly away. Jenny's hand covered her mouth, but she didn't know if her gasp was from stifled laughter or shock.

It was Anthony. A very different Anthony than she remembered from her other visits, certainly not the Anthony who took her to the island.

Anthony hurried his children below deck. Jenny laughed and continued her walk.

Further up the coast she became aware there were fewer boats on the Sound. Instinctively she looked up and realized the sky had darkened. It took another hour to get back to the D'Angelo's.

Mr. D'Angelo opened the door to her. "The radio says there's going to be a storm. There're small craft advisories."

Mrs. D'Angelo came downstairs. "The children had a snack of cookies and milk. They're asleep in the guest room. My, do they talk! Their little hands like tiny butterflies, they move so fast. They're beautiful children, Jenny. I got to love them." She looked out the window. "You're going to stay with us until the storm passes, Jenny. You're not going to take those darling children out in this."

"Of course she's not," said Mr. D'Angelo, offered in Jenny's behalf. "She going to stay right here, you silly old woman."

Jenny laughed.

The weather reports were right. There was a storm. A fierce storm. A typical coastal storm, quickly in and quickly out. They could see the crests of the waves from the store. The wind and rain slammed down the street. The lights along the coast went out. Jenny and the D'Angelo's sat down and had some tea heated on a Coleman stove. Jenny picked up a book. They all turned when a tiny foot stamped.

Cymmi stood at the foot of the stairs, rubbing her eyes and looking at the three of them. Mrs. D'Angelo walked over and picked her up. "What is it, sweetheart?" Cymmi saw Jenny and held out her arms. "Oh, look at this one. Aunt Sadie's no good any more?" She laughed and handed the child to Jenny.

Cymmi cuddled against her mother until some lightning blasted the sky far out over the ocean. She looked up and slid off her mother's lap, walked to the window and looked out over the water. She smiled at the warring winds and waves, pointing at the crests in the harbor and breaking waves. /BEAUTIFUL /WATER /HAPPY /ME//

Mr. D'Angelo asked, "What'd she say?"

"She likes the storm," answered Jenny.

"How about that. Usually kids, they're frightened by the storms."

"No, Cymmi loves them. Back in the city I have to keep an eye on her or she'll try to go outside to see the lightning." The four of them watched the storm. When it was over Jenny gathered the children and left.

Jenny stayed in the cabin's kitchen for an hour after putting the children to bed that night. Before she left, she went back and checked them. She didn't want Davy waking up and following her to the dock.

The path was lit by a half moon just rising over the sea. The coast's sounds and sights blared. She sat down on the dock, the water lapping her feet. A twig snapped behind her and she jumped, expecting Davy to be there. A woodchuck reared up to inspect her, chattered, then trundled off into the woods.

The moon was overhead when she lifted her feet from the water and sighed. "Lovers never return." She slipped her sandals back on and started up the dock when something splashed. It caught her eye. Something small, on the surface, bobbing like a discarded bottle.

It dipped beneath the waves briefly. Jenny could see its movement just beneath the surface. It circled, gathering speed. Suddenly the circle collapsed to a line, parting the waves as it broke free of the ocean's grasp. Her lover leapt high in the air, moving in an arc, like leviathan breaching, from the ocean to Jenny. His body remained perpendicular to the waves through his metamorphosis. Moonlight showed the powerful chest and slim stomach reaching down to scales and fins as he left the water. As he flew the scales and fins melted into legs and feet.

He stood before her, naked, black haired and deceptively well muscled, so different from when she brought him to the cabin, rope marks and burns mottling his flesh. She held her hand out to him and they walked back to the cabin.

She opened the door to the children's room and signed / CHILDREN/ OURS// She remembered his "I don't understand" look from four years ago and tried to explain.

/CHILDREN /YOURS /MINE /FROM /LAST / HERE//
/LIKE /ME /THEM/?//
/DAUGHTER /MAYBE//NO /GILLS//MUTE// NOT / KNOW//BOY /LIKE /ME//
/GILLS/ONLY/ADULTS//

He held her close. She hadn't noticed before, but he had a soggy cotton ball in his hand. /WHAT /THIS/?// she asked.

He answered by dabbing her neck and she led him into her bedroom.

Sometime during the night she realized it was raining outside. She got up to fasten the windows. Cymmi was standing on a chair looking outside. She turned as her mother entered the kitchen.

/BEAUTIFUL /WATER /HAPPY /ME// she signed.

Jenny heard him come up behind her. Cymmi stared at him. / WHO/?//

/DADDY// signed Jenny.

He walked over to his daughter. /NAME/?// he asked her.

/CYMMI//

He looked at Jenny again. /CYMMI/?//

/CYMMI /NICKNAME /REAL /NAME /CYMODOCE// He still didn't understand. Jenny turned to Cymmi /SHOW /NAME-SIGN//

Cymmi signed /WAVE /GATHERER//

/YES// He opened his mouth but no sound came out. Instead Jenny felt something rumbling inside her, similar to something she'd felt watching the trawlers moving into and out of the Sound, but something that rumbled her heart, as well. Cymmi opened her mouth as if in answer. It was the first time Jenny had seen Cymmi ever attempt to speak. Jenny wasn't sure, but she thought she heard something tiny, fragile, a delicate reed whistle piping at the upper edge of her hearing, the sound fading in and out as Jenny breathed. Jenny looked at him. / YES// he signed.

He picked Cymmi up. She didn't fight him. /NOT /WORRY// he signed to Jenny. /GILLS /ONLY /ADULTS//

Jenny pounded the table until he faced her. /WHERE /GO/?// she demanded.

Cymmi answered /GO /SWIM /MOMMY//

Jenny stared at her daughter. Her lover waved his hand until he caught Jenny's eye. /GO /SWIM /NOW /JENNY PACKWOOD// He knew what he was saying. There was no smile and tears slid down his face to land in Cymmi's hair. He started to say something but Jenny turned away.

/UNDERSTAND// she said.

Thunder shook the cabin and Davy called out, "Mommy?"

She went into the children's bedroom. "What is it, Davy?"

"Cymmi's gone, isn't she mommy?"

"What are you talking about, Davy?" she asked, her attention else-where, only realizing his words as she answered them.

"Cymmi said Daddy's here. When we were at the store, she told me she heard Daddy when we got here. She told me she had to go."

She gave him a hug and a kiss. "You stay here. Maybe she's outside. You know how she loves storms." She had to pause between the sentences. "I'll have to go look for her. You stay right here in bed until I get back, okay?" He nodded as she tucked him in.

The kitchen was empty when she returned. She went outside and ran to the dock.

He was in the water, holding Cymmi in his arms. His tail splashed a few times as the waves grew higher and broke with more ferocity in the swelling storm. Cymmi broke free of his grasp and slid through the waters on her own, moving quickly out into the deeper, calmer sea. Jenny stamped her feet on the dock. /CYMMI/?// she called, waving one arm, signing with the other, all the while slamming her feet onto the dock. "Cymmi," she shrieked, knowing neither one could hear. Jenny ran to the shore, picked up a rock and ran back to the edge of the dock. She slammed the rock against the mooring until it fell from her bleeding hands. Jenny slumped against one of the pylons, crying and sliding to the dock, curling and convulsing into a ball of tears. Suddenly his hand was on her back. She looked up. He opened his mouth and she felt the rumbling again. A moment later Cymmi bobbed beside him.

/CYMMI/?//

/SWIM /NOW /MOMMY// She splashed and headed back out to sea.

He started to sign but Jenny looked away. She signed / UNDERSTAND// and let the rain rush away her tears, wiped her eyes and watched until Cymmi disappeared in the waves.

He waved at her, his body half submerged. /LOVE /YOU /ALWAYS /JENNY PACKWOOD// /LOVE/YOU/ALWAYS//

She stared at him, at the fins, the chest, the scales, the arms. Her arms shot up ready to scream "No!" then, farther out, she saw Cymmi leap from the water, her silvering form made blinding by a burst of lightening.

Her hands stopped moving.

A loving father who saw his child as a gift and not a commodity. A parent who would teach and guide his child, who would let her grow into who she wanted to be.

Her arms fell, heavy and weak, her hands clutching each other, not saying a word.

/WHAT/?// he asked.

Jenny turned and walked towards the cabin. She felt him pounding the dock as she walked away.

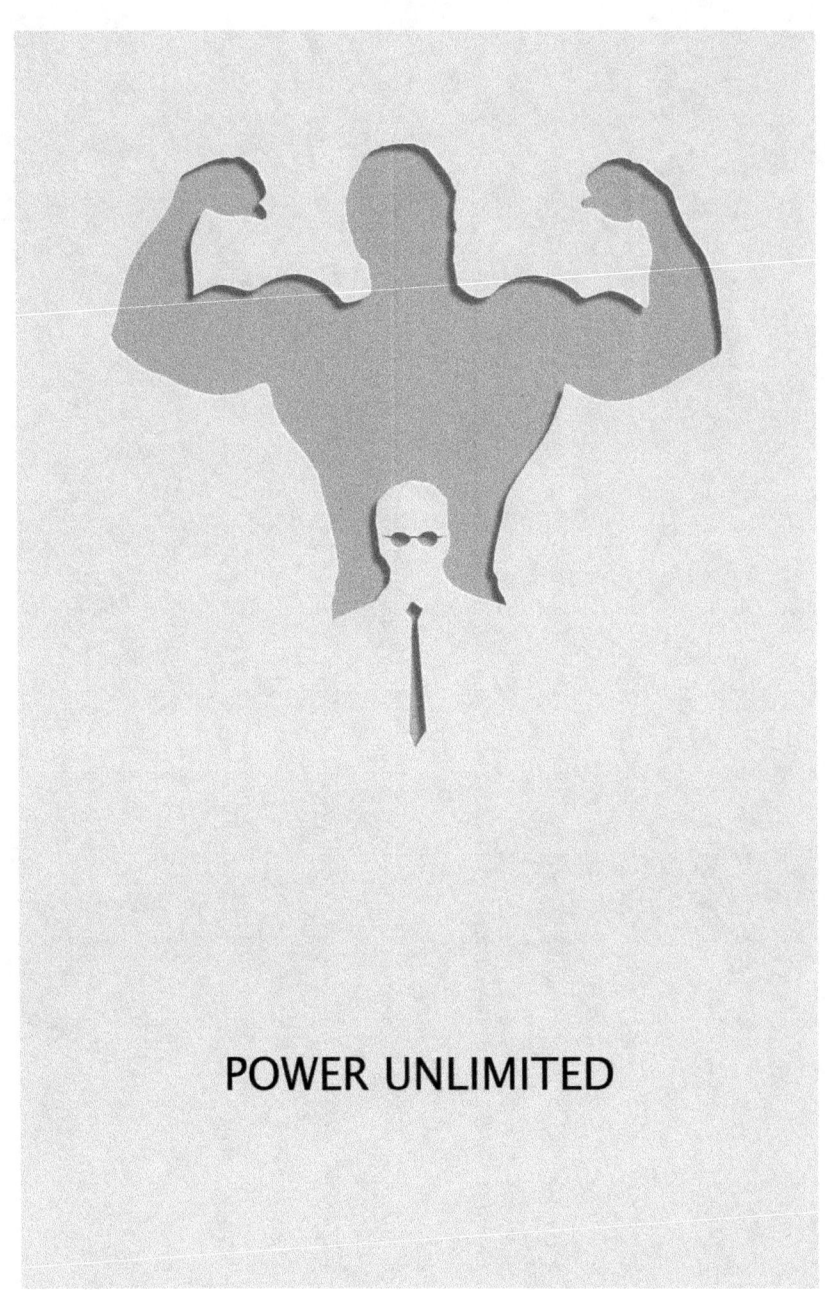

POWER UNLIMITED

POWER UNLIMITED

*T*his is a story about *Tommy Truncero and how I know there* are Martians, but that they're up front guys.

Tommy is Eddie's kid brother. He's okay, now. This all happened last March, when Tommy was still a kid. Not enough fuzz for a cat to lick off if you covered his face with cream. Every afternoon, when all of us were down lifting, Tommy'd come in with towels and soap and those skinny white legs of his hanging out of his superman red gym trunks. And he idolized us, so we watched out for him. We kind of took him under our wing.

Anyway, we were at the iron and Tommy comes in looking like he knows where the last Eskimo Pie is. "Hi, Ange. Working on the lats today? Looks good."

I couldn't answer because it was my third rep with 300 and the sky was getting hazy. Tommy had a way of always talking to you when your guts are busting. If not me, then to Eddie or maybe Benjamin. Benjamin's a thinker. Great guy. Don't like to be called Benny.

Benjamin drops his bar like a trash truck dropping a dumpster. "Hello, Thomas. What do you have tucked under your arm?"

Tommy jumps over the weights and hands him a magazine. "I wanted to show you guys. I hope you won't laugh." Benjamin reads it and "hmms" a few times.

"What do you think?" Tommy says. "Pretty good, huh?"

"Angelo, when you have a moment?"

Benjamin shows me a full page ad for some company called "Power

Unlimited." Under the title is a picture of some guy that you know's been lifting for maybe six, seven years. The guy's got women climbing his thighs. Tommy's got highlights on "30 DAY, NO RISK FREE TRIAL POWER+ PILLS" and "No drugs, no steroids, just EVERY vitamin and mineral YOUR body will EVER NEED!" The ad says it also comes with an exercise booklet.

And all the while I'm reading it, Tommy's pumping me. "Well, Ange, what d'you think? I could give it a try?"

Now, like I say, Tommy's a good kid. And everybody knows these things don't work. But it's free. Thirty days we can set him straight, right? "Tell you, Tommy, I don't go for these things myself. Eddie, you seen this?"

Eddie comes over and reads the ad. He pats Tommy on the back, "Hell, kid, can't hurt nothin' if it's for free."

Benjamin takes the magazine back and looks the ad over again. Now, you got to know Benjamin. He's always reading, and he's the only one of us went to one of those big, four-year colleges. Studied some kind of math. He's got a blackboard in his office and I seen it once. Hell, there wasn't even any numbers on it, just a bunch of triangles and stuff. Some guys make it big, they forget who they knew as kids. Not Benjamin.

Anyway, he's looking the ad over and says, "Thomas, I agree with Angelo. But if it makes you feel better, well, perhaps you should try it. Just let us know if they start asking for money or call you on the phone. Agreed?"

"Gee, thanks, guys. I really mean it," and he's out the door. Kid could make it in track, if he wanted.

Two weeks later Tommy comes back with this box. Inside is thirty elephant pills and a book. I'd never seen the kinds of exercises they had in that book. Neither had Eddie or Benjamin or anybody else. Benjamin reads it through twice and says, "They're neither isometric nor isotonic. But the book does say these are the preliminaries designed to increase flexibility, which makes sense." So I guess it was okay. Those pills were big mothers, though, and they smelled like the water 'back of the paper plant. I couldn't do it, but Tommy pops one right there by the leg machine.

Well, we went back to the weights. Five minutes later, Eddie drops his bar and runs over to the kid. "Tommy, you all right?"

The kid was puke. He's pushing Eddie away, "Yeah, yeah. I'm fine. Those pills work fast." But the kid looks real bad so Benjamin drives us home. We didn't even shower, which made Mrs. Truncero real happy.

Anyway, the kid was golden when we got to his house. Said he felt great. Went straight into the kitchen, sat down and chowed.

Well, a week goes by and nobody sees Tom. Ed was doing Reserves, so we didn't know what was going on. Anyway, one night this guy walks in, clean. Good definition, needs some cutting. Benjamin does a double take, "Thomas?"

I looked again. "Where the hell'd that come from?"

"Great, huh?" He talks like he used to, but now he has more to echo with. Some of the other guys walk over and congratulate him. "Just wanted you to know, I'm sending away for more of those Power Unlimited pills." Three other guys wanted to buy some, too, and he takes their orders.

One of them kids Tommy about his beard. Tommy looks in a mirror and rubs his cheeks, "Damn. That's twice today."

Two weeks later, Tommy's benching as much as me. Now, I'm not jealous, but I know this ain't right. "You still doing that Power Unlimited stuff?"

"Yep." His voice has a barrel behind it and he's given up shaving. And he smells like he's lived in his shorts for a month.

I knew Eddie was coming home that night and I wanted to talk about what was happening to the kid, so I picked him up at the station.

We stop in front of Eddie's house and this big black Lincoln pulls up behind us. When we get out, somebody inside the limo says, "Mr. Truncero?"

Eddie walks over, "Yes, sir?"

The door opens and a beanpole gets out. We practically fell over looking at him. "Mr. Thomas Truncero?"

Now, we know practically everybody around. We don't know any beanpole white guy with a black Lincoln who dresses like an undertaker. Eddie and I stood between Stretch and the house. "What d'you want with my brother?"

Stretch looks at the house and – get this – pushes us aside like we're twigs in a tornado. Eddie tries to blindside him. Stretch doesn't budge and Eddie goes down for the count.

I get in Stretch's way. "Hey, I don't want trouble, but you ain't getting near Tommy till we know what's going on." Stretch stops. Another beanpole, a twin of the one I'm dancing with, gets out of the Lincoln. He shows me a card that says 'Power Unlimited' in big black letters, then underneath is 'Dolman Rigch: 032516-295'. Hey, you know any phone numbers like that? So I says, "You guys work for that company that's been sending Tommy those he-man pills?"

Beanpole #2 talks like he busted his nose and nobody fixed it, "There's been a mistake. Mr. Truncero's name was never on our master list."

Right then Tommy comes out of the house. I only know it's Tommy because he says, "Hi guys. What's up?" He looks like he should be swinging from trees. We're talking severe. I mean the kid needs a body shave, he's got arms like my thighs, a back you could rent ad space on. Unbelievable! And you know Mrs. Truncero, she ain't had it all since that stroke, she follows him out saying, "Oh, my boy's now a man."

Eddie hasn't seen his kid brother in two weeks and goes, "Tommy?" Tommy smiles and waves. Eddie gets up and runs at the beanpoles, "What've you done to Tommy?"

Beanpole #1 catches Eddie with an open hand and down goes Eddie again. Tommy runs over to the beanpole twins. He grabs one in each hand and lifts them over his head.

"Nobody touches Eddie." All I could think of was Ben Grimm yelling, "It's Clobberin' Time," like he does in "The Fantastic Four."

Beanpole #2 says, "Please, put us down. We can explain."

The way Tommy's flapping these two around, I figure they ain't gonna touch Eddie and me. "Yeah, Tommy," I say. "Put 'em down."

They tell Tommy who they are and look him over. "This should never have happened," Number One says. "How could we make this mistake?" And they nod and hum to each other.

Then Number Two says, "Mr. Truncero, you have to give us whatever Power+ pills you still have."

Tommy goes, "No."

"But you don't understand – "

"Understand what? I'm strong. I feel great. That's what your ad said would happen, and it did. What do I have to understand?"

Next thing Benjamin drives up. He's getting out of his car and says, "Welcome home, Edward." Then he takes in the scene and sees Tommy. "Holy Mother. Tommy?"

Beanpole #2 starts up again, "Someone has to make Mr. Truncero understand. These pills aren't for your people."

Benjamin is still checking out Tommy but he says to Number Two, "What d'you mean 'your people'?"

Just then this swarm of bees comes over us. We couldn't see any, but we all ducked anyway. All of us except for beanpoles one and two. They're just looking at each other, waving their long, skinny arms at each other. Finally, Number Two brings his hands down in front of him and they look at us, sprawled on all fours looking for bees. The buzzing stopped so we got back up. "Have you ever travelled to another country?" he says.

"Sure," I nod. "Canada."

The beanpoles got real close to each other and the buzzing starts again, but quiet like. Benjamin is watching them like a hen counting chicks. The rest of us are getting ready to swat bees, if we can ever find them. Beanpole #2 starts again, "No, some other, less developed country, maybe South or Central America or parts of Africa?"

Benjamin takes over. "Go on."

"And before you go you have to take medicinal precautions to insure you won't become ill due to the foreign country's environment?" Benjamin nods. His face has that "Oh yeah, I think I understand" look on it. I hate that. It means he's going to explain the movie while we're driving home. I figure "what the hell" and nod, too. "Some places even recommend you bring your own water and food?" Benjamin's eyes open up wide. I even think I'm beginning to see.

Benjamin says, "Where is home for you gentleman, exactly?"

The bees come back but nobody cares anymore. We're all watching the beanpoles. They don't say anything for a couple of seconds, then together they say, "France," through their noses. Benjamin nods. The second one goes, "We use the ad to contact our people. Names not on our master list get an earth-style exercise booklet and placebos. The pills Mr. Truncero has may do him permanent damage."

Tommy's knuckles are already dragging, so I'm wondering what more damage could they do?

"We're only here to observe," Number Two tells Benjamin, "not to harm. He must stop taking those pills." He hands Benjamin a box of pills, same label as before but they don't smell as bad. "He must take these until he is Earth-normal." He looked real sad. I lean over to Eddie and mouth "Earth-normal?"

Benjamin says, "We'll take care of it," and holds out his hand. The beanpoles hold out their hands and do a soulshake. Benjamin looks at them and says, "Tourists mimicking local customs." The beanpoles smile and nod, then get back in their limo and drive off.

As it turned out, Tommy didn't have any more pills and Benjamin talked him into trying the new ones. Tommy looks okay now, a little heavier than before he started taking those pills. He lifts now, too. Good potential. Late bloomer was all.

Benjamin never offered to explain the beanpoles, Eddie didn't care to know, and I never asked. I figured it out myself.

And people say you can't learn nothing from comics.

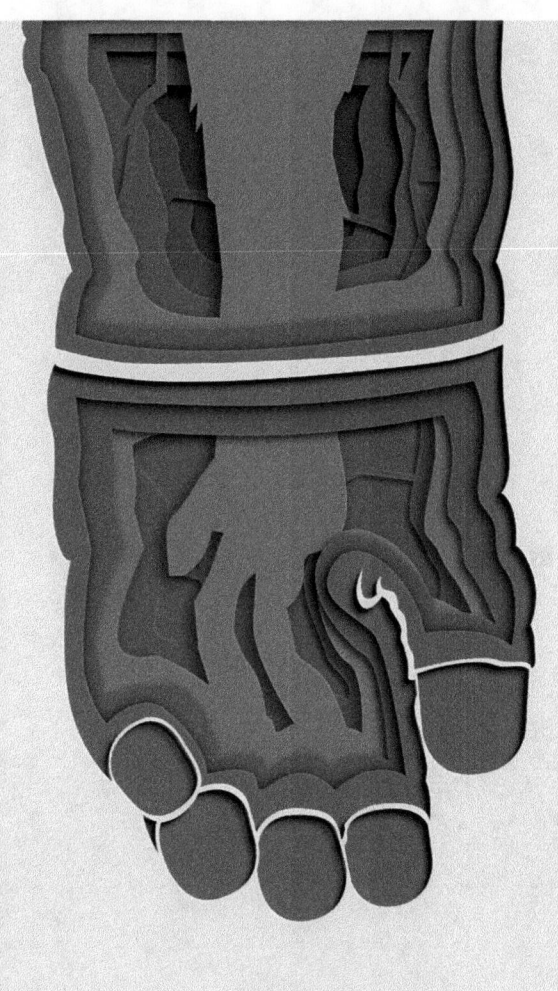

THE GOATMEN
OF AGUIRRA

THE GOATMEN OF AGUIRRA

705015:216 - We've landed in a grotto, near the center of Hochebene's Altiplano, but closer to the Towers of God than not. On one side of the grotto is the only run of clear water for some thirty kilometers, and I've noted with Sanders that this could be a problem as all native fauna encountered thus far follow the same biologies as we. Immediately upon landing, Sanders ordered Tellweiller, Nash, and Galen to construct a blind. We are now a boulder, one among several, that slid into the grotto when we lowered a rumbler to cover our landing.

Nash estimates two standard hours before sunrise.

Early estimates indicated Aguirra was three and a half to four billion years old. Now, with readings coming in about the deep core and mantle, we place it closer to five. Gravity is one-point-one standard and the atmosphere is quite like Earth's only sweeter due to a higher O_3 content. There is also a free floating enzyme, essentially carbolic anhydrase, which explains some of the evolutionary adaptations on the planet. Everything we've observed is based on the nitrocarbon cycle – everything we've recorded from space and robotics shows up as a variation on some earth fauna – and the carbolic anhydrase probably helps redaction and reduction in the O_3 rich atmosphere when a stressing agent is introduced.

Due to the atmosphere there is a perpetual slight pink tint in the sky, much like before an intense electrical storm back home. This area, Hochebene's Altiplano to the Towers of God, is a paragneiss formed we're not sure how long ago by glaciation. It is difficult to estimate because the atmosphere mediates the planetary temperature such that weathering is neither gradual nor minimal – Hopkin's Bioclimatic Law doesn't seem to apply. There are seasons in the temperate zones but without the fluctuations of four true seasons. Summer temperature extremes range from -19°C to 33°C. Winter temperatures also vary by about twenty degrees, from -25°C to 5°C. These temperatures are for our current location, 43°N, 8000m altitude, and, as I've mentioned earlier, shrouded to the west by the Towers of God.

To our immediate east is the rock wall we worked hard to resemble, the rise of the grotto, then the expanse of the high plain for several kilometers. Although comprised principally of paragneiss and granite with only slight eruptions of soil, a hardy tundral grass grows in clumps all around. Our guess is the grass serves to anchor what little soil there is in place. There are wind storms – one is due in another hour – when Astarte 217 rises over the altiplano and begins churning this high, thin air with the thicker, deep valley air far below.

These grasses are richly verdant, their tops a slight yellow as if gently burned. Galen collected some samples when the blind was completed and says the yellowing is a pollen. Thus we learn immediately that these verdant clusters aren't true grasses and that there is some pollenizing agent, perhaps only the wind, which is at work. If the robotics sent into these highlands hadn't met such abrupt and catastrophic ends, we might know more about Aguirra's highland life, at least in this area.

There is still a carpet of snow, albeit thin and frayed in some areas, stretching a kilometer from the entrance to the altiplano to the Towers of God even though this continent is now in high summer. The snow, Nash says, is due to the altitude and rarified atmosphere. Even with the carpet of white, this is a desert, with cold, dry steppes leading to the Towers.

In contrast to earth flora, there appears to be no treeline. While there are no trees on the altiplano, there are five here in the grotto ranging from two to two-fifty meters in height. They appear something like succulent scotch pines, kind of chubby Christmas trees. They have no root systems and, according to Galen, all five trees are extensions of the same growth and are more like vines than trees, growing like Sequoias in the northern California forests. If they are vines, it explains their limbs being naked on one side and holding fast against the grotto's walls. They're being succulents so close to a clear water supply indicates that the water might be seasonal.

There are several similar although much smaller trees, these resembling elms and birch although Galen's report might show different, growing to our west and in the runoff fissures of the Towers. From there these trees grow up to the crowns of the Towers, becoming deeper and denser with altitude, giving the appearance of twin green-haired giants out in the distance. Based on this and other evidence Galen claims these are not true "trees". If Galen's contention about the succulents is accurate, there are but one or two of these "trees" sending their shoots, binding and girding like some giant's phylacteries, up the Towers.

The most noticeable feature of the landscape, the one we all knew would be most breath-

taking, are the Towers themselves. We are eight kilometers above sea level and the Towers rise another eight above us. They are the largest vertical features on all of Aguirra, even and symmetrical in every geologic detail, with their expansive flat plained plateau heads, each five-point-five kilometers in diameter, separated by zero-point-five kilometers horizontal and a four kilometer drop. There are a few passes down the Towers, more like torrents than actual passes in their slope and grain, and various hanging, piedmont, and steppe glaciers coming down the Towers' sides. The best climb, if one were necessary, seems to be along a bergschrund on the immediate faces of each.

Tellweiller has no explanation for the Towers' formation, although it is obvious from their age they were formed in the prebiologic days of the planet.

Although I am not a religious man, standing at their feet and hearing the winds, it is not difficult to imagine the whispers the ancient Greeks heard about Mt. Olympus. I can understand why these features were named the Towers of God.

705015:323 - The winds are fierce now that Astarte 217's rays are directly on this moraine. Instruments indicate speeds in excess of one-hundred kilometers per hour and the sudden inversion is creating torrential rains which are creating waterfalls down the faces of the Towers and flooding this gorge.

These rains reminds me, in some ways, of New Orleans, where Robin and I lived briefly while she attended Loyola. In high summer it rains every hour, suddenly, violently, then stops after ten minutes. There are no clouds in the sky, then they gather up, release their hold and go away.

As the clouds gathered Sanders ordered the caster to ground. At the time it was flying over the run off fissures on the Alpha Tower. It continued transmitting and, thanks to the floor and angle, we witnessed incredible rains and winds clearing the skies and scrubbing the canopy. The only difference here is the color.

Despite the rain and wind, we can see Astarte 217 rising far to the east on that edge of the altiplano. It is peering over the precipice at us like some Indian scouting the fort. The clouds are higher over the plain than the precipice's edge and this gives 217 a green crown. Nash says this is common here but uncommon on earth. Nash. Never-late-for-dinner Nash. Of all on this mission, he's the only one who grumbles when I sit next to him for meals. No one else seems to mind my being a lefty.

God it is glorious here.

705015:500 - Wind and rain have stopped. They lasted about one and a half standard hours, about point-seven-one dechours on this planet, and Nash says we can expect something similar at dusk and dawn every day.

Sanders sent up some more casters to scout along with the first when the storm broke. They are coursing through the far away valley and are sending back holos of the several species inhabiting Aguirra.

Closer to our blind but still some distance down the altiplano Aguirran insects are busy. Their buzzing and clicking reminds me of apiaries and formicariums back home. Typical to robotic and remote sensing, the true aromas of this country weren't captured in their entirety, or were captured with the typical burnt-metal tinge which all such equipment imparts. Considering the waxing and waning humidity, there is no smell of decay, detritus, humus, or their like. Whatever moisture lands is quickly recaptured and, as noted previously, behaves more like some kind of planetary scrubbing action than rejuvenating rain. I've noticed, at the leading edge of each storm recorded, there is a smell similar to a good late spring rain in a forest. The smells of the flora are highlighted and accented, hitting one high in the nose not unlike a pleasantly bitter coffee.

The Aguirran insects disturb me. More correctly, it is their mammalian eyes which disturb me, eyes you're more accustomed to seeing on your dog or cat, eyes which you can believe have some hint of intelligence behind them. Galen further noted that the clearly arboreal species have blue eyes. "Same as you, Banks," he said.

"Why is that, do you think?"

"Adaptive biology, I guess. A blue iris in this atmosphere could cause less ocular distortion over distance. I wouldn't be surprised if everything living eight-k and up's eyes were blue."

Nothing else lives this far off the planetary floor.

Sanders brought me another message from Robin's attorneys today. There are advantages and disadvantages to being in a jumpship. This message, received as quickly as possible, is still months too late for me to respond. It appears I won't be allowed to see Jeremy.

Again, there is nothing here which hasn't been reported before.

7 *15015:030 - The alarms woke us, although there seemed to* be no reason. The casters were called back and found nothing, which our shipboard instruments confirmed.

The casters also indicate thermals on the steppes and higher on the Towers, although the vegetation is too dense for the casters to gather much information due to their altitude.

Sanders is staying up to perform a redundancy on the grid and has ordered the rest of us to sleep.

*7*15015:430 - *The alarms woke me again. It is time to be* about my duties, anyway. Only Galen and I still slept. A moment after the alarms sounded, Sanders called me to observation.

There was another message for me, this one from Jeremy. How an eleven-year old boy could manage to get a message off and properly through channels onto the Net and out to this sector of the Ring...

Still, he was always a clever child, far brighter than either Robin or I. He cried through the transmission. He begged me to come home.

Sanders, god bless him, left me to scan the transmission alone. This, even though every message delivered shipside is reviewed by him, SOP. The only exception are those registered "Private" which the net delivers sealed to a ship's commander for dispatch. These the crew members may open first but only in the captain's presence. Normally it is enough to open it there. I've never had a commander ask to read their contents. Jeremy could not have known.

I had just finished Jeremy's transmission when Sanders came hurrying over to me, swiveled two externals and opened some viewers, pointing wildly to the screens and ports. "This is it. This is what the alarms are about."

Twelve bipeds stood twenty meters from our blind. In appearance, they can only be described as Satan in a snowsuit.

All are male, all stand from one-point-seven-five meters to two-point-one-five meters tall, their mass varies from one-hundred kilos to one-thirty kilos. Their bodies are built low with a powerful, blocky musculature and legs slightly more than one-third their height. Their torso starts with a broad, rounded abdomen – either these creatures eat well or are starving. I won't know until I can autopsy one – and progresses into a broad, massive thorax, with shoulders, chest, and back so well muscled they appear padded like football players. Their arms are equally powerful, ending in hands with two fingers and an opposing thumb.

All have elongated faces, long, prehensile ears emanating from slightly above the middle of each side of the skull, two large, vertebrate eyes – blue. If these creatures are here by evolutionary chance Galen is right – which protrude slightly from the skull, and two horns rising from midway between the eyes and the ears.

Their coat is shaggy white hair, although some have elements of brown, gray, red, blonde, and cream. The only black on their bodies being their hands, their horns, their noses, and their feet.

Robotics showed some bipedal fauna, but merely evolutionary adaptations for food gathering.

Detailed analysis and holos will be transmitted later.

They are staring at us.

725015:600 - They stood outside the blind for a full day, leaving only when the inversion storms formed on the horizon and coming back when the storms dissipated, seating themselves in the extended root systems of the succulent where their coloring makes them damn near invisible. We realize now they may have been there since before our landing, hence the blind is moot.

As I stated earlier, Aguirra is a testament to adaptive evolution. These creatures – we call them 'Goatmen' now that we've been able to observe more about their physiologies – are the best blend of North American mountain goats and South American camels.

In this land of high, thin air, little food, cold, and treacherous terrain, these Goatmen have developed enlarged hearts and lungs – my guess is that they couldn't survive at sea level.

Their coats are fine and dense with two layers; the outer layer is comprised of long, oily, water repellent guard hairs, the inner layer is comprised of dense hollow hairs to provide both thermal insulation and protection from parasites. At least the insects don't seem to bother them. The coat won't collect moisture and sheds condensation, the principal elements of the best insulations known, and is thickest across the shoulders where the guard hairs may be ten to fifteen centimeters long. The coat thins as it moves out to the muzzle and legs.

Toe walkers. Their feet are like their hands, although the toes are broader, flatter, and rubbery in their ability to grasp the surface they walk on. Their legs obviously evolved from something quadripedal in recent evolutionary time.

Chromotographic analysis of their respirations – only two to three per decminute while observing us, apparently a resting state – shows a ninety percent CO_2-O_2 exchange. Without dissection I can't be sure, but I would guess they can force oxygen into their tissues in much the way deep diving cetaceans do.

I would almost believe they live on the Towers, although there is no evidence of this other than the telemetry of the casters.

It is obvious they know we are here. This blind serves us nothing. I've asked Sanders to allow attempts at communications. Although they haven't made obvious communication amongst themselves, their behavior leads me to believe them intelligent.

745015:390 - Two days of observation by the Goatmen. They do nothing but stare at us.

Things happen more quickly than can be imagined back home. Robin has excised herself from my life like a tumor. She, of course, would believe the growth benign. Such a fool. I still feel the hole in me where she and Jeremy lived. To her benign, to me a cancer the traces of which haven't all been removed. It is good I'm here, on this far away world, far away Aguirra, so far even jumpships take weeks to reach us.

Galen and Tellweiller talk to me to comfort me. Neither of them are Earthborn although both are only four generations removed from home, long enough to notice the hints of alien gravities and atmospheres and oceans if you know how to look, not long enough to make them foreign to the species which bred them. Galen is simply too powerful for an endomorph without obtrusive musculature, and too pale. Tellweiller a little too tall, with all his features and extremities slightly longer than they should be to maintain healthy proportion. Nor have they been to Earth, except in holos and on projections, although I have been to both their worlds; Galen's Stratton and Tellweiller's Devereux.

Jumpships may take weeks, but messages still come in days; relayed along the net by semismart repeater stations.

Sanders asked if I wished to reply. I think he really wanted to know why, if my marriage was destroying itself from within, I signed on for another exploration.

He doesn't understand. His life comes to him via a meter, I think. He puts in a credit and garnishes an hour in return. His pinched face beneath cropped, mouse-colored hair atop that tall, thin body, the way he moves as if always stretched in below-standard G, makes me think he's constantly inspecting that meter, perhaps believing he got fifty-nine-mark-fifty-nine minutes instead of the hour he thought his due. I remember watching him as he stood in uniform – the first time since we left – outside my door in the ship's outer ring. Emotions are difficult for him, I think. He doesn't understand them nor those who use them. For him, for as long as I've known him, emotions are something kept in a bottle on a dusty shelf, taken down once a year when socially or politically appropriate, looked at, stirred and shaken, but never opened or expressed, then placed back on the shelf until next year's inspection. Perhaps he feels he was given only a few at birth. That may explain why he's so niggardly with them.

Perhaps he should have married Robin.

But then they would not have given me Jeremy.

In any case, having spoken his due about space exploration and family obligation and how *his* wife understood such things and encouraged them – he breathed hard once, as if to show that talking about her stirred things deep inside him. The bottle of emotion came out and was displayed. "See? I have them, too," then quickly put away – he retreated to the clustered confines of C3I, back to piloting the ship, slinging his way through asteroids with a mathematical precision which, like a grossly integrated curve, showed its discontinuity even if you didn't look.

After hearing my arguments for communication with the Goatmen, Sanders has decided to dispatch a rumbler. I've told him this is a mistake.

745015:400 - The rumbler rolled from behind the blind and out towards the Goatmen. Set on low, its pseudopod extended and thumped the Aguirran plain lightly and rhythmically.

A strange thing happened which I haven't shared with the others but am willing to recount here:

All of us – Sanders, Galen, Tellweiller, Nash, and myself – sat at the great table in Common and watched the monitor. On the screen we saw all the goatmen save one turn and stare at the rumbler. They watched it with the same blank, seemingly mindless expression with which they watched the blind previously. They showed no aggression, no offense, no territoriality; nothing. No display of anything with which I'm familiar.

All except one. He turned to the rumbler, puckered as if in thought, as if he were trying to come to some decision about it, then turned back to the Blind. It didn't end there. If it did there would be nothing more to tell.

When he turned back to the Blind, his eyes – those damn near human eyes everything seems to have on this planet – came to a focus they had not achieved before and he stared – if that word can be used – not only directly into the blind but at me, as if I could be seen by him as separate and distinct from the blind, our ship, even my fellows in the crew. I was about to mention this to the others when I noticed none of them was aware of this singular fellow. All of their attention was on the rumbler, waiting for it to cause an aboriginal scatter. None of them seemed even aware of the lone Goatman.

I looked back at the Goatman whose eyes were fixed upon me and he opened his mouth as if to say "oh". It seemed he breathed rapidly and I...I felt my surroundings fade. As I sat there meeting this creature's unintentional stare, I peripherally watched my compatriots moving off as if into some great distance, becoming wisps and shadows until they, the table, Common, and even *The Merrimack* itself were gone from me.

I am squatting by a fire, just outside of a cave and close to a mesa edge, warming my hands and haunches even as the cold of the high, rarified air and clear, moonless night sky bristle the hairs of my back, neck, and flanks. I note that my hands aren't mine. They are a Goatman's, as is the rest of my body which I can see, and note with surprise that none of this disturbs me. It seems natural and good that I see myself as such, and the shock quickly fades as I let this versipellic vision continue.

I take a step closer to the fire, until my penis is almost hanging in it. I reach behind myself for more chigarro – how do I know that word? What does it mean? – to throw over the flames. There isn't much left, and I season the fire with half of what I have. The dry root burns slowly, sending black, sooty smoke into and over me, making my eyes water until a nictitating membrane covers them – now, at last, I understand how the Goatmen see, what those hideous eyes show them – and my nostrils flare – how wonderful their sense of smell is compared to ours. Aguirra, if this is Aguirra I see myself on, is alive with scents our robotics could never have known – as the chigarro's smoke burns into me. I look around although I know I'll find none of the scrubby chigarro trees; the winds of the mesa don't bite my nose, high up and between my eyes, bringing the tell-tale scent of the chigarro ready to harvest, a scent which always made both me and my father sneeze – what nonsense is that?

Earlier today, I remember, I'd been lucky. I found a bubbling mud-pool while hunting – what? – and, dropping my weapons, rolled in it, covering myself with the mud and letting it cake heavily on me as I climbed back home. Now, under the clear night sky, I let it dry until I feel the fire's heat mold it to me.

My eyes are half open, my eyelids cover the upper half and the lower half are covered by the nictitating membranes. I sing quietly and rock, gently, towards the fire and away, my voice a low roll which works its way across the plain facing me and my cave.

Another low rolling sound comes down from the sky and settles around me, my kin and the kin of my brothers answering my song in prayer, hearing my song in answer. I welcome the sound, adding it to my voice and adding this sound to my own. Slowly, as the chigarro rises into me and the earth is baked into hardened clay upon me, the sound grows louder. I let the sound move through me, patiently harmonizing and deharmonizing with it as I learn its flavors, its colors, its movements, waiting as all the voices merge and separate to reveal themselves to me, each voice revealing the one who made it.

I stand, my eyelids rising on top and my lower lids coming up from below, covering the nictitating membrane and blocking the light of the fire from my eyes. As I stand, the fire-hardened mud cracks and chips away from me. My fur comes away with it, leaving only my heat-reddened, all black skin underneath. The Chigarro root flares as some of the sulfurous mud catches in the flames and its smoke and odors etch my naked skin. Slowly, my eyes grow accustomed to the night sky.

There, up where Old One parted the skies while the People dreamed, a Walker new among the Bright Eyes comes down. This one, he walks over the edge of the mesa onto the plains on the other side of home. I do not know this Walker so he has come far. A Journeyer, he.

Old Ones, Bright Eyes, Walkers, Journeyers and their kin are good allies.

Naked, my fur baked off me, my black skin starts to twitch with chills in the late winter air as the fire quiets to embers glowing in the wind. I take a moment to admire my naked flesh, the new cuts and grooves in it where the fire has spoken to me.

The sound stops. I look back to where I last saw the Journeyer fall. There are no indications of it anywhere.

My ears, still focused on the sound, now turn and scoop after the Journeyer, listening. I hear nothing.

I walk back to my fire and throw some more Chigarro on it, stirring it slightly and letting it grow once again. I squat with my back to my cave, the mesa edge on my right. All around me are hardened furry mud packs. One by one, I throw them into the fire, letting the smoke and stench of my burning fur bathe me, some ritual I know but the ceremony of which I can't remember.

Quietly, I continue my song, now singing the sounds of Journeyer with me.

Sanders recalled the rumbler. His motion on the control board before me seems to have brought me back as everything in *The Merrimack* comes into focus around me.

The Goatmen are staring at us again.

Galen brought to our attention the insects. Or to the lack of them. We studied the recordings of the past few days and discovered that the insects have neither parasitized nor symbiotized the Goatmen from the latter's advent to the present. Perhaps time has taught the insects that the Goatmen's thick coat is too much to get through.

Strange. Co-evolution should not have allowed that.

755015:500 - Sanders consented to an attempt at open com-munications. Aside from the robotics and the collar, I'll be going alone. I suggested a holo for first contact, in case these creatures are hostile. Policy and the others went against my suggestion, and I was selected as Odd-man-out. No robotics indicated anything like these Goatmen, so no xenopologists were assigned to this crew.

This isn't what I was trained to do and I don't like it.

755015:940 - When they saw me walk around the Blind, all immediately lowered themselves to their knees with their arms at their sides and hands on thighs, fingers pointing inward, their backs straight and their faces always towards me. I felt like I was entering an Aikido class. The way their arms arc out from their bodies I can only think of "I'm a little teapot short and stout...". Jeremy so loved that song. I would sing it to him and dance, positioning his little body to the lyrics of the song. Ah, well.

As I approached, in unison they held out their left hands and bent slightly towards me. One of the Goatmen communicated. The com-munication was audial, but was in the infrasound range as I felt it more than heard it, like feeling the vibrations of a big bass drum as a parade marches by. The vibrations stopped and, again in unison, they extend-ed their right hands, still bent slightly in my direction. I was told by a friend from Nambia that most white men smell like goats. The wind has changed and, if this is how we smell, we should bathe more often.

If they used audial communication, I would try the same, hoping my voice was neither beyond their hearing nor painful to their ears.

"My name is Gordon Banks."

They communicated amongst themselves, this time in the audible range. What I immediately noticed was the physical cues to communication. When one spoke, he leaned towards his listener and extended his left hand, then showed he awaited a reply by extending his right hand. The listener kept his back straight until he spoke. During conversation – as opposed to communication – both leaned into each other and their hands darted forward and back quickly but rhythmically. During oration (if that term can be applied) the listeners sit with their backs straight. The patterns for conversation and communication followed when more than two Goatmen were engaged.

I remember that my reaction to their physical cuing was the amount of respect it showed for speaker and listener. I wondered if this physical cuing was ceremonial or cultural.

Their voices remind me most of excited horses and sheep, a combination of high bleating, neighing, and low bellowing. It is obviously a complex language. As they went through their posturings the wind brought several subtle smells to me. Could there also be an vomeronasal component to their communication? How I wished for a Goatman's nose! Is the grotesque physical animation necessary due to the torpidity of the face? Does their vomeronasal sense supplement that? And if so, how subtle and sophisticated is it?

Why did none of the robotics reveal this culture here? Why are there no other such creatures or cultures anywhere else on this planet?

They extended their left hands again (a sign of placation or offering?) and bent towards me. When the one Goatman – I've decided to call him Gomer, it is as close as I can get to his name – spoke, I tied in the translators. He is, I think, a middle-aged male of some importance. "You are from the ..." He made a sound at the end of his question that the program couldn't translate.

Again their right hands came forward. All stared at me, waiting. I spoke into the collar, "Can the computers give me anything on that last phoneme?"

Sanders answered me, although I could hear the others in the background and imagined them all huddled around the holo watching and taking notes. "Something tied to their mythology is the best we can do. Some kind of primary cultural icon, we think."

I wanted to echo "We think?" but know Sanders was incapable of an original thought unless the flight manual expressly indicated it. Instead I said, "Thanks. I'm talking with fifteenth-century Christians and am about to say, 'Jesus Christ? Holy Spirit? Sorry, I have no idea what those are.' I hope their culture is more aboriginal."

I tied in the translators and spoke. "Can you understand me?"

Their left hands came forward, all grunted which the translator expressed as "Yes," and their right hands came back.

"Sanders, can you get me covered if what I'm about to do doesn't work?"

"You're covered, Banks."

I kneeled down and leaned towards them, extended my left hand and prayed the translators had integrated enough of their language into its core. "Our languages are different, friends, and your words are strange to me. Perhaps my language has different words for..." and here I had the translator echo back the phoneme it could not parse.

The Goatmen became agitated.

I spoke to the collar, "What's going on, Sanders?"

"Why don't you start backing up. They don't look happy."

They stood up and so did I. Then, one by one, their eyes ever on me, they walked away.

7*95015:500 - We have not seen the Goatmen for four days,* although the casters clearly showed them going into the brush on the steppes rising to the Towers. I've run several linguistic routines through the computers, but there wasn't enough conversation to develop much lexicon, grammar, syntactical rules, etc.

Sanders just called me up. A Goatman is outside and the computers have identified him as Gomer. It is just as well. This morning Sanders handed me another communique from Robin, this one Private. I left it unopened on my desk.

795015:620 - He started in the standing talking posture. "Come to see our homes, Journeyer."

So I was 'Journeyer'. A name I could live with and one which made me laugh. Robin, I think, would agree with that name.

So be it! I would be 'Journeyer' and I would go with them. For once, I told myself, Robin could be right.

I mimicked their talking postures and said yes, I would come but had some things to do first. He'd have to wait until I returned.

His left hand came forward. "Just you. Not the others..." and again the program returned that impenetrable word.

"What others?" My first mistake. Just because they're simplistic doesn't mean they're simple.

Gomer stood up straight and stationary. The only indication of life the occasional flecking of nictitating membranes over his eyes and slight steam jetties rising from his nostrils. If he pawed the earth I would have run.

Slowly he leaned towards me and his left hand came forward. "The others like you who are in the home who wants to be a rock." Then, as if weighted with finality, "Are there those like you other than those in the home who wants to be a rock?"

And here is where it happened, I realize now; I lied. This, I think, was a gift of Robin's; to lie with such easeful facility. I shook my head no and heard Tellweiller over the collar, "Say it, Banks. Shaking your head might mean you want to date his daughter."

"No. There are no others like me except in the home who wants to be a rock. There are things I need to travel."

He stared at me, those damn cerulean eyes of his never leaving me and, at the same time, giving me the feeling he might not have been looking at me at all or perhaps seeing more than me standing there.

I left him sitting as I returned to the Blind. When I returned to *The Merrimack* I saw him on the monitors, staring at the home who wants to be a rock.

Sanders came to me as I prepared my quarters for departure. "Have you read that last transmission?"

I gazed around me. "What transmission?"

"The one from your wife. It seemed pretty important. I –"

I know my gaze interrupted him. He could not know the contents of a Private message unless he believed the mission in jeopardy and expressed his concerns to CenComm. I felt color leave my face. "How have I jeopardized this ship or its crew?"

If he answered, I don't know, for it suddenly became clear to me that this log was under his inspection as well.

795015:790 - This is the last record I'll make on the ship. From now on, my only connection to the ship will be via the grid strapped to my back. The ship will receive holos of everything around me, the collar I'll wear is linked directly to a translator in the grid, and I'll be able to extend a two-hundred amp field ten meters around me thanks to Galen's and Nash's tinkering. Other than that, the ship will be a passive witness to my fate. I won't be taking food as Galen says the vegetation is high in both digestible carbohydrates and protein, vitamins and minerals, and it might be good not to eat ship food for a few days.

Jeremy and I once played a game called "Circles". One person named something and the next had to somehow link that thing to another thing. So on the game went until you had come full circle and the first thing was named again. Perhaps that is what's happening here on Aguirra. Soldier to husband to father to xenopologist. Ha! What am I to become when the game ends?

805015:700 - I am exhausted. Gomer could no doubt have made the trip from the blind to the top of Alpha Tower in an hour, maybe two. Rarely have I seen an animal so uniquely adapted to its environment. Because of me the trip took a little over a day, and I'm considered in good shape.

Gomer led me up and away from the blind in what I think was a slow pace for him. As the incline increased, he dropped to all fours and moved like a North American billy high in the Canadian Rockies.

His toes act exactly as flattening rubber pads, thick soled and slightly prehensile, that spread and grab the rocks for support and balance. Walking bipedally, it wasn't unusual to see him leap against a rock wall, one foot flatten against it like a hiking boot and filling minute crevices to obtain purchase, and push off and forward with his other foot literally grabbing an outcropping which normally would block the way. All this and maintaining forward locomotion! At another point he had gone around a rivel ahead of me. When I came around he was suspended upside down from an upper ridge with no apparent support. His attention seemed fixed on the steppes leading to the other Tower.

I gasped and his attention was broken. I heard two pops and he fell – a drop of several meters – twisting in the air like a cat and righting himself. The place where he "stood" under the ridge was moist but evaporating quickly, and there was moisture under his footprints now as he walked. It was then I noticed the extremely pronounced musculature and venous markings between his knee and ankle and ankle and pads, markings and musculature which previously hadn't been apparent. I'm guessing these creatures have evolved the ability to control the contour of the soles of their feet and excrete a mucous, thus creating a suction cup.

He looked towards Beta Tower. "Tomorrow," by which he meant today, "they begin their Passage."

The climb only grew more arduous and I told Gomer to stop often. He didn't seem bothered by this. Perhaps he considers me a juvenile?

A curious thing did happen, once. I started to slip and Gomer stared at me. I flailed at the edge. Suddenly he was between me and the precipice, gently butting me back into the direction I should travel, his butting as gentle as a mother covering her young in a blanket yet as forceful as a cat chastising her kits. From that point on he always walked between me and the fall line of the Tower. When the path wouldn't support two abreast he fell to all fours and moved over the edge until more trailspace became available and he could again join me on the path. One could believe they evolved from quadripedal spiders until you see their eyes.

Later, at a particularly difficult pass for a biped, I told him I could go no further. He sat and, of course, stared. Eventually I could draw a breath without rasping. My legs, I knew, would ache for several days due to the lactic acid build-up in them. In addition, the rarified air was forcing me to hyperventilate in order to force enough oxygen into my system and I was starting to feel the cold through my suit.

I looked up at him, silhouetted by the setting sun, the sky clear above but a gentle mist settling over the Tower. On three sides of us were gray crags and skettles of rock. Underfoot and in occasional mounds were bluish green scrub plants. To the other side was the high plains of Aguirra and, far away and below, the lowlands were the colony would one day be. A wind blew, smelling of O_3 and summer storms and my attention went back to him. As the wind blew, his fur ruffled and filled, swirling around him and protecting him, bleeding away the cold the way a hirsute man's pelt bleeds away water as he rises from the sea. All the while his impassive, immutable face stared down at me, the only change in it being the nictitating membranes that covered his eyes when the winds blew directly into them.

I saw myself clearly in his eyes, then as if surrounded by clouds and mists when the membranes came over them, then clear again, and wondered how he saw me.

The winds started to grow more violent and I realized that, indeed, another storm would soon be pummeling the altiplano and all that grew out of it. What oxygen I had been able to glean before seemed to be robbed from me as the pressure dropped and the winds increased. The pain in my lungs was tremendous as they struggled to ventilate me, my blood to irrigate me. My heart began pounding in response to my body's demand for more oxygen.

Why hadn't I thought to bring O_2 shells with me? I could feel my vessels dilating within me to carry rich red life where it was needed and my brain felt as if overcome with fever as oxygen starvation took hold.

On my knees, the Goatman standing on a rock a meter or so over me, I leaned towards him and reached, genetics moving my left hand forward more than any understanding of his culture, and fell unable to speak, unable to look up at him due to the setting Astarte's rays piercing into my skull.

His three fingered hand swamped about my wrist. I was suddenly aware of his strength the way one is suddenly aware of a powerful undertow, being caught and going under, panicking, either to drown or to ride the wake and rise later, eventually making for shore.

I remember feeling the nails of his fingers against my skin. They were hard and cold, like the hooves of a cow in a winter field, but his fingers and palm were warm, near hot in this fairyland through which he guided me. His grip was strong but not violent as his fingers wrapped about my wrist and up my forearm.

He brought me forward, his muzzle a few scant centimeters from my face, and stared intently at me for a moment, as if inspecting me, unsure of what I was or what he was with me, then pulled me closer still until his lips engulfed mine, and he breathed. He pushed his own air into me, filling my lungs with oxygen his body didn't use. His free hand he placed on my belly, feeling my respirations through my suit, monitoring just how much to exhale before letting me breathe again. His eyes never wavered from me as he did this, as he resuscitated me, all with one long, shallow breath like a diver rising without tanks from far beneath the sea.

My body and brain, craving the life he gave me, took too much too fast, I think. I remember him ripping the flesh of his arm with one of his horny nails, making a gouge just wide enough to cover my lips, then making a fist until he bled. He gripped me by the neck then and held my mouth over his wound, holding me there and squeezing his fist. I fought at first but there was no point. Even at my best he was many times stronger than I. He held me there until I drank one, maybe two mouthfuls of his blood.

The skies turned red and I felt myself falling completely into his arms after that. I don't remember if he picked me up, led me, or carried me. I remember nothing until waking up some moments ago. I checked the equipment and all is functioning within specs, so I'm assuming Sanders and the others got everything on holos.

When I awoke, there were several females surrounding me and I was covered with their hairs. I can only guess that, realizing I was going into thermal shock, they lay around me to keep me warm. I was in a depression in the rock surface, not exactly a cave, but leeward, deep enough and with enough of a leading overhang to keep one relatively free of wind and rain. The rock surface itself was covered by plaited hairs, I think serving as a rug. Branches and leaves of some strange tree were woven into walls and roof around me.

I am in someone's hut, I suppose. Someone important, no doubt.

My first impression is that the females are built like diminutive males. All about me have narrower muzzles and foreheads, thinner necks, slightly shorter legs, and less massive shoulders than the males I've seen previously. They have four teats clearly visible due to hairless areas in their undercoats. This is not evidenced in the males. The females around are obviously of different ages although I have no way of knowing what their exact ages are as yet. Also, there is neither reddening nor swelling of the female's teats. This leads me to believe there are no nursing kids in this camp, unless none of these females are mothers. I can say that, as a whole, they stink. They exude an odor similar to an overripe, rotting melon which seems to lodge like a wedge in my sinuses slightly behind and immediately between my eyes. This odor is stirred or freshened when they move and they move a lot. It's damn near killing me.

Shortly after awakening, they brought me a heavy, bluish green porridge. I buried my head in it as doing so alleviated the scent of these women. It filled my nostrils like a fine but foreign liqueur, was sticky to my lips and tasted like sweetened cauliflower; all in all quite invigorating. I drank three good size bowls before it occurred to me I might be depleting their stores. They continued to offer, however, so I continued to drink five more bowls full. As I finished the last bowl I realized my breaths were coming easier. It wasn't until I had finished the last bowl that I realized how much better I felt. The porridge, I think, is sedative, elixir, and re-oxidant. Small wonder!

Gomer came while I ate. He assumed the kneeling position I've described previously, my little aikidoka, and waited. His nictitating membranes rose from the corners of his eyes slowly, near eclipsing his irises, and his lids lowered. I did not know if he could even see me. His nostrils flared and he breathed slowly, evenly, the calm power in his body a mockery of the lack of it in mine. A moment later he got an erection which he stroked slowly and shamelessly. The females left, taking their musky scent with them. Do the females control the matings here? Again perhaps through some vomeronasal sense? Are their matings ritual, ceremony, or purely atavistic? That they have a culture is obvious, how much that culture has stripped them of their genetic coding is not. Do they divorce? Do the females take the young and leave the males lonely and far away? Perhaps that was the hallucination I had. For that matter, what is going on with Robin and Jeremy? Sanders, I'm sure, will know. By-the-Book Sanders who, probably even as I enter this, is asking for a psych addendum to my files.

Ha!

Gomer has spoken. The translator was not hooked in so I had to ask him to repeat. "You talk when there are none who will hear you."

"What do you mean?"

"Your sounds are not our sounds. There are none here to understand."

"The sounds are for myself."

"You sing your own history."

What an interesting phrase; to sing one's own history. Yet it seemed so true, so accurate. "Yes, I do."

"Share them with me. Teach me to sing your songs."

Ah, so social contagion finally rears it's ugly head. That I could not allow. "There's nothing to share. I make it up as I go along."

Gomer, who was kneeling while we talked, sat back at that. He stared at me with those damning eyes and unreadable face, then picked up the last bowl I'd been given. There was still some porridge sticking to the sides of the bowl and, lifting the bowl to his face, his tongue flipped out and rasped the bowl dry. He seemed to bow then, placing first his left hand on the ground before him then his right so that a triangle was formed between the first fingers and thumbs of each hand, then bowing at the waist, next sitting up and placing first right then left hand on his hips and finally rising. He took the bowl with him and left.

What have I said?

Could it be that his culture has no concept of stories or songs for entertainment? Are all their traditions oral? If they have writing, I have not recognized it as such. Are all their oral traditions morality lessons, history and folklore? Are none of them purely for entertainment? Robin would be proud. I've happened upon a planet of Presbyters.

Or at least a plateau of them.

Before Gomer came I was commenting about the porridge and the effect it's had on my breathing. I've also noticed there is no pounding in my ears and my heart isn't racing. At these altitudes, I am not surprised to discover they feast on plants which are both water and oxygen retainers.

*8*05015:0800 - *A brief walk around the village reveals little.* There are no family dwellings as such, although there are some common constructions. The one I was in is evidently for the sick and infirmed. One seems to house foodstuffs. I have not ascertained what the others are for in detail, although it seems one is a common sleeping hut. All are marvelously constructed to withstand the elements, as are the goatmen themselves. Perhaps their physiology precludes the need for dwellings. Even so, I would think that over time they'd come to prefer them.

Which brings up an interesting detail. I asked Gomer what they call themselves. His nostrils flared and released, flared and released, as if beating with his heart. With each flaring he gave a name. He was signaling them by scent, I believe, and perhaps expecting me to be able to do the same, much as we would point to one person after another.

"No, no," I said. "What are you named all together?"

His level of confusion demonstrated there was none. Again, if I were a xenopologist I would have expected that. This also demonstrates there are no other sentients on the planet, I think. If there were others, wouldn't the Goatmen have developed the language to separate themselves from these hypothetical others? Or is this my prejudice placed upon them, By-the-Book Sanders versus Not-By-the-Book me.

Or perhaps there are no other intelligences who have revealed themselves to the Goatmen.

I then told him what we called ourselves – "human" – and his left hand shot forward. "How many of you are there?"

I told him I didn't know.

"There are enough so you don't know each one?"

"Oh, most definitely."

"And all of you are in the home who wants to be a rock?"

He waited for my answer.

Damn my lies. Damn them. Damn Robin. Damn Sanders, Tellweiller, Galen, and Nash. Damn the Goatmen.

"Oh, I misunderstood before. No, many of us are in the ..." and I used that word.

He brayed, something which the translators evaluated as laughter, and gave me a gentle butt. I am sure it was gentle for him. It damn near cracked my skull. "Go on."

They know when I lie. Perhaps my scent gives me away. Yet the gentle reproof. Am I teaching them that some stories can be fun?

I told him we call them "Goatmen". What he heard was "Goat Men" and he laughed again.

"Can half a people hope to survive?" he asked, still laughing.

The last thing I remember was him giving me another gentle butt. Soon after I slept.

The village is multi-generational from what I've seen so far and the divisions are fascinating in themselves. I wonder if these creatures come into a mating season, still tied to some ecologic bio-rhythm, so clearly are the generations demarcated.

Lactating females seem to have longer hair, or perhaps they simply haven't shed their winter hairs as easily as do the males and non-lactating females, of which there are few. Around the nipples of some lactating females there is a bloody stain. Perhaps some of the kids don't give up the tit soon enough.

Closest to me is one female still suckling a young. There is a tenderness common to all sentient creatures between parent and young – and yes, I'm aware of my many assumptions.

I surmise I'm witnessing a parent and child simply by the interaction between them. It reminds me of Robin nursing and nuzzling Jeremy. There was a tenderness between them which did not extend to me, often intentionally excluding me.

I remember, there was one time, I watched her holding him crooked in her right arm, unbuttoning her blouse and folding it down, then pinching her nipple as he rooted back and forth, his little mouth open and reaching, until he found her. His eyes slowly closed as she sang to him, almost too quiet for me to hear. Once she was secure he had found her milk, her eyes, like his, slowly closed.

She rocked then, rocked in rhythm to her song, and his mouth went lax without ever loosing her teat, every now and again his cheeks would tense and he would suck, perhaps six or seven times. She would smile and then he would sleep again.

That these creatures are sentient there can be no doubt. They have long since passed Keiger's Porpoise Test – another anthropomorphic egocentrism, if you ask me. Twentieth century sociologists learned to be participant observers to best understand a culture. Agreed! Goodbye Robin, farewell Jeremy, my son. Sanders, you were my commander, never my superior, even as an officer. To Tellweiller, Nash, and Galen, serve him as best you can if not at all.

Ha!

Robin had plenty of milk for Jeremy, it seemed. Not once can I remember did she ever nourish me.

*8*05015:1280 - *There are no other animals up here. I just* noticed that. More accurately, I just noticed I hadn't noticed. Hopefully the robotics I'm carrying are noticing things I'm not.

There is vegetation and it seems highly ordered although I don't know if it's cultivated.

Joseph Carrabis

Gomer approaches. There is another billy with him. This one's horns are broken off and he appears to have cataracts. Strange.

"I have spoken of the strange things you do and Tenku has offered to ..." another word the translator could not understand.

According to one of my old college professors people learn when they either develop or acquire new language for what they're doing. What is it the translator needs to learn?

Or is it I who has not the language?

I then noticed that Tenku – that's as well as I can do the new billy's name – was holding a black root.

Participant observation, yes.

They came and sat. Gomer never moved from the neutral position except to say "Tenku", at which point the new billy leaned forward, left hand out, and started talking. "We use this when we wish to – " again the translator barked, this time a string of garbled sounds as if it were cursing in a foreign language. I can't believe it hasn't developed sufficient vocabulary yet!

Tenku placed the root between us.

How is it used? Because I'm not an anthropologist, I'm assuming it's some kind of narcotic and, because I'm not an anthropologist, I'm probably right. But how is it used? Chewed? Swallowed? Smoked? Injected? Inhaled? Mixed with something else? Rubbed into the skin? As an enema?

Gomer and Tenku strip a piece of the root then rise and motion me to follow. Each holds a piece of the root, its black juice streaming down their hands and dripping onto the ground. "Where are we going?"

Tenku starts chewing the root. One question is answered. Gomer says, "We speak with the Theisen."

"The Theisen? Who are they?"

"The ones who answer."

It is sweet.

I am naked. Totally naked. No survival pack, no environment suit, no food, nothing.

How did they know to strip me?

Who stripped me?

I am on the ground. How long have I been lying here?

It is not cold nor is it difficult to breathe, yet I still feel myself to be on the Alpha Tower.

I must remember all this for later. To record it. I hear Tenku's voice, what equates to their laughter, the braying, but he's not around. His voice is close but he is not.

The black root must be some kind of hallucinogenic. Gomer is before me. He is standing at the foot of a path, narrowed and marked by azure and deep maroon stones. There are trees further up the path. Real trees. Pines, mostly. Christmas trees with some birches. One or two elms. There are pine needles on the ground. The path leads up a slight rise then disappears between the trees, moving further up a hill and into the woods.

I thought we'd climbed to the top of this tower, but clearly it goes higher.

Gomer is at the foot of the path, staring at me and holding out his left hand. It is covered with milk. His horns are black against the sky and his eyes, always impenetrable, now show me naked before him, goat's eyes with rectangular pupils like huge picture windows looking out onto my soul. He stares at me with his left hand out, slightly bent at the waist with one knee forward, reaching out to me, helping me from the ground and patient for me to follow him, an alien Mephistopheles offering me an unknown Cleopatra at the price of some xenopologic Hell.

I am scared.

Gomer is still waiting, his hand outstretched and still dripping milk. He leans closer and slaps my face. God it stings. The pads of his hand rip my naked face. His hand is still outstretched but now it drips blood. This is familiar. How long have I been here? How long has he been waiting?

I wish I had something to drink. I wish I sucked the milk when it was offered.

Gomer leans forward, coming closer and I fear he will strike me again. Instead he wipes my face. It is covered with sweat. Tears and blood and sweat. He stares at the mixture as it pools in his palm as if he were reading a history of my life.

Again I hear Tenku laugh.

Gomer opens my mouth and lets my history fall in. It tastes like milk and quenches my thirst.

I can't move. My arms and legs are free and yet I cannot move.

Again there is Tenku's laughter. Where is he?

Blood runs down my arm and into my hand and now I can move it. I can taste it. I can breathe. I take Gomer's hand. It is rough and tender. Both facile and feral as it swarms about mine. It takes a while, a few tries, but I get up.

We start up the path. I hear a voice. It is Jeremy's. It comes from Gomer's lips, speaking in the Goatmen's tongue. I look into Gomer's face and see he has Robin's eyes. Now they look at me without judgment, without regret.

I am still naked and it is cold.

*T*enku, Gomer, and I are back, standing in the circle with the black root between us. Their jaws, chests, and hands are covered in streaks of black juice. Their teeth are blackened, as are their tongues. They look like two kids – pardon the pun – who'd been eating and drooling licorice.

Their breath smells like...well, like blood. I doubt this is the case, as they are herbivores and even the billies don't have pronounced canines. A possibility is that they self-mutilate by biting their own tongues, perhaps as part of the black root ritual. I have no idea if sublingual ingestion works for caprins as it does for humans. The pain involved in biting one's own tongue, however...

I am fully clothed again and wonder if I was ever naked. There are black stains down the front of my suit and on my hands.

*8*15015:0800 - *The recorder signaled The Merrimack's re-* quest for my immediate return sometime during my study of the black root. Has my intention for participant observation caused Sanders concern? Has Robin conscripted my pay for this rigging and Sanders needs my consent before he'll approve? Damn him, By-the-Book Sanders. For the first time in years I feel useful, like I'm accomplishing something, and I'll be damned if any petty squabbles will keep it from me now.

I had not noticed before, but some of the billies are not in the village. Have they gone back to inspect "the home who wants to be a rock"? Is this Sanders' concern?

835015:1700 - No entries yesterday. It seems I slept. Gomer tells me this is common for those first exposed to the Wa'asis, the proper name of the black root. He also tells me we didn't get to the Theisen. I could not make the journey, he said, something which is also common. When I asked why he said nothing.

More of the Goatmen have left this village, some even as I enter this, and I note that the majority of those leaving are the young ones. Regarding that, several of the females are pregnant and, Gomer tells me, will start kidding soon. I asked him if there are any natural abortions or stillborns and he answered no, but not directly. There are no words in his language for either stillborn or abortion. This is the strongest evidence such things don't exist.

I've also asked about natural predators. The lowlands have several, he tells me. Original planetary findings confirm this. "Is that why your people came here to live?"

"No, we have always been here."

I haven't as yet heard any of their oral tradition or myths – if indeed they have any. I'm sure they would be fascinating.

This opens our discussion again to Tenku and I question him about the Wa'asis. Whatever it is, only Tenku and a few others have it and administer it. What happens when these others are no more? Then one like them will chew it. "Will you chew it?" He has no answer.

This brings up another point. Are these the only goatmen on all of Aguirra? Where are the other "tribes"?

I ask about the Goatman – here again Gomer laughs at "Goat Man". He butts me but this time knows I'm delicate and it is a tap, barely felt yet frightening never-the-less – the individual who stared at me when we sent out the rumbler.

Gomer tells me no such person – Goatman – exists. I describe the individual in detail and he asks me to go on, to tell him more. It is here I realize something else about these Goatmen and perhaps all aboriginals I've ever known.

The Goatmen's observational skills are based on a delicate yet pervasive matrix of focused attention directed to minute detail, the constant exercise of a rich cultural memory, and the predication of all experience into oral history. This latter is prevalent in all pre-ecririen societies. This could be true of all aboriginal peoples but I have no way of knowing.

845015:0430 - Gomer has returned with Tenku. Tenku asks me to tell him who I saw with the other People when they came to the Blind.

It is not that he's dissatisfied with my description, it's simply that he feels there is more. He doesn't question what I've told him, only asks "Where are you?"

"I am here."

Quickly, he lifts me. I think he is old and still he demonstrates formidable strength. Holding me against him, I smell his scent quite strongly. It is the same and subtly different from the others and the community smell I'd gotten used to. He smells, I realize, of the Wa'asis. His breath is sweet with the stuff, and being this close it is intoxicating.

"Where are you?" he asks me.

"I am here, I told you."

He put me down. Something strange happened then, something I'd noticed but had not referenced in this work before.

There is, I think, a far less obvious kind of communication these creatures employ, something beyond the perceptual ranges of both myself and my immediate instruments. Perhaps even beyond the vomeronasal. Tenku and Gomer moved off in the same direction although there was no clue or communication between them which I discerned. That would be enough, except that several of the other remaining males moved simultaneously to a common point, one of the common shelters, and all entered.

845015:1000 - Extremely cold last night. These creatures know about fire, yet don't make much use of it. Nor do they make use of the common dwellings. It is a matter of perception. By tucking themselves with their backs to the wind they can sleep in the open at forty degrees below zero. Cold to me. I don't know what it is to them.

I have discovered more via some telemetric readings. In extreme cold they reduce epidermal bloodflow to conserve heat, with hands, feet, and exposed facial features maintained just above the tissue freezing point. Warmth to these possible contact points is regulated independent of the rest of the body, an efficiency of design emphasized greatly on Aguirra. On warm days they flair themselves out to keep cool, exposing as much of the body surface as possible to the air, or they roll in the dirt. The younger ones do this quite a bit and I believe it to be some kind of game or play.

Coat ranges in color from almost pure white through white, through various shades of blond cream and ocher to grays, blonds and blacks. Most striking are the slope blue coats of the older goatmen, whom I collectively call 'Silverbacks'.

The recorder is transmitting a caster response signal. Sanders must be serious about my return. He's sending a caster to find me and bring me home. What could he want now?

845015:2200 - Tenku has returned. There is another billy with him, a young one just starting his horns, and not Gomer. They assume the talking positions, not including me. Tenku asks this other Goatman, "Where are you?"

"The Theisen ... " and a bark. Perhaps I would learn more if I didn't rely on the damned translator. "Tenku has asked me to be with him and Journeyer. Gomer agrees this will help us know Journeyer and where he is, as Journeyer, we believe, is lost.

"We sit with the sisters and children of Hepob…"

This new billy's recitation continued for fully forty minutes, at which time Gomer came over.

Before continuing note his reference to "The Theisen." This seems odd to me as he did not smell of Wa'asis and I thought such was necessary for communication with "The Theisen" to begin.

Most disturbing to me was what he said as he came to the end of his speech; "…and there are some fallen stones. The Old Ones, placed without asking by the others from – " the untranslatable word again "– those who dwell in the home who wants to be a rock."

The young billy got up and Gomer took his place. Tenku asked, "Where are you?"

Gomer started, "As Shika said and…"

His recitation of where he is took days longer, even starting as it did from where the other Goatman left off and continuing far down the Towers, across the Altiplano and ranging over the continent.

The missing third leg of the triangle. I believe I have it. The oral history is truly rich and greatly diversified, everyone in the village has their own. They define where they are by their experience, starting at their immediate present, continuing throughout their personal histories and including racial histories when it is relevant to their personal recounting. Gomer, for example, recited a story about a Goatman called 'Denihé'. From what he said, I suspect Denihé might be the Goatman I and I alone perceived when the others stood outside the Blind and Sanders dispatched the Rumbler. If not that, then Denihé is the creature who I became in that dream.

It is fascinating, this concept. To define your existence by your experience. Perhaps I was mistaken in thinking these creatures have names so much as they have icononyms, a single sound which acts as an arrow to a racial or cultural memory of their entire existence. It may explain why they laugh at 'Goat Man'. The name denies them half their experience. To them, "history" is by its very nature an individual's song.

I wonder what they made of "My name is Gordon Banks."? Has that simple statement, denied of cultural references and identity, defined our interactions since?

Tenku sits facing me. There is black root in his hand.

We are moving up a steep incline. There are several males with me. I am walking without paying attention to how I move, much as these creatures themselves do. Several of us turn towards something at once. I know I am to look, to see, to feel, taste, touch, smell, whatever this thing is.

My nostrils open wide and carry the scent to me. I feel my legs twitching, vibrating, as if there's something older here than I should rightly know, a racial memory which others will have to tell me about.

There are a few tracks with a scent mark, although I was unaware of the scent mark. Four of the older billies suddenly surround me, their blue pelages sheening in the sun. I am filled with knowledge, knowledge I know I didn't have, knowledge accumulated and indexed and presented in small, digestible chunks, knowledge of the area, knowledge of animals in the area, knowledge of this season, knowledge of this time of day, details upon details upon details.

There is so much. As it comes into me I can't breathe. I hear the voices of my brothers, my sisters, my family, my children - my children? - long distant, summoned to talk to me now from throughout time. Things heard from others. Histories sung.

My four acolytes leave me, as suddenly as they came, moving back into their ranks in our procession, and ahead of me one other male slows. As I'm about to pass him he butts me. It is the male who watched me at The Merrimack, although now his horns are broken like Tenku's and their edges cut me. "Make a guess," he says. "What do these particular marks, these specific trail clues, mean? Tell me what and who has been here. Where were they before? Where are they headed? When? Will they come again?"

I answer his questions, surprised at my knowledge, astounded by my experience. My guess is correct, for all that I tell him, then realize I'm not answering out of my own experience. I'm answering out of the experiences of others.

He laughs at me. It is Sanders' laugh. He has an Old One's face.

At night, the air around the Towers grows still and quiet. There are no raptors or other predators at the altitudes governed by The People. How ever long they have lived thus, they have grown calm and accepting of their environment. No guards or watches are posted. Of course, with their ability to communicate vomeronasally, I doubt any threat would long stay such to these creatures.

The sky, at night, is darker than the darkest desert night on Earth or many other worlds I've seen. The constellations, Tellweiller told me, are those the dinosaurs on Earth once saw.

I heard something coming up from the altiplano. When I got up, half the people of the village were up, at the edge of this Tower and looking down to where I long ago left the blind.

A meteor rose from the ground and rode through the skies. Half way into the darkness it exploded.

85015:0010 - A caster lies wrecked about two hundred meters from me. When that happened I don't know. The transmitter's indicators show only that it records.

Only that it records.

Damn.

There is no indication that it sends. *The Merrimack* is gone. Without me.

Damn.

Damn Sanders and Galen and Nash and Tellweiller and Robin and the Corps and...

How do I know what an Old One looks like? For that matter, what is an Old One?

I'm overcome by a feeling of melancholy. My notes are no longer transmitted to the ship. Who hears them? Who reads them? I mourn the loss of my objectivity. I mourn my participation in their primitive rites. All has become nothing more than my history song.

I want to tell them more will come, that the Pilgrimage Council will find a way to deny them their aboriginal rites. With no natural predators, how can they prepare? How could they understand?

*9*05015:0830 - *How many days of recording does the transmitter have without The Merrimack close by to bleed power from?*

Gomer is back with Tenku. Both are playing with the kid whom I witnessed nursing earlier in this narrative.

Yes. They have become distinct to me. I can recognize and individuate them.

I've noticed The People seem to pick up cues from each other even when there is no obvious contact. They can have their backs to each other, even at extremely distant parts of the village from each other. Something will catch the attention of one of them, usually something outside of that individual's experience, and as that individual's attention quickly becomes hypnotic a common anxiety moves through them all. Others respond by moving without hesitation to look at the area where the first individual is staring. They respond simultaneously, as though some group consciousness comes "on-line".

I ask if we'll try to reach the Theisen again and Tenku shows me the black root, the Wa'asis. The ceremony is much like the previous one. It is ritual to me, ceremony to them. There is a meaning to them, a history and a reasoning. To me there is only the placing of the root, the stripping with the teeth, the chewing. With all other cultural iconography gone I suppose I must make it more than mere ritual soon, I must not repeat the mistakes of the Europeans colonizing the world. They wanted to prove their god was the match of any pagan idol and took tobacco, alcohol and more powerful hallucinogens, all aboriginal vectors to the gods, and bastardized them until they became addicted, proving the old gods greatest of all. They forgot the ceremonies behind the rituals.

I must not. I can not.

"Who are the Theisen? What happens when we chew the root? Where do we go?"

There are no answers. Tenku offers me the root. "Wait. I have questions," I say. It is too late. They have already started to chew.

I'm losing my objectivity. I decide to sit and see what happens to them. I watch their breathing, their eyes, watch their bodies relax and sag.

The nanny comes over. The kid, who sat watching us, sniffs the air, turns to his mother, and butts her belly and thighs. She squats – the Little Teapot – and he raises on toe to nurse.

She's staring at me. Her eyes aren't like the others. They are deep, and black. Like Robin's. And also, I think, beautiful.

Without meaning to, or perhaps meaning to without knowing I mean to, afraid to be left alone as it were, I lift a root to my mouth and chew.

No knowledge of time or date. I am naked. In the same place I was before, only closer to the path. Gomer is here and Tenku is not, although I feel Tenku is near.

Gomer stands over me, at the foot of the path. All of my training, all of my knowledge, all of my experience avails me not, and I am terrified by the newness of it.

This is the magic I believed in as a child and denied as an adult.

Gomer offers me his hand. It is easier to reach this time and I stand quickly.

Tenku laughs.

"Where are we going?" I ask, wondering how Gomer can understand without the translator to mediate.

He points up the path.

"Are the Theisen up there?"

He says nothing and begins to walk. I follow.

Whatever experiences I have, I'm unaware of them. The only thing I am aware of is my terror at being a child.

I wake and find myself holding Gomer's genitals. How this came about I don't know. Gomer waits for me to sit up then tells me we traveled far.

"Did we reach the Theisen?"

Tenku, sitting with his back to us, answers, "No. Not yet."

"Do you journey with us? I think you're there but you're not."

"No."

They leave me. I check my recorder. Nothing of the hallucination has been recorded. Then I am chilled.

Tenku spoke with his back to us. The normal postures were ignored. What has happened? What have I done?

The nanny, Hepob, has taken on the task of feeding me.

*T*enku *has awoken me. We go to the edge of our Tower closest* to the other. The ground is uneven and churned here. If there were more moisture it would be muddy. The sun has risen enough to heat the two plains of the Towers of God. Gomer joins us. There is a great mist rising from the altiplano table and atmospheric venting is creating a turbulence between the Towers. It reminds me of a high speed oil and water separation. I can make out the other Tower through the turbulence but not enough to determine details. The wind gusts up the edge of this Tower and the other like the updrafts beside some coastal shelf.

There is a rumbling in my gut. All the males join us, all of them Gomer's age or older. The only other males in the village are prepubescent kids and those not yet off the teat.

How old do they think I am?

I still don't know how old Gomer is. As more and more older billies join us, the rumbling grows. It feels like a sonogram with too much power. The billies are panting. No, I see now they are taking rotary breaths.

Are they purring? Is that the sound I feel? They line the churned earth, leaving a great center space between them.

My god it's deafening.

They all face the other Tower. All the males seem joined in this chorus. The earth, this Tower, quakes beneath us. The mist clears in a column, as if some great tube were being laid between this one and the other, a passageway with invisible walls. The mist rises around it but does not pierce it.

This passage, this sonocasting, grows warm, although no sunlight penetrates the thickening cloud.

There is another rumbling, another purring, an answering chant, from the other Tower and, as I watch, the young billies start to come across.

Some walk although it is clear they are afraid. Some run. Others leap. Some leap but not through the passage and you hear their separate cries ascend the Towers as they descend to their deaths.

A few walk and show no fear. Some hold onto others, some help others.

They are braver than I.

"What is going on?" I ask Tenku.

He doesn't answer, his concentration on his breathing, on the direction of his voice, his eyes holding onto the passageway their song has made between the Towers.

*T*he translator is failing so I use it sparingly. The recorder I use because I can. I will take a guess and record the date as 916015.

Funny how much lighter these units have become without *The Merrimack* to power them. The mists cleared. The earth is churned more than before due to the leaping and running of the young billies. Most of the elder billies have gone, as have all of the young. There is no more rumbling. I peer over the edge of the Tower and make out the bodies of those who didn't make it.

Tenku is staring at me.

"What happened here? What was this?"

He grabs my genitals. I don't know if that is the answer, but it is the only response I get.

He doesn't seem surprised by them. I am surprised at the gentleness of his touch. They must seem a child's, weak and ineffective in his hands. How did an ancient Hebrew oath right find its way here, I wonder.

Back in the village, Hepob offers me the same porridge as when I arrived. It tastes slightly different and I see scrapings of the black root in it.

After I eat, I rest.

I slept long and deeply, yet my sleep was fogged by dreams as thick as the altiplano's Aguirran gnats. I no longer know how reliable or intelligible this redaction has become.

I remember several dreams, although only a few clearly. In one, I was back at the ship. Sanders, Galen, Tellweiller, and Nash walk through me and past me as if I don't exist, nor can they hear me even though I scream at them. The Old Ones have advanced. *The Merrimack* was called home.

In one dream, I watched Galen and Tellweiller on one of Dave's C3I monitors, then realized I was Dave watching the monitor. This wasn't a common dream, where you know who you are and have a sense of yourself no matter what you are in the dream. Here, I was more a passenger along for the ride; not David Sanders, but able to experience his environment, thoughts, and emotions along with him. Not a pleasant journey. He seems a lonely, fearful man.

On the monitor, I watched Tom ask Bob if he'd like to join him in a little exploring. "Care to come along?" I sat with Dave in C3I as they finished lunch in the Common. Dave tapped in the commands for a two-way screen split and zoomed a separate window onto each man's face. His eyes, always quick, looked down and over his nose at the images on the screen. They went out of focus momentarily and he "hmmed", bridging his fingers against his mouth and nose. His eyes still out of focus, he titled his head back further, just enough so he could see the tip of his nose in the foreground of their faces. This is an unconscious habit he has when talking to people.

As the two men cleaned up their table and left the Common, Dave adjusted the Eyes to follow them out of the ship. They hadn't travelled far when they stopped. Without even looking for any remotes or robotics, they fell into each other's arms, laughing and giggling, pulling off their suits and, making themselves comfortable against each other, finally ... finally I looked away, not so much embarrassed as wanting to afford them their privacy. My only thought was "How could they have kept this secret so long?"

Dave continued to watch and I felt him dissociate, fighting to have no emotions, finally losing so that the only emotion he had was disgust and even this one he denied himself. In the end, Dave made a note in his log about each of them and included a special adjunct to talk privately with Bob. Dave, I now realize, lives by the book because he is terrified to do otherwise. Within those paper-thin walls he is safe. Outside of them he is open to the attacks with which he attacks others. Seeing others outside the book is a threat to him, a constant reminder of what he has not.

Nash, brown hair and beard, brown eyed, tall and heavy, leaves *The Merrimack*, calling Bob and Tom back to the ship before the storms come. I watch him through Sanders' eyes then suddenly am him and suddenly realize he tends to direct his words towards some space over people's heads.

Tom and Bob return and I am them, my mind hearing both their words and their thoughts, feeling their emotions, moving their bodies, and I note as I-Bob answers Nash that I-Bob tends to look over our head as if to read our words as if they appear in the old style cartoonist's speech ballons. Although I was never conscious of it before, I now understand I thought this gazing was due to self-consciousness over a speech impediment which tended to leave certain words swimming in saliva back around his molars.

Back in the ship, my equipment looks foreign to me and there is a young billy dead in my chamber, lying on my couch.

In the next dream I am back on Earth, back in New York City. I meet an old lover there and, in the magic traveling of dreams, we are suddenly on the Towers. She is on the far one from me. She starts to walk towards me and I scream at her to wait, there are no billies with histories to create a bridge. I open my mouth and tears fall from my rasping Goatman tongue. The tears fall down the side of my Tower and swell into a rising mist. She leaps and falls. I do not hear her scream. I only hear her hit.

Then I am back home, in my apartment on Earth, and dream that I woke up in the middle of the night to go to the bathroom. I went into the bath and turned on the light. On my way to the toilet, I passed the mirror and looked into it. An Old One with my face stared back. I remember being terrified of it. The Toelitchte didn't recognize me and was angry, near enraged at me.

The Toelitchte?

The last dream was the most vivid of all. I was somewhere on Aguirra, although I didn't know where exactly I was. There were massive trees before me, far grander in size and age than even the oldest Sequoias or any tree in any rain forests on any world. Yet they did not smell of forest floor. Instead the air reeked of human sweat, tears, and blood.

They talked to me. More correctly, they talked around me. I could not speak their words although I know they could understand mine.

"Who are you?"

They didn't answer. Or if they did I was unaware.

"What are you?"

No reply of which I knew.

"Talk to me," I shrieked.

Their branches ruffled. They made sounds in the wind. I looked up and could not see their tops, so high were they in the sky.

A great catlike creature, one of the ones Gomer mentioned to me, came out from behind one of the trees. It was more like a cross between a tiger and a bear, with the great lumbering body of some monstrous ursus yet the swiftness and retractile claws of a feline. Its eyes, also, were those of a cat. Its belly was white and the rest all brown, with small tufts of white at the tips of both ears.

It came at me. There was nowhere to run or hide and, in one breath, it was upon me. Its first swipe of those six toed claws opened me. The second broke through ribs. The next three cored me deeper and deeper until there was nothing left.

Then it left me there, bleeding on the ground, as it walked away. I felt other things, smaller things, tickling me and entering me. They were the roots and shoots of the trees, spreading through me as if I was the earth in which it grew. Suddenly I was one of those massive trees, looking down at myself on the forest floor.

Only it wasn't me I saw. Tenku was there, his body eviscerated as was mine, only mine was not to be found. The air changed its smell. I was engulfed by the black root.

That's what I remember of my dreams.

I will be more careful what I accept in my porridge.

I don't know how long I've been here at this point. I've been making records as often as I think to, always when I wake up, but have no idea of how long it has been.

Hepob and all the other females of kid-bearing age are due soon, if not today. I wonder who Hepob's mate is, or if she even has one. For that matter, why are there only two sexes here? Why not one, or ten? There is a life form on Chalderon that was at first thought to use seven hosts before it could reproduce. We discovered too late there were seven sexes and each played a significant part in the fertilization and development of the embryo.

Unfortunately, only the last sex was sentient, and when your life cycle is several thousand years and your planet is colonized right before the end of your mating period?

It is too horrible to think about.

Tenku is here. It's black root time.

I have met the Theisen. I had met them before but had not known it.

Trees. Light-year spanning, world bearing trees. Trees with leaves big enough to shelter a sun. Trees so vast their being spans the multiverse. Trees that root in universes we do not know and gather light in universes we can not name. The youngest is the age of my race and the oldest form the Towers of God. They talk to me in words I won't live long enough to pronounce and tell me of their people, the Aguirrans, and my own.

The Theisen travel the stars multigenerationally. They have no concept of time or space. To them everything is here and now. Yet they have memories, race memories, of seeding a hundred billion worlds.

Each Theisen is a history of their kind, yet everything they know is happening to them as they speak of it. Is this where the Goatmen learn their songs?

They know they have travelled and there is no place other than "here" to them.

"How can you know everything on all worlds, even ones I've never seen? You're parts of my dream, aren't you?"

"We dream each other. You are part of the millennia long dream of trees."

I say nothing because I desperately need to believe I sing to myself.

"Do you know where you are?"

I turn to walk away and see the Alpha Tower across a great divide and in the distance. Many elder Goatmen are there. There is much turbulence in the air between us. They start to sing and a pathway forms.

"No!"

"Do you know where you are?" The Theisen's leaves shake at me although I feel no breeze.

"How?"

"*Do you know where you are?*"

I understand the words and they are not really a question. It comes as the sound the translator couldn't parse. This is the cultural icon, the mythic symbol of which the Goatmen speak.

I take a step onto nothing but sound, nothing but song, and I'm back aboard *The Merrimack* looking at Galen and Tellweiller. God. I never told them they kept me sane. They were the epitome of the Pro-Choice movement's slogan at the turn of the 21st century; Life begins when you mind your own business. Galen – Tom – was athletically thin, something I attributed to his being the youngest of us and always able to find good looking, intelligent women he genuinely wanted to spend time with. Pale skinned, clean-shaven with freckles, aquiline green eyes and copper hair, he had the uncanny ability to answer questions which were asked rather than the questions implied. I envied him that.

No guile. What a gift.

– Why am I thinking of him in the past tense? –

Nash, definitely the oldest of us, was also the most talkative and often engaged you in conversation unless you asked him not to, then it's "Oh, I'm sorry," and the next thing was, "Do you think Tom's around?" If not Tom, then Sanders or Tellweiller. He was an old Texan with a square face and a slight hump which he'd never allowed Fleet-Med to reconstruct. Part of this I blame on his arcane religious beliefs, part on his sense of independence, and perhaps a little on his "fear of the knife" as they use to say.

I liked his drawl.

– God Damn It! Stop! –

He's traveled so much you can't really notice it anymore, except when he laughs and talks immediately after. His laugh is loud and abrupt, high in his head and right in your face. He is the kind who genuinely laughs and whose whole body shakes when he does, which is interesting to watch as he is a field geologist and grisly hard and permanently tanned from exploring half a dozen worlds.

I left them in Common. "Damn, it's quiet out there," Nash said, his eyes so wide on the screens. I had to laugh. If he'd been looking out a window, he'd be at home in a horror-vid.

"Probably just your ears getting use to the lack of wind and rain," Sanders said.

"No. Christ, I wish Gordo were here," Nash said, wanting an ally, I think. "He's the xenopologist. You watched his reports. He understood more than any of us what all these biologic anomalies were about."

– I dream – dream? – Now they talk of me in the past. What is going on? –

"Listen," he continued. "It's *quiet*."

"Huh? Maybe. Whatever." Sanders shrugged. "I'm going to C3I. We'll find out in a couple of days what the fauna's circadians are. We can analyze the last of Bank's transmissions then if we want."

A moment later I'm in C3I with Sanders as Tom walks in. "Sanders, I have something for immediate uplink."

Sanders didn't respond. He sat there, his face flushed and his eyes red, until his breathing, which had been harsh at Tom's entrance, was more normal. Finally he stood up.

"What's wrong, Sanders?"

"What's wrong?" Sanders eyes opened wide, as if Galen were an apostate and his sins should be obvious. "What's all this...crap – Crap! – in your personal logs?"

Tom's stared back at Sanders. "You went through my personal logs?"

"Damn right I did, and a good thing, too. All this talk about how beautiful Aguirra is, all these poetic descriptions about the land, the sky, the birds – the fucking birds? Number One, a lot of this is from Bank's observations. And he's dead as far as we know."

"– I noted where *my* observations are substantiated or reinforced by what Banks transmitted."

"And Number Two, I decide what goes out, not you."

Tom stood for a moment, his face showing the effort of trying to understand. "Wait a minute. Do you mean to tell me you haven't uplinked any of Gordo's transmissions? None of his holos? You had no right – "

"As commander of this mission I made it my right. With all the stress he's been under I had to make sure he could still carry out his duties, didn't I?"

Tom was speechless. He kept his eyes fixed on Sanders. "You had no right. No regulations allow for this."

Sanders grabbed the holo-cube away from the younger man. "What's this that you need uplinked so quickly?" He popped it into a viewer and adjusted the controls. Holos of the Goatmen appeared, life size, between the two men.

The audio came on and I heard my own voice, rich and full, with more life and strength than I'd heard in it before. "It is worth studying the transmitted holos against holos of terrestrial goats. For males of the same age and weight, the goatmen's head is wider, longer, and generally larger, their necks are about the same. With the goat being bigger in the chest by several centimeters. The goatmen are five centimeters taller, eight centimeters longer in the leg and twenty centimeters longer in the body. The goatmen have no tail, and the feet are twice the size of terrestrial goats."

"Captain, I'm demanding a Level Ten Field Transmission. Give me the cube, please."

Sanders hesitated. I think if there'd been a weapon near by he would have used it. Instead he backed away from his console. Tom's fingers raced over the pads then dropped the cube into the reader. He pressed another tab and said, "Append: The decision may be called questionable when taken with respect to any previous transmissions regarding Xenopologist and Acting Mission Redact Gordon Banks. It is my belief, based on many years experience as mission personnel and a long relationship with Banks, the increased responsibility assigned by acting Captain David Sanders has jeopardized both the life of Xenopogist Banks and this mission. At the time of the assignment, Banks was not fully capable nor a totally productive member of the crew. It is my belief that the lack of confrontation with his problem and non-acceptance of his familial status impeded his re-adjustment to *The Merrimack*'s five-man society."

In another step I am on my mission previous. Another step takes me on the mission previous to that. There is a rustling above me and I am standing on sound canopied by Theisen. Part of me fears their singing will stop and another knows it won't.

If you live knowing only a process, you can never have all your options. If you live knowing there are options, one of them can be to partake in the process, they tell me.

I agree.

Would I like to see my world? they ask. I accept. It comes at me like a newsview montage, everything at once, because that is how they feel it. There are little wars claiming the peace, tiny exultations where one doesn't think the other is right. Companies, vast multi-systems, their employment records reading like census briefs from minor and not so minor worlds, deciding political strategies for planet-nations fighting planet-nations. Peace only exists where it generates acceptable profit.

The Theisen tell me no memories come from there now and the montage stops. How so? I ask. Our children there now are not, translates their one word reply.

What? The Earth gone? Were there no warriors for her in all the people I knew there?

They do not.

I am leaving Jeremy one last time. I am playing with him on the gold hills of Teindien.

My leaves are folding through space, mapping it like the back of a hand I don't really have.

I am with Robin at his birth.

My shoots and roots engulf the stars and suns burst from dust, blaze, then grow cold instantly.

I am with Robin.

Mother, father, sister, come quickly then are gone.

Grandparents.

Oceans like worlds and worlds frighteningly like first oceans.

Seeds and vines burst from me and grow free of me. They float through space, gripping worlds and running through them.

My foot lands on churned, moss covered ground.

The singing stops.

Listen. I ask the Theisen. Listen to your children. Don't they call you?

We know not.

Tenku takes my hand. He leads me away. I'm not sure where we're going. My eyes are cataracted with blood and tears.

Tenku wakes me early in the morning. He is as excited as I've ever seen him.

"Where are we going?"

"Yes." He gently butts me.

I know what he means. The nannies are kidding. The field behind the village is littered with nannies on their sides, their legs folded slightly up towards their bellies and their eyes glazed. They do not scream or weep. There seems to be no pain at all. Tenku leads me to Hepob. Gomer is with her.

I ask questions, the xenopologist in me still strong even though I'm sure my transmissions are no longer reaching any ship.

Kids are born one hundred twenty-eight Aguirran days after conception. Kids are always born in the village. They're only single births with twins being very rare and it is unusual for any individual pair to have more than two children. If there is a methodology for deciding which partners will have more kids it alludes me.

It is dawn and the kidding begins. Like popcorn in an old style popper, the plateau pops with the bleats of first one kid then another, the sky filling with bleats and nays and hinnies as the kids pop from their mothers, the air turning first rich then acrid then pungent as puddles of blood and bowel and afterbirth meet the rising sun. The kids' coats are damp, matted flat and mucousy. They steam as they dry. This is perhaps why they are born so early in the day; to ensure their coats being dry and fluffed before the night's cold and rain. Close my eyes and I can hear the nannies' tongues licking, scraping, and cleaning their kids, followed closely by the hollow sucking as the nannies consume the afterbirth.

It is the first time I've seen kids this early in their life. They more closely resemble goats back home –

Home.

Where am I?

There is a cracking sound inside my head and I feel myself drawn into the ground, my spine and legs fused into a trunk and roots reaching deep.

Where am I?

– although their craniums are noticeably larger and the eyes more obviously placed for binocular vision. But male and female kids walk on all fours and follow their mothers around just a few moments after birth, butting their mothers legs, near knocking the nannies over to get at their milk.

Hepob is on her knees before me, a newborn billy nipping her coat to get at her teats. Gomer comes over to me and places his left hand forward. "She is yours now. I have given you a son."

"What?"

He leans forward and grabs my testicles in his hand. His left hand. He takes his hand away then grabs me with his right. He says something, an untranslatable word but now its meaning is clear to me. Home. The untranslatable word is "I-Am-Home." The meaning is not transitive but transcendental. It is an equivalence.

*D*oes this thing work anymore? The lights come on. I know it records. I just don't know if there's anybody listening. Or anyone to listen.

Tenku is dead. Gomer, soon, I think. Age, when it comes, comes quickly to them. Gracefully, though. He has left me his Wa'asis. Hepob is teaching her daughters how to grow and cultivate it. What was once so unique I now know as ordinary. Unlike us, Goatmen mate for life. A mate's passing is announced with a song. I suppose it would be translated as "He/She waits for us" that starts with the mate and finishes when the youngest has chorused that line.

The Theisen are always with me now. They've told me about their technology, one we had long, long ago and forgot because something inside us didn't let the blue-eyed Neanderthals live.

I have blue eyes.

Our technology, they tell me, was developed because we feared the unique, the different, thus we created a science which ultimately made everyone equal without and did nothing to make us equal within. We developed the means to give everyone equality then mocked and mistrusted those who used the means.

How is it here the Neanderthals lived? How come evolution provided no challenges?

A young nanny has asked me to take her to the Theisen. I was afraid of this. As soon as she asked, by a communication I do not yet understand, Gomer was there. "Come," he said. After some walking we are near a cave I recognize but don't know where from. "You go in. I'll stay here and watch."

There is no need for Wa'asis this time, but I take some anyway.

Dutch Courage for what's inside.

I'm climbing the Theisen. There is no indication of how long I've been doing it, although I feel many days and nights have passed. As always with them, I am naked.

Long before I see their tops, I see Aguirra fall away below me. Shortly after, stars dwindle in the distance. Galaxies come and go. Nebulae bathe me then recede. The gravity storms of blackholes and radiation tides of pulsars wash over me without affect as I pass them, one by one.

Still the tops of the Theisen aren't in sight. There is something, though. A barrier of some kind. It is semi-solid, firm yet yielding, and like Ezekiel breaking through to see the mechanisms of the Universe, I go through.

I know where I am. Robin is gone. So is Jeremy. So is *The Merrimack* and her crew. Earth is no more. There is no taste or scent of her.

Definitions are by what, not by who, and at the top of the Theisen the what and the who are one.

I see myself reflected in the whirlpools of this space, a goatman with broken horns staring at me. He waves and smiles.

And I remember. When I was a child. Shopping for Christmas Trees. It was a large lot. A field. Acres and acres of trees. Getting lost. Not hearing my parents voices or the voices of any elders or other children at all.

Just hearing the voices of the trees.

Screaming at what they said. Not wanting to accept or believe but knowing it was true.

I let go of the Theisen and start to fall, unafraid of the descent, knowing where I am and knowing now which direction is down.

I emerge from the cave and know many days have passed. Gomer, my first-friend and -brother, has died outside the cave. Hepob seeks comfort from me and weeps. Between sobs she whispers "He waits for us" and, not understanding, dimly aware, I quietly join in.

*M*y kid is ten years old now. He is strong and fine and makes me proud. Gomer, too, I think is proud. In my dreams he offers to go into Hepob again if I wish another child.

Not yet, I tell him. There is something first I must do.

*T*his tower is cold. Colder than the other. Around me are many billies, one of whom, my kid. Across from us, on the Tower of our People, the other, older, billies have gathered.

The singing starts. The histories come. The young billies around me are scared. They snort and stamp the earth. This Tower is higher and lower than the one across from us. I am in the lead with my son. A column forms, like the root of a great Theisen, reaching out to us. My kid is afraid as we walk across.

I sit atop the Theisen and at the mouth of Denihé's cave, my cave, and watch the skies, waiting and listening for the gentle quaking of a Rumbler leaving a ship, hoping it will wake me if I sleep at night. They always land at night. I remember, when *The Merrimack* came here, waking at the sounds of the Rumbler being dispatched and going to my console, adjusting my Eye until the Rumbler's coal-black combustion flare arced past and made its way through the cold lights of space towards Aguirra.

That was long ago.

Now I aim the transmitter's beacon towards Canis. It is cold. I motion Tika's daughter, Keke, to throw some more of Hepob's blue-green berries into the fire along with some of the Wa'asis I'd left here to season. Keke forces a few berries into my mouth and I swallow without chewing. The berries in the fire ignite like Chinese Tallow, albeit more evenly, and burn white hot as their oxygen catches the flames. I wonder what the berries do to my gut.

"Look. I'm setting it on passive attract. It'll transmit everything in its core once a year. You'll be able to hear it when it transmits, so don't worry.

"But you have to remember to let it remain here, on top of the

Tower, until another Journeyer comes."

Should the Pilgrimage council ever again corridor this world, I want someone to know what they'll find here. Which dream of trees they may destroy. Checking the transmitter's power supply, I pull my survival suit's flaps tighter around me. Most of my own clothes are long tattered and mostly fallen from me. There's not even enough left to provide some dignity if I were to meet another human. Still I wear them, partly out of habit and partly in case anyone else ever comes.

My eyes wander from the power supply readout to the fire. It had burned down again. I remember being in college, back on Earth, and going on an expedition up K2. I'd gone with the goal of climbing to the summit, being able to say I'd been there. At seven-point-five kilometers, with slightly more than another kilometer to the summit, the sherpas gently took me aside, sat me down, said no, told me I could go no further.

"I'm fine."

They pointed to my holometer and shook their heads.

"What? What'd'you mean? I've been taking pictures all the way up. I was just changing picture-paks."

Yes, they nodded. And it had taken me thirty-five minutes to change a picture-pak which, at base camp, I'd done in not even as many seconds.

The fire flickered again, almost out, and Keke grabs a fistful of Hepob's berries, brings them to my mouth and forces them in. I hope their oxygen finds its way into my blood before I pass out for good.

Blue-eyed Keke, Tika's daughter, is beside me without my noticing. Did I black out again? She selects specific pieces of Chigarro and places them on the fire, along with some of her great-grandmother's berries, blows gently and quickly the fire grows. Next she pulls skins of bear-cats I've killed tighter around me and lifts me closer to the flames, propping me by the fire so I squat the way all the males do.

Her hands on me cause me to snap my head up and I leave the Theisen, perhaps for good this time only to join them another. She knows I'm fully with her and I let her move me, her hands, with their two fingers and opposing thumbs, feel good on me. Their natural suppleness and strength massages my blood through me. She takes some berries and raises them over my head.

I'm back with the Theisen, resting comfortably on their tops, outside Ezekiel's machinery, watching Keke and a male of The People, broken horns and with cataracts, far below.

She's trying to feed him something. When he doesn't follow, she forces his chin up and opens his mouth. She massages his throat and he swallows quickly.

He doesn't fight her. He seems barely aware of her.

I feel time slow for him. I feel his life leave him.

He catches her out of the corner of his eye as the fire's flames first silhouette her then flicker to show her features and he wonders, when he can see her, who is this Satan in a snowsuit?

His hand comes up to her hand at his throat and he feels the fur there, so much like the coat Robin wore when he first met her in New York. Her fingers, even now, feel so warm and tender. He remembers his wife, Robin, and wonders, looking at Keke, why is Robin dressed so strange?

Keke, holding the berries over his open mouth, crushes them in one hand even as she holds his head up with the other. He starts to fight her, to struggle, and she increases the pressure, helping him swallow. The black juice from the berries oozes like pitch over her hands and into his mouth. Her fingers and palm sticky with the juice, she shoves her fingers under his tongue, wiping them under, over, and around his tongue and all along the inside of his mouth.

His struggles cease. His eyes clear and color leaves his cheeks. Her eyes tear. She releases her grip on his throat. She sings his song.

Another billy appears beside her as I fall from the trees. It's Jeremy, the dying Goatman's son. There are black streaks down his face, chest, hands, and sides.

MANI HE

MANI HE

Anthony Morelli saw the badger across the street as he came out of South Station, where the MBTA's southern terminus washed people towards One Financial Place. Anthony wore his St. James suit – bright grays with a black pinstripe – with cream oxford shirt and red and gold pumped satin tie, diamond studs, stockings which blended with his trousers, and black wingtips. It was an early Boston Fall and Channel-4 forecasted light drizzle. Morelli's raincoat was draped over his left arm and his accountant's case pulled down his right like a ship's keel in a storm. Today he made the presentation showing the errors in Thompson's plan.

The badger sat on a pretzel wagon. People were buying soft pretzels with mustard, soft pretzels with cheese, soft pretzels with extra salt. The badger was passing small talk and change and nobody else seemed to notice.

Morelli stopped and stared. The smell of coal-cooked chestnuts, peanuts and pretzels came over the diesel and street-level smog of Boston. His mouth watered and he remembered his father teaching him how to flip peanuts and catch them in his mouth.

The badger looked at Tony and hollered, "REDhots! PRETzels! GETcha-GETcha REDhots! PRETzels!"

If Anthony wore his glasses, he'd've adjusted them. Today he wore his contacts but his hands went to his face anyway. The badger waved at him and laughed, mimicking Tony's hand movements. The badger started pedaling his pretzel wagon and rolled away, calling out

"REDhots! GETcha REDhots!"

Tony went into One Financial Place, made his presentation, shook hands, got his back patted, and was thanked personally by the Old Man. Brumhall, the Old Man, looked fifty and was well past seventy-five. His eyes were clear and sharp and his mind had never dulled. Haggedorn, Brumhall's number two, stopped Tony outside Thompson's door. "Anthony, excellent! You planned this? Excellent. Impressed me, right here," Haggedorn tapped his heart. "The Old Man and I gotta talk. It'll be excellent. Thompson. Have to let him go. Too bad. It'll be excellent."

Just then Thompson opened his door, stared at the two men, excused himself, and walked towards the restroom.

Tony looked at Thompson, the way the man's shoulders sagged, the way his chin quivered. Tony swallowed and felt a lump like a badger claw etch its way down his throat, crashing into his stomach like a bus into a pushcart. He wanted to say releasing Thompson wasn't part of his plan. Instead he dug into his pocket for the roll of TUMS his wife, Grace, gave him when he left the house, popped one in his mouth, and made a note to pick up a fresh roll when he went for lunch.

The Old Man came up to them a few moments after Thompson returned to his office. "Mr. Morelli, take the afternoon off. You come in tomorrow, you stop here." Brumhall pointed at Thompson's door and nodded to his number two, acting as if Tony no longer existed. "Mr. Haggedorn." The Old Man opened Thompson's door without knocking.

Haggedorn nodded. Before entering Thompson's office and while the door was opened, he said, "The American Express office. Third Floor. Our branch, right there. Excellent. Stop in there. Big surprise. It'll be excellent."

Tony said, "I need to get my things."

Haggedorn said, "Already taken care of. Third Floor. American Express. Excellent," and closed Thompson's door.

Tony, still stunned and feeling hollow, took the stairs.

There was a Platinum Plus card with the company name on it waiting for him on the third floor. He smiled, lifted the card to his nose and inhaled like it was a roll of bills and he was an old-time gambler. Another whiff and the smell of platinum plastic rubbed the sting of Thompson's misfortune away. "Excellent." He sniffed the card again.

He took a cab home. From the Financial District to dying but ethnic Revere, even though his mail went thirty miles away to a PO box in affluent and upscale Newton. As the cab went through the Callahan Tunnel the lights went out. The cab starting bucking and kicking, as if the gas and brake had suddenly become alien to the burnt-ash-black West Somalian cab driver. The cab started to weave and horns blared in front, in back, and to the sides of them. Tony leaned forward and tapped on the glass. The burnt-ash-black man looked over his shoulder and Tony slumped back into his seat.

The West Somalian driver was a moose, the driver's dreadlocks weaving through the moose's antlers. He bellowed apologetically in the driver's pidgin English, "Sorry. In my country, we have nothing like this."

Outside his home, Tony gave the West Somalian moose a fifty dollar tip. The moose lifted the bill to his nose much as Tony had done with the Platinum card, inhaled, kissed the bill, then inhaled again. He smiled at Tony and Tony thought he said "Ganja." Tony couldn't be sure because there were grasses and weeds dripping from the driver's mouth. He pulled a U-ey, waved at Tony and left.

Tony waved until Grace called him inside. "Why're you home? Are you okay? You didn't get fired, did you?"

He explained. They celebrated. Later, they went to a quiet little bistro back in the North End, a place they knew from childhood, a place where they were part of the family. They spent the day sipping espressos and talking their first generation Italian-American English with Danté, the owner and the man who introduced them. Tony jumped up from his chair and hurried Grace into her coat when Danté brought some antipasto and linguine pesto.

"Anthony, what's wrong?" asked Grace.

"Nothing. I...I don't feel good. Too much strain. I have to go home."

A long, thin, pink tongue snapped out of a lizard's face atop Danté's body. "*Antonio, stai male?*" The lizard said.

Tony's face blanched and he wouldn't look the lizard in the eye. The lizard grabbed the water pitcher and a bowl from an empty table. He put the bowl down in front of Tony and poured some water in it, then sprinkled some olive oil on top of the water and placed the salt shaker beside the bowl. He made the sign of the evil eye and motioned Tony to pick up the salt. "*Malocchio.*" The lizard stared fixedly at the bowl of water and oil, waiting for Tony to finish the evil eye ceremony.

At hearing the intervention against misfortune, Tony looked up again. Danté was once again old Danté, the man they'd both known since childhood. The scaly lizard's face and great round eyes, seen for a moment, were gone. His tongue was hidden in his mouth and not whipping about casting for flies as it had been a moment before.

Not believing in the old ways but honoring his friend, Tony sprinkled some salt in his hand, pressed it to his forehead, made the sign of the Cross with his thumb against his forehead and dipped the thumb into the oily water. The oil separated, fleeing from the salt as it lowered the specific gravity of the water. Tony knew the science but couldn't bring himself to shatter the old man's faith. "*Si, amico mio. Si.*"

Late that night, Tony and Grace lay in bed. "It sounds like you've been working too hard, Tony. I don't mind being rich, but I don't want to be rich alone." She rolled on top of him and straddled him. "You die, Mister, and I'll have somebody else in this bed before your breath is cold."

It was an old joke. They both laughed. Up against the wall on the other side of the room and in a line of sight behind Grace's head, a spider built a web above Tony's closet. Tony's eyes focused and zoomed on the spider as if they were camera lenses. Grace was still laughing and rocking on his hips. He saw the spider look up from her web building, hold a pedipalp in front of her eyes and shake it like a finger, shaking her head, "no", as if in warning.

Then the spider was just a simple spider, building a web. Tony's last thought as he went to sleep was, "How did I know it was a 'she'?"

He woke up before the alarm went off. It was daylight and he saw by the clock he had about ten minutes of sleep left. He rolled over, towards his dresser and away from his wife. The badger was picking through the things on his dresser.

It looked up at him and said, "You got any juju-bees?"

Tony shook his head, no.

"How about toys, you got any toys? Coyote likes toys. That dumb shit's always playing with toys."

Another voice called from the hallway. The voice echoed and Tony knew it was coming from the pulldown stairs that led to the attic. "Found 'em." He heard something bumping up in the rafters then the same voice squealed, "Hey, look at this! Tonkas™! The kid's got Tonkas™!"

The alarm brizzed over Tony's head and Badger said, "See you later, kid. Gotta go."

Grace swacked the alarm silent and said, "Wake up, hon. Time to make me a millionaire."

Tony opened his eyes and reached on his dresser for his glasses. They weren't were he left them the night before. They were shifted a few inches to the right. A coldness shivered him despite the warmth of the bed. On his way to the bathroom he saw the attic stairs bolted and secured in the ceiling and laughed at himself. "Probably got up last night and moved my glasses myself," he mumbled.

In the bathroom he started the shower, turned to the toilet and fell backwards into the tub when he lifted the seat.

Grace called from the bedroom, "You okay, hon?"

"Yeah. Yeah, sure. Just slipped." He turned the shower to cold and held his head under the blast of frigid water. "Okay. I'm awake," he whispered. Drops of cold water trickled down his face, chest and shoulders as he looked back in the toilet. A child's bow and arrow were wedged in the seat.

His old bow and arrow. The bow and arrow which he'd packed under the Tonkas in his toy chest in the attic. The old bow and arrow his grandfather had given him. Holding them he remembered his grandfather's smell, a laborer's smell, his grandfather strong like a farmer. "My people use to be warriors," he once told Tony. "That was long before I met your grandmother." He remembered going to meet other old men with his grandfather, other old men who wore the strange turquoise and silver, bone and bead jewelry his grandfather wore. Then, too soon it seemed, Grandfather John died and the bow and arrow, the old men with the funny jewelry, were no more.

The arrow was rubber tipped and the rubber suction cup was old and cracked. The plastic feathers were stripped in places. The bow was also plastic, with a string made of heavy thread. Feathers and thunderbirds and Indians on horses were painted on the bow. He picked them up and memories of playing Indian as a child came back, as if the memories were waiting like mountain lions in the bow and arrow, waiting to pounce as soon as he touched it.

He lifted the bow and arrow to his shoulder and took aim, hearing himself and others chanting childhood rhymes and verse, mixes of broken English and Hollywood Indians, as he swept the bow and arrow around the bathroom, his arms somehow tiny once again so the toys became big and real and he wasn't Tony Morelli anymore but Little Chief White Feather once again.

He stopped smiling when he took aim at himself in the bathroom mirror. Behind his reflection, a mountain lion pulled back the shower curtain, held out a paw and pointed at the sink. "You wanna hand me the soap there, buddy?"

Tony skipped breakfast and went to work. Haggedorn met him as he got off the elevator at the eighteenth floor. "Anthony. Excellent. New office. Right here. It's yours. It's excellent." It was Thompson's office. A corner office. Two walls of floor-to-ceiling tinted windows with blinds tied to the environmental system. All Anthony had to do was set the amount of light and heat he wanted and the blinds would open and close to accommodate. When necessary, lights and ventilators took up the slack. The name plate on the door – his door, his name. Excellent! – was gold, as was the one on his desk, which was huge. The desk was as big as his bed and the office – his office. Excellent! – was the size of his living room. Along one wall was a multiplexing entertainment system and, at the press of a button, a bar which could rotate from fully alcoholic to totally dry, depending on who you were trying to impress. The other wall had a full length black brocade leather couch. The walls were dark oak, matching the desk. The upholstery of both Tony's chair and the two opposite his desk matched the couch's black. The rug, an inch-thick plush, was gray. He had two computers on his desk and a twenty-channel phone system. The phone's listings were all the ones he'd had in his old office. His accountant's case was there. Along the walls were plants and floral arrangements from various people in the firm and clients he didn't know he had.

As Haggedorn left, the office procession began. Several people came through, all shaking his hand and congratulating him. He looked into their faces as they came and left; this one was too hungry, this one would wait. This one would ally with whoever offered the most, this one would remain loyal.

He stayed late, enjoying the feel of a vibrating, reclining, twelve axes of movement, heated chair and kicked his legs up onto an oak desk so thick it would take six strong men to lift. Somebody knocked on his door. "Yes?"

"Cleaning crew, Mr. Morelli."

Tony checked his watch, a gift from Grace from their dating days when wishes were horses and the two of them rode. "Come on in. You guys don't waste any time, do you? Office has only been closed about an hour."

The door opened and a hawk pushed a cleaning cart into the room. A hummingbird followed in behind the hawk. Both were dressed in clean and neatly pressed "Ace Cleaning Services" uniforms. The hawk's uniform had a white name tag over the right breast pocket which held an Ace Cleaning Services pocket-protector filled with pencils. Stitched in red was "Sparky". The hummingbird was obviously new because he had no pencils and his name was a red-on-white iron-on tag and not stitched in, therefore showing no permanence. He was "Bob". The hummingbird wore earbuds and hummed a tune Tony couldn't place.

"We try not to waste any time, Mr. Morelli," said Sparky the Hawk.

"Sometimes, though, people keep us waiting their whole life."

Hummingbird Bob nodded, "Yeah."

They took out spray bottles and stain removers and went to work.

Haggedorn came in with the Old Man. He looked around the office, told Sparky the Hawk and Hummingbird Bob they were doing a good job and he appreciated their consistency as if there was nothing strange about them, then faced Tony. "You like it here, Mr. Morelli?" asked Brumhall. "This office satisfy you?"

"Yes, sir, thank you. And please call me 'Tony'."

Brumhall nodded slowly, measuring Tony with some internal gauge. "May I see your watch then, Tony?"

"Beg pardon, sir?"

"Your watch."

Tony peeled it from his wrist. Brumhall inspected it. "This watch have any significance to you?"

Tony, his eyes on the watch, swallowed. "No."

"Good." Brumhall tossed the watch into the trash basket on Sparky the Hawk's cart and turned back to Tony. "Mr. Haggedorn."

Tony watched Haggedorn open a black case. Out of the corner of his eye he watched Sparky the Hawk grab Hummingbird Bob's hands as the latter dove for Tony's old watch. Brumhall said nothing until Haggedorn gave Tony the black case.

A new watch. Rivier platinum, with more dials and gauges than Tony imagined he'd find in a fighter cockpit. The back had his name, the date, and "Welcome to The Club."

"You play tennis, Tony?" Brumhall asked.

"No, sir."

Brumhall brow creased. "No? What about Racquetball?"

"No, sir, not that either."

Brumhall turned briefly to Haggedorn then back to Tony. "Golf?"

Tony was about to answer in the negative when Haggedorn interrupted, his voice slightly higher and his face a little whiter than usual, "Outdoorsman. And excellent, Mr. Brumhall. Our Tony. Gun in hand. Right, Tony?"

Before Tony could answer, Haggedorn continued. "Hiking. Camping. Being alone. One man against nature. The outdoor thing. And excellent."

Brumhall considered this for a moment. "You like to hunt?"

Behind Brumhall, Haggedorn stared into Tony's eyes and nodded vigorously. Tony answered, "Yeah."

Hummingbird Bob dropped his spray bottle into the bar's sink. "Sorry."

Brumhall stared at Bob for a second then said, "The company's got a cabin up in New Hampshire." His looked back at Tony, "Did you know that?"

"No sir."

"Is it hunting season, Haggedorn? Is there something he can go up there and kill?"

"Yes, Mr. Brumhall. Something. Something excellent."

"Good. Give him the keys, Haggedorn. Call ahead and make sure he's got provisions for three days. I'll see you on Monday, Mr. Morelli. I'd like to see something strapped to the hood of your car when you come back. Am I understood?" The Old Man's eyes were clear crystals bearing into Tony's face.

"Yes, sir. I think so."

"Good."

*T*ony rolled on the cot and almost fell off. Badger nudged him, "Come on, Mani He. Get up. Grandfather Sun is awake. See? He's yawning and stretching his arms way over the eastern mountains. Get up." Tony mumbled something and rolled back the other way, away from Badger and the sunlight coming in through the cabin window.

"Mani He. Get up. You're the one who wants to take this journey."

Tony reached behind his back and swished his arm back and forth until he felt Badger's warm, soft, thick fur. Then he pushed Badger away.

Badger curled into a ball and rolled with Tony's shove, then came back, ripped off Tony's covers and buried his teeth deep and quick into

Tony's rump.

"Ouch!"

"Ah, you're awake."

Tony sat up and realized suddenly, forcefully, that he wasn't home and he wasn't talking to Grace. He snatched the covers back and held them tightly against him, one hand at his throat and the other at his groin. "You bit me."

"Oh, that I were Coyote. I could look at you and say, 'Me? Never,' with such a straight face. But I am Badger. Now get up." Badger bit Tony again. "Besides, you'll meet Coyote later."

"I'm talking to a badger."

"No, no. You're talking *to* Badger. No 'a'. This is me. I'm it. Now get out of bed."

"Where are we going?" Tony asked as he filled a basin with water and washed.

"I don't know. All I know is that I'm Badger. And it's morning. See?" Badger pointed out the east facing window. "Grandfather Sun is winking at us. Soon he'll be smiling." He stood beside Tony as Tony toweled off. While Tony dressed, Badger pushed the soap down into the water and watched it pop up again. He laughed. It was a chittery sound. "I love this stuff," he said, pushing the soap down again. "Besides, when we find the others, they'll know."

"The others?"

"You don't think I'm going to do this all by myself, do you?"

"Do what?"

"Not what, who. Go."

"Look, I haven't dropped acid since '79 and it was out of place then. You're a hallucination at best, you're work-related stress in the least. I'm going to make myself some breakfast, go into town for a paper, then you'll be gone."

Badger slashed Tony's face with his claws. "Get going or I do the other cheek." He raised his other paw.

"I'm up, I'm up."

"Ah, yes. Give them a little pain and they'll believe anything."

"Where are we going?"

Badger sighed. "Follow your nose, Two-Legs."

"Are you going to bite me again?"

"Not unless I have to. You don't taste too good. Besides, my nose is much longer than yours and I follow it. It doesn't usually get me in trouble. You have eyes, too, you know. I wouldn't expect you to listen to just me, why should I expect you to listen to just your nose? Now," Badger pulled back a paw. There was a slight click as his claws spread, "You going to move, or what?"

"I'm talking to a fucking badger."

Badger hissed at him.

"To Badger. I'm talking *to* Badger."

They'd walked through the forest with Tony in the lead most of the morning, up hill and down yet never leaving the mountains. Near noon Tony stopped. "Okay, that's it."

Badger stood beside him and looked around. "What's 'it'?"

"Where's the cabin?"

"The cabin?"

"Yes, the place where we started."

"Gee, Mani He, you've got lots of traveling to do before you can get back to where you started."

"Listen, Badger, or whoever you are, I've purposely walked in a big circle –"

"Good for you!"

"– and I know we should have reached the cabin by now. Where is it?"

"I'm glad you're interested in circles, Mani He, but we can't create them. All we can do is become aware of them and make good use of them. Besides, with me, with you, we go east."

"Do we ever stop to eat?"

"Plenty of things to eat, Mani He." Badger pointed at the beetles, snakes, mice, and other things crawling around them.

"You expect me to catch things?"

"You expect me to feed you?"

"What am I suppose to do, then?"

"You can do what I do, if you want. It works for me." Badger closed his eyes briefly. When he opened them, a small snake scurried in front of him. He snatched it up and put it in his mouth. Half the snakes body whirled around his nose as he crunched the other half. "See?"

"No, thanks."

By late afternoon they'd traversed what seemed like several mountains. Tony wasn't even sure if they were still in New Hampshire. "Can we take a break. I'm tired."

"Hmm. Grandfather Sun is almost home. Are you a little bit tired or a lot tired, Mani He?"

"Grandfather Sun?"

"Not tired at all, eh?"

"Just a little tired. Maybe. And what's 'Mani He' mean?"

Badger stopped and stared at him. "It means you, Mani He. I mean, it must. You answer to it."

"Yeah, right. But what do the words mean? For all I know, you could be calling me 'shithead'."

"No, no, no, Mani He. That would be 'ceslí natá'. Trust me. There's a difference."

Eventually they stopped at the edge of a marsh so vast Tony couldn't see the other side. "A marsh? We're still on the top of the mountains! Where'd it come from? And what'm I suppose to do, cross it? Look, I'm tired. I need to rest."

"Oh, so now you're a lot tired. Okay. We'll rest. Besides, we're here." Badger lay down and patted the ground beside him.

"Anything I can eat here?" asked Tony.

Moose rose from the marsh and stood on legs like tree trunks. He bellowed deep and resonant. The sound made Tony tremble and cover his ears. Badger rolled on his back and laughed.

"Plenty to eat here," said Moose. Moose dipped his head down and came up with all sorts of grasses and twigs hanging from his mouth, mixing with his beard and dripping down. "But first you must ask."

"Ask you?"

"No, no. Ask who you're going to eat. When I'm hungry, I ask the Standing People," said Moose, nodding at the trees. "They tell me which is safe and which isn't. Sometimes they play tricks and make me a little crazy, sometimes and just a little. Sometimes, when I don't ask, they reach down and grab me by my antlers until I apologize. Sometimes they get bored and grab my antlers anyway. Then I bite them, nibbling off their bark so they'll have something to talk about. Sometimes I rub my antlers against them to make them raw. I do that when the Standing People act too wise.

"But when I eat, I ask, and they show me."

"Badger never asks."

"Yes, I do," said Badger.

"I never heard you."

"You never listened. That's why you went hungry all day. You never asked."

"How come you never told me this?"

"Hey, people who don't ask for what they want deserve what they get. Besides, I teach you my lessons," Badger pointed to Moose, "he teaches you his."

"Okay then, I want to go home."

"Which is exactly where we're taking you," Badger said.

Now Moose laughed. The sound was deep and wide and moved through the marsh like ripples on a pond.

"So what happens now?" Tony asked Badger. "Do you leave and I go with him?"

Moose turned to Badger. "Did you tell him about his eyes and his nose?"

"A-yuh, I did."

Moose turned back. "Who are you?"

Tony folded his arms across his chest, "Anthony David Morelli."

Badger's claws clicked open and Tony held his hands up. "Don't worry, Mani He. No wounding this time. You have to decide who you are, who you'll be. That's always been up to you."

Tony looked at his watch. "Mani He?" he whispered.

Badger smiled over Tony's shoulder and Moose looked back at him. "That's a real fancy watch, Little One, but I don't think it can answer you."

"I just remembered. 'Mani He' was what my grandfather use to call me. What's it mean?"

Grandfather Sun fell over the western mountains just as Grandmother Moon came up in the east. "Badger, Moose, who is that with you?"

"He's finding out, Grandmother," said Moose.

"Oh. I thought it might be Grandfather Sun disguising himself again."

"No, no, Grandmother. If this were Grandfather Sun," said Badger pointing at Tony, "I would have burnt my tongue when I bit him."

"He went that-a-way," offered Tony. Standing behind him, Badger held his paw low and palm up. Moose gave him five and both smiled.

"Thank you, grandchild."

Tony snapped the watchband against his wrist. "Are you looking for Grandfather Sun?"

Moose held his hoof out and Badger returned the five.

"Of course. He either chases me or I chase him. Often, when it is my time, I hide. Then my magic is strong and might kill him, and without him where would the Day-Eyes be? Once in a while we embrace. If I catch him the sky goes dark as I bring Night with me. Sometimes he catches me and I cover my face to delight him. Always, when we embrace, we make our children."

"Your children?"

Grandmother Moon laughed and it covered the marsh like feather-blown rain, "Great Star Nation, Mani He. They are our children." She laughed and continued on her way.

Badger and Moose called out, "Good night, Grandmother. Happy hunting!"

A moment later Tony whispered, "Good night, Grandmother."

Grandfather Sun was just starting to reach over the east when Tony woke up sneezing and cold. Beside him was a heavy blanket or rug, he didn't know which. He tried to slide under it. It didn't budge. The rug smelled like a swamp, but it wasn't wet or damp or even mildewy. Despite its smell, it was warm. "Stinking or not, I'm cold." He gave the rug a firm tug.

"Ouch!" bellowed Moose. He rose and peered down at Tony, now quivering with more than the cold. "You wake up a little bit grumpy?"

"It wasn't a dream."

"No," said Moose. "I think you really pinched me." He waded into the marsh. "You hungry?"

"Yeah, kinda."

"You remember your lessons from yesterday?"

"Yeah, yeah. Okay, who do I ask?"

"Who's the one being you know you can always trust, Mani He?"

"I don't know. God?"

Moose kept walking into the marsh. Tony hesitated in the early dawn as Moose moved into the still, gray shadows. Soon Moose would be out of sight. Tony, kneeling at the edge of the swamp, slammed his fists into the mud. "Damn it, this is crazy."

Moose called over his shoulder, "You think this is crazy, you wait 'till Coyote."

Tony waded into the swamp. "Can we wait until it's light out?"

"We could. Or you could use your feet to feel ahead of you. When you feel firm footing, step. When you don't, keep feeling until you do."

"Is this part of that follow your eyes and nose stuff?"

"Good boy, Mani He. Everyday a new lesson." Moose dipped his mouth into the marsh to drink and blew bubbles through his nose. When he lifted his head, water dribbled down his chin and beard and mucous globbed under his nostrils. He licked them clean with his tongue.

Tony, up to his chest in the marsh, stopped beside him. "Eeech."

Moose smiled, revealing lots of stump-grinding teeth. "Bet you wish you looked this good in the morning, huh? Now, where's this god you're talking about?"

"I don't know. Up in the sky, I guess. Heaven. You know?"

"And you're in touch with this god a lot?"

"Well, that's the idea, anyway."

"This god ever steer you wrong?"

Tony stammered, "Well, uh, you see...What am I talking philosophy with a moose for?"

Moose gently nudged Tony with an antler. "Mani He, if you learn no other lessons, learn that those you meet on this journey take no indefinite articles. In fact, every thing else is a pale and shadowy image of the real thing. Brother Badger is more real than any you'll ever find in a woods. I am what all other moose are compared to. If nothing else, learn that lesson well."

Tony considered this as they sludged through the marsh. "I'm cold."

"It's those wet clothes, Mani He. You'd be warmer if you took them off."

"You mean, get naked?"

"What, you think you got something you can brag to me about?"

"Well, no, I –"

"Trust me, Mani He. The sooner you get naked on this journey, the better off you'll be."

"Okay. We were talking about God. If things are working right, you do what God wants. If things aren't working right, you go ask God for forgiveness."

"Do I have this right? If things are cool, you give your god the credit. If things aren't cool, you take the blame?"

Tony nodded.

"Nice deal. I'd like to be your god. Mani He, I don't think it's fair to divide the 'attaboys' and the 'ohshits' up like that. If things are going well and you give this god the credit, give that same god the credit when things suck. The other antler is to take all the credit for the 'attaboys' and 'ohshits' yourself. There's lots in between, of course, but I'd go for that last one."

"So who do I ask for food?"

"You got to grab that antler, son, then you'll know."

Tony grabbed Moose's right antler. "This one?"

Moose stared at Tony a second. He smiled and his smile broke into laughter. Ripples moved across the surface of the marsh. Moose laughed harder and the ripples became waves. Tony felt the winds from Moose's laughter lift him and he held tightly to both antlers as he and Moose flew through the air to the far southern shore of the marsh.

Grandfather Sun was now mid-morning in the sky and Moose was lying beside a fire. There was a spit with some smoking meat over the flames, Moose took one end of the spit and turned it in his mouth.

"Where'd this come from?"

Moose mumbled, "You trusted and showed innocence, Mani He. You learned the lesson faster than I could have taught it, although you probably don't know what lesson you learned." He lifted the spit from the flames and mouthed it to Tony. "Here. eat."

Tony was too hungry to argue. He tore at the still smoking meat with his teeth and nails, letting the juices bleed down his cheeks, neck, and chest. "This is good. What is it?"

"The only thing I can offer, Mani He; moose."

Tony gagged as some of the meat stuck in his throat. "Oh, Christ. I didn't know. I'm sorry. Oh, Christ."

"Mani He, it's okay. I offered. You probably don't know it, but in your innocence, you asked."

"So if I'm hungry again, and I want to eat moosemeat, I should ask a moose to let me eat it?"

"No, Mani He. You should ask me to provide you with a moose. You're not eating me. I'm not one to give my body so easily. But I will give you one of my shadows, probably one who can walk no further or who grows too tired to see Grandfather Sun again, one who is willing and ready to leave the Red Path and follow the Blue.

"But always you must ask. If you take without asking, soon I leave, just go away."

"Go where?"

"Just go, Mani He, go where even Grandfather Sun can't find me, to a place where I'll cast no more shadows. It is like that for all of us."

Mani He placed the spit and remaining meat over the fire. "Brother Moose, I am hungry. May I ... Is it alright if I ... I'm new at this so bear with me; can I eat this?"

"Surely, Mani He. Partake and enjoy."

It didn't take him long to finish. He kept the fire going until Grandfather Sun had set, then stoked it large. He lay on his back, his feet towards the flames. Soon Great Star Nation appeared. "Where is Grandmother?" he asked.

"I don't know, Mani He. She comes when she comes."

Suddenly Tony sat up. "What the hell am I doing? Tomorrow's Monday. I've got to get back to the office. I've got to kill something." He stared over the fire to Moose.

"You can ask, but I'll give you no more because I know you're not hungry or cold. Hopefully, though, by the time we're done, something will be dead. That's the whole point of this. Don't worry. These are the real days, everything else is a shadow. When you return, you will have never been away."

Slightly more at ease, Tony asked, "So what happens tomorrow?"

"See those mountains in the west? That's tomorrow."

Tony put more wood on the fire and went to sleep.

He awoke feeling limp and powerless. The weight of his body hung from his neck. The ground, about a foot beneath his feet, was moving rapidly and he could see enough of what was in front of him to know he was going uphill. Occasionally he caught a glimpse of great catlike paws silently slapping the earth under him but he couldn't turn to see what beast it was. Hot breath coated his back and neck and he felt a gentle shaking run through him.

Something chewed delicately on his neck and he heard a low, sultry, muffled female voice ask, "You awake now?"

"Uh-huh."

The grip on his neck released and he fell to the ground. "Hold on while I tidy you up and get your circulation going." A wet, fleshy rasp gently scraped up his back and bobbed his head from side to side. "What the –," he looked up and screamed.

Mountain Lion leapt back and spun with her back to him, snarling and baring her fangs and claws, her hair raised and her tail poofed. After a few moments she sniffed the air then turned back to him. "What was it, Mani He? I see nothing." She approached him quietly, with lidded eyes. When she was close enough she sat and stared off into space, as if watching something he couldn't see, then licked one of her paws. Her head snapped at him suddenly, as if she'd just noticed he was there and she stretched close enough to kiss him. One paw fell on his leg. Her eyes defocused and she sniffed him, her nose twitching with each breath. She purred, huskily and heavily. "What'd you scream for, child? There's no one here but us. I might kill you, but before I do that I'll love you." She rasped him lightly with her tongue, starting at his belly and running up his chest.

There was something in her eyes, something in the heat and sweetness of her breath, that blurred Tony's vision.

She licked him again, running her tongue up the inside of his legs. "What is your name, child?"

He felt an erection growing and told himself it was a dream, a bad trip, too much Scotch and not enough water. He shook his head until it cleared. "Mani He. Are you my teacher today?"

Mountain Lion purred and laughed, flashing her teeth and pulling her whiskers back flush against her face. It didn't make him feel better. "Today and everyday, Mani He. Just like everyone else." She rolled onto her back and stretched, revealing her white furred stomach to him. "Be a dear and give a scratch, would you, love?"

He did and was surprised. The fur was much coarser than he thought it would be.

"Mmmm," she purred. "We decided to do it this way because we thought it best for you. Not all the lessons at once, you know. You did good, Mani He. If you gave me your shadow name I'd've killed you."

"That'd be one hell of a lesson!"

She rolled away from him and stood up, paused and licked her side where it had touched the ground. "A powerful lesson, yes." She started walking further into the hills and he followed. She called over her shoulder, "But this you'd learn anyway, and probably too late; If you continue to live only in shadow, you'll die."

After a day of walking further up the mountain, Mani He sat on a rock and rubbed his thighs and calves.

"What's wrong, Mani He? Why have you stopped?"

Mani He tried to stand and fell back to the rock. "Mother, I can't go on. I have to rest. My legs are burning worse than an hour on a StairMaster at max." He squeezed his thighs with his hands and sighed. "We've walked up these trails all day but we don't seem any higher or deeper than when we started." He tried to stand again and fell forward with his first step.

Mountain Lion padded back to the rock on which he sat. "You called me 'Mother'. Thank you." She brushed his face with her whiskers then groomed his sweat from them. "What made you call me mother, Mani He?"

"I don't know. I just came out of me, I guess."

"Excellent, Mani He. You've learned another lesson, child."

"Then maybe you can carry me like you did this morning?"

Mountain Lion laughed. "You've grown far too big for that already, Mani He." Her eyes widened as she stared at him. Her irises pulled open and wide until he could hardly see them. "Besides, now we do something else."

Before Mani He could move, Mountain Lion swiped across his belly with her paw. Her claws opened him up in five shreds. He looked down in shock as his stomach and intestines began to spill out.

He screamed and began shoveling his entrails back into his body as the blood drained from him.

"No!" hissed Mountain Lion. She knocked him on his back and rested a paw on each of his arms so he couldn't move.

"Get off, you dumb bitch," Tony screamed back. "I'm going to die. You killed me, god damn you." He turned his head and saw his stomach and blood sliding down the mountain trail.

"Relax, Mani He. What kind of a mother do you think I am?"

He struggled less, although he wasn't sure if it was because of lack of blood or what Mountain Lion said. Shortly he stopped. The pain, intolerable at first, was gone. She got off and he looked at his gut. There were no marks, no blood. Nothing. It looked fine. Actually, it looked better. A word from the gym came to him and he fought not to laugh – he looked "ripped".

"Am I dead?"

"Hardly, child. How do you feel?"

"I feel great." He patted his abdomen and chest. Next he patted his buttocks and, trying to be demure, ran a hand over his crotch.

"Don't worry, Mani He. Everything's where it's suppose to be."

"What did you do to me?"

"Do you think you can continue walking now?"

He nodded, surprised at the strength he felt.

"That, little Mani He, is what I did to you. You must remember, none of us will ever harm you. We're way different from most Two-Legs when it comes to that. What I did may have hurt you, but only because you had to let something out before you could let something in."

Again they walked. Grandmother Moon was well up and smiled upon them, lighting the path to help Mani He see where he might trip. "I'm not tired, Mother, just curious. How much further is it?"

Mountain Lion, who now walked beside him, said, "That depends on you, little one."

"You mean I can rest if I want to and you won't cut me?"

"You can do whatever you want and I'll make no promises. We walk to the West. Walk far enough and you'll find the place where your Red Path and your Blue Path meet, where this life goes into the next. But we also walk to where ever you want to go. You have to decide where you want to go and how far you're willing to walk to get there.

"I'll tell you now, though, child. You've walked as far as you can as you are. If you want to walk further, if you feel where you want to go isn't where you are, you'll have to let more of where you want to go in."

"That sounds like a riddle, Mother. Is it a riddle?"

"Only to those who can't understand it."

In her eyes, Mani He saw his own reflection and that of Grandmother Moon. He saw himself nod and, as Mountain Lion's eyes followed him, lay down on his back, his stomach exposed.

"Are you afraid, Mani He?" she asked, her whiskers again brushing him.

"Yes, Mother. A little. I'm a little afraid."

"It's okay to be afraid, little one. It's okay." Mountain Lion nuzzled her way under him so she made a comfortable cushion and blanket for his back and head. "When you awake, I'll be gone, Mani He. Another awaits you."

"I understand, Mother. Thank you."

She licked his face and her breath covered him like a warm perfume. He closed his eyes and cried out only once, when her claws ripped open his ribs and pulled out his heart.

Grandfather Sun was high to the south when Mani He awoke. He was on his back, stretched out on what felt like a huge rock. Before moving, he felt for scars and wounds. There were none. He sat up and saw he was on a plain, not a mountain any longer, like a desert with cactus and weathered stone outcroppings everywhere. He started to roll off the rock when a long, heavy, white, brown, and yellow scaled tail knocked him back against the rock.

"Where'd you think you're going?"

He rolled over. The tail, attached to some kind of crocodile or alligator or gila monster or something, made moving difficult. Whatever it was, it rolled its eyes and yawned as a fly came past. A long, pink tongue, sticky with mucous, whipped out and brought the fly back into the mouth. The creature's eyes rolled forward and it burped. "Excuse me." The tongue came back out and licked its right eye. "So, where'd you think you're going?"

"I'm hungry and thirsty. I wanted to get some food and water."

"Plenty of flies." Its tongue whipped another fly back into its mouth.

"No, thank you." He felt something crawling at his feet. A small lizard waited there, flattened against the rock. "We can only give each other who we are, not even what," said the creature.

Remembering Moose's lesson, he asked. "Are you Lizard?"

"Very good, Mani He."

"May I eat, uh...May I?"

"Enjoy."

Mani He snatched the lizard and, quickly breaking the neck, swallowed it whole.

"So you're Lizard?

"Yes, I'm the original."

"Is it that way with all my teachers?"

Lizard laughed. When he laughed his eyes rolled back and his tongue snapped out flat on the rock. "It's that way with any teacher, Mani He." Lizard shifted himself to a warmer part of the rock. "And as soon as you stop thinking you know what you want to learn, everything becomes your teacher. Truth waits for eyes unclouded by longing."

"So what are you going to teach me?"

"To be quiet and enjoy a good, warm rock." Which is how they spent the entire day, dozing on their rock until Grandfather Sun kissed the mountains to the west.

"May I ask you a question, Father?"

"May you not?"

"If this were a dream, would you teachers be Jungian archetypes?"

"Can you dream a dream? Is that the question, little one?" Lizard's tongue whipped back in and out as a fly buzzed past. He burped and laughed. "You have to answer that for yourself, Mani He. We believe the only limits people have are those they put on themselves."

Mani He's head ached. He let the pain go and said, "I'm getting cold, Father. How can we stay warm?"

"Tonight you stay warm the way I do; you crawl under a rock and into the sand."

Mani He considered the heaviness of the rock and the scratchiness of the sand. "I'm not sure I can do that."

"You have to be like me. What you have to do is let the me inside of you out."

"Is this going to be like Mother did last night?" Mani He looked at Lizard's claws and teeth.

"Sorry, Mani He. This one you've got to do yourself. But I'll give you a hint: Every one of your teachers is."

"Is what?"

Lizard crawled off the rock and buried himself in the sand.

"Father, don't leave me here. Help me. Please?"

Lizard's tail flicked out of the sand and, like someone beckoning with their finger, invited him into the ground.

Mani He cried out, lonely in the cold desert night, "I can't. I don't know how." He didn't know if Lizard heard him. He sat against the warmest side of the rock and cried.

"What is wrong, grandchild?"

Tony opened his eyes, realizing he'd fallen asleep against the rock and was now bathed in moonlight. His body was curled tightly into a ball and still he shivered. Even as he slept, tears covered his face and he whimpered through his dreams.

"Father Lizard left me here in the cold. He told me to follow him but I don't know how."

"Stand up, Mani He, and walk towards me."

Without thinking, Mani He stood and walked towards Grandmother Moon. "Will you show me how to stay warm?"

"Quickly, Mani He, how did you do that?"

"Do what?"

"Look behind you and see." She shined bright beams of moonlight on his footprints in the sand.

"Do what? Walk?"

"Exactly."

"I don't know, I just did it."

"And that's how you should follow Lizard."

"I don't understand."

Lizard's tongue lashed out and flicked back a scorpion crawling on the rock. "She means you should just do what I do. Don't think about it. Like walking. You don't think about walking when you do it. You just do it. Not everything works that way, though. Some lessons are learned by doing, some by thinking, some by feeling, some by seeing, tasting, sniffing, hearing, still others by teaching."

"I thought you were somewhere in the sand."

"No. When you didn't follow, I came back onto this rock, to protect you from other things which might come in the night."

"I didn't see you. Were you there all along?"

"Yes, just as soon as you didn't follow. Your fear blinded your eyes to me. Did you forget Mountain Lion's lesson?"

Mani He lowered his eyes. "Forgive me?"

"It's not my lesson to forgive. You'll have to ask her to forgive her lessons forgotten."

"Will I see her again?"

Grandmother Moon washed the sand from him with bright light. "I'm sure. Now I must go. Grandfather awaits."

Mani He waved as Grandmother continued her journey through Great Star Nation. Lizard dropped off the rock and, with a wiggle and a shake, dove under the sand. Mani He jumped as if from a diving board and, wiggling and shaking the best he could, followed Lizard to where the sand was a warm blanket protecting him from the night.

He awoke the next morning on a high desert plateau to the feel of warm water and the smell of strong urine on his neck and chest. He sat up quickly. Coyote lowered his leg and said, "You're my little puppy now," then rolled over, tucking his legs into his belly and laughing.

Mani He didn't know if this was the same desert he'd met Lizard in. He was high up. It felt higher than even Mountain Lion had brought him. The edge of the plateau wasn't far off and Mani He started towards it.

They were indeed high up. So high, in fact, that Grandfather Sun moved through the skies beneath them. Far to the west and below, Mani He saw Grandmother Moon going beyond the mountains. On the northern and southern horizons he saw the people of Great Star Nation. Tony stared at Coyote with respect and awe. "Are you the greatest of all my teachers?"

Coyote puffed up his chest. "Of course I am." Then he laughed again, but this time not so deeply, more tenderly. "No, I can't do that to you, little Mani He. I'm not the greatest of them all. None of us are. I'm just your teacher for this lesson, same as Badger, same as Lizard." He paused and looked over his shoulder, then whispered conspiratorially, "Of course, if you want to act like I am, we'll get along a lot better." Coyote looked into Mani He's face and once again belly laughed, now so hard his eyes teared with his mirth. After a few minutes he stopped and wiped his eyes with a paw. "Come on, kid. Lighten up."

Mani He asked, "What's today's lesson?"

"This is it."

"What's it?"

"This is. This plain. This plateau. Where it is is what it is, and why it is me is how it is for you."

"You forgot 'when'."

"No, little one, I didn't. But since you asked, when is now and now is always."

"You like riddles, don't you?"

"Do you always hide in shadows when you don't know what's going on? And that's not a riddle. Even Lizard stays out in the sun in the middle of the day."

"You're right. I'm sorry. I don't understand what you mean."

"Good. When you're confused – and you're willing – we can teach you. Now, come back from the edge before you fall. We've got places to meet and people to be." Coyote howled at his joke and his voice carried across the plateau.

"Don't you mean...oh, forget it."

They came to the middle of the plain. "Sit," Coyote said. "Now, look up. What do you see?"

"Nothing. It's dark."

"Such a bright boy. Look down."

"Yeah, it's dirt."

"Two for two. Good. Now comes the tough one. Look around you."

The plateau was covered with balls of light, some small, some big, some bright, some dark. They came in all different colors. Some looked like they had acne. "If I didn't know any better, I'd say these things were stars."

Just then one of the balls of light flew up to his face. He could feel its warmth and had to shield his eyes from its light. "Greetings, Mani He."

Mani He looked under his hand to Coyote and back.

"Say 'hello', Mani He."

Mani He held out his hand. "Hello". The bright object hopped into it and he felt himself grow light, as if a wind might blow him away. "What's going on, Coyote?"

More of them came around, covering Mani He in their light and warmth. Each one greeted him, each in a different voice. Some voices were like children's, some were like adults. Some spoke like grandparents and some spoke like mothers and fathers speak to a newborn.

"Coyote, I'm afraid."

"Really?" Coyote said it deadpan.

"Help me."

"Tell me what's going on."

"All these...these...these things are covering me. Their light is blinding me and their heat is burning me. I can't breathe."

Coyote spoke from behind him, "Wow, that sounds horrible."

More and more of the objects surrounded him. Mani He felt himself go higher and higher into the air. "I'm going to fall. Make them stop!"

Coyote's voice came from his side. "Might kill yourself from that height."

One of the bright objects popped in Mani He's mouth as he was about to speak and he gagged. "I'm dying," he cried.

Coyote spoke from his other side, "Badger warned me about this."

"Help me!"

Coyote was once again in front. "You don't need my help, Mani He. You're doing a fine job of tricking yourself without my having to do a thing."

"Are you up in the air with me?"

"Nyes."

"Which is it, damn it? No or Yes?" He felt teeth sink into his thigh and yelled at the pain.

"Watch it," Coyote said.

One of the bright objects whirled into the wound. The pain left.

The wound was cleaned and sealed and the bright object asked, "Better, Mani He?"

"Yes." He felt his thigh and realized no harm was done. "Thank you." More of the objects swarmed over him. "Coyote, I don't know which you mean, no or yes."

"Not 'either-or', Mani He, 'Both-and'."

"Both-and? No and Yes? You are up in the air but not with me?"

"You're cold."

"You're with me and I'm not up in the air?"

"And Moose said you'd be trouble."

"But I feel light."

The objects chorused, "Thank you, Mani He."

"They are stars!"

The stars pulled away from him. He saw Coyote in their light, sitting outside of them and spitting something onto the ground.

"What's wrong, Coyote?"

"Badger was right. You don't taste good." Coyote walked into the circle of light with Mani He. "Now, son, let's take an inventory. You thought you were dying. Are you dead?"

"No."

"Are you in the air, flying around?"

"No."

"Did you suffocate or have any other real trouble breathing?"

Mani He took a deep breath. "No, not really."

"You got any burns?"

He shook his head, no.

"How about blind? You blind?"

Mani He lowered his face and continued to shake his head.

"Did you blow away?"

"No, no, and no."

"Feel pretty foolish, don't you?"

Mani He stopped shaking his head and sighed. "Yep. Sure do, by golly. Big joke on Mani He, right?"

Coyote jumped up and licked Mani He's face. "That's for knowing your name. Know what I do when I feel foolish?"

Mani He shook his head again.

"I throw back my head and laugh. It's the best thing for you. Try it. Like this." Coyote howled. He howled and laughed so hard he started hacking and coughing. "Quit smoking!" He yelled at himself, which only sent him laughing more and more. "Come on, Mani He. Try it. Throw back your head and laugh. Laugh at yourself. It's the best thing for you and you're probably the only one who knows how funny you really are."

He started with a soft chuckle. The stars, who had been quiet throughout this, began to chuckle as well. A few minutes later he was on his back and clutching his sides, rollicking at fears he'd given himself, fears and beliefs which he had no evidence of but which ruled him anyway. The stars joined him, rolling and laughing. Their laughter came out as different colors in their lights. He saw and heard himself reflected in each one and laughed at that, as well.

Eventually he quieted. Coyote said, "Feels good, doesn't it? To not take yourself so seriously?"

"Yes, it does."

"Good, Little One, good. Come on, now. Time for us to go." Coyote headed them towards the edge of the plateau.

The stars called out. "Good bye, Coyote. Good bye, Mani He. Remember us and come back when you need to. We're here any time you need us."

Coyote called back to the stars as they neared the edge of the plateau. "Thanks, guys. That was great, really. We'll do lunch." He howled again.

At the edge Coyote said, "Remember this always, Mani He. You came from the stars and you'll return there. Honor them. No joke. Whenever you need to get to them, or anywhere, anywhere other than where you are, you close your eyes and come get me. Okay? Some places, they'll be like nightmares. Other places, they'll be like your sweetest dreams. Go towards your sweetest dreams, Mani He. Stay away from the nightmares. And always – Always! – know which is which. Got it?"

"Got it."

"Good. Have fun tomorrow," Coyote said and hip-checked Mani He over the edge.

As he fell into the sky Mani He heard Coyote call after him, "Sleep well, Mani He, and don't worry. Remember what Mountain Lion taught you."

Mani He screamed, "I'm afraid," and his voice faded as he plummeted through the clouds.

Mani He woke to a gentle swinging motion, a rocking. He was in a branch-lined hole somewhere. The hole was about twelve feet across at the top and nicely bowl-shaped. He climbed on the larger branches to the top. When he cleared the top of the bowl, he froze.

It wasn't a hole in the ground. It was a nest in a tree.

"I'm not sure I want to know what kind of bird builds a nest this big."

A whirlwind caught him from behind with winds so strong and steady he had to clutch the branches to keep from toppling out of the nest to the ground.

"Obviously," came a great bass voice from the direction of the wind, "a great big bird."

"Are you my teacher?" Mani He hollered.

The booming bass voice and blasts of wind continued. He had to hold the branches tighter and tuck himself into a ball not to fall. "Are you my student? Turn around and let's find out."

Mani He let go of the branches and slid back down to the bottom.

The bass voice laughed. Two huge claws, each big enough to crush him if he was caught in them, clamped onto the far side of the nest's rim. Two huge wings, wings broad and strong enough to blot out the sky, stopped beating and tucked against the great bird's brilliant blue and orange body. Two eyes large and round as auto wheels and black as skyless night stared at him. The bird had a long beak like a spear, and Mani He knew it could pierce him before he could move.

"What kind of bird are you?"

"Let's get down and you tell me." The huge wings began beating so fast Mani He couldn't see them any longer. The bird flew up and grabbed him in its terrible claws, lifting him and carrying him to the ground.

The winds grew less and less as they got closer to the ground. When they touched down, Mani He turned and his eyes went wide. "Bob?"

The great bird was a tiny hummingbird, flitting and flighting back and forth before his eyes.

"Howdy, Mani He. How you doing today?"

"But you looked so big before."

"Of course, I did. That's because I am. Even more so when you're in my nest."

"Did you get smaller or did I get bigger?"

"Nyes."

"Got'cha. What're we doing today?"

Hummingbird flew up and said, "Brothers and Sisters, attend!"

The trees moved closer. "This is like Great Star Nation, right?"

Hummingbird stared apologetically. "Well, no. These are The Standing People."

Mani He was surrounded by various "Hi'"s, "Hello'"s, and "How are ya'"s.

"They're part of what you have to learn today."

Various vines and flowers grew up along the trunks of The Standing People. Hummingbird sang as he flew among them, dipping his beak into the flowers and sucking out the sweet nectar. Mani He followed him and did likewise. Before he dipped his head into each flower and as he stood before each tree he whispered something Hummingbird couldn't hear.

"What are you saying, Mani He?"

"I'm...uh...I'm asking the flowers if I can drink their nectar, and The Standing People if it's okay."

The Standing People concurred with various "Yep'"s, "Huh-uh'"s, and "Sure is'"s.

"Good," said Hummingbird. "You're remembering what we teach you. Remember it forever and you'll be here always, any time you want and any time you need."

Grandfather Sun, directly overhead, reached his sunlight over all The Standing People. They twisted and turned and lifted their branches and leaves and flowers up to him.

"Hello, Grandfather."

"What are you learning today, grandson?"

"I don't know."

"Good," said Hummingbird. "A perfect place to start. Look at The Standing People."

Mani He watched the trees and plants and flowers, all the green things of life, bury their roots deeper into the soil while they waved their branches and leaves and flowers higher into the sky. All the while they sang and smiled and delighted in the richness of the earth and the warmth of the skies, showering Hummingbird and Mani He in seeds.

Mani He picked up a handful of the seeds of the different trees and flowers and was startled when an old willow spoke to him. "Our seeds are our ideas, Mani He. Changes in our lives are the children they bring."

"It's wonderful," he said.

"Yes," agreed Hummingbird. "It is. Now, do you know where you want to go? You don't have to tell me. I already know. All that's important here is that you know."

"Well, I, kind of. I think so."

"Is there a problem?"

"I'm not sure how to get there."

Hummingbird laughed. "That's okay. That's not what I asked. All that's important right now is, do you know where you want to go."

"Yes."

"Do you know where you are?"

Mani He thought for a moment. "Yes."

"Good. Here's your lesson. Take what you learned from The Standing People and remember it always. Take what you learned from me and throw in a little Coyote – not too much. Laugh at your own joke but don't be your own joke – and remember that you heard my song and The Standing People's song together. Keep all those together and your feet will lead you where ever you want to go. Just like Badger, only now you don't have to know the direction. The direction will know you."

The Standing People parted to show a path lighted by the first rays of Grandmother Moon.

"Go ahead," said Hummingbird. "That's part of my gift to you, trusting in yourself to find the direction you must go. It's been within you all along, all you have to do is let it out, like Mountain Lion said. All you have to do is walk it."

"Good bye, Father." He started. Before he got far down the path he felt whirlwinds climb the skies behind him.

He hadn't walked far when he tripped over something and fell down. He grabbed for a nearby vine and, once it was in his hand he couldn't let go. Suddenly there were several vines around him, whipping around faster than he could follow and tying him up as if he were in a cacoon. Another vine went splat against his back and he was lifted into the air.

"Now what?"

He looked up into eight cold eyes and two wicked looking fangs.

"Hello, Mani He," said Spider. The web thrummed with her words. She crawled down until she was in front of him and stretched her legs out along the lines of her web. She looked common enough for a spider. Her body was hairy and, where there was no hair, shiny. Her eyes were dark and Mani He was surprised to see her focusing on him with them. "You're doing well, child. Most people are frightened by me."

"I'm pretty scared, Spider. You frighten me, too."

"Yes," she quelled. "I can feel your quaking in my web."

She crept closer and Mani He could see her pedipalps on either side of her fangs. The end of each pedipalp had a large spongelike pad which she used to carry things and eat with. Looking at her, feeling her so close and feeling himself trapped in her webbing, he grew even more afraid. "Please don't, Mother. You...the way you look...what you are...terrifies me."

She raised her fangs over him.

"Are you going to kill me, Spider?"

"Only you can decide if the penetration is a bite or a kiss."

Her fangs came down and Mani He slept.

He awoke still in the web but out of the webbing which held him. He discovered he could move about it easily and enjoyed the sensation it gave him. How high up he was, or where he was in relation to anything else, he didn't know. He was swinging from thread to thread when suddenly he saw Mother Spider leap up from under a leaf.

He lost his grip and started to fall. All about him he saw The Standing People, now far larger than before, and far below the ground rushing up to him.

Six strong legs, thin as swords yet strong as steel beams, wrapped around him gently and firmly. "Mani He," exclaimed Spider. "You frightened me. I was afraid you'd fall all the way before I could catch you."

With strong tugs, Spider lifted herself and Mani He back to her web. Her legs came away from him as something wet and sticky splatted across his back. "There," said Spider as she placed several turns of her webbing over his shoulder. "Now you can explore without killing yourself. Very important, you know." She tied off the other end to the center of her web. "If you need me, just tug on this. I'll come a' runnin'."

A fly buzzed past them and got caught high up in her web. "Ooh," she said, her excitement thrumming her web as the fly struggled. "Lunch, lunch, lunch. You hungry, little one?"

"No, thank you, Mother. The way you eat is," he tried to be tactful but opted for honesty instead, "kind of gross."

"To some, yes. But I make no excuses for it. I know who I am and what I am and am comfortable with it. I know my own truths and never deny them. What would be the point? To lie to myself? If I don't have myself as a friend, child, there is no one to befriend me."

The fly's struggles drew her attention away. "Would you excuse me, child?"

He nodded and she scuttled up her web to where the fly lay in wait.

As night came over the web, Mani He gathered his safety line and tied it off to make both a hammock and a web cave, thus keeping himself out of the wind and any rain, should it come.

Halfway asleep, he had strange visions. A city, the place where he worked and the people he knew. Old Man Brumhall appeared as a raven and a rabbit wore Haggedorn's clothes. He felt a gentle shaking of his web home and woke up. "Yes?"

"It's me, Mani He," said Spider. "You were crying out in your sleep and I grew concerned for you. Are you alright?"

"Just a bad dream, Mother. How come you didn't come in to wake me?"

She laughed. It made her pedipalps and fangs clang and rasp together. "I can't come in there, Mani He. That's your space. You made it comfortable for you. That means it's a mirror of your Sacred Space, the space within you where only you can go. Only you and others by your invitation. So I can't enter. I can stand and guard. And you were asleep. When you sleep – when *you* sleep – that's Coyote's time."

"I had a dream about Coyote. Actually, about Raven and Rabbit and Coyote. Are Raven and Rabbit my teachers also?"

She wiped her eyes with a pedipalp. "Everything is your teacher, Mani He. You have to decide the lesson."

"Could you help me with this lesson?"

"Of course, child. You have Coyote, and of the three I think he's best. Coyote'll laugh at you and laugh at himself, and you can learn to laugh at yourself before any others do if you learn him well. Rabbit can laugh at himself, but only if others show him the joke. Raven is a trickster, as are the other two, but Raven can never laugh at himself and doesn't like others to, either.

"You dreamt of men who trick themselves and don't laugh at their own jokes, men who think they are incapable of being jokes."

"Sounds like Haggedorn and the Old Man."

"If they are your teachers, what is their lesson?"

"I don't know."

"Then you must go inside, into your Sacred Space, to find the answer."

"No, I...no."

"Your journey isn't always going to be an easy one, so take your time. Remember what Hummingbird taught you and let your goal be your guide. Now your goal is to find the place inside you you've lost. Take all the time you need. I'll stand outside here and guard you. No one will pass until you are through."

It was morning again. Morning on a desert, similar to Lizard's and very unlike Coyote's. There were different color stones all around, the ground wasn't sandy but was dry. Cacti, the kind called "Mexican Old Men", were everywhere. The sky was clear blue without a cloud and Grandfather Sun was chasing Grandmother moon on the horizon.

He took a step and tripped on a rock.

"Sorry," said the rock.

Mani He jumped back. "Oh, my gosh. I'm sorry. I didn't know you were there."

The rock sprouted legs, a tail, and a head, and Mani He saw it was an armadillo. "Did I hurt you?"

"Nope, not at all. Come on." Armadillo waddled off towards one of the cacti. "Heard you had a dream last night. You thirsty?" They stopped at one of the cacti.

"More like a nightmare. And yes, very."

"Dig at the base of this old man, will you?" Before Armadillo could say another word, Mani He had dug half his body into the ground. "Pretty good, son. Lizard teach you that? Now, tell me about your nightmare."

Mani He told him, now adding his journey into his Sacred Space and his beliefs that the men in the dream were himself and some of the others he worked with.

"Sounds scary, especially if you don't like the way you saw yourself in that dream."

"It is scary. I don't want to be like that."

"What did Coyote teach you?"

"To go after the sweet dreams and avoid the nightmares."

"Good. Now, let me show you how to do it." Armadillo curled himself into a little ball and once again looked like a brightly shining rock.

"How will that help me avoid going towards my nightmares?"

"Don't worry, we're getting close. What did you learn from Spider?"

"My Sacred Space will keep me from going towards my nightmares?"

"Close, and this is where I come in. Everyone goes towards their dreams or the nightmares in two ways. The first way is the way everybody starts going to one or the other, they reach for it; you want to become your dreams, you reach for them. You want to become your nightmares, you reach for them. Eventually you become them, one or the other. You can never be both. If you try to be both, Nightmare always wins."

"Okay."

"Once you've started reaching, others see you reaching. Those who go towards their own nightmares pull you and push you towards yours. Those who travel towards their own dreams help and guide you towards your own sweet dreams. Now we put everything together. Your Sacred Space, if you listen to it and feel it moving inside you, if you're willing to learn – in your case – Spider's lesson, you'll know when you've gone too far towards your nightmares and not far enough towards your dreams."

"Mmmm. I realized that last night," Mani He said, rubbing the wounds where his Sacred Space dwelt inside him.

"So when you go too far towards what you don't want, when others pull and push you towards your nightmares, let your armor shine like the blackest nights. Show them your warrior spirit, tell them to beware your boundaries."

"Usually it's not that easy."

"That is when you must have courage, Mani He. Warriors fight many things and all of them are afraid."

"I know it's okay to be afraid," said Mani He. "How do I get courage?"

Armadillo laughed. It wasn't as unpleasant as Spider's. His armor rattled and his tail thumped against the ground. "By saying you're afraid and letting your fear guide your path. If you listen to it, it will bring you back to where ever you're safe. You're supposed to have fear, Mani He. It's a gift from the Great Mystery. It lets you know when you've gone too far. The more you accept your fear, the greater your courage will become."

Mani He noticed that Great Star Nation had come out. He sat and scooped some water into his mouth. "It's been a long day."

"Sure has. You hungry?"

Mani He nodded.

"You ever eat chicken?"

"Yeah."

"Then you'll love armadillo. Chicken tastes just like it. Armadillo's a little sweeter. 'Course, you'd have to expect that from such a glorious animal, wouldn't you?"

He woke to the wind rushing past him and pains in his shoulders. He looked up and saw fierce talons piercing him. He followed the talons to the legs and further until he saw he was carried by a great hawk. He peeked down and gulped. "Sparky? Is that you? Damn we're high up. How high are we?"

"You know your voice doesn't hide your nervousness at all, not one bit?" Hawk had a distinctly female voice, kind of like Mountain Lion's but higher and whispier.

"Mrs. Sparky?"

She chuckled. Her laugh wasn't bad at all. Her eyes closed and her beak opened. That was all. "Hawk will do."

They flew to a mountain. It was different from all the others he'd been on since Badger came and got him. It wasn't like Mountain Lion's and it wasn't like Coyote's. "Is this your mountain, Mother?"

"No, Mani He. It's yours."

"Am I going to meet my other teachers there?"

"You've met all of the teachers you have. I'm the last."

"You mean, after I do what ever I have to do with that mountain, I'll wake up?"

"No, Mani He. If you leave that mountain, you'll sleep forever. The only reason you started on this journey was to get here. Remember what Hummingbird taught you."

He was about to ask another question when Hawk let him go. He fell, but not down. He fell towards the mountain. As he neared the mountain's side he began to fly, like Hawk, up its side, gaining speed and feeling the wind move him until he was soaring scant inches above the mountain's face up to its peak, flying even though his body walked.

When he thought he would shoot beyond it and be lost in the sky forever he slowed and landed on the summit, a table of stone barely wide enough for him to stand upon. "What am I supposed to do up here?"

Hawk circled the summit below him. "You're supposed to remember all your lessons."

"But what am I supposed to do?"

"Look around you, tell me what you see."

Mani He started to turn but the narrow summit forbid him. "I can't turn around to see what's behind me."

"What would you need to see all that's around you?"

"Faces in all directions, I guess." Mani He screamed as three more faces erupted from his head, one in each direction of the compass. "What kind of trick is this?"

"No trick. That would be Coyote's job and it won't do here. Accept you'll be given what you need when you ask for it. There's no magic in that. Now, look around you. Can you see everything? Can you hear everything? Can you smell, taste, and touch everything?"

The four mouths answered in unison, "Yes."

"What is there?"

He looked. He saw Thompson placing a gun into his mouth. He saw a young girl, someone no older than Grace when he first met her, punching her stomach and repeating "You bastard, you bastard, you bastard," feeling her blows in his own stomach as she learned her own ritual for destruction, an echo and an answer to his own. He heard some children crying because there was no profit in feeding them wholesome food. He heard some bankers helping druglords to escape because cocaine was the only cash crop their countries had. He felt others dying because the companies where they lived were more willing to pay penance than finance safe industry. He tasted flesh eaten by others, the flesh of species as sentient and thoughtful as he, because it was cheaper to destroy than to preserve. He smelled gunpowder as explosions rocked the mountain where he stood.

There were other things, too. He saw a man holding another, someone the first man didn't know, as the second died of AIDS, and felt the second man's joy in knowing someone cared. He heard a rock singer who gave half his earnings to plant trees and saw the young shoots tear through the ground. He felt his belly fill as a woman ordered all the restaurants in her chain to give their daily leftovers to the homeless and helpless. He tasted the first harvest of some people who'd learned to cultivate their land with enough to provide for others, others who'd been their enemies through time. He smelled Grace, the first time they slept together, and remembered how it had been when there were horses to ride.

"I can tell you, Mother. I can tell you what's there."

"Yes, Mani He. Tell me. But not just me. You're here on top of a mountain," she cried up to him. "Listen to Spider, listen to Hummingbird, listen to Badger. What is Moose's lesson for you here? What is your way to the West, the way Mountain Lion taught you? Remember Lizard's words, Coyote's, and Armadillo's. Think of what I teach you.

"This is where everything comes together for you, Mani He. This is where you're meant to be. This is where you've always wanted to be. You're quite lucky, Little One. Most two-legs never know either the one or the other. If they do, they never know how to make them meet."

"But how?"

Badger formed to the east, patted him on the back and said, "Hi, kid."

Mani He said hello. Badger said "Coming in!" and dove in Mani He's mouth.

He felt a poke from the south as Moose spoke, "Glad you made it,

Mani He," and entered him.

Mountain Lion purred to his west and entered him. Next came Lizard from the north, followed by Coyote above, Hummingbird below, and he felt Spider's webbing within. What he thought was a stone whacked his foot to his right and Armadillo climbed in.

He opened his mouth and Badger called out, "Hey, Hawk, room for one more!"

"Use the abundance you have been given to give to others," cried Hawk. "There are opportunities all around you, Mani He. All you have to do is use them." She folded her wings and entered his chest.

Mani He, feeling Badger and Armadillo, hearing Moose and Mountain Lion, seeing all his teachers within, began turning his head, first right then left. Faster and faster, right and left, until suddenly it went all the way around. Then again. And again. And again and again and again. Faster and faster until his senses were finding out everything around him, everything that happened on the world far below.

All there was in the world filled him, building up in him, until finally his mouths opened and he spoke, telling all the world what he saw, sharing what he felt, describing what he heard, giving names to what he tasted and smelled.

His Rivier watch throbbed against his wrist, letting Tony know it was time to get up and head back to Boston, to Old Man Brumhall, to his corner office.

He sat up on the cot and scraped the sleep off his shoulders, having slept through the entire weekend. An hour later, the sky still dark, star-filled and with the moon climbing through the trees, he finished packing his car. The last thing was the rifle Brumhall had ordered him to use. Touching it, he remembered the Old Man's demand.

As he held the rifle crooked in his arm, a mountain lion broke through the trees and landed on all fours, staring at him. The moon cleared the trees and cast its bright night light on Tony and the cat.

He asked himself, "What are you going to do?"

The rifle grew heavy in his arm. It was loaded. He knew he could snap it up and fire before the Mountain Lion moved either towards him or away.

"What are you going to do?"

The moon came up higher over the trees. The sky began to brighten as the sun made its presence known. Stars began to fade and the moon continued to spotlight the distance between himself and the mountain lion. The big cat didn't move.

"What are you going to do, Morelli?" he said out loud.

He lifted the gun up, swung it like a baseball bat and smashed it against his car, breaking it in two and severely denting the hood and fender.

The cat sat down and cocked its head left, as if curious about this odd behavior and trying to determine what it meant.

"My name is Mani He, Mother. I'm having trouble finding my path and I'm afraid. I'm sorry I forgot and hope never again to forget your lesson."

The cat stood, scratched the earth where it sat, circled and scratched the earth again. It ran off into the woods and Tony saw it had left some scat. He ran his hand over the damage to his car. "It was just a cat. A big fucking cat."

A badger ran out from the woods, stopped about twenty feet away and sniffed in his direction, then continued on its way.

The sun came up and he realized there was going to be an eclipse. He hadn't known about it. Surely someone would have mentioned it at work or he'd have heard about it on the radio. A hawk cried high overhead. When he looked up at it, it circled down and perched on a tree, some fifteen feet over his head. Something fluttered in the trees near it and he saw a hummingbird perch next to the hawk without fear, as if the hummingbird and hawk were old friends.

"Not quite the lion and the lamb, but close enough," he said.

Somewhere down in the valley he heard a moose bellow. He asked himself again, "What are you going to do?"

He considered setting fire to the cabin and his car. "I don't think that's necessary, do you?" He asked the hummingbird and hawk. They continued to stare at him. "That's what I thought."

The woods grew quiet as the eclipse began. "Somewhere," Mani He whispered, "stars are being made."

At the eclipse's peak, he felt wounds on his body, wounds where his teachers marked him with their lessons. He didn't feel the wounds as pains. He felt them as lessons, memories, teachers, and time.

As the eclipse past, when the moon and sun gave each other their last kiss for this time of passion, he shaded his eyes and looked into the sky. "It's a new day, Grandmother, Grandfather."

He looked at the dents in his car and laughed, then laughed at himself laughing. He took off his Rivier watch, strapped it to the hood ornament on his car and laughed again. "Yes, Mr. Brumhall," he said. "I killed something, all right."

He got in the car and left.

THE SETTLEMENT

THE SETTLEMENT

*T*he Vega *parked over Mars' northern pole, a small pleasure* shuttle attached to one of its docking pods. Occasionally the shuttle clanged against *The Vega*. The other docking pod was exposed but empty.

The little woman sitting at the table, packed in makeup like a parody of a Hollywood star, seemed much smaller than he remembered. "You look good, Ma. It's nice to see you again."

She nodded but said nothing. Her shuttle clanged and she stood up.

"Don't worry, Ma. My docking collars lost their smarts a while back and I haven't had a chance to repair them. It's nothing. Now, are you sure I can't get you anything to eat? Maybe something to drink? I can make some coffee, no problem."

She looked around. "I...I didn't think a ship this small would have a kitchen."

"Normally it wouldn't, but there were some things I wouldn't give up. The smell of fresh brewed coffee first thing in the morning, for one."

"Yes. Coffee would be nice." She looked up as some lights winked on a panel beside her. "This is a Scimitar ship? It's awfully small."

"Scimitar class. You can't be too big when you're moving between asteroids. Just lots of power for scything and towing, lots of facility and equipment for artifact extraction, and lots of smarts to know when to do one or the other."

"You...you look good," she offered, her eyes moving from panel to panel in the small cabin.

"Yeah. Thanks." He let it hang for a few moments. "So what's this all about?"

"Your father and I are getting a divorce."

"All right! It's about god-damn time."

His mother started crying and he concentrated on the smell of the freshly brewing coffee, waiting until her tears passed. "Let me guess. This is Pa's idea, right?"

She pulled out a handkerchief and nodded as she wiped her eyes. "We're fighting over the settlement."

"So these impromptu calls from you and the old man are for what, visitation rights?" He laughed, but there wasn't any humor in his voice. "Neither of you so much as send me a birthday card in twelve years and now I get two calls in two days, 'Come in to Mars North Polar, family emergency'."

"What am I going to do? I've always done whatever your father said. He always said he knew what was best."

He didn't answer at first, gauging his own emotions, wondering if he should let his feelings out. "You believe he always knew what was best?"

She nodded.

"For you?"

She continued to nod, sobbing into her handkerchief.

"What about for me?"

"What? What do you mean, for you?"

"Look at me, Ma," he raged. "You think this is the best for me?"

"He's your father," she screamed back. "He didn't know what he was doing."

"First, neither you nor Pa know what a father is. As far as I'm concerned, my father is E.J. Oerstad down at Space Flight Systems. He got me this job. He took care of me. He nursed me back to health after that bastard you call a husband beat me so bad – " he waited until his voice calmed before he continued. "Second, even if he didn't know what he was doing, you sure in hell did. Or are you going to tell me you thought it was normal for fathers to beat their sons to the point where they bled, where their legs were broken, their faces smashed?"

"I didn't know," she wailed, tucking herself into her chair.

"You didn't know?" he laughed. "You stood there and watched. Every fucking time you watched! I remember your standing at the door to my room and pleading with him to stop but doing the same thing you're doing now."

"I was scared."

"Here's your coffee."

She took a sip and made a sour face. "God that's strong."

"You're welcome. I don't have a lot of guests. The kitchen needs a new servo, anyway."

"Son," she said, staring into her cup. "Whatever you think of your father, whatever you think of me, we were a family. We may have not been the best family, but we were a family. You had it bad, but so did we."

"That's not an excuse, Ma. If you didn't like what happened to you as a kid, you go talk to your parents about it. And I don't know what you call a family, but what I had wasn't a family, it was a concentration camp. You always in the kitchen and him always in the garage? You didn't need a son, you needed a mediator. I always wanted a family. I never had one. You going to tell me now I still might? I never will, Ma. Never."

An alarm sounded. "That's Pa coming to tell me his side of life. Don't worry. I don't take sides. I can't. All I can do now is see to my own needs and wants." Her pleasure shuttle clanged against *The Vega* again. "As soon as I get around to them, anyway. You going to stay or leave before he gets here?"

She looked around for a sink. Her cup was still full of coffee and ringed with lipstick marks.

"Don't worry, Ma. I'll take care of that."

She nodded and placed a folded paper with a Space Court jurisdictional seal under the cup. "Goodbye, son."

"What's that?"

"A claim. A subpoena with writ to a claim."

"A what?" he screamed. "A subpoena? How the hell am I going to appear in court?"

She had her back to him, straightening her dress and clutching her bag tightly to her. "You don't have to appear. It says you're my property. Your father threatened to lay claim to you when we found out how much you made as a Scimitar. I told my lawyer to lay claim first to make sure your father didn't get a cent. He'll probably lay claim, too."

There was silence as she moved towards her ship, then, "Don't worry, son. I'll take care of you."

His mother's shuttle disengaged from the docking collar. He watched through camera eyes as she made a wide berth on the far side of him from her husband.

His father called on an open channel, "Hey, son. Those docking collars look damn sloppy. Is it safe for me to come over there?"

He closed the communications to his mother and father and watched them continue their dance; one toward and the other away and him always in the middle. "I will never have a family. I'll never have the family I wanted."

Part of the system which allowed him to see to his own needs fired briefly and he registered the change in potential as "The hell I won't."

As his mother's ship started to fall planetside, *The Vega*'s caterpillar engaged, holding both shuttles in toroidal plasma arms. Scything lasers began to carve out pieces of the ships. Alarm calls pinged from both shuttles. He hummed through the comm as his lasers sliced their communication pods before they could signal planetside. Steadily, his lasers moved towards the passenger bays, at which point needle-thin lasers made their cuts slowly, delicately, almost tenderly. In a few moments, his parents' bodies, bloated and ruptured, were drawn into the forward observation bay.

"They gave me the knowledge to be self-repairing, so let's see how much I can repair." Waldoes rolled the bodies over a few times as he scanned memory, calling up anatomy, neuro-physiology and neuro-topography charts.

Satisfied, his manipulator arms and lasers went to work.

The frozen space high above Mars' northern pole made the work easy, keeping tissue in stasis as he adjusted cameras and lasers and manipulators and waldoes to do the sensitive work of removing the necessary brain functions – only the necessary ones – and wiring them into the kitchen and docking subsystems. "Memories? Some. Definitely need motor skills. Some sensory input. Yeah, that's good."

Two hours later, he began reheating the kitchen servo and docking port controls. "Ma? Pa? Can you hear me?"

Her voice sounded from the kitchen servos, "Yes, son? What can I do for my wonderful boy?"

The docking ports moved silently for a moment, then answered in his father's voice. "Huh? Sorry, son. I guess I was napping. Beautiful day, huh? What'd you say the three of us go on a picnic?"

The Scimitar broke out of Mars North Polar. "Sure. Let's."

THE WEIGHT

THE WEIGHT

A little shopkeeper's bell dingled as I closed the door behind me. I looked up at it and wondered what kind of place this was. The sign out front read *The Mythic Center*.

A woman's voice came out of the shadows behind the bar. "You're a long way from home."

The place had a look that made me comfortable. The tables and chairs were light maple - all local and hand made, nothing imported and nothing with a machined #7 of 7,000 look. The place had a good, solid, well-worn feel about it. Whatever wasn't maple - the paneling, the bar and stools, the booths - was oak, ash, or thorn. Some of the tables had chess and checker boards carved into them, a few others had cribbage boards carved into them. Serious gamers came here because the gaming tables had green-shaded, metal poker lights suspended from the ceilings over them. Between those and the bar and booth lights, the place was well lit without being blinding, what I'd call soothing, never too much light unless you needed it.

The woman moved out from the shadows so I could see her clearly, a waitress' apron tied neatly and knotted in front and a towel with blue edging slung over her shoulder. "We're more tavern than bar." She checked me over, a seasoned waitperson's eye determining what kind of tipper I was, and smiled. "More a way station, actually," she added, her evaluation over. "Been traveling long?"

I nodded and smiled back, rubbing my hands against the cold they'd gathered in the day's walking. I could have sworn I left the city in late

255

Summer but Fall seemed to come fast in my wake. I was the only other person in the place so I'm sure she didn't mind the company. "Seems a little lonely with only the furniture and walls to keep you company."

"Alone, maybe. Never lonely."

I walked over to a wall with several built-in bookracks and ran a finger over the spines.

"Are you a reader?"

"I thought so but I don't know any of these titles: *Moral Calculations* by Laszlo Mero, McFarlane and Saywell's *If²*, Lattimore's *Acts and Letters of the Apostles*, Smith's *The Essential Kabbalah*, Barks' *The Essential Rumi*, Margenau's *The Nature of Physical Reality*. What are these?"

"Philosophy, mathematics, folklore, religion, ..." Her voice trailed off.

I looked up at her, shrugged and shook my head.

"They're mainly to keep up *The Mythic Center* image."

The opposite wall sported a genuine British competition style dart board, well used. I stared at it and my face must have lit up because the waitress asked, "Do you throw?"

I shook my head, no, although I walked over and lifted a dart from its rack. I ran my fingers over the flight feathers - again, no plastic and the darts were competition weighted. "No, just an admirer of good things built to last."

She stopped drying down a Monopoly gaming table and stood up to look at me, one hand on a hip and twirling the damp towel with the other. "Thanks."

She was pretty in an older kind of way and I wasn't sure I expected someone in their late thirties to, oh, late forties to be tending bar on an old country crossroads at the northern edge of the New York-Mass border. The light over the table captured her in a spotlight and she let me take a long drink before she reached up for the chain and turned the light off. Salt&pepper hair that made a long, thick braid down her back, cerulean blue eyes that my dad used to call "ice-eyes", a wide face with lots of freckles but no wrinkles except laugh lines, and no makeup to disturb any of it. When she smiled there was a gap in her front teeth and I caught myself thinking of Chaucer's *The Miller's Wife*, then quickly shook my head.

It showed, I guess. The way she smiled at me, running her tongue over the gap in her teeth absentmindedly, looking down and to the side as she shook her head.

Under the full length apron she wore a blue tanktop matching her eyes. Her jeans were torn at the knees and faded from work, not from some designer's idea of what work did to good clothing, and red high-top sneakers like I used to wear as a kid.

She quoted Bob Seger's *Nightmoves*, singing it like a question, "Little too tall? Could'a used a few pounds?"

I wanted to say, "Not from where I'm standing" and, ever cool beyond measure, instead I sneezed, the smell of strong - not burnt - coffee finally making its way through the frost in my nostrils.

"Bless you."

"Thanks."

She continued to stand, one hand on her hip, the other still twirling the towel but now in the dark of the bar with that table's light off. The music switched from Judy Collins' *Since You Asked* to CSN's *Suite: Judy Blue Eyes* and she went back to washing off tables.

"You closing? I know it's late but this is the only place I've seen with lights on - hell, it was the only place I've seen, period - since dusk."

"Been this way before?"

"About thirty-five years ago but I don't remember any of these roads and I'd rather not keep exploring."

"We got time for one more. Besides, the only people who come here this time of night are worn and tired." She finished the next table and stood up, twirling the towel again. "Or lost."

"Lost I get."

She pulled a blue bandanna from her hip pocket, wiped her brow then lifted both arms to tie it over her hair. The bar lights cast shadows over the curves of her body as her hands shaped a butterfly over her head. She kept her eyes on me the whole time, watching me watch.

"I'm dyeing my hair scarf," she said.

I laughed. "Where is this place, anyway? I noticed it's not exactly a real happening burg."

She laughed. "'Happening burg'? Jeez, are you dating yourself. I haven't heard that since, let me think, when, '75?"

"Obvious, huh?" I laughed and checked myself out in the mirror behind the bar. Burgundy felt hat pulled low, light parka, strong, clean face that needed a shave, sharp, clear brown eyes, still tall and broad, iron-gray flannel shirt. What I couldn't see I knew from memory: faded jeans bottomed by crazy quilt wool socks and double-laced Tyroleans. Everything like it was on my original trip, everything I could remember.

Talking with her, I'd forgotten I still carried my pack, although now the straps were damn near separating my arms from my shoulders.

She nodded at the pack. "Take it off. Nobody here's going to bother it."

I unhooked the belt and slid the pack off my shoulders. As it dropped down I fumbled a grab for it. It swung around and knocked into some chairs. My shoulders ached now the weight was relieved. "Sorry."

"Must be quite the weight, carrying around all these years."

"Excuse me?"

"Nothing. Want something to drink?"

"What you got that's free?"

She laughed again. "Everything in life comes with a price tag on it. You just got to decide if you want to pay the price."

I shrugged, partially in answer and partially to soothe my neck and arms.

"Tell me something," she said. "You got a new pack, new boots, that jacket's not army issue, and you look health club strong. You didn't get that build working on a farm. You look like you got money. What're you grubbing for?"

I looked at myself in the mirror again and could feel her flattery working. "You think I look good?"

She turned to face my reflection, leaned against the bar and scowled. "For somebody in his, what, early fifties? Sure, you look good enough."

She turned quickly to face me and reached across the bar for my arm. "Hey, I didn't mean that the way it sounded. You look great. How about a cup of coffee? On the house."

"You working alone tonight?"

Her smile changed slightly. Her nostrils flared and her eyes took on a hungry look. Not a good hungry, just a hungry. In the back of my mind I heard, "Warning, Will Robinson! Danger! Danger!"

"Me and Cook," she said.

I held up my hands. "Hey, no problem. I was just going to say 'How about a bowl of chili and I'll do tonight's dishes.'"

She looked down at the dish towel in her hands, shook her head and the smile came back but, as Harry Chapin said, it was a sad smile, just the same. "Just working your way through?"

The music changed again, this time to Joni Mitchell's *Woodstock*.

"Jesus Christ, what station are you listening to? Those tunes bring back memories."

"Hang on a second. I'll go ask Cook if it's okay."

She went through the kitchen doors and came back out with a one-eyed German Shepherd at her heels.

"Oh, jeez," I said. "Accident?"

"Ran into a tree. He likes it if you rub the spot where the eye used to be."

I sat down on the floor and did as she suggested. She jumped up and sat on the bar. "Hey, buddy." I scratched the dog's ears and looked up at her. "Buddy?"

"Budless, actually."

I turned my attention back to the dog. "Happens to the best of us. What's your name?"

"Cook," she said.

I laughed again. "What do you say, Cook? Can I have some chili if I do the dishes?"

The dog woofed.

"That's a 'yes'," she said.

An hour later she was still washing tables and I was tying on an apron. "Damn, that was good chili."

"All food's good to a starving man. You had two bowls full."

"No, I mean it. I haven't had chili like that since '74, the last time I was through this way. It was a place called 'Ms. Ruby's Inn'. I remember I went in there and asked to see a menu. The waitress looked at me like I was from the moon then disappeared into the kitchen. She came out a few minutes later dragging a blackboard with food and prices on it and apologized for taking so long. She said they had to go find some chalk. There was chili on their menu and I didn't have a dime to my name." I threw my head back and gathered the memories. "I made them the same offer I made you. I didn't even know you had chili here."

She stared at me, her blue eyes exploring, evaluating, wondering, deciding. "I thought you saw it on the menu."

"What menu."

She pointed to a chalkboard on the wall behind the cash register.

"I didn't get any nachos this time. Ms. Ruby made these wonderful plate size nachos, paper thin."

"I ran out of those a long time ago."

I stared at her, unsure of the joke. Besides, Ms. Ruby'd be in her eighties now.

"Was I wrong about you and money?" she asked.

Cook was giving me belly. I was rubbing his missing eye with one hand and ruffling his chest fur with the other. "One eye gone, you should have named him 'Odin'."

There was a loud caw from the corner opposite the bar. A raven was perched there and I nearly leapt off the floor at his call.

She nodded at the raven. "That's Odin," she said, then pointed at the dog. "He's 'Cook'."

The raven cawed again.

"How long's he been there? I didn't see him when I came in."

She was looking at me again with that evaluating, exploring, wondering, deciding, 'What do I do with this one?' look in her eyes.

Odin cawed again but it was almost a whisper. The glow of the outside lights went out and the night outside the windows got noticeably darker. The waitress looked from the raven to me. "They're on a timer."

"Isn't everything these days?"

Her eyes relaxed. The inspection was over. "You got a place to stay tonight? It's gonna start getting awful cold out. First snow in a few days."

"*Odes to ancient children gone –* "

"*we are one,*" she finished the line and smiled that *Miller's Wife* smile.

I looked at her, unsure. Odin cawed again. He'd been damn quiet until I'd said his name.

"I'm asking if you'd like to come home with me."

"Umm...what's happening here? It's been years and I'm not sure I know the game anymore so...are you picking me up?"

She came over and guided me up off the floor, putting a finger over my lips as I was about to speak. With her other hand she pulled the apron knot free.

I put on my parka and picked up my pack as she shut off the lights. "Come on, Cook."

"What about Odin?"

She pointed at a raven sized, heavy plastic door in the wall by his perch but said nothing.

I heard the lock click on the door as the dog led us into the night. Odin laughed overhead.

*S*he was gone when I woke up. So were Cook and Odin. "Hello."

Nothing.

"Hello-o-o?"

Still nothing.

"Huh. She must've gotten up real quiet." I chuckled. "But she wasn't that quiet last night."

Daylight came in through two lace curtained windows. Out the windows I saw a dirt road and a field. I took a deep breath. The place smelled and looked like a farmhouse, at least from this one room.

Comfortable, like the tavern and most of the furniture constructed from the same woods with the same handmade feel - the wardrobe, the dresser, the mirror frame. The nightstand was draped with pitch black towels. There was a brass moon-and-star candlestick with a beeswax candle on the dresser - I looked around and noticed there weren't any lights or lightswitches in the room - and a fine, white china bowl and cistern with blue glazing the color of the waitress's eyes - and typical, I'd never even got her name - of *Red Riding Hood and the Wolf*, except Red was a guy and the Wolf was voluptuous and not in the vulpine sense.

I shook my head and stared at it. "Freaky."

The bed was a three-quarter four-poster. It didn't seem that small last night. The sheets were still crinkly fresh and both the quilt and comforter were back over me (we had kicked them off during the night). Steam blew from my nostrils. I stretched under the covers, scratched my stomach and slowly worked my way down.

I stopped at my balls and used both hands to explore. Finally I threw back the covers and checked myself like the doctor taught me. The small lump was gone. My dad died of prostate cancer and mine was just beginning. I was so excited I couldn't even find my vasectomy scar.

The cold air was making everything pucker so I pulled the covers back over me. "Hello," I called. No answer. "Hel-lo-o?"

I rolled away and pulled her pillow over to me, just to make sure, smelt her there, and for a moment relived last night.

Half an hour later I had sponge-bathed, dressed, and filled my water bottle from the kitchen pump. I hefted my pack, adjusted the straps, stepped out the door and stopped, looking for something familiar. The road went east to west. There were no cars.

To the right was a barn in such a state of disrepair that I smiled. My dad used to say "I think we got one more mortgage payment on that one" when we drove past such relics on country drives when I was a kid. Nothing had used that barn in twenty-five, thirty years and I couldn't believe that the waitress I'd slept with would have let it farrow so.

I called out again, "Hello!"

No answer. I looked east. "We came that way, didn't we?"

A wind blew and something rattled. A shutter was loose and about ready to fall off. I walked over and noticed it was the shutter to one of the bedroom windows. "The least I can do is fix this."

I didn't trust the barn, though. "Maybe there's tools in the house?" I turned back to the door and stopped. The house, the house I'd slept in, was in the same state of decay as the barn.

A raven perched on a joist protruding from the barn hayloft. It cawed and flew off to the west. I adjusted my pack and followed.

Two hours of straight walking later I was still on the dirt road and beginning to not like it. The road wasn't graded which told me it wasn't heavily traveled. I hadn't seen a school bus, car, truck, tractor or another farm since I started walking. I hadn't seen the field or farmhouse where I started since the first bend and that was early in the first hour. The woods didn't get heavier but they didn't thin either. I got to a crossroads and dropped my pack.

The tavern had been at a crossroads.

On the far side of the crossroads from where I stood was an old highway marker - a sign this must have been a heavily traveled road in its day- but the signs were broken off in all directions. "Great. Don't know where I'm going and not sure where I've been."

A raven landed on the marker. "Odin? Is that you? I thought I lost you way back in the woods. Which way is out, buddy?"

Odin or whoever it was just stared at me. "Not even a 'Nevermore'?" Nothing.

I hadn't had any breakfast and my body knew it. My dad use to say that any direction's the right one when you don't know where you're going, so I started west anticipating a forced fast and a march.

Last night's memories grew dim.

The day was cool without being cold and that made walking decent. I didn't bother listening for cars. I hadn't seen one since yesterday and didn't think any'd come by now. The road itself had enough turns and dips to make the travel interesting without being occupying. The surrounding woods and fields were quiet. Eventually I found myself remembering the last time I'd strapped a pack on my back.

It was great. I was a kid, a little too young for Woodstock and a little too old for much of anything else. I'd had a few years of college and that went nowhere, except to get me a wife and a kid, both of whom I adored but neither of whom I wanted. I remember coming home one day and watching Paula - my ex - playing with David-Jeremy in the backyard where we lived. She was a great mother. She just knew how to be with a kid. She wasn't older than me, but she was, if you know what I mean.

So one day I asked if she'd like to go down and visit her mother in Virginia. Her mother hadn't seen the baby, so that seemed like a good idea.

"Let's stay a couple of weeks. Give me a chance to see if there's a good job down there."

I think she knew. She must have. How could she not know?

The third day there, I told her I was going out for a pack of cigarettes. She looked at me for a a minute but said nothing. Finally she just kissed me and let me go.

I don't know why I said that. I've never smoked cigarettes.

I drove as far north as I could on the gas I had. When I stopped to get gas, I sold the truck and used the money to buy a good pack, some hiking boots, whatever I thought would be necessary gear and supplies, and headed up the Dragon's Spine. Those were some of the best years of my life. Worked when I needed to, met some good people, some bad. Got into some pretty bad fights once or twice when I started out. Met a lot of fine ladies. Met some pretty important people, too.

One time on that trip, high in the Catskills, I needed to get into a town to pick up supplies so I could continue north, making my own underground railroad, thinking 'the norther you get, the freer you get'. I came down out of the hills and walked into this town called Acra.

Jesus, that was a time.

It started to cloud up. I quickened my pace.

I'd been walking most of the day and it grew dark. The sky never cleared, and cloud covered nights on dirt roads in heavily wooded foothills weren't the most comfortable. I could barely make out the road in front of me and kept hoping it didn't branch before I got to whatever town was listed on that signpost I'd seen earlier in the day.

That's when I heard the guitar up ahead and coming out of the dark, so faint I had this image of encountering the toothless hillbilly from *Deliverance*. Whoever played experimented with chords and fingerings, like they were searching for some melody they weren't sure of.

The wind picked up and blew the guitar notes at me. Something rattled off to my side. An old wooden town marker. I brushed off some dirt and had to feel the letters carved into it.

Acra.

Acra?

You've got to be fucking kidding.

But right now I was too tired, hungry, and thirsty to do anything but laugh. I swallowed my last protein bar, gulped the last of my water, and followed the music in.

It had changed a lot since my last visit. There are two for real ghost towns in New England and both are in Massachusetts: Dogtown just outside of Gloucester and Purgatory down by the Rhode Island border. Both towns have similar histories and both are spooky as hell.

The Acra I stood in qualified for number three.

There was a general store in front of me and not much else. To the right was an Esso gas station — that shows you how old it was — and to the left an apothecary. All three buildings had broken windows and doors falling off their hinges. The whole town shimmered briefly as if warm air had risen from it. The music came from the general store and I went in.

The general store was pretty clean inside. One side was set up like an "open-mike" bar although there was no bar to be seen. There were tables and chairs with ashtrays and those little votive candles in holders on each table. The stage — more a platform wide enough for a stool and a mike — was against the wall and draped with purple cloth. That's where the guitarist sat.

If he saw me come in he didn't show it. I picked a table near the middle, pulled out a chair, turned it so I could keep my pack on - you never know when you have to leave these kinds of small town places quickly - and sat, hoping somebody would be by with a menu or something. Coffee would've been fine.

All that happened was that this guy played. I recognized his style and form but the actual tunes he played were new to me. His blond hair was shorter than I remembered and darker, now just bright blonde strands amongst the darker rest. Same beautiful blue eyes, same killer smile. Somebody once told me it was a shit-eating grin and I smiled, remembering. His playing was smoother, more relaxed. The last time I'd heard him was thirty-five years ago in Acra and back then his playing had this bizarre intensity, as if he had something to say but didn't know how to say it and his music echoed his frustration. He lost a lot of his baby fat since then and had the look of someone who'd been physically working for a long time. His sleeves were rolled up and I could see veins and the movement of his muscles as he played. The last time I watched him his arms still carried some baby weight and there was no clean separation of muscle movement. His skin was darker, too. Tanned, like someone who'd been out in the sun. I couldn't see any tan lines but the fact that his face, neck, and what I could see of his chest matched the color of his arms told me his work was real, not just for relaxation or performed as leisure. I looked for a watch mark and saw none. He was timeless.

Then, my jaw dropped. I'd only eaten a couple of protein bars all day so maybe my mind was weak. I didn't think of it at first, but now it came on me like a strong waterfall - I remembered this guy.

"Frampton!"

He looked up at me and smiled. Without a break he went from whatever he was playing to *Show me the way*, acoustic. His voice still had the power and intensity I remembered but now, hearing just him and his guitar, it seemed like he'd found out where he was going.

He sounded great.

"*You-ou-ou, show me the way.*" His bright eyes fixed on me. "Hey, Joe."

All I could get out was "Frampton! Jesus Christ, Frampton."

He laughed and put his guitar down. "That's twice we've been confused."

"You remember me?"

"I remember then."

I leaned back and felt my face flush. My breaths came high and shallow. The whole place shimmered again and I laughed like I just took a major hit of some Acapulco Gold. My eyes ached and started tearing before I could cover them. "Prove it."

"You came into town just like you did this time; you walked. You came in for food. That's the same. I was playing and you listened. Same. You said, 'You know you look like Peter Frampton?' I said, 'People have told me.' You said, 'You even sound like Frampton.' I said, 'Thanks. I work at it.' You listened some more and said, 'Frampton. Jesus Christ, Frampton.' That puts us back on track, I think."

I was still breathing fast and high and getting dizzier by the minute. "You said, 'That's the first time we've been confused.'"

He continued, "I asked you if you played. You nodded, but when I asked you to join me you said no."

"The stage," I said. It was getting hard to see. Everything was bubbling and fading in and out. "There wasn't enough room for two."

"Back then there was barely room for one." He came over to my table, grabbed my hand, and pulled me towards the stage. A foot away from the table he stopped and pointed at my pack. I didn't let go of his hand and unfastened my straps with my free hand. My pack fell from my shoulders and crumpled to the floor like some animal hit while crossing the road.

I lifted it and leaned it against the table. He watched me and smiled. "Not going to let go?"

"There were others," I said, confused.

"While you listened, David, Steven, and Graham came in. We started to jam. You listened."

"I remember."

"You stayed a few days."

"I needed time."

"Joni came in the next night. You were on your way to Montreal, maybe further. You had a decision to make. Arlo came in the night after."

"*Ode to ancient children gone, we are one,*" I mumbled. The stage got bigger with every step.

He supported me in his arms as we walked. It felt like a good friend helping me home after a good drunk. Except I never drank. Never drank and never smoked. Cigarettes. Helped a lot of other people home, though. Just like this.

So this is how it felt.

"That wasn't the song."

His statement shook me. I wondered if the waitress had given me something because the stage ended at the curvature of the earth. I kept shaking my head to clear it, looking at the floor instead and nodding. "I know. I got this far and couldn't go on because I wasn't really sure. Robbie Robertson, Richard Manuel and some of The Hawks came in and started playing *The Weight* and...I don't know. I made my decision here. I made my decision and I could go on."

Beside his guitar was another. I hadn't seen it before. He sat me down on the stool and put the guitar in my hands. There was another stool beside mine. Then another and another and...

"I still can't play good."

"You play good." His arm swept over the audience. Where did they come from? Everybody I'd ever helped, everybody I'd ever cheated, everybody I'd ever hated or loved and right there in front, Paula and David-Jeremy. "All the world, huh?"

"What?"

"Not to worry. Besides, we'll decide if you play well."

"Huh?"

The audience was applauding.

The stools filled. CSN, Joni Mitchell, Maria Muldaur, Robbie Robertson and Richard Manuel.

Neil Young walked in. "Arlo won't be able to make it so I came instead."

"Thanks," I said. Frampton adjusted the mike for me. The lights went down and somebody caught me in a blinding spot. I cleared my throat and pulled the mike closer. "It's 2005, not 1974. What are you folks doing here?"

"Not yet, Joe."

"That woman from the tavern?" I looked at Frampton. "She coming? That'd make this complete."

He smiled. My head cleared and the room settled down to where and what it'd been, although it was still awfully warm considering the doors and windows were all busted and first snow was coming soon.

The door opened and Frampton pointed at a young man standing there. "No. He makes this complete."

He was a handsome kid. Just shy of too tall, nice build although towards thin. Long brown hair, brown eyes. His beard had blond highlights. He looked like he'd been on the road for a while.

A waitress came out from behind the bar. Not the one from last night, the one from thirty years ago. I could feel my eyes bulging out of their sockets. "How - "

Frampton put a finger over my lips. The boy looked up at her. He had a terrific smile. I bet that smile got him into lots of beds thirty years ago. Nowadays, I only hoped he carried protection.

"You got any chili?" he asked.

A dog barked outside. A moment later I heard a raven's *caw*.

Frampton smiled. "Your ride's here, Joe."

The store shimmered again. Everyone was gone and the place looked deserted, like it should have when I first entered. I put a hand to my chest. It felt like my lungs were closing inside me. Somebody was softly crying and I saw the kid was still in his chair. In front of him was some chili in a cracked bowl. There was a scene on the outside of the bowl. It was the same as was on the farmhouse cistern.

The kid sobbed as he shoveled the chili in.

I reached for Frampton. He was melting. I could feel him radiating heat, like he was burning from the inside out.

"Am I dying? Is this it?"

Mouths formed where his eyes had been. "I don't think so," his eyes said.

I couldn't get any air and the pressure was killing me. "That boy. He's me?"

Frampton's features and clothes were completely gone. All that remained was a white, human form, as if beeswax had been given human shape. There were no flames but the heat stifled me.

"No, not you."

"Who?"

"A boy, needing time to make a decision. Unfortunately, I got in the way."

I put out a hand to him for support but he wasn't there. Talking took too much energy, too much of what little strength I still had. I shook my head. I didn't understand.

"What you call thirty years ago, I came through here, through what you think of as this place, just a traveler. A tourist, really. You came through here, too, passing me as I rested. You entered my dream and found solace there. That was fine. But we exchanged unequal weights. You took some of my reality and I took some of your dream. Neither of us could survive. My people carry our realities wherever we go. Your people carry your dreams. I used one of my realities to bring you back."

"Where?" I sobbed. "Here?"

"Yes, here, where your dream ended. You needed to come back to your first great decision, to that moment when you first dreamed of how different things might have been."

I wanted to cry, scream...I wanted to do something to get this ache away from me and onto someone else. My first great decision. Made here. In a place like this. My decision to leave my wife. To not hear and relish and comfort the sobbings of my son. When I dreamed they would be better off without me, with someone else. A young boy's dream. A dying man's sadness.

"I give you back your dream. I take back my reality. Your kind can not know different yesterdays, you can only accept those you know you had."

The ache was ripped from me. That weight, my pack that I'd carried for thirty-some years, caught fire, burned bright for a moment then died. It went dark.

A strong light came through the cracks in the wall. The dog barked again, the raven *cawed*, footsteps and dancing lights outside.

The waitress opened the door and caught me in the spotlight she held in her hand. "Joe? Christ, we've been looking for you all day and night. I went out to get some stuff for breakfast, I come back and you're gone."

Cook trotted up to me. Odin flapped in and landed on his back. "Caw!"

The waitress reached out for my arm. "You okay? You look like shit. Where's your pack?"

Caw!

"I dropped it. Somewhere."

"Yeah, well, it can't be far. You're only about two miles from the house. But you must've walked some crazy trail to get here. Cook zigzagged and doubled back half a dozen times."

Caw!

"Leave it. Let whoever finds it have it. I don't need to carry that weight anymore."

She dimmed the light and shined it in my eyes. "You sure you're okay?"

Cook nuzzled my free hand. I scratched him behind the ears. Odin hopped forward and I smoothed the feathers on his head. I took the waitress' hand in mine. "What's your name?"

She laughed. "Sheril. Sheril Anne. With an *S* and an *i*, not a *C* and a *y*."

"May I come home with you, Sheril Anne with an S and an i, not a C and a y?"

She walked beside me. Cook walked ahead of us. Odin flew overhead.

THEM DOORE GIRLS

THEM DOORE GIRLS

Y*ou hear that? Kind of like a ship's horn, waiting to get* piloted into land. Starts low and keening, then suddenly high. Won't do much good looking. You can look everywhere you want in these parts and you'll never find it. Ain't none of us could ever find it, and we looked some. Pilot Farley, he took his skiff out far into the fishing waters and found nothing. He'd be able to find it if any could, that Pilot Farley.

You wait right here, though. Few minutes is all. You'll see them Doore girls come out that shop across the way and start walking to home.

See, I know what makes that noise, and it ain't no ship fetch up on the rocks. It's what's calling them Doore girls, and it ain't nothing human, at all.

I found out long time ago when I was just about your age – you're being what, twenty? Twenty-five? You just rest a while, sip that soda pop slow and give that fancy car of yours a rest while I mind the store, and maybe I'll tell you. I'll tell you because there ain't nobody around here going to listen. You can ask, they won't say nothing. Women want their husbands and sons home at night.

Ya. That's them Doore girls. They ain't hard to look at, are they? That's Ruth and Livy, front door and back door, if you get my meaning.

Now Ruth, she's right comely, ain't she? Ruth, she's my age – don't roll your eyes, son. There's more to this town than you could know.

Livy, she's being a year and a half younger. But that Ruth, she's always the kind of woman, somebody'd see her walking and we'd all get up from the card game just to have a look. Some of the others of us, some like Johnny Walker – his parents weren't too proud when they named him, were they? – come outside and sit like we're doing now, right on the porch, and he'd keep right on looking as she'd go past. Ain't known much pleasure, that boy.

Always had a warmth for Ruth, I did. When I was a young man, I had my own boat and a home right up on the bluff. I protected my home good against both summer and winter. Now-a-days they call that "solar design". Don't matter. Just knowing where you live, is all. Sold my boat so long ago I don't hardly think of it. Don't go out on the water now. Them others, they don't mind. They'll go out 'cause they know their children's safe. They got them Doore girls to thanks but none of them will.

I was shy back when I was young. Wouldn't talk to no one. But I'd known them Doore girls since we was born.

The Doore girls live by themselves. They lost their parents to the water when the sisters were entering their teens. That ain't odd, people dying on account of the sea. But ain't nobody died on the sea since then, neither.

Come when I was thirteen when their tragedy struck. Ruth and Livy and their Ma and Pa went out to the island to do some clamming. It was a big church supper and we was all bringing something.

They won't tell all, that I know for sure. But as they'd start coming back, here comes that sound like something looking for something it can't find. The Doores were caught out in it, no more than a mile from shore either way, something every newborn pup knows how to swim, and their Ma and Pa is gone. Next day we found Ruth and Livy fetch up, looking terrified and sick, and both of them, their eyes got a fear couldn't be described. Old Evie Halpren took them in, but they wouldn't hear none of it. "We got our own home to look after, Mrs. Halpren," they said. We all thought they still had the sun in them. Pilot Farley said letting them live alone was about as sharp as a sack of wet mice. But they wouldn't hear none of it, and being they's Doores, just like their parents, – Tommy Doore, God bless him, many's a day we'd see him standing in his field, arguing with a stump – we nodded and let them be.

Well, they grew up, was all. But they grew like I told you, front and back door alike. That Ruth Doore, the way she moved, stay with a man like the taste of strong licorice on the back of your tongue, or maybe that first taste of coffee after pulling up the morning's nets in a too heavy fog. And that Livy – and this ain't showing no disrespect for the wonders God's done – you just know she'd keep a man warm and awake at night. Ruth, she knew how I'd feel. Never told her, but let her know the best I could with a look and a nod when the church socials was over. She'd always smile back, but kind of sad, and I kept my words to myself cause of that.

But when ever they'd walk past, we'd all go see then shake our heads and smile. We'd all come back in and sit down to the game again. I guess my feelings must have showed strong one day, cause Old Farley – You'll know him when he comes. Got a stump like Ahab. Warn't no whale, though, just caught his leg in the ropes pulling up the nets. That's when they started using Diesels. Didn't know about no clutches back then – he'd whoop his stump under the table; whack, whack, whack, then look at me and smile. The other's joined in and I could feel my face getting hot then cold.

"Wouldn't be the first man or boy asked to sit beside a Doore in church, or maybe brought them the pride of his catch," he said.

Clem sighed, "Would be the first they invited in, though," and they all laughed again.

I was about to throw my cards down when Pilot Farley puts his hand on my arm. "Don't mean no harm, Noah. Don't want to shame you none. But you can't sell what you don't advertise, son. You got a feeling for one of them girls, you go tell them. Ain't no shame in hearing a 'no'. Only shame is in not hearing anything at all."

Clem and the others nodded, not looking at me but looking at me over their cards. I put my cards down and left.

I walked the shore then, from the docks down to Indian Point and up east to River's Spring. Thought maybe they'd be clamming, but they weren't. Went to their home then, but they weren't there neither.

Now about this time, it's getting dark and a heavy fog's coming in with the night. And from low beyond the island, there comes that sound. I could hear the lobster boats churning and making back water, pulling for the dock rather than sit out in the bay waiting for Farley to lead them home.

Easiest way home for me from their house was on the shore, so I headed down the path until I was walking on gull tracks and sand when I heard their voices.

It was full dark now, and the fog was hanging on you like a sweater soaked in snow. But I saw them Doore girls down by the water. I looked, thinking to call to them, but stopped and watched. They weren't clamming and they weren't swimming. They was waiting, was all.

I lay down in the grass just to watch, thinking maybe they had somebody coming from one of the towns east or south, and maybe that's why no one got close to the Doores.

Then that sound come again, deeper and nearer, like it was carried on the mists of the fog itself. Them Doores, they start moving like cattle expecting a storm. There was one more blast from whatever it was coming across the water, then I saw it.

Something big and dark, looking like a man and rising like the crest of a wave, coming close to where the Doore girls watched. Bigger than night and darker than the pitch we poured on Old Farley's stump when he got his leg twisted in the Diesel.

A wave like a man's hand washed up against them and Livy shook, shook hard and her legs opened so the water could go high. Ruth's blouse was pushed against her, flattening her breasts against her chest. The next wave took Livy down to the ground and the wave after tore open Ruth's blouse and pulled off her dress.

I jumped up then and shouted, "Ruth, Livy, what is it?" and like a fool wanting to shake hands with Devil I ran down thinking I was to save them.

"No, Noah. Don't. Go back," yells Ruth, and they both started crying and covering themselves, their voices sounding so sick like what ever's happening to them is the worst curse out of God's own mouth.

They started backing away, though I couldn't tell if they was backing away from me or the sea which was surrounding them.

"What's happening?" I hollered.

"Go back, Noah! Go away before it finds you!"

Something dark come up out of the water then. Something like I'd never seen and don't want to see again. Something looking like a man, but no man could move like it did. I backed away and slipped, falling into sand wet with the tide. Whatever it was, it didn't have no face that I could see, but you could tell it was looking at them Doore girls as they moved up into the grasses and out of the reach of the water.

Next thing I know I'm deep into the water and it's feeling like a stone cold vise pushing the life out of my chest. I hear that noise, too, deep inside me, and I'm thinking for sure Jonah's whale's got me in its jaws.

I come up out of the water once, something holding me in its hand above the waves, and again that sound bellows through me. Ruth, I heard her call my name. Heard both Doore girls, crying and shrieking, and this thing bellowing and shaking me, until finally them Doore girls started back down to the water.

Whatever it was moved up against the Doore girls. First one, then the other. Until they were washed in the waves and this thing was rolling with them, moving onto them and finally into them. And they was screaming, screaming as if making love to the tides.

Next thing happens, I'm thrown far up onto the rocks. When I woke up it was morning and them Doore girls was gone.

That's it, that's the story. Ain't no one else around here going to tell you why them Doore girls lost their parents and them two survived, or why ain't no others died on the sea since them Doore girls washed up. Something was looking and found what it wanted. Something took a liking to them. Something that's keeping them all for itself.

They ain't changed much since then. Ain't got a gray hair between them, least not one as you'll ever see. And that ain't showing no disrespect. It's the truth.

I'm telling you this because, boy at your age, you should know there's some things made just for looking, ain't never meant to be touched, ain't never.

No.

SEMA

SEMA
(A TALE OF THE NORTHERN CLAN)

*I*felt the pulse before I saw her. The next thing I knew, she was obvious in the crowded concert hall, walking up to me, the same wide mouthed, full lipped smile she had when I'd roll out of bed and she knew she only had to throw off the covers to get me back beside her. There was some guy walking with her who didn't mean much.

"Jeremiah!" she called.

What's going on now? I wondered. She's using my true name.

Cathy glanced at me immediately. "Who's she that she knows your real name?"

Sema's use of my true name, Jeremiah, put me on guard. Most people know me as "Jim." Most people know Sema as "Sandy."

"Sema," I whispered. Cathy nodded. I could feel her trying to remember when I'd said the name before.

"Jeremiah," Sema said, closer now, her hand on my arm. She leaned forward and gave me a friendly kiss on the cheek. That was for the world to see. I felt her body rush forward and try to get into mine. But I am the Shield, and there was no entry. Still, she pushed her body over my shield, hoping the feel of her thighs and breasts would weaken me, perhaps force me to rut. Among our kind, those who are younger, it is common. Around us, people saw two friends greeting.

"Sandy." I gave her a hug. "I'd like to introduce my wife, Cathy."

Cathy smiled and extended her hand. Sema extended hers and I felt her scan Cathy quickly, neatly, sharing Cathy's memories of standing by a mirror, naked. *Not bad,* Sema pathed. *Buxom and full hipped. She's got strong thighs.*

She rides horses.

She does if she married you.

I don't know if I blushed, but I extended my hand to Sema's date. "Hi. I'm Jim Risman. You're?"

She has an hourglass figure, Jeremiah.

I know. She's also intelligent.

And?

And forgiving.

Sema smiled at that.

"Tony Newfields. Nice to meet you." Sema's date shook my hand. He had a good grip, but I knew he wasn't for Sema. He would never understand. Sema knew this, as well, I'm sure, but I could feel Tony's needs within him. That explained Sema's spending time with him. The four of us chatted for a few minutes as Sema and I conversed on our own.

Is she a good wife for you?

Yes, I couldn't have found better.

She seems happy. Does she know? Does she understand?

She doesn't know everything, but she knows enough not to be frightened by me. She asks me where I go at night, sometimes. She knows when I leave and keeps my body covered until I return. Does she understand? I don't think any of them do. They can guess, but they can't know unless they can do.

Sema nodded at something Cathy said. She nodded at me, too.

Have you seen any of the others since the last Calling? I asked.

No, she replied. *I felt Jedediah and Ezekiel pass over one night, scanning for remnants. I don't know if they found any.*

It was my turn to nod, this time at something Tony said. Sema smiled.

I guess we did a good job, then.

Sema nodded, but only for me. I felt a tear inside her, released my

Shield and held her close.

You saved my life that time.

I know, I pathed. I did. It was true.

I t was a little over twenty years ago, during the time from January to February when the real cold of winter hits New England. Each night, Cathy and I would walk my dog, Maschaak, a hundred and eighty-three pound Newfoundland. The pup and I love the cold, but Cathy doesn't quite take to it as we do. We'd be almost through walking before she'd start to warm up. She used to be jealous of the dog. Eventually she realized how much he meant to me, although she could never understand what he was for me. All she would ever see was a big, black, drooly dog.

As we walked, she'd ask questions; "What are you listening to?" or "What's out there?" or "Who you talking to tonight?"

"Nothing," I'd say, as I did that night.

In truth, there was a lot of activity up in the ether, the overhead where we communicate. Everyone was jumpy, although none of us knew why. I don't know if I was the first one to figure it out, but I was the first one to path it openly.

The Earth was warming. To your children, a respite from the cold. A welcome thaw and lower heating bills. Not so to ours.

A Venting! I pushed the message so hard I almost fell down. The dog was with me and I drew from him. Cathy held my arm. Normally a signal wouldn't go out so vibrantly, but I am the Shield. Often I have no choice how these things happen. As soon as I caught my balance I began tracking to find their access points. The dog started growling, sensing my activity, and I welcomed his additional energy.

Jedediah, who is the Lifter of the Northern Clan, was the first to respond. I could feel him coming up as if from heavy slumber. *Jeremiah?*

Yes.

Where are they?

Local.

Ezekiel joined in then, *How can you tell?*

The Earth warms, I pathed.

Why local? asked Jedediah.

Ariel, who Sees, answered for me, *There are no temperature aberrations elsewhere.*

All this occurred while Cathy, Maschaak, and I took a single step. Then there was silence until we finished our walk. Occasionally I would see the dog looking intently or sniffing the wind, and I would listen for anything he might find.

We got back to our house and started taking off our coats. The dog stayed beside me. Normally he either goes over to his bed and lies down or goes to his water bowl for a drink. Cathy told him to go lie down and he just looked at her. She turned to me and said, "You're going out tonight, aren't you."

"Do you mind?"

"No," she lied. "You'll be okay?"

"Aren't I always?"

She didn't answer and we headed for bed. The dog, who usually sleeps at the foot of our bed, begged to sleep on top, beside me.

I fell asleep quickly, pushing my body down through the levels of rest until it reached a stasis that would keep it active until I returned.

About sixty miles up I felt Jedediah, Ezekiel, and Ariel waiting. Aaron and Malachi awoke from the south, Rhode Island and the Connecticut shores respectively, and joined us. Aaron Talks to all that is and Malachi Moves through things.

Jeremiah, Aaron pathed, *what can you tell us?*

There wasn't much. *Central New England seems to be the locus of the heat.*

And your shielding? Ariel now. *What do your shields tell you?*

I've felt a surging along my shoulders and spine, I mumbled the path.

How long? Jedediah asked.

Ezekiel's healing flooded me, making the words come easier. *Too long. A week, perhaps. I didn't want to respond until I was sure.*

Ariel, who Sees, stated it non-judgementally. *You have a human wife.*

No! I pulsed. I threw my shield up so fiercely it hazed visibly for a moment. *I haven't denied my first love for her. She knows this and accepts it.* Under the cloudless sky, under the light of the stars, my shielding forced them back. Without thinking, Jedediah, who has helped stars pass when their time is near, engulfed me in his strength, fearing I might harm myself as well as them.

Far below us, the moon, a cap of orange on the horizon, framed Ezekiel's thought, *Peace, brother. It was a question we had to ask.*

Malachi tried to change the subject, *Are any of us ready?* Unfortunately, his question threw attention back on me. None of us would be fool enough to force a challenge without a Shield. This was a Venting. They would be legion. There were only six of us.

I've been doing some ranging with the dog. I can be ready in two days.
Jedediah again, *Do we have that much time?*
We don't have much choice, pathed Malachi.
I won't be able to find where they come from, but I can lay down a gentle shield and see where it waffles, I offered. They all thought that was good. *In two days then.*

Cathy was half sleeping when I came back. The alarm went off after I'd been in bed for thirty minutes. I shut the alarm off and let her get an extra half hour of rest before I said, "Babe, time to get up."

She put her arm around me and buried her head in my chest. "Not yet." Her free hand tugged on my shorts. I told the dog to get off the bed.

Two nights later I had my answers. There was a mild disturbance in the Berlin, NH, area, and a tremor in Marlboro, Mass, pushing the Assabet river from I-495 to Rt 9, forcing the heat track of Rt 85 to take a wide curve around Browns Corner.

Ezekiel, Jedediah, Ariel, Aaron, Malachi! They each answered. *A Calling.* I placed a spoor where we were to meet and when.

Not much later Ezekiel, Jedediah, Ariel, Aaron, Malachi and I stood beside a snow covered field off Rt 85. The moon was strong and bright in a cloudless sky. There was a ring of pines and birches encircling the field that started about fifty feet to our right, went straight back as far as you could see – which was pretty far, it was near a full moon – and around then back to the road, ending the semi-circle about 350-400 yards down the road from us. The field was huge and hot.

"Well, brothers. Time's a' wasting," I said. I wasn't in a hurry, but I was anxious. I wanted things over, done with. We moved into the field and alarms went off. I threw a shield up in front of us and pathed for them not to walk through. My senses told me something else had entered the field.

I let my brothers share what I was feeling. "Mortal?" Ariel asked.

"Barely," I replied. Whatever I was picking up was human, but not in the sense that yours are human. "Hold on, I'm checking."

I was having trouble because what I was picking up had the shape of yours but the feel of mine. Your shape and my feel doesn't normally throw me. It was the female form – a very female form – that threw me.

Something came towards us from the line of trees. Ezekiel said, "It's a woman."

Ariel asked, "What's she doing here?"

It was indeed a woman. Fair skinned, dark haired and brown eyed. Her eyes were wide and almost tear shaped, almost oriental, and her nose was slight, but was shaped either for a southern Italian or for a middle European Jew. Full lipped and wide mouthed, and even before she was close enough for me to make out facial features, I could taste her build. This woman is made for the night, I thought.

"Who are you?" I asked.

"Who are you?" she demanded in return. Her voice told me she was use to being answered.

I could feel Ezekiel put a calming on her, although I didn't feel she needed one. That was strange and should have warned me. She was overly confident in what most women could consider a potentially dangerous situation. She looked at him as he put her to sleep.

He asked Ariel. "Are you looking?"

"Yes." We waited. Then, "A candle surrounded by gusting winds. Some kind of hybrid? More human than we are? No, she has abilities. She's sensitive," he directed this comment at me, "but no more so than she needs for her own protection."

"Can you tell what her abilities are?" I asked.

"I'm getting there, be patient."

I wondered if that was just something he said or did he feel what I was feeling. Looking at her, watching her lying there on the snow, standing near her, almost over her, drawing her spoor deep into me, I wanted to join her on the ground. I was ashamed at my urge and hoped the others didn't know.

"She's of the earth, some kind of Linker. I'd say her talent has to do with earthquakes."

Jedediah pathed for all of us, *Earthquakes? What do you mean 'earthquakes'?*

Ariel relaxed his Sight. "That I can't say. All I can tell you is that her talent has to do with earthquakes. Something strongly and intimately tied to the earth, anyway. Also that she has some human in her. Either that or she's something I've never seen before. Almost looks like she's one of us but can remain hidden, but not like Jeremiah can. It's as if hiding, but not shielding, were one of her talents. I'd say she's more like us than not, but she has strong human ties."

"What shall we do with her?" Ariel asked. I had some ideas.

Ezekiel, the oldest and wisest, decided for us. "Tonight's a wash, at least until we know why an unknown near-one entered the field we chose for gathering." He looked at me, then, and said what he had to, "We need to know more about her."

I nodded.

"Shall I wake her before we go?" he asked.

"No, thanks. I'd rather be the only one here when she comes to."

They'd been gone about five minutes. I kept scanning for things either leaving or entering the earth, some kind of activity to alert me to danger, but there wasn't a thing. Suddenly I sensed her gaze upon me.

"You alright?"

"No," she said. "I'm half left."

I laughed. "You came over to us and fell. You took a nasty bump on the head, I think."

"Help me up."

As Shield, I am suspicious of many things. Because I am suspicious, I tied myself to the earth before offering my hand. She grabbed it and tugged, trying to make me fall. Instead I picked her up without strain. She focused on where I was standing but kept quiet about it, saying, "You're a strong one, aren't you?"

I smiled again. "Can I offer you a ride home?"

"No, thanks. I don't live far and can walk from here. Where did your friends go?"

"They went home. We didn't expect to find anybody here. You kind of threw us."

"So what were you doing out in a field in the middle of the night?"

"We're astronomers. Amateurs. I saw this field and thought it would be a good spot to bring our telescopes."

She wasn't buying any of this and probed me. I kept a tight, quiet watch and let her mind run its hands over my body, partially because I wanted her to think I was a human male, partially because I enjoyed the feel of this woman's touch. Her mind ran its hands over my thighs and buttocks several times. At first she did this to see if my musculature would allow me to link to the earth as she did, but soon I realized she enjoyed what she felt.

"I have to go," I said. "If you don't need a ride and you'll be okay, I'm going to take off."

"Good night, then," she said, and left.

I was halfway home when Ezekiel called, *Jeremiah?* I closed myself and didn't answer.

I heard her calling over the next few nights, feeling her wanting me at the edge of my mind, trying to find me. That would be impossible for her to do, of course, because no matter what happens to me I can't stop being a Shield. But being a Shield didn't stop me from contacting her. I never asked her name nor could I reveal any knowledge of her. Instead I gave her the idea I'd be at a specific place at a specific time, a public place, a shopping mall close to where she lived. The dog came with me.

She was waiting for me. "I knew I'd find you here," she said. We made small talk.

When I felt it was right, I said, "I have a lot of questions to ask."

"Here?"

"This is as good a place as any," I said.

"Follow me." She grabbed my hand and led me back to the parking lot. "You drove, right?"

"Yes."

"Where's your car?" A couple of minutes later I was following her. The dog was jumpy. So was I. She was leading me towards her apartment. "Have you eaten?" she asked once we arrived.

"No, but I'm not hungry."

"How about him?" she nodded at the dog.

"He's fine. A bowl of water, perhaps."

"Then sit down in the living room and you can ask all the questions you want." She went in the kitchen and I heard the faucet run.

She came back and chose an overstuffed, green chair in a corner of the room. The room was homey, but sparse. The TV had lots of dust on it, but the radio – and I do mean radio, not a stereo or even a boom-box – was neat. There were large, green leaved, flowering plants everywhere, especially behind and around her chair. A knitting bag lay next to her chair. Lots of needles stuck out of it with lots of balls of yarn strewn around it. She picked up something in the process of being knitted. It was flat as it came out of the bag but assumed a fluid, undulating shape as she placed it on her lap. I thought it was alive, that maybe it was a kitten or something that'd played in the yarns. But it wasn't a kitten, just something she was making. It took four needles of various sizes, and yarns trailed from it to the floor. She picked up several of the balls of yarn and placed them around her on the floor. I noticed that each of the balls – I counted eight different colors and thicknesses - had a thread leading to the thing on her lap.

She sat there, relaxed but waiting, her legs crossed underneath her, her wide, brown eyes always on me, her tongue running her lips as if it were a hot August night and her lips oozed lemonade, her breasts filling her shirt, moving slowly with her breathing, light dancing off the needles, the thing in her lap writhed as her needles passed through it, trapped in her lap by the webbing that surrounded it.

"What do you want to know?"

"Your name would be a good place to start."

"Sandy. Sandy Fuller."

"What name do you call yourself when you don't speak it?"

She looked at me, more intently than before and with fear. I was glad for that. She showed no fear when she met us on the field. Now she did. The needles drew tighter, the knitting writhed less. "What do you mean?"

"When you're with other people, you can look at them and know what they're thinking, right? Maybe not the exact words of their thoughts, but you know what they'll do, how far you can go, when to be afraid, when to stay away from people and not go places, right?"

She didn't move.

"And there's more than just knowing what people will or won't do, isn't there? You can do things that you've had to keep secret, things you couldn't tell anyone." I did some looking myself. Surface looking. Like viewing the surface of a lake. You don't know how deep it is or what's under the surface. You only know there's water there. "Things you've never even told your sister, Trisha. Isn't that right? Things to do with the ground?"

She was definitely frightened at this point. I was glad. This Sandy Fuller was too use to being in control of situations, or at least being able to steer them.

"You're like me, aren't you?" she asked.

"Am I?"

My name is Sema.

I didn't respond. As a matter of fact, I talked through her path.

Sema, she pathed a second time. I continued to ignore it. I felt her push herself around me, but kept my shields in a tight ordering, filtering things around me, giving the scent of a common man.

Sema, and you are a fool, and I will no longer be afraid of you.

JEREMIAH! I brought my shields up, shaping their energies into probing and grasping fingers and hands, crushing the parts of her brain that she used for pathing. I wanted her immobilized, unmaneuverable, motionless and optionless. True, I am the Shield, but much of Shielding is offense.

Sema rocked back into her chair. Her knitting fell as she grasped the sides of her head, the needles dropped, the threads of yarn limp, the thing in her lap part of a sweater once again.

I stood up as she sat there, her mind still recoiling from my thought. She wasn't as strong as I surmised and passed out as my projection reverberated in her mind.

I was sitting on the couch when she awoke, groggy. "I need some water," she said. As she passed in front of me her legs gave out. I caught her before she'd fallen far and pushed some strength into her. She looked at me, then, her eyes clear and the pupils wide, her irises almost not showing, so that her eyes appeared as black and deep as fissures in the earth. She pushed me back onto the couch and straddled me. Her left hand grabbed my hair and pulled my head back so that my neck was exposed. No vampire could have looked more frightening. Nor more seductive. She sank her teeth into my shoulder, deep into the muscle, burying her teeth slowly, gently, until blood erupted from my skin. I didn't make a sound, but the dog, quiet and sullen until now, growled at her. She hissed at him and I laughed.

"He is mated to me in ways you couldn't understand. Your threats mean nothing to him." As if to prove my point, the dog growled and bared his teeth. *Good puppy. It's okay. Go lie down.* The dog looked from me to her and back. If a dog could shrug, he did, then went back into the kitchen and slept on the floor.

She rubbed herself against me and I could feel the rut beginning. But there are codes by which we live, ethics which none of us will pass. Originally the codes were to keep your kind safe from us, now they're used in all things, even in communicating among ourselves.

She was kissing me, arousing me, moving things in me that my dear Cathy did not know I had, but I kept my arms at my sides, my hands limp, using all my mind to keep my body unresponsive.

"I want you," she said. I smiled. She pulled back from me then, the enormity of the thought clouding her features. "You don't want me?"

"I will not do what I am not asked to do. I will not go where I am not invited."

She breathed deeply, as if pulling my words into her body and making them hers. Before I knew it, her shirt was off and her hands were behind her back, unfastening her bra. "You're invited, lover." She pulled my face into her breasts, forcing a nipple into my mouth. *You are invited.*

I've always been gentle with human lovers, but not so with my own. She drew blood from me, and now it was time for return.

I reached for my clothes two hours later, not wanting to see the look of triumph in her eyes. She lay on the floor where I left her, modesty neither a question nor a concern. She wore her bruises, where I'd bitten and scratched, like badges of honor. "You're getting dressed?" she asked. I nodded. She stood on her knees before me and grabbed my buttocks in her hands. "Not yet, lover. Not yet." I had only my shirt on. Nothing else, and it was unbuttoned. She wrapped her mouth around me. I closed my eyes, listened to the dog's breathing in the kitchen, felt the outer cold on my chest and thighs, filled myself with her musk, and guided her head until her tongue made me weep.

Eventually she was satisfied she'd taken everything I could give. I remember thinking then that Ariel voiced truth, this woman was more like us than not.

"What is your talent?" I finally asked, when she sat back from me, her own needs sated.

"I don't know. What do you mean?"

"What can you do that no one you know can?"

"I think I can read minds."

"So can we all. But to each of us is given a uniqueness, a singularity, a gift that is at best mimicked by others. What is yours?" She knew what I meant and tried to hide the information from me. "You will not tell me?" I asked.

"I don't know what it is."

"Your body gives you away, don't you know? Each of our talents belie themselves in our shape. Your thighs and calves are the only thing about you obviously out of proportion to the rest." She opened her mouth to protest but I kept on. "I know, you weightlift and exercise to balance yourself, but it won't help. Your talent is earth-bound. You can either tell me or I'll find out for myself."

She looked at me then, and I could feel her determining strategies, trying to determine from my morphology exactly what my talent might be. I wanted her mind focused on my question, but gave her an answer I felt she needed. "When I spoke my name, it was an unspoken whisper."

She drew back and didn't hesitate her answer. "I can make earth-quakes."

"We thought as much. Can you control them? How intense can you make them? Do you have to make earthquakes? Every once in a while, perhaps?"

"I can control them, to a degree, yes. I don't know how strong I can make them. One time, when I was a child, I got angry at someone and destroyed their house."

"Then you are directional?"

"Directional?"

"You can control the path the earthquake takes as well as the intensity?"

She nodded. "You wanted to know if I have to make earthquakes. I'm not sure what you mean, but I know I get sick if I don't make them for a while. Sometimes I go down to Connecticut, there's a place where the earth rumbles. They call the rumblings 'Moodus noises'. Sometimes it's the earth. Sometimes it's me."

There was nothing else I needed. "I have to go."

"Will you come back?"

I had no choice. I nodded, but didn't say anything.

Cathy had left for work when I returned.

There was a note, "Call me when you get in. Love you," on the kitchen table. Still slick from Sema, I showered instead of calling. I called later, told her I loved her, hung up and cried, enraged at my choices.

Half way through the day, Ezekiel called, *Well?*

She can control and direct earthquakes. She is also quite like us, more so than she is human, I think.

A talent like that could be useful right now. I noted that he didn't comment on my second statement, but I pathed agreement.

Would she help us?

I'll find out.

We gathered at the field that night. Sema was there. She wasn't use to so many voices inside her head and it fatigued her. Ezekiel was concerned. *Are you well, child?*

This is new.

I'm a Healer. I can help. His eyes closed and you could see the confusion leave Sema.

What did you do to her? I asked

Nothing to her. I made the rest of you talk tighter. That was Ezekiel's "I will not go where I'm not invited." Sema didn't say, "Okay, come into my head and help," so he wouldn't.

Sema, I pathed, *can you detect any earth activity?*

Yes. I'd already explained the situation to her. It also answered a question I'd forgotten to ask; how did she end up in the field where they were moving? My brothers were listening, and it made them feel better, too. *So that's why you were here that other night?*

She stopped thinking for a moment, as if the question were so foolish that it shouldn't be asked. *Yes, of course.*

Can you lead us to their Vent? asked Ariel.

She started trudging through the snow. Jedediah pathed me, *She can't even lift herself?*

Malachi cut in, *She's not completely like us. More like them than us in some ways. What can you expect?*

How would she feel about being lifted? Jedediah asked.

Let me. Then to Sema, *Sema, can you move objects?* I felt a "no." *Can you move yourself, I mean up into the air, kind of like flying?*

There was a laugh, then, *Give me a break, will you? You going to tell me you guys can do that, too?*

My brothers must have thought I'd already started lifting Sema because as soon as her thought finished they floated past her. She looked at them, pathed, *Hey, wait,* and noticed their feet weren't on the snow. "Oh shit!" she said.

I don't know if that was a response to seeing my brothers lifting themselves or suddenly feeling herself weightless. I could tell by the way she began spinning that she couldn't bend gravity the way we could, so I gave her enough mass to keep her food down, lifted myself beside her, and went after the others. *Is there anything you can't do?* she asked.

Still have trouble pissing into the wind.

She laughed.

Can you still tell where they're coming from?

She pointed to the far edge of the field, behind a small knoll that hid the beginning of the forest from the road.

Suddenly my senses flared: *Link to me!* My brothers threw themselves, their energies, into me, absorbing my gift to strengthen themselves. *Forming!* We became a thing of six arms. Sema was next to me, looking at me, and didn't need a separate linking. I hit the ground, taking her with me, and pushed my armor like a sunburst past my brothers.

The field was alive with them. The creatures we had sensed these past few nights. Creatures with the shapes of men, but men enlivened by a wounded god. Small, round, twisted cherub-like things. Large eyed and fanged, with horns the same color as their bodies, coming out directly over holes that served as ears. Monopods with hooves the reverse of horses', and of many colors. There couldn't have been this many if they had been waiting for us.

The waves of aggression were incredible. I could feel myself being hammered as they sought to enter us.

Jeremiah, Ezekiel pathed. *Can you take this?* None of my brothers had ever asked me that question before. The strain must have showed. It is said among our kind that nothing can pass a Shield unless the Shield so wills it, but I came upon my talent early and am still young in its use.

Presently, my youth was leading us to downfall. Superior strength often falls prey to superior experience. My shields have absorbed the power of tidal waves before they could claim a coast, but so many skilled foes I was not used to. Jedediah was powerless to go beyond my shields, and to drop them left us open to the enemy's attack.

Ariel Saw me and cried out, *Jeremiah*. My body started phasing between your world and ours as I cannibalized myself to strengthen my shield. I felt Ezekiel's arms lift me and listened to his body dissolving to replace the parts I lost. He wailed as he assumed my pain, pain he could endure because it is the Healer's gift, the near ultimate sacrifice. The agony was for his own, as parts of him died to renew me and were replaced, I feared even faster than his body could stand.

Jedediah thrust his hands into my head, phasing and linking to me. *Use me,* he demanded and I was too weak to resist. His massive form began to collapse as he moved towards all life's destiny. Crying with pain and rage and my own weakness, I channeled the strength of this starquaker through me.

Our minds claimed the thought together. *Starquaker.*

I'm looking, Ariel called. *There!* His mind pointed to a planetless star so far away you will not know of it for millennia yet. I opened a pipe where my shield had grown weakest and Jedediah, Aaron, and Malachi rushed out. Aaron told the star of our need and, with its agreement and acceptance, Jedediah clutched and crushed it until friend star raged anew. As the star quaked its last, Malachi raced through its heat gathering the energies of its furnace into himself. A new mystery for your philosophers to ponder. An average, sun-like star, in less than a second collapsing to a hole in the sky, yet no radiation given off.

The evil, the insanity, of the creatures before us was draining me of what little life I had left.

As my body baked itself into a final form one shield was breached. Suddenly Ezekiel was there, his body arcing as the Terrors raced through him, his body replicating with each strike as he used his talents to fortify my wall.

Then our brothers returned with a Sacrifice of Innocence, a power no evil can face. It was this willing sacrifice that saved us, as it always has been and, we fear, always shall be. This is how wars will always be won or lost. Not with tanks and bombs, but with hearts, and minds, and the Sacrifice of Innocence.

I started to fold my shields around our attackers. I gathered them, Jedediah grouped them.

Ariel, can you See a place to put them? Jedediah asked, tightening his lifted grip until it seemed these small ones would burst like fleas between his unseen fingers.

Sema cut in, *Let me.* She lifted her right leg, as if to step over something in the snow. Instead of stepping forward, however, she stamped it down, tucking her arms and bending her knees when her foot hit the snow. She looked like a petulant child stamping her foot, about to pout, defying a parent when it is time for bed, but the quake forced all save Jedediah and I to lift ourselves from the ground.

There was a clean rift in the world, starting at Sema's foot and extending some thirty feet into the woods. At its widest it was ten feet. Jedediah released his grip and the creatures plummeted into it. Sema faced the rent sideways, raised her left foot and pushed it slowly into the snow. The earth sealed and covered itself over as if it had never opened at all.

We fell, exhausted. All save Sema, who watched us and waited, and Malachi, who retained enough starstrength to feed us. My body started re-energizing, reshaping and reforming so that I could again walk among men. Sema watched us, stood over us, and smiled. She probed me then, abruptly and viciously. My secrets would remain hid, as they must, but I was too weak for anything else and let her look.

Eventually, one by one, the rest of us regained our sense of self.

Any more for tonight? Ezekiel asked. None of us could find anything. One by one, we left.

Cathy wasn't up when I got home, but she woke up as I got into bed. I got beside her, held her close and played spoons. She held my arm in hers and placed my hand on her breast. I lay beside her, and I wished with all my heart that I, and not friend star, had died.

There were fewer of them the next night. So few, in fact, we were suspicious. They do not come and go so easily, especially not when it's our time, the deep winter. It was a time for Aaron, Ariel, and Malachi to use their crafts. These three went high into the air, Aaron asking, Ariel looking, Malachi to go where they told him. Ezekiel, Jedediah, Sema and I stayed in the field. Ezekiel and Jedediah were describing their talents to her, joking and kidding about things in their past, acknowledging things in hers. Finally she turned to me. "But what is it you do?"

I said nothing.

"Tell her, Jeremiah," said Jedediah. I think Ezekiel realized then that something about Sema unsettled me. It might have been nothing more than her power to seduce me. I wasn't sure.

Don't be ashamed, brother, pathed Ezekiel. *We've each had the blood burn and ache within us. You're fortunate there is someone to satisfy your need.*

Sema asked again, "Jeremiah, what is your gift?"

"It is nothing."

"Nothing!" howled Jedediah, his mind echoing the word into the cosmos. I suddenly felt myself lifted in his hands and tossed, a paper-doll in a hurricane, high above the clouds. *Baby brother, tell the little one your gift!*

Jedediah, started Ezekiel, but too late. Jedediah so loves me, and my shielding makes me invulnerable to his play, so he does not fear to delight in what I can do. *Do you not know, Sema? Jeremiah is the greatest of us all!* He tossed me into the Great Winds, the atmospheric Rivers encircling the earth. *He is the Watcher, the Guardian, the Keeper, The Watchman in The Tower, He Who Stands and Never Sleeps, Lord of the Swift Warning.* Jedediah's joy was sending me the the edge of the atmosphere as he continued the litany of names both your kind and mine have given Shields throughout time. *He is the Singer in the Woods, the One Who Speaks in Silence. He is the Runner, the Hunter, the Shield Against Which Nothing Can Stand!* Jedediah was hurling me like a comet, whipping me around the sun. I enjoyed his delight, but had had enough. When my feet touched the ground, I drove them deep into the earth, drawing strength from the old and deep things there, things your kind have forgotten. Jedediah wasn't prepared for the shift and cantilevered himself, like a toy airplane from a child's elastic, racing through the sky. His laughter surrounded us like warm spring rain.

Sema looked at me. "You need the earth," she said.

Where the earth is, I am.

She smiled then. I should have explored, but Aaron, Ariel, and Malachi came back. Behind them we felt Jedediah creating gravity wells to hasten his return.

And? I asked.

Aaron started, *I asked the Old Ones what they could tell. There is a place, not far, perhaps a mile or so, along the river. The earth pitches down there, not much but enough. They said the quaking most often comes from there.*

Ezekiel, *Did you go look?*

Ariel, *I did, yes. I couldn't find anything there. There was nothing to See except a cave, a natural cave. If they use that as a Vent, it would take Jeremiah to know it.*

Malachi cut in, *I could go there, if all agree.*

No.

They all looked at me, surprised. But all knew not to deny me.

All except Sema. *Why not?*

Jedediah, who had returned, pathed, *Little one, none of us violate baby brother's warning.*

She didn't understand, but kept silent as we went our separate ways.

I was back home walking the dog when Ariel's voice, an agony in my head, rocked me, *Jeremiah! I can't See Malachi. And he is the least of us.*

The others?

I called you first. Shall I call the others?

Ezekiel, for sure. Aaron, to Ask the earth and stars where our brother's gone. And Jedediah, to help Lift him if the need arises. The dog came up beside me. *Very well, pup. You can come, too.*

Thus my clan gathered again, far up among the stars, and called to our lost brother. There wasn't even an echo of his mind to be found. But this is also where older men can teach the young. *Jeremiah,* pathed

Ezekiel, *you can shift his shield matrix, can't you?*

Of course, why didn't I think of that?

Can you do it now? asked Aaron.

I gauged my remaining strength. *I would need to draw from you,* I explained. *Even then it would leave me weak.* The sun was coming soon. We'd have to be about our lives among men. I pathed to Ezekiel, *Do you ache for him?*

He is alive. There is no sense of passing. There is fear, and pain, but no direction for me.

Tomorrow then, unless you feel him fading sooner. I will alter his shield then follow your mind to him. We all thought that was best and parted for the morning.

The night didn't come too quickly. I told Cathy the situation and she knew she might not see me for a day or two. The dog came with me, for which I was glad. I left word for my brothers that I would meet them later, I wanted to explore some things myself.

There was no one and no thing in the field when I got there, so I went to Sema's. She was gone also. Aaron and Ariel said there was a scar in the earth somewhere close by. Malachi had offered to go there. He wouldn't go against my words, but I thought to look anyway.

It was easy to find, close to the highway and rising slightly by the roadside. There was no snow anywhere around it, but scrub brush, a vertical earthen opening, barely wide enough for a man to fit through, deep with blackness and something cloying inside. Directly in front was a hollow in the earth. To either side rills ran at angles, like giant's legs gently covered by earth. Here was their true Vent, totally hidden by not being hidden at all. The earth pulsed, rhythmically, under my feet. The Vent quivered, as if giving birth to something moving deep in the earth.

Malachi? Nothing. I told the dog to wait up on the hill and went inside.

I'd walked about five feet when I was forced to squeeze through a narrow. Something moved against my leg, ran up the side of my thigh and was gone. I clenched my fists on the other side of the narrow, turned, and put my hands on the walls of the cave. The narrow twitched. I pulled my hands back and lifted them to my face. They held Sema's scent.

Something moved further in the cave and I followed. There was a reek of fear and nausea now. I was about to leave when I felt Malachi's scent in front of me.

Are you here, my brother?

Of course he is. Sema pathed, behind me. I turned and she was there, smiling. *Here is your brother. I've kept him all neatly wrapped for you.* She tapped her foot on the ground and part of the cave wall fell, exposing luminescent ore. Malachi was twenty feet in front of me, trapped in something that could have only been made by a spider, but no spiders could grow so large. I looked closer and he saw me.

Help me, please. His scent ached out, almost too weak to touch me.

I energized, locking on the webbing that held him. Something moved behind him, revealing itself as it came around to face me. Something heavy, something old. A spider's body, to be sure, but only to the thorax. From the abdomen a human form sprang, as black and bristly haired as any spider's body could be. The arms were shaped like a man's, but ended in a spider's scapula and claws. The head was also shaped like a man's, but had a spider's eight eye array, and the chelicera and fangs of all Arachne's children. I could tell it didn't fear me as much as I feared it.

Maschaak, come!

The dog shaped before me, first a pup, then my dog, then a lion, finally emerging as a manticore, the body of a great lion, the head of a man with a lion's mane, a mouth of razor and needle like teeth, and a tail ending in a mace of poisonous darts, the shape this angel most often uses to protect me. The old thing backed away from Malachi, going deeper into the cave. My guardian followed.

That leaves you and me, lover. Sema called.

Why?

These things... her mind wavered, unfocused. Something small and colored ran around her, laughing, and left. There was a greater coldness now, something untouchable in her. *I can open the earth for them, even in this cold. They protect me from others like you.*

That was what Ariel saw as "hidden." They had found and seduced her. I was saddened, having come close to that path myself, but pity wasn't something I could presently afford.

I don't know about your friend, she nodded after the dog, *but you I do know.* She raised her foot, preparing to drive it down and rock the earth around me. *You must be in touch with the earth to be all that you are,* she smiled as she brought her foot down, *and I control the earth.*

I lifted myself off the ground, as if surfing on a sea of air. Her quake opened a fissure, but it passed harmlessly beneath.

You did not hear, nor understand. I pathed, softly, sad for what I would do. *I am not where the earth is. Where the earth is, I am.* I do not link to the earth, the earth links to me. It reaches out to me, not I to it.

She was not prepared for the shock I sent through her. It caught her like a lightening bolt, going up through her legs and imploding her mind. She was thrown back through the cave, tumbling and unconscious, finally stopping outside, near dead in the snow. I faced Malachi. He was weak. I freed him and he fell in my arms.

My brother, I pathed, sending some energy into him.

When I left, I felt her moving into the earth. No others among us share my gift, so I thought to explore.

Rest, Malachi. Then, *Jedediah, Ezekiel.* I felt Jedediah around me as Malachi was lifted from the cave. Ezekiel's pain passed through me, briefly, as he healed our brother. The dog trotted past me, the old thing's blood dripping and a bone hanging from the puppy's mouth. *Good boy, puppy.* He growled in return.

I met them all in the field, Sema in my arms. *What shall we do?* I asked.

Ezekiel, always the wisest, said, *Ariel, now that their wrath is broken, can you See more clearly?*

Yes, he answered. *She was bent to them, but only because she knew none like us. Thinking there were no others, she was seduced by those she thought could guide her.*

Ezekiel turned to me. *How come you didn't kill her back there?*

She could be one of us, couldn't she? Ezekiel nodded, turned to her, and healed what I had done.

And that is how I saved Sema's life. Cathy tapped my shoulder. My eyes cleared and I was back in the concert hall, the lights dimming to let the audience know it was time to return. Sema was looking with me and at me, sharing the memory. *Now, Sema?*

She kissed me, my mind, then. I let her, and returned it. It wasn't a passionate kiss, just one of memories shared. *You were a good lover, Jeremiah. You are a good friend.*

As are you.

"Earth to Jim. Hello, Jim?" Cathy said. Everybody laughed.

"He does that, too?" asked Tony. "Sandy always seems to go away for a while. Especially when she's asleep."

Sema blushed and I turned away.

"Nice meeting you," I said.

"Can I ask you a question?" he said. I nodded. "How come you use 'Jeremiah' as a nickname? Nicknames are usually shorter than proper names."

Sema shrugged an apology. Like I said, he'd never understand.

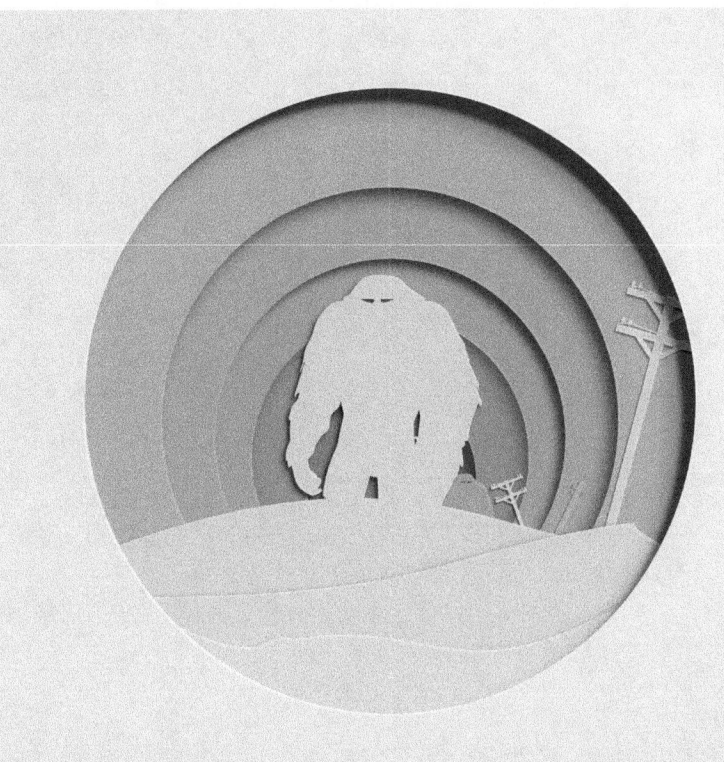

WINTER WINDS

WINTER WINDS

It occurred to me, as I sat watching, that the scene was not as it should be. The winds played oddly on the landscape, and even the patterns of the falling snow were different. However, it wasn't until I turned off the floodlights, which are white, and turned on the ground lights, which are pink, that the entire scene was revealed to me.

You must remember that this was a very typical wintry night. The snow was falling in one of the worst – or best, according to my son – blizzards of the decade. But it was one of the heaviest snowfalls in the century, according to the weather service.

Anyway, my son and I stood by the glass doors that led to the back-yard patio. We were watching the snow fall. He and I talked about skiing and sledding and tobogganing – I from memory and he from anticipation. As we talked, he pointed to something out in the field. We looked, but I couldn't see anything. He wasn't sure that he had seen anything, either, so we went back to a discussion of which broom to use to sweep off the pond.

We fell silent then, the late-night stillness of the house being inter-rupted only by the slurps of hot cider. We had pulled my big lounge chair around so that we could be comfortable. Suddenly David leapt to his feet and pointed out to the field. "Dad! Dad, look! What is *that*?"

His excitement startled me, and I jumped up from the lounge chair, nearly spilling my hot cider. I rubbed my eyes and looked. Then I rubbed my eyes and looked again. Something was moving out there on the field. Something...

"What is it, Dad?"

My first reaction was to take off my glasses and clean them. When I put them back on I saw the same basic picture. Only now the form – whatever it was – had moved farther across the field. "I'm not sure, Dave." That was an understatement.

I pressed myself up against the door to get a better look. It didn't help. David came up beside me. He sipped his hot cider, evidently more curious that frightened. That was good. At least one of us wasn't alarmed.

Whatever it was, it was huge. I couldn't make anything out clearly, but the snow formed a silhouette, and I could judge its size by the trees that it was near. The thing stood about twelve feet high. At one point, I remember, I wished that I were outside so I could see its shadow. Maybe then I could have had a better view of it, perhaps a better idea of what it was.

We stood there, watching, and it stopped. I swear if it had moved toward the house I would have been out the front door in seconds. There was more turbulence in the air around it. Once again Dave's eyes were better than mine. "Over There, Dad! Look!" This time I could tell that David was fascinated.

Now something moved in the snow over by the edge of the field. I hoped that it was just the snow swirling. No. I could see more clearly now. There were several of them! Most of them were as large as the first one I'd seen. Others were shorter; only eight feet tall. They all moved across the field in some kind of slow march.

At this point I turned on the pink lights and shut off the white ones. "What do you think they are, Dave?" I figured it couldn't hurt to ask.

"They're snow giants."

His reply was too calm, too knowing. "What makes you say that, Dave?"

"Just watch. You'll see."

Ok, I figured, maybe I *would* see. In the pink light their shapes were more defined. They appeared to be bipeds, but the proportions were a bit off.

In the midst of my analysis, Dave said, "See, Dad, I told you they were snow giants!"

I saw more agitation in the air. More gusts of wind? No, the pink lights showed differently. "What are *they*?"

"Those are the storm gnomes, Dad!" His voice was taking on that childhood air of contempt at their parents' ignorance.

As the snow swirled into the lighted area, I saw more shapes, different from the first ones. These were small – perhaps four to five feet long – and they were flying on leathery, batlike wings. At that point I became glad that I couldn't make out any features. Things really got bizarre then.

It seemed there was a battle going on in my field – some kind of invisible warfare. But why? I played coy. "My eyes aren't as good as yours, Dave. What are they doing out there?"

"Oh, come on, Dad. What do you think?"

"David, Don't talk to me like that."

"Well, gee, Dad. You mean you don't know?"

"Son, tell me what you see."

"Ok," David sighed. "In the winter, when snow has covered the ground and the temperature stays below freezing for a long time, the snow giants can move south. The snow giants – large, powerful, hairy beasts – move like men and are very friendly. Few reports, however, have been made as to actual encounters with humans, as snow giants tend to prefer the company of their own kind. At first it was proposed that they moved south for food or shelter. This was dismissed since their natural habitat is the extreme north. Only after close observation was the reason for their seasonal migration discovered."

I nearly laughed at this – it sounded so farfetched.

"One observation team," Dave continued, "noticed that the snow giants come out of hiding only during heavy storms. When they do, they either attack or are attacked by another set of creatures – the storm gnomes. These creatures ride the winds of the winter storms, existing in ice-laded clouds. When heavy snows come, the storm gnomes ride the winds to the ground to do damage; knocking down trees, tearing shingles off houses, breaking windows, breaking off gutters, and in more recent times pulling down transmission lines and towers, satellite receivers and the like.

"*Why* the show giants travel south to destroy the storm gnomes is not fully understood. No storm gnomes have been reported in the pole regions, so it is not known if these two groups are natural enemies. However, fortunate observers have reported seeing disturbances in the storms of winter and have noted the actions of these creatures."

Previously I had been too fascinated by the lecture and the display to look at David. But this was a bit much. Children are supposed to have imaginations, but this? Then I noticed that he had his reader in his hands.

"What are you reading?" I asked.

"I couldn't remember everything from class, so I was reading to you from the book. Come on, Dad, this is break time!"

I was having a hard time remaining calm. "All right, son, you've done well. May I see that for a minute?" He gratefully handed his reader to me.

Animals of the World was in the titlebar. Are there some I didn't know about? Didn't know about, sure, but this? Whatever happened to lions and tigers and bears? I tapped the reader to the page he'd been reading. Sure enough, there was a list of the observed habits of the snow giant. On the next page was a list of the habits of the storm gnome. I looked from the reader to the scene out on the field and back to the reader. Everything fit. I looked at the title again, read the jacket chart, and looked outside once more. Just as the reader said, the snow giants were catching the storm gnomes as the gnomes flew to the ground. They didn't eat them; they just threw them down. After a while the dead bodies began to pile up. Do you know what they were forming?

Snowdrifts!

I thought I was dreaming. Dave and I watched the whole night. At some point we must have fallen asleep because Janet woke us up in the morning. She said that we looked cute – David curled up with his face buried in my beard and the comforter pulled around us as we snuggled together in the lounge chair.

The first thing that David said was, "Come on, Dad, let's go see the tracks before the sun melts everything."

"What tracks?" asked Janet.

"Railroad tracks," I answered.

She looked at me and laughed. "No, really, what tracks?"

"Dave and I thought we saw something out in the field last night, that's all." I didn't look at her, but started pulling on my boots.

"What was it, Dave? Snow giants, maybe?" she asked very nonchalantly.

Was I the only one who didn't know? It must have shown on my face.

She laughed at me while helping David on with his suit. "Don't be upset, Jeff. I was born on Mars, remember? You've lived here a mere two years." She put on her own boots and tossed me my suit. "You're not expected to know everything about the place."

Did you enjoy **Tales Told Round Celestial Campfires**?

Please write a review on Amazon http://nlb.pub/TalesV1 and Goodreads http://nlb.pub/GTalesV1 (and our thanks!)

Become a member of Joseph's blog and read more

http://nlb.pub/JoinJoseph

Follow Joseph on
BookBub http://nlb.pub/BookBub
Goodreads http://nlb.pub/Goodreads
Facebook http://nlb.pub/Facebook
Twitter http://nlb.pub/Twitter
Instagram http://nlb.pub/Instagram
Pinterest http://nlb.pub/Pinterest
LinkedIn http://nlb.pub/LinkedIn

CURIOUS ABOUT JOSEPH'S NON-FICTION?

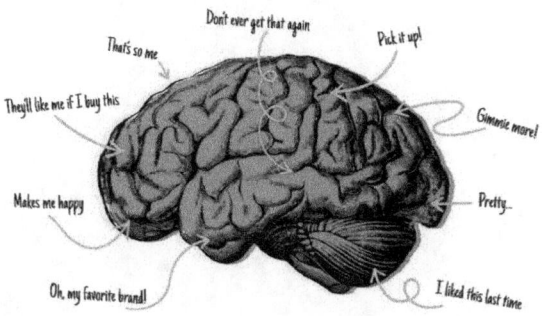

Avoiding Self-Destructive Behaviors

The first thing you need to know is that the best way to avoid self-destructive behaviors — those things you do which you don't mean to do that sabotage your work, your partnerships, your life. That's why such behaviors are also often called self-sabotaging and self-defeating behaviors — is to not have them.

That's kind of like "Just say 'No' to drugs," isn't it? Don't want to sabotage yourself? Then don't.

The good news is that just about everybody on the planet has some self-defeating behaviors. Self-defeating behaviors — in their more useful form — are known as our *protective instincts*. Protective instincts are those things that stop us from walking off cliffs, intentionally touching live high tension power lines, things like that. Protective instincts stop us from doing things that might hurt us.

Very useful, don't you think?

Then how did something so very useful become something so ... unuseful? Basically self -destructive, -defeating and -sabotaging behaviors are given to us (that's right. They're given to us) in childhood. We hear our mothers say things to our fathers, our fathers to our mothers, a much older and probably care-giving sibling to someone else. We see something done that should not have been done or seen. We believe we did a good thing, something to be proud of, and are punished for it.

Any and all of these things (and many others) occur repeatedly and when we're too young to understand them, to separate the people from the acts or the words, we get wounded in ways too penetrating and permanent to recognize.

The wounding is psycho-emotional, the most difficult to heal. The body, luckily, doesn't remember pain. When the body is wounded it sends a message to the brain, "That hurt! Don't do it again", but it doesn't remember the pain itself. That's the brain's job, to remember to help us avoid.

Which is what happens when we're older, supposedly wiser, going after a job, a promotion, a client, a lover, a friend

Then, suddenly poof, for reasons hidden away, not recognized because we as adults can't access the childhood memories that caused these kinds of trauma (without help and training, anyway), the memories and pains associated with them reveal themselves in behaviors that cause us to put on the brakes, to stop the win, to avoid doing whatever it is we're doing, to defeat, sabotage, and destroy our best efforts by turning them into worst efforts.

Triggering Events

Any behavior is a response to an internal or external event. More accurately, all behaviors are external manifestations of internal responses to internal or external events (what are called BMIRs - Behavioral Manifestation of Internal Response). We drive our cars, cook our dinners, hug others, and push still others away because our lifelong memories dictate how we respond to events happening around us now.

The same is true for self-defeating, destructive, etc., behaviors. We respond in the moment with a life time of experience. What we need to do is recognize what events trigger which behaviors.

An Example

A small company CEO always seemed to take vacations whenever a client was ready to sign, a product was about to be released, a milestone was about to be achieved, ... , whenever anything critical to company progress was going to happen, the CEO ... well ... vanished. Couldn't be reached by phone, by email, knocks on the door or requests to family and friends.

Company success was unobtainable because the individual leading the company psycho-emotionally refused to lead when the need for leadership was at its peak.

And it was all traceable to a mother who never honored a father's best efforts, demonstrated that lack of honoring in front of her children, and, as this individual grew, refused to honor this individual's best efforts as well.

When the repeated message is that no best effort is worthy, the desire to put forth a best effort fades — after all, it won't be honored — so while the conscious mind wants us to achieve, the lifetime of experience instructs us to avoid.

Changing Responses

Knowing your personal history of self -destructive, -defeating, -sabotaging, ... behaviors is part of the solution and is best done with professional help. After that knowledge comes learning to recognize what events trigger those behaviors. This takes a willingness to become self-aware that in itself can be a difficult and painful journey (although an incredibly worthwhile one (in my opinion) for those so willing).

It is while on this last journey that we learn to control our behaviors, to respond to events as we wish to rather than how we used to, to change what we were to what we can be.

It is up to us as individuals to decide.

Addendum

The person who taught me these things has long passed and I'm writing this post to pass on that learning to a friend, the CEO mentioned above, and including another lesson from this same master: My journey is my goal, my path is my prize.

Knowing, learning and changing is what life is all about. No matter where your path takes you, rejoice in it. No matter what your journey entails, relish it.

Fear of Rejection

I was contacted by someone whose personal life is interfering with their public life.

First, in a Facebook, LinkedIn, YouTube, Twitter world, I detect some kind of oxymoron in the thought that public and private lives are still separate.

Second, throughout all history it has been impossible for most people — barring sociopaths — to keep their private life and public life separate. I've known some people who are remarkably adept at compartmentalizing things and this doesn't mean they're keeping things separate, only that they're letting specific things through.

The reason it's impossible to keep different aspects of our lives separate is because all aspects of our lives are "powered" by our core psychologies and beliefs. Someone who's a joy on the job and a terror at home is simply bringing their work frustrations home and letting them out there. The reason people act out at home (private life) more than at work (public life) is because the relative safety of the home allows for more of the core to manifest itself.

Usually.

But this chapter is about *Fear of Rejection*, so let's get to it ... This individual's family-of-origin (the core family group that raised you) didn't support open emotionality (Note to parents: unless children learn how to express their emotions openly they'll never learn when it's not safe to do so). This lack of support planted a seed of emotional confusion and frustration.

Such seeds usually sprout polarity type demonstrations. The individual either grows cold (never having learned how to demonstrate emotions healthily the safest thing for them to do is shut theirs down when presented with yours) or demonstrates their emotions too easily and often (never having learned how to demonstrate emotions healthily they've never learned boundaries and limits to their own emotional displays). At the best of times there's a median ground where the individual doesn't grow completely cold with certain individuals or learns with whom it is safe to be emotional.

In this case, that seed was watered when a poor partner choice paired them with someone who could not honor commitments and philandered. Often.

And what sprouted is a fear of rejection.

As noted above, this fear wasn't compartmentalized to one aspect of life. What happened in their private life manifested in their public life. Seeking a new job, they decided the potential employer was not interested (and worse, if you know how these phobias make themselves known).

So they contacted me for some advice, and I share that advice with all those possibly facing similar fears.

Advice to the fearful

Your partner (I assume now an ex-partner)'s philandering was an indication of their psyche, not yours. You've decided their actions were due to some lack or inability on your part hence you've "developed a fear of rejection".

"Fear of rejection" isn't something that happens overnight. Nobody wakes up one morning, stretches, throws back the covers, looks smilingly into the sun and declares, "Yes, from this day forward I shall fear rejection!" This response - because that's what it is, it's a response to your environment - was something taught to you and learned over time. Because it was taught and learned, because it's not part of how you're designed to work, it can be unlearned, untaught, and more useful responses can take its place.

By the way, you were designed to be wonderful. Just like everybody else. If you're not wonderful right now, it's someone else's responsibility. Your parents, your partners, your co-workers, your supervisors, your friends, ...

But (*BUT!!!*) if you're reading this right now, you are being invited to take responsibility *from them* - they're obviously not good stewards of you - and put it where it belongs, *in you*.

Scary, I know, that "taking responsibility for yourself" part. We are what we've put our greatest efforts into creating and it took us our whole lives to become the way we are. It's tough to re-do a work of art so far along in its creation and that's okay, we're designed to be able to do it. It's part of that evolutionary process that's in our DNA.

I would offer that you've created a tool for dealing with certain types of information. Now you must decide if the tool you've developed — a fear of rejection — is the best tool for dealing with the "no information coming in" type of information, the "negative" information, and other certain types of information. Dealing with negative information - the type of information we'd rather not have - is pretty easy. First determine if it's valid information. It is? Then change the reason for the negative information (maybe it's time to change a job because of a harsh boss, change a partner because they don't care about you, change your brand of soap or laundry detergent, ...). It isn't valid? Ignore it and its source.

Right. Now let's deal with the "no information coming in" type of information. Often when people are waiting for a response from someone or something and they get no response whatsoever, they imagine the worst. In relationships (professional and personal) this becomes fear of rejection.

So first recognize you're using the fear of rejection tool to deal with "no information coming in".

Next, recognize that information is coming in, simply not information you have a good tool for. The information is "no information" because (without boring you with jargon) an information "vacuum" can not exist. The vacuum is being filled with information from your past experiences, and specifically your "fear of rejection" experiences.

As with your partner, so with this potential employer: whatever their response, they're making a statement about themselves, not about you. Your life-partner's philandering was a statement of their limits, their lack, and how they sought to fill them. It was a demonstration of their lack of tools and had nothing to do with you.

Really, truly, it is so. Believe it.

There's a tool I use, not specific to "fear of rejection" although I'm betting it would work quite well because it is a "fill the vacuum with correct information" tool. I contact people and ask them, "Have you made a decision yet?"

I know, you're shocked that I would be direct and to the point, yes?

This tool is built on another tool, an Eliadean tool, known as "choice is better than no choice". I believe knowing is better than not knowing, hence my desire to know as a fact that I'm "rejected" is stronger than my desire to remain ignorant of such a fact because knowing facts allows me choices. Not knowing limits my choices.

Knowing something is a fact allows me to make decisions and choices based on that piece of information. Not knowing makes me a victim of my ignorance, traps me in a well of uncertainty, and forces me to stop functioning until I learn what fact applies.

More to the case here, it causes me to live a life of fear rather than a life of joy, bliss, happiness, love, ... And I do know that how I choose to live my life directly affects all those around me. Living a life of fear will cause me to demonstrate fear-based behaviors to everyone I'm in contact with, especially those I love. If I interact daily with children? They will learn the "fear of rejection" lesson and the more I interact with them the better they will learn it.

So for me I'll chose a life of bliss, joy, happiness and love because I'd rather people drink those things from my cup than any others.

Rewarding Your Critical Actors

Do you have a little voice inside your head that warns you about things you're about to do? Maybe it goes beyond warning you, perhaps it out and out chides you or even yells so loudly it stops you dead in your tracks?

Congratulations, you've been in touch with what people studying learning models call your *critic* (not a surprising name considering what it does, is it?).

Do you have a little voice inside your head that makes suggestions on how to get the most out of whatever you're about to do? Maybe it goes beyond suggestions, maybe it reminds you of what worked and what didn't in the past? Maybe it demands this path be followed over that path?

Congratulations again, now you're talking with your *actor*.

Want to learn how to confuse them or even shut them up completely? It's probably obvious (once you think about it) that our mind's actor and critic come from different parts of the brain. The critic comes from the front part of the brain where reasoning occurs, the actor from the rear of the brain where we process vision and memory (generally speaking).

Both are necessary. They're part of what's called *instrumental conditioning* and constitute the most basic form of *adaptive behavior*. Adaptive behavior and instrumental conditioning are very important to our survival as individuals and as a species. We adapt how we behave in order to maximize rewards and minimize punishments, and that process of adapting is done in (hopefully) small steps by conditioning ourselves to our environment.

The actor reminds us what happened before in similar environments and helps us predict what to do in the present environment. The critic predicts future gains and losses by evaluating present conditions and information out of our direct experience. We need both of them. They work in tandem for most of us and people lacking one or the other tend to take unnecessary risks or avoid new situations altogether.

But what if your critic-actor is too critical or too ... umm ... actorial?

Both critic and actor cause the brain to send hormonal signals through the body. Most often these signals are survival oriented — great for the jungle and possibly night walks in a city, not quite the same as deciding what you should purchase or whether or not to get on that really big roller coaster.

So here's how to deal with both and let you — your hopefully rational, thinking, intelligent self — make the decisions.

First, Agree

People think this is an odd suggestion and it comes from lots of studies. When your critic is saying "No, don't! Danger, Will Robinson! Danger!" respond with "Thanks. That's good advice. I appreciate your letting me know that" or something similar. Strangely enough, all the critic really wants to know is that you're paying attention to warning signs in the environment. Letting your critic know you're doing so is often enough to either shut it up or quiet it down, at least for a while. Similarly, agree with your actor. Same rules apply.

Second, Take a Deep Breath

Remember those hormonal signals I mentioned? Those signals are survival based, as in fight or flight. Taking a deep breath, centering yourself, maybe even closing your eyes for a second, all send counter-signals telling your brain and body "It's okay. You can relax now. I'm here." Think of something funny, a joke or some such. Put a smile on your face. A real smile, not just a polite one. You'll find you can think clearer when you do.

Third, Act Intentionally

Your critic and actor are exerting all sorts of energy to tell you what might, possibly could, or should happen. The truth is neither they nor you know what will happen. What you do know is what's happening right "now" in the moment of the decision. This is where you take control of your adaptive learning and instrumental conditioning to your own best benefit. Decide what option looks best "as far as the eye can see" so to speak and make a deal with your actor and critic. Ask them to cover your back and let you know if something needs your attention. Nothing quiets these primitive parts of the mind more than asking them to help. Seriously.

Lastly, Take Small Steps

You've chosen a path, now move in that direction. Just a little, not a lot. Are you still okay? Everything still good? Great. Lather, Rinse, Repeat. The moment you can't see what's going on or things stop being okay, back up to your last safe spot and decide if you want to continue or not.

Summary

Your actor and critic are there for a reason. The goal is to use them rather than letting them abuse you.

Enjoy.

CURIOUS ABOUT JOSEPH'S OTHER FICTION?

BY JOSEPH CARRABIS

When we dream we speak a language which is also employed in the most significant documents of culture: in myths, in fairy tales and art, recently in novels like Franz Kafka's. This language is the only universal language common to all races and all times. It is the same language in the oldest myths as in the dreams every one of us has today. Moreover, it is a language which often expresses inner experiences, wishes, fears, judgments and insights with much greater precision and fullness than our ordinary language is capable of. - Erich Fromm

http://nlb.pub/EmptySky

Please enjoy this preview of *Empty Sky*

Synopsis:

The Moon embarks young Jamie MacPherson and his dog, Shem, on a quest to save the world's dreams. Along the way they must find Jamie's disappeared mother, Ellie, help his father, Tom, come out of coma, and stop the NSA's Earl Pangiosi from weaponising dreams to control society.

Excerpt: Chapter 1 - The Cabin

Jamie woke to Shem's tail thumping his legs. The big golden retriever sat at the edge of their bed and stared out the cabin window.

Jamie reached over the quilt and grabbed his tail. "What, Shem?"

Outside, peepers and crickets chirped. Raccoons chittered. Opossum and skunk hissed. Owls hooted and loons called. A wolf howled in the distance.

Shem looked back at Jamie and whined softly.

Jamie's tiny hand ran through his ginger hair and looked past Shem to the oak, elm, and pine of Michigan's Upper Peninsula forest. The moon, full and bright, illuminated the trees and the small, one-room vacation cabin at their center.

"Shem go pee?"

Shem jumped off the bed and scratched at the door.

Jamie glanced at his parents, Ellie and Tom, asleep in their own bed on the other side of the cabin and put his finger to his lips. "Shh. Mom and Dad sleeping." He crawled out from under the quilt and tip-toed in his stars-and-moon print Doctor Denton's to the door. Standing on a chair, he drew back the bolt and lifted the latch.

Cool winds changed rustling treetops into brooms sweeping low-hung clouds from late September skies. Dust devils spun mists where night air met day-warmed rocks. Trees bowed to the rising moon as its face changed from meteor-impacted gray to a beautiful, white-skinned woman's.

Shem walked into the night. Jamie followed.

The Moon continued her ascent.

The woods fell silent.

Silent.

Ellie sat up in bed. Her hands clenched the blanket and held it tight against her. A cold, dank wind swirled through the cabin, lifted things slightly as if inspecting them then putting them down, and drew a musk of old earths in its wake.

Moonlight entered the cabin's single room.

Ellie's eyes fixed on Jamie's empty bed.

"Jamie! Shem!"

Tom's eyes bolted open. He followed her gaze then rose and put his boots on in one motion. "Where are they?"

She hurried with her own boots. "The door's open."

Tom threw Ellie her coat. "They must be together. Shem won't let Jamie out of his sight."

"Something's got them. Some wild animal."

"There's no blood anywhere, Ellie. Shem'd raise hell if something got in the cabin or near Jamie." He grabbed an iron poker from the woodstove.

Ellie stopped at the door, a silhouette in the moonlight. "Shh."

Tom came up beside her. "What the...?"

"Shh!"

"What are they doing?"

"It looks like they're playing."

"With whom?"

Jamie and Shem romped in a grassy clearing twenty feet from the cabin. Moonlight cast long shadows everywhere as they danced about, the sole performers under a celestial spotlight.

Tom looked to the rutted dirt road that served as the camp's driveway. No cars but theirs. He scanned the shadows.

Ellie whispered, "Can you hear that?"

Tom pulled back. "He's laughing?"

Jamie danced in circles and laughed as if being tickled, his arms up as if waiting to be lifted, little hands grasping, little fingers curling.

"Shem's bowing."

"Isn't that dog for 'Let's play', bowing? He's not facing Jamie. Who's he playing with?"

Shem jumped and bowed and ran around as if playing catch with someone throwing his Frisbee.

The Moon rose above the trees and lit the clearing from above. Jamie's and Shem's shadows crept underneath them. The wind stilled.

Ellie grabbed Tom's arm. "Do you see that?"

Other shadows entered the clearing, some Jamie's size, some slightly larger. Shadows with nothing to cast them. Shadows where there shouldn't be shadows. Shadows standing upright, not cast on the ground.

Jamie danced with them and they danced around Jamie. Shem ran among them, played tag with them. Jamie laughed. Shem barked.

Not a warning, not an alarm.

Recognition.

Something twinkled in the shadows, prisms breaking the intense moonlight into hundreds of bright, tiny rainbows.

On the edge of the clearing, in the dark where the trees stood in ancient vigil, eyes gathered in the moonlight.

(one line space/not intro to new scene)

Ellie woke, the covers clenched in her hands.

She looked across the cabin and saw Jamie and Shem, sleeping together as always, in their bed.

She let out a breath and shook her head. It was a dream. The full moon's light came in through a cabin window. It must have disturbed her, woken her, worried her in her sleep.

She rolled over, away from Tom to give him a little more room.

Dew-laden, toddler-sized footprints and paw prints made a path across the floor from the cabin's door to Jamie and Shem's bed.

She sat up as the cabin door closed.

From Chapter 15 - Empty Sky

A cold wind ruffled Jamie's bathrobe against his pajamaed legs. Thick animal fur warmed his face like a blanket, its smell filling his nostrils with each breath.

But not Shem's fur. It smelled...heavier than Shem's fur...more urgent than Shem's fur.

He raised his head, his hands stiff from clenching Graywolf's coat.

"We're almost there, Jamie."

They moved through a rush of trees. White-barked birch and scotch pine, gray ash and winter oak towered over him, their branches alternately pine needle and leaf and snow covered and offering a canopy through which the night sky, its stars and planets, could still be seen.

High overhead the moon sailed through the sky, full and rumbling like a big church organ. The Aurora walked back and forth in the cold night, crinkling like cellophane candy wrappers, sounding almost like words just beyond his ability to understand, like the Aurora was people talking at a party, like when Mom and Dad had people over and Jamie and Shem listened from the top of the stairs.

The wind moved through the trees and sounded like long, low, breathy, conversations, as if the world talked all around him, ignorant or perhaps unaware or maybe even uncaring that he and Graywolf *ruddaRump*ed underneath.

Jamie whispered, "It sounds like everything's talking."

"Everything is, Jamie. The world just waits for someone to listen."

Something moved quick and clean, a snowhare, down and ahead of Graywolf's steady gait, leaping out of his way. Jamie wondered that he could hear it, wondered what kind of magic was in this place that he could hear things so.

Overhead, he heard the beating of great wings. Many of them. Large birds, and in a flock. From the island of trees ahead, wolves. Hundreds and hundreds of wolves. Howling, their calls drilling across the frozen arctic plains. Their howls answered from somewhere high up in the sky. From the forest of pine and birch trees up ahead came howls and the sounds of other feet, padded like Graywolf's, *ruddaRump*ing across the wilderness, gathering, all of them baying at the moon, some sounding like they came from the moon.

"We're here." Graywolf stopped running so quickly Jamie tumbled from his back, rolling in the hard-packed snow, rolling where many feet had pressed it down. He yelped and put his hands out to stop rolling. They came back cold and wet.

What's going on? Why wasn't Dad waking him up?

Tall pines and birch, ash and oak, continued their rumbling talk all around them, their breath filling the air with the scents of their saps and spines, their voices washed back and forth like waves on the snow. The moon continued its deep organ trembling high overhead. The Aurora he was right about. It did come down, right into this clearing. He could see there were lots of different lights moving back and forth, not just one big one. All the different lights had different colors and sounds associated with them. The ocean sound became a breathy sigh as the lights came and went.

Jamie stood and brushed snow from his bathrobe. The lights stood aside and he stared into the clearing's center.

Many eyes stared back.

From the ground and the air above it.

The beating of wings didn't come from birds. It came from wolves. Each wolf had great feathered wings. When folded, they tucked so tightly against the wolves backs and sides they practically hid in the fur. When extended, each wing was twice as wide as its wolf was long. There were birds in the air and in the trees, too. Owls and eagles and cranes and more, but none of them as big as the winged wolves.

Jamie's legs wobbled.

Graywolf came up behind him, supporting him. "Easy, Jamie."

Some of these creatures hovered with great windy wingbeats over the heads of those on the ground. Others came and went, trotting and galloping along moonbeams, rays from the Aurora or sometimes flying with their peers like puppy-dogs at play.

"What kind of wolves are these?"

From the center came an old, gruff voice. "We are not wolves."

Graywolf had his doggy-smile again. "Oh, now you've done it." With his long nose he pushed Jamie in through the winged wolves to the voice at their center. It came from a very old, very white, winged wolf.

The old creature sniffed at him then ruffled his wings the way an old man might pull his coat tighter around him after seeing some unpleasantness. "Hmmph. Human cub."

Several of the winged wolves rose up from the snow and ambled towards Jamie, their noses twitching as they approached. Clouds of warm breath rose from each as they moved silently on the snow, their pads making marks like white whispers while their tongues hung over long, sharp teeth.

Other wolves rose, their noses twitching as well, their ears flicking forward and back. Their eyes and coats glistened in the ever brightening moonlight, brown eyes and blue eyes shining and watching from faces of gray and black and brown and white winter fur.

Sweat dampened Jamie's robe. It entered his slippers and slickened his feet. His heels, steaming with sweat, melted the snow, like sand shifting under his feet when ocean waves came to lick them.

The wolves circled, closed.

A familiar voice, not Graywolf's voice, came from behind him, from the direction of the ever brightening light. "Enough."

The voice came again, "Enough." But this time the voice carried every sound Jamie'd ever heard at night. Owl calls and wolf howls and trees rustling and rain and snowfall and bats crying and crickets tittering and things he didn't want to know grunting and running.

The winged wolves stopped, their eyes and ears and nostrils and tongues fixed on what stood behind him.

"Of all that dreams, of all that rests in the sleeping world, he alone hears me."

Jamie felt something rest gently on his shoulder. A hand? He didn't want to look and find out it wasn't. As it rested there, the voice resolved itself into one from long, long ago, a woman's voice. "In all the sleeping world, he alone hears my voice. It is enough."

One of the wolves not far from Jamie raised its muzzle and howled. Soon some others joined in, each wolf lengthening its throat and lifting their muzzles skyward. Within moments all the wolves sat on their haunches, their eyes open yet seeing nothing in the cold, night sky, each one hollowing its muzzle and lolling tongue until the arctic plain echoed with the trumpets of the night.

Finally the old wolf rose and walked over to Jamie, licking its lips and running its tongue over its fangs like a barber stropping his blade. It knocked Jamie to the ground and licked his face, just like Shem, only the old wolf's tongue was a little rougher as it ran along Jamie's cheeks.

"Yes," it said. "It is enough." The wolf's breath filled Jamie with thoughts of deer kills and things chased through the snow.

The howling stopped while the old wolf spoke. Now it rose again twice as loud as before. The wolves howled, their tails thumped the snow-covered ground, the Auroras sang and waved and lifted up into the night, merging to become a multicolored nightcloth. The trees spoke a single word that came out as a deep, shaking thrum.

"Where am I?"

A woman, dressed completely in white, walked from behind Jamie to beside him.

She was the most beautiful woman Jamie ever saw.

Everything about her was white: white skin, white lips, white mouth and tongue when she spoke, white hands at the end of a billowing white sleeves, white hair flowed like a lion's mane and almost touched the snow covered ground. Her white robe had the faintest lines of nightsky-blue edging. Jamie was sure if she wore shoes or slippers beneath her long robe, they'd be white with the fine blue edging, too. Only the fine lines of her features and shadows on her face gave clues to where lips ended and nose began, where nose ended and eyes began, and so on for her ears and chin and brow.

Except her eyes. Deep and dark, almost as if she had no eyes at all. Jamie stared but couldn't be sure. It almost seemed as if there were stars in the dark of her eyes.

"You are in my garden, Jamie," she said. "You see these men and women around you?" She waved a hand. The gathering of wolves was replaced by men and women, easily as many people as there had been winged wolves a moment before, dressed all sorts of ways. Some looked like they worked in cities, some in the country. Some looked like they came from far away. Some wore clothes Jamie had never seen before, some wore almost no clothes at all. Some looked like they drove trucks and some looked like they flew planes. Two pups, their wings not yet fledged, wrestled at the edge of the group until a woman cuffed them into silence. They stood up and became young men. The people were of every color, as if their skin had taken on the colors of the winged wolves' fur.

But all of them shared one thing in common. All had their right eye blue, their left eye brown.

"Yes."

"These are my guardians, Jamie."

An old man dressed like a woodsman, a green hunter's cap pulled down tight around his ears, a red and black plaid jacket with its collar pulled up and buttoned tight around his neck so only his scruffy, unshaven face showed through, walked up to him. "Aye," he said. "Guardians of The Moon. Children of a King your pack has long since forgotten."

"Who are you?" Jamie asked the woman.

The clearing brightened as she spoke. "I am The Moon."

Jamie looked at her. He knew the moon he saw in the sky was only a reflection of the moon he saw here, much like the moon in the sky was only reflecting the light of the sun.

"Why did Graywolf bring me here?"

The old man took off his cap and ran a rough hand through thick, white hair. Jamie could see his face clearly. His eyes. The right blue, the left brown. He lifted a pipe from his pocket, tamped tobacco into it, and lit it. A cloud of smoke blew in Jamie's direction and a sweet smell like mornings in a forest filled him.

"Because, cub," the old man said between puffs, "you listened."

"I did?"

"You heard when I spoke, Jamie," said The Moon. "You did not know it was me, you did not know what you heard, but it was my voice and you responded to it. For all the time that men and wolves, men and the children of wolves, have walked together, those who've heard my voice are asked into my service."

"You want me to become a wolf?"

Graywolf laughed and Jamie looked up at the sound. Graywolf was a man again: long black hair, dark skin, right eye blue, left eye brown. "No, Jamie, not a wolf."

"Come, child. There is much to tell you." The Moon held out her hand to Jamie, the sleeves of her robe filling the sky like sails sown from the Milky Way.

Jamie looked at the creatures around him, some winged wolves, some human, Graywolf, tall and silent, the trees now quiet, the birds and hares and moles and voles, rabbits and fox, even the Aurora stopped crinkling. All grew silent, waiting.

He reached out and took her hand.

"Jamie, do you believe you will see your mother again?"

"I don't know. I hope so."

"Yes. You don't *know*, you *hope*. Imagine how you'd feel if you knew you'd never see her again."

Tears filled Jamie's eyes and made icicle rivers down his face.

"You do not know, you hope. Hope goes beyond knowledge. Hope sees more than knowledge can reveal. Hope lies in dreams, in imagination, in the courage to turn dreams into realities. It is what the Old Ones of your kind called *Elp*.

"When people lose hope, when you believe you'll never see your mother again, that is despair. It, too, has an ancient name: *Vön*."

"I don't understand. Are Elp and Vön people?"

Graywolf said, "Not exactly. Remember what I said about always finding the center? You can see Elp in the eyes of a baby in the arms of its mother, in the voice of a father teaching his child to play games, in the sounds of a village working together to bring in a harvest. Elp is what's in people's center, what holds them together."

The Old One spoke, "Aye. Vön is what drives them apart. It is a wolf that never had a pack, never fed from a hunt, never had pups who played. Old beyond time, its coat matted and unkempt, never hearing a mate's or kin's answering song in the night." He pulled on his pipe, pursed his lips and exhaled a cloud of smoke. It coalesced into a lone wolf on a hillside, thin, hungry, afraid, but always wanting to be strong and not knowing how, then floated away. "When the world was young, when your pack first stood on two legs and saw farther horizons, hope ruled the world."

He became a winged wolf again. "Now they look no further than what they hold in their hands, their eyes never cast to the heavens and it's the heavens that's your tribe's destiny."

All the wolves, winged and wingless, howled in agreement.

"Some's dreams go no further than their next meal and they forget the rest of the world dreams of being warm, being fed, being safe, being dry, ..."

Graywolf spoke, "Being loved." He paused. "People are losing the ability to dream, Jamie. To imagine. Without that, humanity is lost."

He knelt and rested his hands on Jamie's arms. "We would like you to help us, Jamie." He stared deep into Jamie's eyes, ran his hands up and down Jamie's arms as if warming him. A tear slid down Graywolf's cheek.

"Are you okay, Graywolf?"

"We can not ask for your help and leave you unaware, Jamie. You must know what you'll face."

Jamie met Graywolf's eyes. He blinked and looked up at The Moon.

The old winged wolf spoke up. "No one serves the Queen under force, cub. It is your decision to make but make it you will before you leave this place. If you decide to walk away you'll wake up on the train and all of this will have been an interesting dream. If you decide to walk with us you'll live your life seeing things as they wish to be seen."

"What's that mean?"

Graywolf shook Jamie's lightly. "It means you'll always see things' centers. The real meaning of things. What people really want, not just what they say they want."

Jamie's face scrunched, deep in thought. "You mean like one time when I didn't want to give Bobby Games any of my HotWheels™, but he didn't have any and I gave him some of mine anyway?"

The Moon glowed brightly. "You shared even though you didn't want to. You chose compassion over fear, kindness over conceit. That is Elp. If you chose not to, if you feared your having fewer more than his having none, that would have been Vön."

Graywolf held Jamie at arm's length. "To do what you must do, Jamie, you must lose your innocence, and it is better I show you than a world of others who love you less." Hot tears became snowflakes drifting down to the snow. "You can't do what you'll be asked to do unless you know the enemy you'll have to face: Hopelessness. It is your decision to make, Jamie. If you are willing to help us, you'll be changed forever. There's no going back if you say yes. Do you understand?"

Jamie nodded. "Yes."

"Look into my eyes, Jamie."

Jamie did. He saw things. Horrible things. Bombs falling on mothers running, their children in their arms. Boys no older than him and Bobby Games carrying weapons into fields and on city streets.

His vision swirled around him, engulfing him in what he saw, a hellious dancer pulling him on to the dance floor.

Soldiers came into his home with long knives called machetes, killing his baby brother and sister before his eyes, before the eyes of his parents, then running their blades through the rest. The last thing he heard was the soldiers laughing as they walked out, bloodstained.

People came at him with clubs, beating him, beating the people with him, beating them because they looked different. Or thought different. Or spoke different. Or prayed different.

He watched people half-buried in the ground, unable to move, screaming as wild animals came to feed on them.

He watched boys his age and younger, girls as well, walking streets, standing under streetlights or in dark alley corners, getting in cars.

He held his hand out for food and heard laughter from behind before being knocked to the ground.

Someone grabbed him and threw him in a van, left him in a dark room, chained to a bed, until someone came in.

He was a teenager. He was with a girl. They left their baby in a dumpster and ran, hoping to outrun its screams of hunger.

He was a man. He watched his wife and children torn from him, torn from each other, never to be seen or heard or felt or known again.

He forced his sister to leave her baby on a bench in a park in the dead of night.

He was old. He lived in fear. He slept, woke and lived with nothing, his mind, heart, and stomach empty.

He felt hunger. Pain. Cold. Thirst.

But never love.

Never, ever love.

Graywolf closed his eyes.

Jamie's world stopped swirling, the dancer let go. Jamie shook, his little hands shaped into claws, his eyes darting, his chest heaving yet unable to breathe.

He screamed.

From Chapter 21 - Nighthorse meets Ann

Nighthorse, it seemed, could *dream*. Half an hour after entering one of Dr. Lupicen's sleep chambers Ann's QLCs pulsed deep forest green to keep up with him.

When he woke up Dr. Lupicen tapped on the door to his sleep chamber and Nighthorse waved him in. "Mr. Nighthorse, you are a most remarkable man."

"Oh?"

"We have had many people come in and dream a little or a few for us, but none has dreamt the way you do. Do you dream this way on purpose?"

"How do I dream?"

"I'll show you." Lupicen left the chamber returned and with a large tablet showing some moving EEG-like images. Different color lines zigzagged back and forth next to a time-axis, but they mostly remained together with only a few oddities here and there.

One line, purple, went all over the place.

Lupicen pointed to the purple line. "This is you, Mr. Nighthorse. All these others are other guests we have today." He pointed to a green line. "This is Mr. Carsons. He sleeps soundly now and doesn't dream at all, see? His line shows his mind needs to be quiet for a while. He dreamt quite busily before. Maybe later we'll see something he needs us to see. This orange line is your friend, Mr. Sally."

"Captain Sally," Nighthorse corrected.

"Ah, yes. This he has told me many times. Captain Sally sleeps hardly at all and when he does, it seems he stops himself from having dreams. But you are quite busy when you sleep, Mr. Nighthorse. You dream, yes, but it is *how* you dream that is so interesting to me. Do you know, Mr. Nighthorse, that you have no PEA in your sleep?"

"I went earlier."

He laughed. "Ah, you joke with me. Very good, Mr. Nighthorse. May I sit?"

Nighthorse nodded. Lupicen pulled a small chair next to the sleep chamber's bed and sat, tucking the back of his labcoat into his lap as if it was a tuxedo with tails. He placed the tablet on the bed between them. "P-E-A is a neurohormone like an amphetamine. It tells our brains when to be emotional. It is why we can fall in love and out again. Dreaming is usually a highly emotional state, but not for you."

Nighthorse said nothing, gave nothing away, his eyes always on Lupicen's.

"My computer monitors people while they sleep, you know, including the expressions on their faces. This we told you before you began. You remember this?"

"Yes."

"She - "

"She?"

Lupicen blushed. "I think of my computer as Ann. She is an 'Articulated Neural Net,' so Ann, a child's name. She - Ann - looks at emotions. She recognizes facial expressions and their meanings because she sees action units, 'AUs'."

Lupicen's finger traced the purple line.

"You, Mr. Nighthorse, have none. There are usually two reasons for this." Lupicen stared intently at Nighthorse's face. He reached out and touched Nighthorse's cheek and jaw line tenderly, almost lovingly.

Nighthorse smelled clove aftershave mixed with electrolytic gels and hospital adhesives on Lupicen's hand. His cheek twitched like a horse flicking off a fly.

Lupicen pulled his hand back. "The first is Möbius Syndrome and this is not you. An individual has no movement of the facial muscles, they have drooping and wide eyes, and a narrow open mouth. Also they have a problem with the sideways movement of the eyes. They move the whole head to gaze at something. Most people experiencing Möbius Syndrome are unable to express any feelings with the face. Their appearance is mask-like."

Lupicen stared intently at Nighthorse's face. "This you do not have. For one, you were not awake. For two, your face responded when I touched you."

He sat back. "The other is what I think we must investigate. It is the twin potentials of 'protention' and 'retention'. Retention is when we keep active information from the immediate past, such as hearing sounds and, when enough are heard, recognizing the collection of sounds as music. Protention is when we make information active in the immediate future, such as deciding what someone is going to say before they've said it and mishear them. Or we missee or missense something because we make incorrect information active. Most people rely on their pasts to create their futures."

Lupicen's finger lovingly traced the tablet's purple line. "You do not do this, Mr. Nighthorse. You have no emotions when you dream because you don't protend. You let things happen without bias."

Lupicen's gaze returned to Nighthorse's face and he sat forward. "How do you do this, Mr. Nighthorse?"

Nighthorse shrugged.

"You are a quiet man, Mr. Nighthorse. Words do not suit you?"

Another shrug.

Lupicen looked at Nighthorse's trace on his tablet. "Your dreams are under neither conscious nor nonconscious control. They are most like my Ann's dreams. But her dreams exist in branches of superpositioned quantum realities. She can decide a dream will be real and essentially 'wake up' in that world. You do not protend, Mr. Nighthorse, and because you do not protend you, also, can travel between worlds as they come to you. You do not anticipate, only respond."

Shrug.

"At least in your dreams."

Nighthorse chuckled. "Traveling between worlds. Sounds like my grandfather's lessons. He knew the old ways. *Wovoka*. Spirits came to him in his dreams."

"Your grandfather is alive?"

"Dead a long time, now."

"Pity. To lose such gifts."

"Yeah. Funny, though. I've been thinking a lot about him lately." Nighthorse swung his legs over the side of the bed and sat there, his hands slightly above his lap, fingers up and palms outward as if pushing something only he could see. He stared at his hands as, wondering what they pushed against. "He taught me. Must have stuck."

"What is it that stuck, please."

"Oh, stuff about the spirits. Good spirits, bad spirits. Not bad, just tricksters. Maybe that's what my purple line means. Maybe that's why I could hear it but not see it. I'm waiting for the spirits to return and first up is a Trickster spirit?" He looked at Lupicen and smiled. "Grandfather would really laugh at this. He'd say, 'It only took you white guys two-thousand years to catch up?'"

Lupicen frowned. "Tell me about this Trickster spirit, please. What did you hear but not see?"

Nighthorse described his dream, sharing every detail.

"What has changed, Mr. Nighthorse? Before you were a quiet man. Now..."

"I don't know. Thinking about my grandfather? I haven't thought about him in years and now I can't get the old man out of my head."

"You think you can do this," Lupicen hesitated, unsure of the word, "Woowoo?"

"*Wovoka.*"

"Thank you. *Wovoka*, yes."

Nighthorse smiled. It felt good to be doing such things again. A set of muscles he hadn't exercised in years. It might help him figure out what to do with Pangiosi when the latter showed up.

"Sure, Doc. I can try."

COMING SOON FROM NORTHERN LIGHTS PUBLISHING

Stay up on early reads, special offers, and gift opportunities! Join our mailing list at http://nlb.pub/nlbmailings

June 2023: The Inheritors

Tommy was told he was different by his family, his friends, and his teachers. He was special. Then one day he disappeared, prompting a mystery that would span millennia and bring together individuals from all walks of life from the distant past to the near future. Reaching out across all the world's civilizations through all time, The Inheritors tells the story of the hidden costs of immortality, the innocent lives exploited in its pursuit, and the unlikely heroes who make the ultimate sacrifice to exact justice.

September 2023: The Shaman

Gio Fortuna, a boy spurned by his parents for being "slow," is raised by his grandfather in the ways of the Practice, a rich esoteric discipline drawing upon mystic traditions passed down over thousands of years from a multitude of cultures. Written in five parts chronicling Gio's life, The Shaman sees Fortuna embark on a journey from initiate to adept, young boy to old man, as he navigates a network of teachers, each with their own unique lessons and challenges. Steeped in wisdom applicable to all, The Shaman is an inspiring story that proposes a unique path to self-discovery and growth unlike anything written before.

December 2023: Search

Two young boys and their guardian go missing in the Maine woods. No one has a clue, no one comes forward offering information, and the police are powerless to provide the boys' family with any answers. The boys' older sister learns about Gio Fortuna through a friend and asks him to help. Search chronicles one life-changing event in The Shaman's life, an event causing Gio to realize the use of his grandfather's teachings and their purpose in both his life and the lives of others.

THREE QUESTIONS FOR YOU

1. *Did you know most readers rely on other readers' reviews and comments to make their book buying decisions? Ongoing research begun in mid-2022 indicates reviews and comments are better decision drivers than video teasers, author interviews, author blogs, and everything else combined.*

2. *Did you know most on- and off-line bookstores - from the smallest indie to the largest megastore - rely on reader reviews and comments to decide which books to put on their shelves?*

3. *Did you enjoy* Tales Told 'Round Celestial Campfires*?*

Help Northern Lights as a publisher and Joseph Carrabis as an author by reviewing Tales Told 'Round Celestial Campfires *on Amazon http://nlb.pub/TalesV1 Goodreads http://nlb.pub/GTalesV1, Barnes&Noble, BookBub, NetGalley, your favorite reader Facebook and LinkedIn groups, TikTok, Instagram, anywhere and everywhere.*

Let's Kick It Up A Notch!

Send a link to your online review of a Northern Lights Publishing book to Reviews@NorthernLightsPublishing.com and we'll give you a 35% discount on your next Northern Lights Publishing ePub or Print book.

Not Enough? Let's Kick It Up Another Notch!

You can share that 35% discount with up to ten friends, family, neighbors, we won't mind, and you'll have our thanks.

Join Northern Lights Publishing's Journey
http://nlb.pub/JoinNorthernLights

Do You Know Where You Are?

How do you keep track of where you are in your reading? A paperclip? A napkin? A pencil? Maybe a highlighter if you're reading a textbook or non-fiction self-help? How about dogearring the last page you read?

How would you like three (3) high-quality, nice, stylish 7"x2"color bookmarks? (our choice)

They're easy to get:

1. Take a high resolution picture (minimum 2500 px in jpeg, png, or gif format, please) of you holding or reading this book (or another Northern Lights Publishing print title), this or another Northern Lights Publishing book in your favorite space (no bathroom shots, please), one of your pets reading it, …
2. Make sure we can see both the book cover and your smiling face (if you're holding the book) in the picture (and recognize we may need to crop/resize the image for space consideration).
3. Email the picture to bookmarks@northernlightspublishing. com.
4. Remember to include your postal address so we can mail you the bookmarks.

That's it! Get us that picture, you get three (3) high-quality, nice, stylish 7"x2"color bookmarks for free!

(and our thanks for helping us grow our publishing program)

Please note (things our attorneys told us to include):

A) By accepting this offer you give Northern Lights Publishing the right to use your image on our site on our Happy Readers (http://nlb.pub/HappyReaders) page (and add you to our email list).

B) Offer limited to one reader/email address/book.

C) No crank, prank, vulgar, questionable, or offenses images, please, and we get to decide if something is crank, prank, vulgar, questionable, or offensive.

D) We may cancel this offer without notice.

ABOUT NORTHERN LIGHTS PUBLISHING

Northern Lights Publishing/Press is an association of five professionals (one graphic artist, one marketer, one editor/book designer, one copyeditor, one editor/educator/author) and a rotating group of ten published authors and poets all of whom are passionate readers. Financial backing is provided by a small group of investors led by Susan and Joseph Carrabis through the NextStage Evolution Corporation. Everyone receives remuneration and owns an equal share of the company with the exception of Susan and Joseph Carrabis.

We're developing our publishing/marketing model so we're not accepting submissions at present.

We'll open our doors to submissions (and announce it through various social networks) once we're sure we can break even and preferably turn a profit. Until then, wish us well.

It's an exciting journey and one we'd love to share, but only after we're sure we can successfully navigate the publishing seas.

ALSO BY JOSEPH CARRABIS

Non-Fiction

That Th!nk You Do - http://nlb.pub/TTYDv1

That Th!nk You Do is based on a series of blog posts Joseph wrote between 2008 and 2016. They dealt with ways his research in fields as diverse as neuroscience, linguistics, psychology, sociology, anthropology and other disciplines could be put to practical use to help people better their lives.

If you ever wonder about how to think like an expert, the difference between your inner critic and the actor within, your ability to be heard, the value of being a musician, how to protect yourself from liars or how to overcome fears, you will find answers in this book..

Reading Virtual Minds Volume I: Science and History - http://nlb.pub/Minds1

The science and history behind NextStage Evolution's Evolution Technology

Reading Virtual Minds Volume II: Experience and Expectation - http://nlb.pub/Minds2

Learnings and Take-Aways from NextStage Evolution's research and studies

Reading Virtual Minds Volume III: Fair-Exchange and Social Networks - http://nlb.pub/Minds3

Learnings and Take-Aways from NextStage Evolution's research and studies applied specifically on on- and off-line social interactions

Fiction: Novels

Empty Sky - http://nlb.pub/EmptySky

What if you're a young boy, Jamie McPherson, whose mother has been missing for over a year and whose father starts falling in and out of coma? What if you hold onto your aging dog, Shem, who's always been with you and always protected you, because the world isn't safe anymore?

And what if in the midst all that's happening, The Moon asks you to help her save the world's dreams?

Earl Pangiosi's greatest desire, since childhood, has been to control and manipulate people. Working for the NSA, Earl learns that people's dreams - their nonconscious minds - guide their conscious decisions. Control their dreams - weaponize them - and you control people at an unprecedented level.

Jamie will not face Pangiosi alone. The Moon sends her Guardians, winged, shapeshifting wolves; and her children, The Oneiroi, little black silhouettes, shadows in the darkness of night, whose multicolored, multifaceted, crystalline eyes serve as kaleidoscopic Gates — little rainbow bridges allowing humans passage from one dream reality to the next, to help Jamie.

Pangiosi sends the Native American giant, Nighthorse, to stop Jamie. But Nighthorse's grandfather introduced him to Wovoka, the DreamWorld, as a child. Going after Jamie, Nighthorse finds one of the Oneiroi's Eye-Gates and realizes his grandfather may not have been such a fool after all.

Meanwhile the Moon brings together a team of "Dreamers" to help Jamie. One such Dreamer is ANN, a supercomputer who can blend dream and waking realities via Penrose Consciousnesses, quantum superpositions.

If they fail, Pangiosi and the NSA will control the world.

The Augmented Man - http://nlb.pub/Augmented

What do you do with a deadly weapon when it's no longer needed?

Nicholas Trailer is the last of The Augmented Men, beings created first by society and completed by a political group the public can't even imagine exists. Captain James Donaldson takes severely abused and traumatized children and modifies them into monsters capable of the most horrifying deeds without feeling any remorse or regret.

But the horrors of war never stay on the battlefield. They always come home.

Battling what society and science has made him, Nick Trailer discovers he is loved. From the horrors of childhood to the horrors of a war, what does it take for someone to find true love and peace? Especially when everyone has their own agenda, from the senators who sanctioned his making to the Governor of Maine who wants to use Nick's struggle to propel himself to the White House.

The Augmented Men were good at war, perhaps a little too good. Now they have to come home ... or do they? What do you do with man-made monsters?

Nick must decide if his friends are his friends and if his enemies are his enemies, all while protecting the woman he loves.

And are you truly the last of your kind?

What if you must remain a monster to defeat a monster? Will you sacrifice love to protect what you love?

Fiction: Anthologies

Tales Told 'Round Celestial Campfires - http://nlb.pub/TalesV1
Includes:

Binky (available separately at http://nlb.pub/Binky)

What if you run an inner-city health clinic and are tired of fighting budget cuts, politics, protestors, police, ... ? And what if you question your purpose because caring is no longer cost-effective? And what if you meet a bright, beautiful child who leads you to a child who died sixty years ago? And what if that child asks you to save its life?

The Boy Who Loved Horses (available separately at http://nlb.pub/ Horses)

What if you're born and raised Hill but got City educated and now you drivin a big state issue Buick back into Hill 'cause you gonna show them you something else? And what if one town you drive through's got secrets it don't want nobody to know? And what if you plan to tell City those secrets and those secrets got they own idea who you gonna tell?

Canis Major (available separately at http://nlb.pub/CanisMajor)

What if you're a WereMan, human when the moon is full, a beast when not, and your father died before explaining your gift to you? And what if your fully human mother did the best she could but couldn't really understand your needs? And what if you're tired of being alone and afraid and once, just once, you want to hold someone and not be afraid of their fear?

Cold War (available separately at http://nlb.pub/ColdWar)

What if your last deployment left you so damaged driving a school bus tops your employable skills? And what if the kids laugh at you because you can't talk right and twitch at nothing? And what if the military calls you back, says they can make you a man again. Or get close. And what if you're so lonely, angry and tired you say sure without realizing they plan to leave you out in the cold, forever?

Cymodoce (available separately at http://nlb.pub/Cymodoce)

What if the only man you've ever given yourself to isn't a man at all? And what if you gave birth to twins, the son wholly yours, the daughter wholly his? And what if your daughter needs to return to her father in order to survive? And what if her survival means never seeing her again, and her brother losing his sister forever?

Dancers in the Eye of Chronos (available separately at http://nlb. pub/Dancers)

What if your love so delights the Gods they grant you immortality. But you learn love is meant to age, to mature, to grow and change in ways the Gods can't imagine. After millennia, they strip their gift from you. But that's what you wanted; to hold your lover's face one last time before darkness falls. Or is your love so strong it outlives the Gods themselves?

The Goatmen of Aguirra (available separately at http://nlb.pub/ Goatmen)

What if you've signed onto a deep space mission and left behind a wife and young son? And what if your mission takes to you a supposedly uninhabited planet that harbors intelligent life that values family above all else? And what if they take you into their family to heal you? And what if, finally healed, your shipmates abandon you when the mission is called home?

Mani He (available separately at http://nlb.pub/ManiHe)

What if you've acquired your dream job but destroyed another man's life and career to get it? And what if the president of your company hands you a rifle and the keys to his mountain cabin with the instructions "Bring me back something to make me proud"? And what if the spirits in the mountains have their own ideas of what it means to be proud?

Power Unlimited (available separately at http://nlb.pub/ PowerUnlimited)

What if Eddie's kid brother Tommy idolizes you guys at the gym and wants to be like you but you know he's not really built for it. And what if he sends away for some "GET BIG FAST" Muscle Pill exercise programs? And what if he starts looking like The Hulk and King Kong had a baby? And what if the people who make those Pills want them back?

Sema (available separately at http://nlb.pub/Sema)

What if a beautiful woman discovers you and your friends are beings living side-by-side with humans since the beginning of time? And what if she discovers you have abilities beyond imagination and she, too, has gifts no mortal should possess? And what if, having no knowledge of your kind, has trained with a Darkness humans can't imagine, never suspecting a Light beyond mortals' dreams?

The Settlement (available separately at http://nlb.pub/Settlement)
What if you're a young, hotshot, wildly successful asteroid miner who hasn't seen your parents since you joined the corp underage? And what if your parents are getting divorced and each is laying claim to guardianship of your fortune? And what if your parents never knew why you joined the corp or what you had to give up to get a ship of your own?

Them Doore Girls (available separately at http://nlb.pub/Doore)
What if the woman you love is the mistress of something else, something so monstrous, so hideous its summoning her creates ocean storms? And what if she knows this entity will destroy her, you, your village and all those you know if she denies it? And what if you know she goes to it willingly because it threatened to kill you, her one love, if she doesn't yield to its wishes?

Those Wings Which Tire, They Have Upheld Me (available separately at http://nlb.pub/Wings)
What if you're a little boy with brain cancer whose doctors say they can cure you by replacing your eyes with an experimental device? And what if that experimental device lets you see your guardian angel? And what if seeing your guardian angel makes you best friends with the class trouble-maker? And what if the class bully finds out you talk to angels?

The Weight (available separately at http://nlb.pub/Weight)
What if you've been a success at everything you've done in your life and decide to retrace a hike you took when wishes were horses and beggars could ride? And what if you met one of your heroes on that

long ago hike and - miracle of miracles - you meet him again? And what if your hero isn't your hero and says you took something from it way back when and now it wants it back?

Winter Winds (available separately at http://nlb.pub/Winds)
What if you're sitting in your favorite chair, your son on your lap, helping him with his homework when you see something in the fields outside your house? And what if you turn on the floodlights and see unimaginable creatures battling in your fields? And what if your son and wife tell you you're the strange one because those fantastical creatures battling in your field are as natural as natural can be?

Follow Joseph's work in magazines and other anthologies at https://josephcarrabis.com/tag/im-published-here/

You can find most of Joseph's work at http://nlb.pub/amazon

ABOUT THE AUTHOR

Joseph Carrabis told stories to anyone who would listen starting in childhood, wrote his first stories in gradeschool, and started getting paid for his writing in 1978. His work history includes periods as a long-haul trucker, apprentice butcher, apprentice coffee buyer/broker, lumberjack, Cold Regions researcher, mathematician, semanticist, semioticist, physicist, educator, Chief Data Scientist, Chief Research Scientist, and Chief Research Officer. He was an original member of the NYAS/UN's Scientists Without Borders program and held patents covering mathematics, anthropology, neuroscience, and linguistics. After patenting a technology he created in his basement and creating an international company, he retired from corporate life. Now he spends his time writing fiction based on his experiences. His work appears regularly in anthologies and his own novels. You can often find him playing with his dog, Boo, and snuggling with his wife, Susan. Learn more about him at https://josephcarrabis.com and his work at http://nlb.pub/amazon.

www.ingramcontent.com/pod-product-compliance
Lightning Source LLC
Chambersburg PA
CBHW070204120726
47909CB00001B/246

* 9 7 8 0 9 8 4 1 4 0 3 1 2 *